ZETA K. PIERCE

The Haunted Warrior

BOOK 2

Copyright © 2025 by Zeta K. Pierce

ISBN (paperback): 979-8-9919274-3-7

ISBN (hardcover): 979-8-9919274-4-4

ISBN (ebook): 979-8-9919274-5-1

All rights reserved.

No portion of this book may be reproduced in any form without written permission from the publisher or author, except as permitted by U.S. copyright law. The Author expressly prohibits the use of this work in any manner for purposes of training artificial technologies to generate text, including without limitation technologies that are capable of generating works in the same style of genre as this work.

This book is a work of fiction. Names, characters, businesses, organizations, places, events, and incidents either are a product of the author's imagination or used fictitiously. Any resemblance to actual persons, living or dead, events, or locales is entirely coincidental.

Cover illustrated and designed by MiblArt

Map illustrated by Vivien Gintner @evilienne16 – www.viviengintner.com

Edited by Danyelle Briggs at In the Write Dyrection

Contents

Content Warnings	3
Map	4
In case you forgot	5
Chapter 1	9
Chapter 2	19
Chapter 3	33
Chapter 4	41
Chapter 5	53
Chapter 6	61
Chapter 7	74
Chapter 8	86
Chapter 9	92
Chapter 10	101
Chapter 11	110
Chapter 12	118
Chapter 13	127
Chapter 14	137
Chapter 15	145

Chapter 16	154
Chapter 17	167
Chapter 18	178
Chapter 19	185
Chapter 20	191
Chapter 21	200
Chapter 22	212
Chapter 23	223
Chapter 24	233
Chapter 25	240
Chapter 26	248
Chapter 27	257
Chapter 28	265
Chapter 29	273
Chapter 30	283
Chapter 31	292
Chapter 32	298
Chapter 33	308
Chapter 34	316
Chapter 35	325
Chapter 36	331
Chapter 37	342
Chapter 38	348

Chapter 39	353
Epilogue	362
Afterword	367
Acknowledgements	368
About the Author	369

Works by Zeta K. Pierce

The Crimson Knight

To anyone who has ever been lost. You will always find your way again.

Content Warnings

Please note before reading that some of the warnings may be light spoilers.

The Haunted Warrior is a dark fantasy intended for an adult audience. It contains elements and tropes that are commonly found in the genre, including but not limited to: graphic depictions of violence, death, blood, gore, torture and dismemberment, alcohol use, animal death, and on page consensual sex. There are also elements of addiction pertaining to corrupted magic that impact a teenage character.

In case you forgot

A refresher for The Crimson Knight, as told by the Soul Reaper

I am the first child born of the Cosmos. I have witnessed the birth of all her subsequent offspring–from the formation of the realms to the creation of life itself. The matters of the Human Realm are but a trifling thing–a mere ripple in an infinite ocean.

But even ripples can cascade into waves of destruction.

This tale begins with a human woman. Like many of her kind, she can wield the power of the Cosmos. Some humans foolishly forbid this, as was the case of her leader, a man by the name of King Rhys, who punished Cosmic Arts practitioners by death.

A band of omens schemed together and brought Beasts into the Human Realm, creating havoc and destruction. Their efforts successfully drew each of the kingdoms' rulers to a single location, where the omens intended to wipe them all out at once by overwhelming their forces with Cosmic magic.

They did not account for a blood mage in King Rhys's ranks.

Haizea brought their attack to a grinding halt—but not without claiming the lives of many of her allies. A necessary sacrifice to fuel her power.

I can still taste the essence of their Souls.

Upon discovering the true nature of her magic, King Rhys called for her execution. Haizea escaped and took refuge in a small, destitute village at the base of the mountain. Here, she met another human by the name of Alastair—a nascent necromancer with unrealized potential.

King Rhys placed a bounty on her head, and word quickly spread amongst the villagers. Violence and chaos ensued in their attempts to capture her. Roughly a hundred Souls were sent to my realm in the fight that ensued. The villagers laid waste to Alastair's home and slayed his entire family—save his cousin, who was dragged away in the midst of mayhem. Intent on saving her, he and Haizea left the village behind in pursuit of her captor.

King Rhys also did not relent in his efforts. He hired mercenaries to drag Haizea back to his domain, but he also made contingencies in the case of their failure.

Back in Arcelia was Haizea's grandfather, Harzel. He received a letter of warning from Haizea, delivered to him by a Soul. Though his blood magic was a mere fraction of its original might, Harzel left a trail of bodies in his wake as he prepared for a confrontation with King Rhys's forces.

As King Rhys's mercenaries closed in on Haizea and Alastair, an unlikely ally came to their aid—the realmdrifter, Kallistê, who spearheaded the attack against the kingdoms' rulers. The duo slipped past the king's clutches, but with each passing moment, his forces steadily closed the distance on Harzel.

They caught up to him at the base of the mountain range. Harzel put on an impressive display of strength, but the king's forces were able to sever Harzel's connection to the vitality and cut off his magic entirely with a plant the humans call 'earth's smoke'. He succumbed to its effects.

Though defenseless, Harzel was not alone.

In the same fashion that Haizea had warned her grandfather, she'd also sent a message to her old comrades, the Bruvian warriors. They'd descended the mountain to assist Harzel in his travels. While the king's men focused their attention on him, the Bruvian warriors descended upon them.

Two warriors struck down numerous men in the blink of an eye. The earth's smoke still lurked on the backdrop—one of the king's men used it to dampen their magic and used the opening to escape their assault with Harzel in tow.

King Rhys showed Harzel no mercy. He tortured him, purposefully drawing out his death before sending him to my realm.

Haizea learned of her grandfather's death via a letter from King Rhys. With it was a basket that contained her grandfather's severed head.

The realm will bear the scars of her wrath for generations.

Haizea cut down the army of soldiers that stood between her and the king. She beckoned young Alastair to resurrect them with his magic, binding their Souls to their broken bodies and turning the king's own army against him.

She found the royal family first–the queen, the prince, and the princess–hidden away in a bunker. Haizea struck down the queen but faltered at the sight of the king's children. Unable to kill them in cold blood, she spared them.

Her Soul wavers in that decision, even now.

She continued onward, finally reaching the king in his castle. He'd laid a trap with the earth's smoke to snuff out her connection to the vitality, but it made no difference–Haizea had prepared for such a scenario. Deprived of her magic, she defeated him with her fists.

Together, she and Alastair sent thousands of Souls to my realm in a single night.

A worthy offering.

With the king defeated, they returned home to the mountains. But threats to their newfound peace still lurk in the backdrop.

The young prince and princess set out to learn transmutation and exact their vengeance. And the islanders from across the ocean have steadily expanded their reach throughout the realm.

I sense many more offerings are to come.

Chapter 1

Human Realm, Mount Illiniza, Windhaven Village

Haizea's boots sank into the blood-soaked snow. The soft crunch of her footsteps slowed as she came to a stop. She tilted her head back and inhaled deeply, giving into the instinct to savor the sight and smell. The vitality awakened within her—a jolt of desire ripped through her veins and manifested into an unrelenting thirst, demanding to be quenched.

Haizea eagerly obeyed its call, though she concealed her zeal behind a level countenance. Even with the flames of her bloodlust furling within, she did not lose her sense of reason–her survival instincts spoke to her just as fervently. Danger lurked nearby.

Harsh winds whipped her hair about, making dozens of her long braids fly in every direction, a handful of which clung to her deer skull mask and obstructed her vision. Haizea squinted, and her fingers brushed against the mask's hard surface as she pushed her hair back. She stood motionless and surveyed the area, her ears straining to pick up sound.

The torches that lined either side of the snow-covered walkway served as her only indication of direction. The fires illuminated the puddle of blood that trailed off to her right. Dozens of paw shaped footprints patterned the snow.

She narrowed her eyes at the sight and tugged at her coat. Beneath her furs was a holster that held her swords. She took a slow, cautious step as she followed the trail before pausing again to observe. When nothing stirred, she advanced and kept her eyes and ears on a swivel.

A dark shape, half obscured by a drift of snow, lay ten paces ahead.

At the end of the trail of blood lay a disemboweled body with its guts splayed across the ground. She halted in her tracks, her heart hammering against her ribs. Haizea took a deep breath to steel herself and crept forward. As a warrior, the duty of investigating fell to her.

This path experienced heavy traffic during the day as mountaineers traveled between villages. To find a dead body here, at the end of her patrol shift, alarmed her. She crouched down beside him to observe more closely.

A jagged, uneven gash splayed across his stomach and puncture wounds riddled his arms and neck. Between the nature of his injuries and the paw prints in the snow, an animal had most likely attacked him. If another villager hadn't already seen him before her arrival, then someone who knew him would certainly report him missing in the coming days. To help with identification efforts, Haizea locked the man's features into her memory—a medium build, beige skin, and graying hair.

Her brows drew together. She wondered what type of life he'd lived and if it had been peaceful. She wondered if either of those things mattered, if in the end, he died so gruesomely.

Despite her healing abilities, Haizea could not change the immutable fact of mortality. However, she could control the *way* death came. Death took many forms, and Haizea had the power to mold it.

She could make it equal parts peaceful and horrifying. She could kill as an act of mercy or a method of torture. A good death held just as much importance as a good life—a fortune that this man had been denied.

Haizea blinked a few times to refocus on the task at hand. The dead body before her needed tending to.

The man's entrails painted the snow in ribbons of crimson—there was no way she could carry him back alone. She'd have to get the other warriors. She knelt beside his head, preparing to bid his Soul farewell as it traversed into the next realm, when his fingers twitched. Haizea froze. Then she lunged forward, pressing her palms against his face. Eyes closed, she reached for her healing magic. There—barely a whisper of life, but it was there. A thread-thin pulse beneath her fingertips.

She began weaving the fractured strands of his life force back together. A faint thrum plucked against her power as his heart fought to cling to life. Haizea sank deeper into the vitality, searching for the source of his bleeding, but wounds riddled every inch of his body. Blood oozed between her fingers and his pulse faded.

She swallowed thickly. Inhaled a deep, calming breath that helped her ignore the cold sweat breaking out across her forehead. Haizea honed in on a major blood vessel that had been ruptured and stitched it closed. She—

A roar erupted from behind her. Weight slammed into her back—claws and fangs tearing through fur and flesh. She hit the ground hard, writhing beneath the crushing mass of fur and muscle.

Haizea turned just in time to see a multitude of wolves attacking her, jaws open wide. One wolf hovered near her face, its hot breath cutting through the freezing wind. Thick saliva dripped down its fangs and splattered onto her cheek. She brought her arm up to protect her face as the wolves bit down. Hundreds of pounds of pressure clamped down and fractured her bones in multiple places–her arm, her ankle, her shin. Haizea's howl of agony echoed through the night.

Haizea used her free hand to reach for her sword on her hip. Her hand wrapped around the hilt, but with the animals attacking, she couldn't maneuver properly to unsheathe the long blade. Instead, her fingers fumbled toward her ankle, hoping to grab the knife sheathed there. Haizea managed to pull it out just as another wolf settled on top of her and tore a chunk of her sleeve away, sending tufts of her fur coat flying.

Crisp air whipped against her exposed skin. Haizea knew that the next bite would tear away a piece of her arm. She wheezed, her chest unable to expand properly beneath the wolves' weight, and she positioned the knife to stab one of the wild animals. She just needed a single break in their skin, a single drop of blood, and this would all be over in an instant.

To Haizea's dismay, her positioning made it difficult to wield her blade properly, and she only managed to glide through the wolf's dense fur.

A wolf bit down on her arm and ripped out a sizable chunk of her flesh before clamping down again. This must have been how the man perished. Attacked without warning and—based on how his body had been torn apart—eaten alive. Her eyes landed on him. His body lay several feet away now. Blood pooled around him and glinted under the torches' lights.

Her magic twitched at the sight.

No. She had to heal him. Had to get him back to his family.

Another wolf lunged for her, its dagger-like teeth sinking into the soft skin of her throat. Bubbles of blood streamed down her neck as she gasped for breath.

Haizea met the man's form once more. Still, his heartbeat pulsed against her magic. Rising bile twinged her tongue, and a pit formed in her stomach. She squeezed her eyes shut to avoid his unseeing gaze—so that she would not have to look what she intended to do in the face.

Forgive me, she thought.

In a fraction of a second, the tendrils of her magic seized the man's life force. It rushed into Haizea's body, and her world transformed. The white, snowy mountainside shifted to a shimmering crimson landscape. The wolf in front of her glimmered red with vitality. Her strength multiplied, powered by his life force.

Haizea's movements blended as she intercepted another wolf before it could fully clamp down on her neck. She wrapped her free hand around its muzzle and squeezed with all her might. Not only did the bone shatter in her grasp, but the vitality within the animal also visibly fractured and dimmed. At the sound of the injured wolf's cries, the wolf gnawing on her other arm released her. Haizea winced as blood poured out of wounds left behind.

A brief stunned silence wafted between Haizea and the wolves as she rose to her feet. Then, they must have decided they were more enraged than afraid because the animals growled and howled as they circled around her, fangs bared, and muzzles twisted into a snarl.

Haizea gritted her teeth against the sound and, relying on her amplified speed and strength, she blocked three wolves as they leaped at her—two sets of jaws snapping at her face, while another grazed her side. She kicked outward, and while the move would have sent a human being flying, the wolf only shifted a few feet.

As Haizea shifted her weight into her fighting stance, her mind and body buzzed from the influx of the vitality. Her reddened eyes zeroed in on the wolf pack, and their positions switched—*she* became the hunter, the predator. Haizea leaned into that feeling—the thrill of her bloodlust and the fear her power instilled.

Her form blurred as she closed the short distance between herself and the wild animals. She snapped one of their necks in two. The wolf dropped to the ground in a heap, lifeless. Haizea turned to the rest of the pack and let her magic flare, wild and unsuppressed—the only warning she was willing to give. The rest of the wolf pack heeded it–they tucked their tails and ran.

The sounds of Haizea's belabored breathing filled the air. She stared at the dead wolf's unmoving form, stunned by the suddenness of the attack. Haizea frowned as her bones shifted–not painfully, but not without discomfort either–and her magic worked to heal the fractures throughout her body. She wiped her face and felt the dampness of sweat beneath her furs. A distant, yet familiar giddiness warmed her from within–the oncoming high of using her blood magic.

Haizea took a few steps and stumbled before she managed to right herself. Her attention landed on where the man's body had been, only to find a partial skeleton in his place–the force of her power had reduced most of his body to dust.

She froze where she stood, lips ajar and fingers trembling as her magic roiled beneath the surface. His life had meaning, yet she'd stripped it away and repurposed it toward her gain. She could have saved him. She was *supposed* to save him.

A ball formed in her throat, choking her. Haizea exhaled a shuddering breath.

"I'm s–" a hysterical laugh cut her apology short.

Haizea's voice, rich and full, twisted with maniacal glee. She did not fight against the high of her Cosmic magic. Alone, with no one else nearby to watch or listen, she let her power wrap around her like a warm blanket and sank into its embrace. A white tint skirted the edges of her reddened vision. The mountainous winds drowned out her laughter and whipped against her blood-soaked fur coat. Only when her chest began to hurt did Haizea work to control herself.

She exhaled slowly to regain her composure. Her quivering hands removed her coat as she crouched down and bundled the remnants of the man's skeleton within her furs. Despite her incredible strength, the pile of bones weighed heavy in her arms.

Haizea arrived at her leader's doorstep, covered in blood and her clothes tattered. When the door swung open, Vendela's brows rose high and her dark blue eyes darted over her towering form as she crossed the threshold.

"What the hell happened to you?"

Haizea sighed.

"Wolf attack. They took down a man on the walkway. I found him partially eaten," she unfolded her coat and revealed the contents.

"*Partially?* Then why is he a pile of bones?"

Haizea's austere expression did not betray the way her gut twisted under Vendela's scrutiny.

"You try fighting off an angry wolf pack, alone and without magic, and tell me how that goes for you." Her words came out harsher than intended.

"I tried to save him, but the pack took me by surprise. Held out as long as I could against them, but it all happened so fast. I felt their fangs crush my throat and...," Haizea trailed off, shaking her head.

Vendela frowned as she looked down at the pile of bones, making the faint lines on her forehead and around her mouth more prominent–a rare moment when her age truly showed. With medium brown skin and her few strands of gray hair carefully tucked away beneath her dark brown tresses, Haizea often forgot that Vendela was in her early fifties–close to the same age her mother would have been if she were still alive. A few moments of silence passed before Vendela spoke again.

"Were you able to identify him beforehand?"

Haizea nodded and described what she could about the man. Vendela sat down heavily at the table.

"That's a start, at least. I'll get the word out later, see if anybody recognizes his description. Hopefully, we can find his family quickly."

"It's my fault they won't have a body. I should be the one to do it."

"Vendela shook her head.

"As the leader, it's my job to do that. There will be plenty of time and opportunity for you to take on the hard tasks in the future. No need to rush into it now. Besides, if he really was half eaten, then I suppose you spared them the horror of having to identify him."

Haizea cleared her throat to respond, but her own words would not form—the Cosmic high still furled in the background, and her irritation added another load that her already overwhelmed mind couldn't parse through. She clamped her jaw shut and took a deep breath to conceal the lingering high as best as she could.

A glint in the corner of Haizea's eye caught her attention. Several boxes lay strewn about in Vendela's home. Their metallic exterior led her to believe that they contained earth's smoke—it was the only way to transport the anti-magical plant in large quantities safely.

Her throat tightened at the sight. If King Rhys had never gotten his hands on the plant, Grandfather Harzel might have survived the confrontation with his knights.

"Delivery from the warriors of Mount Haligus. I asked for a bit more since some of our younger warriors are nearing the age where they can craft their own weapons." Vendela's voice pulled Haizea from her thoughts, confirming her suspicions.

Earth's smoke grew naturally in the southern volcanic mountains of the range. As a result, the northern non-volcanic mountains—Illiniza and Niaby—relied on them for supply.

"You should store that box outside." Haizea pointed at one with a massive dent. "If the earth's smoke starts sapping your vitality, you won't feel it. They should know better than to travel with a damaged box."

Vendela grunted and shifted in her seat.

"They had a run-in with some kingdom dwellers as they traveled between the mountains. Probably got damaged in the fight."

Haizea's brows drew together, further hardening her expression.

"Kingdom dwellers?"

Vendela nodded.

"Every now and then, they need a not-so-gentle reminder about not encroaching on our lands. A few heads on stakes should deter them from trying it again anytime soon," Vendela said.

She paused, her expression sobering as she regarded Haizea. Vendela stood up and came back with a smaller box that had been mixed in with the rest.

"The Niabian warriors came through here the other night to get their supply as well, since it's easier to meet them halfway. They said this is for Alastair."

Haizea opened the box and inhaled sharply at the contents.

"It's still difficult to wrap my head around his own villagers killing his entire family. How has he been?"

"Windhaven is an adjustment for him. It took him quite a while to acclimatize to the high altitude, but he's much better these days. We're taking everything else one day at a time."

Vendela smiled softly.

"The vitality curses as much as it blesses. I'm happy to hear that the scales have tipped in your favor once again," Vendela said.

"Please, send Alastair my best wishes. I'll never be able to fully understand what you two have been through, and I pray to Aaryn that I never do. But I'm glad that you two have each other. I know having something to lose makes it harder at times, but it's important to stay grounded. Especially for us warriors."

Haizea dipped her head in a slight nod, her eyes still glowing a brilliant red. She picked up the box and stood to leave.

"Thank you, Vendela. I appreciate your kind words."

Haizea closed the door, and the brisk winds enveloped her. She closed her eyes and took a deep breath, inhaling the bloody aroma wafting off of her skin—the fact that most of it belonged to her didn't matter. The vitality pulsed within, low and steady like a drum. Each beat pushed the man's grotesque demise to the back of her mind, and her inner doubts about whether or not she truly could have saved him from his injuries fell by the wayside.

She could not reverse what she'd done to him. Best not to linger on it.

Haizea hummed to herself as she continued onward with her walk home, the soft tune drowning out the quiet, nagging voice that told her otherwise.

Chapter 2

Human Realm, Mount Illiniza, Windhaven Village

Dawn had given way to a full sunrise by the time Haizea returned home. The front door gently clicked shut behind her, and she left her boots and swords by the door. She followed the sound of Alastair's deep and even breathing to their bedroom.

A thin ray of sunlight peeked through the curtains, showcasing his sleeping form. He lay on his side facing away from the door, but they had a mirror set up so that he could see who entered the room, no matter which direction he faced.

Haizea crept over to her wardrobe and gathered fresh clothes so that she could wash the blood from her body before he woke up. When a cool breeze brushed against her skin and her magic responded to the sensation, she dipped her head in defeat. She looked up to see Alastair watching her through the mirror. He grunted as he rolled over and sat up properly. His shirt lifted and, before she could stop herself, Haizea's eyes followed the trail of white hair that went down his lower abdomen.

Alastair pushed the curtains back to allow more of the morning light to come through. He turned back to her with a smile on his face, but as his gaze combed over her, it slowly faded. It took half a breath for him to close the distance between them.

He held her arm in his hands, frowning as he ran his fingers over her shredded shirt sleeve. Haizea shuddered as her magic flared at his touch, but her discomfort mostly came from the tenderness within her arm—although her skin had mended itself and the bones wove themselves back together, they still had not fully set themselves yet. On the outside, she looked fine, but it would take more time for the internal aching to go away.

Alastair's hands roamed lower and grabbed her waist. He gripped her firmly, but his thumbs gently brushed against the claw marks on her shirt. Haizea tensed when he pushed her shirt up, and he ran his thumbs over her exposed skin, smooth and unbroken. His mouth tightened as he looked over her. His gaze honed in on the side of her neck before he examined her there too. When he let her go so that he could sign, her vitality calmed, but she quietly yearned for him to hold her again.

~*This is* your *blood*.~

Haizea sighed and then explained what happened on the walkway with the pack of wolves.

~*I thought the warriors always traveled in twos? Where was Shauni?*~

~*We parted ways to head home after finishing our patrol. I'm fine, Alastair.*~

His frown deepened.

~*I'm okay, I promise. I get a little bruised sometimes, but I always make it back in one piece.*~

Alastair's eyes flickered over her once again.

~*Not always,*~ he signed.

Haizea sobered, understanding that he referred to her fight with King Rhys, where she'd fallen from a few stories high. With the earth's smoke suppressing her magic, it left her bones shattered and slow to heal, and she was still unable to walk. Keen to change the subject, she retrieved the box from the dresser and guided him to sit down on the bed.

~*This is for you.*~

Alastair grew still as he opened the box. Tears welled in his eyes, and his lips quivered faintly. He pulled out a portrait and held it up—the picture of Rey that had been in his old bedroom. The other portrait in the box had not fared as well. Half of it had burned in the fire, but the half that remained showed a picture of Alastair's family. He was much younger, a teenager. His mother and father stood behind him, and a few of his siblings and cousins fit into the image before the rest had been burned away.

He pulled out a few more trinkets, most of which Haizea didn't recognize, but with each one more tears spilled over. When he began to weep in earnest, Haizea stepped closer and wrapped her arms around him, holding him against her chest. A crippling guilt clenched deep within.

She had wasted precious time by helping his village with her healing abilities. By allowing her compassion to blind her, Alastair's family paid the ultimate price.

He leaned heavier into her embrace, and Haizea hugged him a little tighter, stroking his hair until his tears finally calmed. When he leaned back to look up at her, his eyes caught on her shirt—shredded, blood-stained and now damp with tears. He peeled it off and the dried blood made the fabric tug against her skin. Her pants weren't quite as ragged, but still not in great condition. Alastair unzipped them and tugged downward on her waistband. The air hit her exposed legs. He got to his feet, and Haizea craned her neck to continue holding his gaze. He grabbed her hand and led her toward the bathroom, where he began filling the tub. Haizea nudged him.

~*Is this your way of telling me I smell bad?*~

~*You've had a long night on patrols. You deserve a relaxing bath.*~

She narrowed her eyes at his all too innocent expression.

~*You know, I'd already be soaking by now if you hadn't interrupted me. You'd be none the wiser.*~

~If you're hurt, I want to know about it. Even if you're healed,~ he paused, and his expression grew stern. ~Especially *if you're healed.*~

In response, Haizea slipped out of her underwear, effectively drawing his attention elsewhere. Satisfied, she stepped into the tub and the warm water caressed her bare skin. Alastair pulled a small step stool beside the tub. He dipped his finger into the water and drew circles along the surface, watching as she lathered her towel with soap and began washing her body.

Haizea winced as she reached down to scrub her legs and feet. It wasn't an intense pain—just a small pinch of discomfort as her internal injuries continued to heal, but regardless, Alastair noticed. He pushed up his shirt sleeves, took the towel from her hands, and grasped one of her legs, slowly lifting it out of the water and scrubbing it for her. A pulse shot through her from his point of contact as her vitality rippled. Haizea leaned backward and focused on her breathing to keep the tides of her power at bay. Small pieces of the tub chipped away as her fingers gripped the sides—residual strength from using her blood magic earlier still remained.

~Do you mind if we display them?~ he signed after he put her other leg back in the water.

Haizea blinked and drew her brows together, still preoccupied by the lingering sensation of her magic responding to his.

~The pictures,~ he added.

~Alastair. This is your home as much as it is mine. You don't have to ask.~

~I know, but the only portrait we have out is the one we took together a few weeks ago. I know you have more. I'm guessing there's a reason you choose not to display them.~

She exhaled a deep, drawn-out breath.

~That doesn't mean we can't put yours on the mantle. There should be some frames in the second bedroom,~ she signed.

He perked up visibly at that. As Haizea got out of the tub, he offered his hand to help her keep her balance. Once her feet touched the ground, he wrapped a large towel around her body.

Alastair pulled a container of moisturizer from the cabinet. Jolts of energy radiated through her as he applied it to her skin.

No longer skin and bone like when they'd first met, Alastair had filled out his frame over the last several months. He wasn't muscular or plump, but he instead looked whole, with a distinct softness–like a once withered flower that now flourished in the sun.

It took all of her willpower to pull away from him and get dressed. They went to her childhood bedroom, which served as more of a storage closet than anything else these days. She rummaged around for some old frames that looked like they would fit Alastair's portraits. Behind her, Alastair huffed and the floor shook from his weight. She turned around to see him crossing his legs on the ground.

A box holding most of her family's portraits rested in front of Alastair. Haizea had only intended to get the frames for him, but by the looks of things, he had more in mind.

~*Is this your mother?*~ Alastair asked.

He held up a picture of Haizea as a teenager. Beside her stood her mother. They displayed an identical glare, with the only notable difference between them being Haizea's blonde coils compared to her mother's dark tresses.

~*Yes. Her name was Ilmare.*~

Alastair looked between Haizea and the picture a few times.

~*She was very beautiful. You look just like her.*~

Haizea joined him on the ground and thanked him by leaning in and pressing her lips against his. Alastair cupped her face with his hands and showered her with more–her forehead, her eyebrows, both cheeks, and her lips once more. Her vitality tugged and pulled in response, her magic amplifying her physical desires.

Alastair gifted her with a warm smile that showcased his dimples before pulling out the next portrait. This time, Grandfather Harzel and Haizea's father, Hadyn, looked back at them. They were both much younger and livelier than Haizea's recollection. Both of them smiled brightly and her father held a small bundle in his arms—Haizea as a baby.

Her eyes stung as she looked at that portrait in particular. Seeing her grandfather—young and rife with life—made her chest tighten.

Tears blurred her vision. The portrait morphed into the image of his severed head placed in a box—sent to her doorstep like a gift, only to unwrap a nightmare. She bit her quivering lip and inhaled sharply, her nostrils flaring as she worked to quell the tide rising within.

She had felled an entire army in the wake of his death. But that feat felt worthless. Her power was supposed to *protect* the people she loved. That was her duty—her purpose.

Grandfather Harzel died because of her inadequacies. He gave her every tool, taught her everything she knew about Cosmic magic, and she'd failed him when he needed her the most. Just like her father had her mother. She couldn't repeat the same mistakes.

Alastair's moving arms caught her attention.

~*I see where you get your smile from,*~ he signed and paused for a moment as he looked at the first picture again. ~*I can also see why you don't do it that often.*~

Haizea hummed to herself in a desperate attempt to mask her grief with amusement. Alastair's bright eyes searched hers, the baby blue overtaking the lavender. He caressed her cheek with the back of his finger.

~*We should put these up too.*~

Haizea nodded and blinked a few times as she fought to maintain her composure.

~*He didn't blame you, Haizea. He loved you...he still does.*~

For some reason, hearing that only made her feel worse.

They set up the portraits on the mantle above the fireplace. A picture of the two of them sat in the center. Unlike the others, which were intricate drawings, a transmuting mage made theirs by creating a flash of fire to burn their images onto paper. They'd passed by the mage's stand in the marketplace and Alastair had never seen anything like it before. Haizea couldn't bring herself to refuse. In the photo, Alastair beamed by her side with his arm wrapped around her waist and Haizea showcased her rare smile—genuine and unreserved in a way that made her expression match his warmth.

Haizea suppressed a yawn as the night caught up to her. The bed called her name, but she didn't want the moment to end.

~*You've been up all night. You should get some rest,*~ Alastair signed.

~*I'm alright.*~

~*How about this? You sit on the couch while I make breakfast and we can eat together once I'm done.*~

He stared her down, but he couldn't muster nearly the same ferocity she naturally emanated. Still, the fact that he even tried tickled her and the slight flicker of her lips betrayed her amusement. She acquiesced with a nod and Alastair slipped his arms around her from behind, his long locks of white hair twining with her honey blonde coils as he rested his chin on her shoulder.

Haizea closed her eyes, swaying gently in his embrace. They stood together for a short while before he shifted. Sparks of energy radiated across her skin when he began planting gentle kisses along her shoulder.

She shifted her head to meet his eyes—the flame's reflection danced in them, rich orange against a soft periwinkle. A gentleness colored his countenance, yet a hint of darkness hid underneath. Her fingers traced over the back of his hand as he toyed with the hem of her shirt.

He trailed more kisses up her neck and grazed her ear with his teeth. Heat from the fireplace hugged her bare skin as his hands slipped beneath her clothing, one roamed over the swell of her chest, while the other ventured between her legs.

A ragged sigh escaped her lips and her vision flickered red under his touch. She reached behind and tugged at his waistband and he quickly obliged her by stripping them away. They joined together, falling into a familiar rhythm while he continued pleasuring her with a well-practiced ease. She rolled her hips to match his movements, intensifying their pace. Alastair grunted behind her and tension coiled in her core before she shuddered in release.

A red hue tinted Haizea's vision. She blinked a few times in an attempt to reorient herself. She turned around to see Alastair's cheeks had small red blotches on them—her magic had pulled on the threads of his vitality. Haizea concealed her healing by caressing his cheeks with her thumbs.

They made their way over to the couch, where he draped a blanket over her. He waited until she rested her head against the couch's cushion before heading toward the kitchen. In his absence, Haizea's attention fell to the portraits. Their family etched their way into her dreams—all of them, gone before their time.

Alastair's face was the last thing she saw before sleep finally took her. A resolve steeled itself within. She would use her power to protect him from sharing their families' fate.

After a full day of rest, the lingering aches of Haizea's encounter with the wolves had evaporated. Dozens of heartbeats thrummed against her magic as she approached the warriors' training grounds.

"Catch!" a voice shouted amidst the crowd.

Wads of fabric flew toward her and she narrowly caught them before they hit her in the face. Haizea's eyes landed on Shauni, who stood several feet away. Her grin broadened as Haizea's glare intensified.

"Hello to you too," Haizea said.

"How about a bit of sparring to warm up?" Shauni said.

Haizea unrolled the fabric and her perception of the pulses around her began to fade. She slipped the bands around her wrists and ankles—each containing earth's smoke within. To avoid the lethality of direct exposure, the plant did not touch their skin, but the close proximity still suppressed their magic. For the time being, Haizea no longer had access to her healing abilities and Shauni could not use her telekinesis either.

Shauni tossed her two wooden swords and they each slipped into their respective positions. The afternoon sun cast a circle of light between them.

Haizea went on the attack, leveling a series of strikes toward her companion. Shauni twisted her torso out of the path of the first blow, while using one blade to block another. Specks of wood drifted in the space between them.

A single step from Haizea put her out of Shauni's range, allowing her to avoid any retaliation while still running her offense. She unleashed blow after blow, but years of training together had wisened Shauni to her tactics. Shauni dodged, her footsteps nimble as she narrowly avoided what would have been a chest impalement had their blades been real. Instead, the blade landed on her shoulder.

Shauni answered with an attack of her own–thrusting her entire body forward to diminish the spacing advantage that Haizea's height gave her. Though Haizea staved off the worst of the attack with a quick shift in position, the wooden blade smacked against her thigh.

She gritted her teeth but otherwise made no show of the pain radiation up her leg.

As Shauni recovered to her base stance, Haizea seized the opening. She gathered her strength and went for a lethal blow to the head. Recognition flickered on Shauni's face at the last possible moment and their swords clashed together in a violent collision. Two of which exploded into a cloud of dust while the other two splintered and fractured. The duo looked at their damaged weapons respectively–Haizea with a level gaze and Shauni with an amused smirk. They dropped them to the ground in unison.

A strong breeze blew between the two women, sending Haizea's braids flying while Shauni's short, tight curls didn't budge. Despite the wicked grin creeping across Shauni's face, her dark violet eyes hardened with focus. Haizea matched it with a cold glare of her own as she shifted into her fighting stance. They went on the attack.

Haizea utilized her height advantage by throwing a bone shattering roundhouse at Shauni's face. Shauni ducked below her outstretched leg while simultaneously side stepping, where Haizea's back was wide open. When Shauni landed a powerful blow to Haizea's kidney, it took all of her control not to cry out. Haizea shook it off, but unlike normal, her pain did not fade right away.

The faster of the two, Shauni closed the distance with a barrage of punches and forced Haizea on the defense. Shauni threw a jab to her throat and Haizea used one arm to block and answered with a powerful upper cut of her own. Shauni tilted her head back, narrowly avoiding the blow that would have cracked a few teeth if it landed–nothing that Haizea couldn't fix afterward.

Their movements blurred as they fell into a familiar flow. Bruises and welts formed on their arms and legs as they struck and blocked one another. Shauni parried a punch from Haizea and followed with an ambitious grab, clearly aiming to throw her companion. Haizea reversed the grab and Shauni landed roughly on the ground with her arm twisted against the grain—just enough to hurt but not enough to break the bone.

Shauni did not give up so easily. She swept her legs across the ground and knocked Haizea off balance. When Haizea hit the dirt, Shauni erupted into boisterous laughter.

"What's our score now?" she asked as she caught her breath.

"Shauni, you're the only one keeping track. If we're not even, then it shouldn't be more than one or two matches difference," Haizea said as she clambered to her feet. She held her hand out to Shauni.

"Well, in that case, I'm definitely one ahead," Shauni winked, earning an eye roll from Haizea.

They each doffed their bracelets and returned them to the storage area where they kept weapons and other supplies. In their absence, Haizea's healing magic rose to the surface. As her body mended itself, she laid her palms against Shauni's skin, melting away her injuries.

Flickering desire pulsed in tandem with Shauni's heartbeat. Haizea's vitality coiled, as the undercurrent of her Cosmic power tried to claw its way to the surface. Before she had realized it, her fingers had curled, prepared to break skin.

Shauni breathed a sigh of relief before thanking her, drowning out the newfound roar in her ears. Haizea swallowed, quickly putting her hands by her side.

"Again, Jassia."

They both turned at the sound of Vendela's voice. A few yards away, she ran the younger warriors in training through sword-fighting drills. This particular group ranged from their early to late teens. For girls whose mothers were warriors, like Haizea and Shauni, they typically began training as soon as they could hold a sword. For those who didn't have familial ties, their training started much later in their adolescent years.

Jassia—the girl at the center of Vendela's attention—was thirteen and she'd begun her training three years ago, around the same time Haizea left for Arcelia.

Jassia repeated her sword drill. Her sword wobbled as she gripped onto the hilts and approached her sparring partner, Covy. Covy tied her long black braids back, her dark brown eyes hardening and she slipped into her fighting stance. Jassia followed suit, but hesitated, her eyes darting to the crowd watching them.

"Come on now," Vendela urged.

Jassia closed the distance and swung at Covy slowly. A translucent form weaved about as Covy's astral projected Soul fortified her defenses. She aimed her next attack at Covy's face, who blocked it with ease.

"We both know you're faster than this, Jassia," Vendela waved Covy off.

Jassia nodded tightly. Her chest heaved up and down and she picked up her pace. Her movements became more fluid, but they lacked the strength required to deal any injury. Jassia completed the first half of the drill before Vendela tested her defenses.

Vendela's wooden sword slashed through the air, not violently, but not without power either. Jassia narrowly blocked it, her grip still unsteady. Vendela sped up and landed a few hits. The sound made even Haizea wince from where she stood.

Frowning, Vendela sent Jassia to stand with the other girls. Covy whispered in her Jassia's ear dusted off her shoulders.

"You all have a lot of work to do. Some more than others. Keep practicing your sword drills in your own time. Tomorrow we'll take a break from weapons work and will do strength and endurance training."

Some of the young warriors groaned, earning a sharp glare from Vendela. They quickly silenced themselves. Others nodded with a somber determination.

Jassia wiped at her eyes a few times, clearly frustrated, but she otherwise maintained her composure. Haizea walked over to her. Jassia craned her neck to make eye contact, her irises glinting a vibrant copper in the sunlight. When the young girl stiffened under Haizea's gaze, she made an effort to soften her expression.

"I just wanted to say I think you did fine in your drill. Your motions are perfect; you just need a little more power behind your blocks and strikes. I can tell that you know the techniques."

Jassia sniffed and nodded.

"I've been practicing every chance I can. I just…," she glanced at the crowd of other warriors. Haizea followed the movement and hummed in understanding.

"Everyone's packing up now. Do you want to try again? You can spar me."

Jassia hesitated for a long stretch before nodding.

They grabbed a set of swords from the storage area and Haizea led her to a quieter area, at the edge of the training grounds. Haizea lifted her swords into her fighting stance and motioned for Jassia to attack.

Jassia started off timidly, her movements lacking power as they did with Vendela. Haizea nodded silently to encourage her. Jassia put more power into her next strike. Still not quite where she needed to be, but closer. By the time they traded places and Haizea put Jassia on the defense, the girl had a spark in her eye and blocked Haizea's swings with ease. Once they completed the drill, Jassia surprised Haizea by continuing and they fell into a rhythm.

"Have you learned how to disarm yet?" Haizea asked while blocking. Jassia nodded.

"Show me."

Haizea held her swords more loosely so that Jassia could knock them out of her hands. One sword chatted to the ground a little too easily for what she wanted, so she made Jassia work a little harder for the second but gave in before the girl got frustrated.

"You've got the foundations of an excellent swordswoman, Jassia. Keep working, and in due time, you'll be ready for your mastery test."

"You were sixteen when you passed yours, right?" Jassia asked as they walked back to the storage area.

"Yes," Haizea answered, taking note of the way she brightened. "But most warriors take theirs as adults. Shauni was eighteen. Many of the others were in their early twenties. Everyone is ready at different times."

Jassia opened her mouth like she wanted to speak, but decided against it. They packed away their supplies in silence before Jassia ran off, her loose curls bouncing with each step. Haizea stretched her arms across her chest, giving her joints a much-needed pop.

"That went better than I expected. Guess she's just got a bit of performance anxiety," the sound of Shauni's voice behind her almost made Haizea jump. Almost.

"I thought you left," she said. "I think so too. Once she grows out of it, she'll be fine."

Shauni grinned and playfully bumped Haizea with her elbow. It stung, just a little. Haizea threw her bag over her shoulder and they walked along the snow-covered path to go home.

Chapter 3

Human Realm, Mount Illiniza, Windhaven Village

Alastair rummaged through his dresser and pulled out a pair of pants. They hung a little loose on his hips than normal. He tightened his belt and, despite his full belly, passed over the well-worn loop where he usually latched it and went for one beside it.

A frown curled his lips. He must have lost a few pounds—a worrisome realization since his current weight was not only the heaviest he'd ever been, but also the healthiest.

He always had plenty to eat here in Windhaven, so there was only one other possible explanation for the weight loss that he could think of: magical wasting was inching its way back.

Wisps of magic crawled across his skin, unleashing a wave of exhaustion that crashed into him at the familiar sensation of someone, or more specifically *something*, looking over his shoulder. Prying open his mind. Peering into his thoughts. Although Alastair could not see it, he knew exactly what and who it was.

The Soul Reaper always kept careful watch over him. The entity's presence served as a painful constant reminder that no matter what Alastair did, his magic would cause his demise.

If he used his necromancy, which required him to pull power from the Soul Realm, then the Soul Reaper would chip away at his Soul as a form of repayment. This corruption would not only kill him but would strip him of his Soul entirely. It meant that he could not continue on in the Soul Realm after death. He would never reunite with his family again.

If he avoided his Cosmic magic altogether, then magical wasting would destroy his body. He had not used his necromancy in nearly a year, not since he helped Haizea defeat King Rhys and his army.

As a medium, he spent his entire life intimately connected with death. Having that connection be severed as a direct result of using his magic went against his very nature. Magical wasting meant an unpleasant death, but at least Alastair could find comfort in spending eternity with his family.

If only it were that simple. Alastair still had one last tether to the Human Realm.

Haizea never asked if he practiced his necromancy, but if Alastair could see the nascent signs of magical wasting now, then certainly she would soon notice it as well. He had yet to muster up the courage to tell her the gravity of his magic. She thought Alastair's choice was between living and dying–between magical wasting and embracing his Cosmic power. In reality, his choice was which early death he preferred.

He knew that he needed to tell her. And he would, eventually. But the prospect of doing so—of impaling yet another dagger into her fractured heart—twisted his stomach into knots. They had a quiet, peaceful life here in Windhaven, and once he revealed the truth about his power, it would quickly come crumbling down. He wanted to hold onto that for as long as he could.

Alastair's focus shifted back to the present. He tugged on his coat and finished off the cup of warm cider he'd had with his breakfast. A bowl rested beside the door, holding coins Haizea set aside for him so that he could buy anything he needed. He had a few hours before she would return from her warrior's duties. The crisp mountain air greeted Alastair as he ventured outside.

It had taken a while to get accustomed to Windhaven's vastness compared to Goldenleaf. Massive, sturdy-looking log cabins made up the residential areas of the village. Well-maintained roads provided pathways to travel throughout the village. A pack of dogs leashed to a sled raced past him, with a person standing on the back and holding onto a handle. Their mouth moved and the dogs made a sharp turn to the right.

Alastair trailed behind, heading toward the village's exit. Unlike his time in Llyr, steam-powered vehicles did not fill the roads here in the mountains. Instead, ropeways with cable cars hung dozens of feet into the air to transport the villagers. Telekinetic mages stood stationed at the various pylons and used their magic to power the pulley system.

To Alastair's surprise, villagers could ride them free of charge. Haizea had explained that everyone paid a tribute from part of their earnings to maintain the cars' upkeep and provide a salary for the mages that operated them. Alastair nodded at one of said mages as he climbed inside. The conductors waited while more people loaded on and then the cars began to move.

About fifteen minutes later, he arrived in a neighboring village called Mistpoint. Many families here worked as butchers, so their food market offered more variety. Alastair had every intention of stopping by the market—he usually prepared supper while Haizea was out—but a cool breeze against his skin nudged him in a different direction. He followed the tug of his magic, his footsteps wandering aimlessly until he finally saw what it led him to.

A massive building was embedded in the rocky mountainside. The structure towered dozens of stories high, reaching toward the skies. People wearing long robes meandered up and down the expansive steps, many of them walking, others floating and some of them flying. Jaw falling slack, Alastair took a step closer. The vitality curled tighter around him as he did so.

Alastair paused, curious about the building, but uncertain. A Soul settled on his shoulder and words echoed within:

Keep going.

He continued onward. With each step he took, the magical pressure sharpened. Alastair burned hot in his coat, and yet he shivered at the same time. He started up the steps and nearly walked into a woman standing there—he'd been so preoccupied with the building up above and the way his magic reacted, he hadn't noticed her.

She pushed her hood back, revealing a bald head and topaz eyes. She looked older than him, probably in her late thirties or early forties.

~*It's a pleasure to meet you, Alastair,*~ she signed.

Alastair furrowed his brows.

~*How do you...? Do I know you?*~

The woman smiled and tapped her forehead with her finger.

~*No. You told me.*~

A light pain pinched inside of Alastair's head and memories rose to the surface. The day he met Haizea. Bickering with Alina. A rare, hearty meal with the rest of his family. His desperate attempt to resurrect Rey.

~*You're a seer?*~ Alastair asked. The woman nodded.

~*My name is Diora. I keep an eye out for any wanderers who arrive at the monastery looking for help.*~

Alastair gained a sense of understanding when she mentioned that this was a monastery. Mountaineers came here to worship. Which meant that the robed woman in front of him was a monk. Alastair did not follow the practice of worshiping the Demons, and neither did Haizea, so he never had any reason to come this way before.

~*I don't need help though. I'm just...a Soul guided me here.*~

Diora's smile softened.

~Precisely. All of the Soul Reaper's children make their way here eventually.~

He wrung his fingers and shifted his weight. He'd never heard of anyone paying obeisance to the Soul Reaper—only the Demons—but Alastair understood very little about the entity.

~What do you mean by the Soul Reaper's 'children'?~ he asked.

~That's a question best answered by another medium,~ she frowned as she considered him. ~Actually, in your case, another necromancer. Though I must admit you're quite young to be one.~

Diora waved at him to follow. Alastair ascended the steps and mirrored her grimace with one of his own. Young to be a necromancer? Haizea had taken up blood magic at the age of eighteen and Alastair was around nineteen or twenty when he first used his necromancy, although it was by accident. That aside, it didn't seem out of the ordinary.

He looked at Diora, knowing she'd heard his thoughts and hoping she would explain further, but she kept walking. The closer they got to the monastery, the tighter vitality constricted around him. Once they crossed the threshold and entered the temple, a towering statue of Aaryn peered down at them. She looked exactly as Alastair remembered—vibrant golden skin and hair and wings as white as snow.

Alastair moved to wipe a bead of sweat from his forehead and the air itself seemed to ripple from the movement. He stopped short. Another wave cascaded through the atmosphere and a shiver ran down his spine as it tugged against his magic.

A cluster of parishioners passed by, the atmosphere around them shimmering. One of them slowly levitated from the ground and the distortion intensified, sending another surge through his vitality.

Diora tapped his shoulder to get his attention.

~Hundreds of parishioners visit the monastery every day. The vitality is more concentrated here due to the high usage of magic.~

She motioned for Alastair to wait and darted off before returning with another monk in tow. As they approached, Diora's mouth moved rapidly and the man nodded, occasionally glancing at Alastair. He was also bald like Diora, but looked older than her, probably in his late fifties or early sixties, with faint wrinkles adorning his eyes and face.

~Alastair, this is Pamin. He'll be your guide,~ she said, and departed just as swiftly as she had appeared.

~Diora tells me you have many questions,~ Pamin signed.

Alastair hesitated, uncertain of where to begin. ~Diora said that I'm young. I'm not sure what she meant by that.~

~How old are you, son?~ Pamin asked.

~I'm twenty-five. Almost twenty-six.~

Pamin pursed his lips.

~Most mediums do not touch the Cosmic Arts until they are well into adulthood. The earliest being in their thirties, but many choose to wait until their forties or even fifties. Necromancy cuts the life short, so it gives us a chance to spend more time in this realm before traversing to the next,~ Pamin's frown deepened. ~That's something you should have learned in mage school.~

~I grew up at the base of Mount Niaby. Too far to attend mage school.~

Pamin's chest heaved up and down in what looked like a sigh.

~Tell me more about how you came to use necromancy for the first time.~

Alastair told him about Rey and how he'd tried to bring him back to life and instead found himself trapped in the Soul Realm, with the Soul Reaper. Pamin perked up, his brows arching higher.

~Very few necromancers are blessed with a visit from the Soul Reaper while still in the Human Realm. You must have his favor,~ he signed.

When Alastair stiffened, another cool breeze brushed over him. Pamin must have read his Soul once more.

~*Tell me, what are your encounters with the Soul Reaper like?*~ Pamin continued.

Alastair swallowed heavily. He wrung his hands together before continuing.

~*The first time I saw him, he didn't say anything to me. He just watched. The second time, he explained to me what happens to my Soul when I use Cosmic magic. Another time, Aaryn pulled me into the Soul Realm and the Soul Reaper...I'm not sure what she wanted, but the Soul Reaper stood between us.*~

A smile crinkled the corners of Pamin's eyes.

~*He protected you,*~ he signed.

Alastair's gut twisted and he scowled as irritation flared within.

~*How can he possibly be* protecting *me when he's corrupting my Soul?*~

~*It's true that necromancy comes at a hefty price, but that is the case for all Cosmic magic. The Cosmic Art takes what's precious to us and corrupts it, but that isn't exclusive to necromancers. Take blood magic, for example. All blood mages originate as healers. They're trained to restore life, but their Cosmic magic forces them to extinguish it. Mediums are intrinsically tied to the Souls around us, but as necromancers, our power ultimately untethers our Souls if we allow it to so.*~ Pamin said.

Alastair studied him, his brows drawing together.

~*What do you mean by 'allow'?*~

~*I think we should start with something simpler. Smaller. In order for you to understand the complexities of necromancy, you need to have a strong foundation as a medium. Your meetings with the Soul Reaper were beyond your control, correct?*~ Pamin said.

Alastair nodded.

~*The most gifted mediums can read the Souls of beings far across the realms. With practice and proper training, you'll be able to hear whispers of the Beasts and the roar of the Titans. You can even call upon the Soul Reaper at will. This is all without even touching your necromancing abilities. We can focus on that later,~* he paused, considering Alastair. *~Full mastery also means having the ability to block it all out in total silence.~*

Silence. That resonated with Alastair.

~Is that something you'd be willing to teach me?~ he asked.

~Of course. It's what we monks are here for. Besides, you were sent here as an act of divinity. The Soul Reaper may very well call me home if I refused,~ Pamin signed.

Alastair tilted his head and idly wondered if Pamin was mad, but the prospect of homing in on his control and maybe, just maybe getting rid of the ominous feeling of being constantly watched was enough to make him overlook it.

Chapter 4

Human Realm, Kestramore, Khisfire Province, Tarnow City

"Have you heard from Lotus recently? She replied to my letter regarding our meeting, but it's unlike her to be late," Premier Eryx asked, reaching for her wine glass.

Kallistê straightened her shoulders and smoothed down her dress—a brilliant gold with a plunging neckline and thigh-high slit.

"Lotus has her hands full with Olysseus. Despite eliminating Sovereign Jasver, the kingdom still has a functional army–and, a result, an emboldened populace. I suspect that's the reason behind her tardiness. My spies informed me that dissenters have begun concentrating their forces and setting up a base there. There's even been a sizable exodus from Arcelia," she said.

"Viltarin gave me the impression that he had Arcelia under control," Eryx quirked an eyebrow as she returned her drink to the table.

"That's precisely why people are running to Olysseus. Arcelia has no army. Without a formally trained fighting force, he's brought them to heel with ease."

Kestramore had offered an alliance on the condition that someone who represented the islanders' interests took a place on the open thrones. Somedays, Kallistê wondered why she bothered herself with this political merrymaking, but just as she needed spies within Llyr, her plans to build an empire relied on others advancing her interests when she could not actively be present.

It also didn't hurt that setting foot on Kestramore's shores reminded her of her love for the island. The vitality settled weightily against her body, rife with Cosmic magic. A warm breeze brushed against her skin and the sun shone brightly through the windows. The thought of returning to Llyr after this made her feel homesick.

Premier Eryx considered her for a long moment. Rays of sunlight danced across her face, highlighting the richness in her terracotta skin. She brushed an errant strand of gray hair from her face and smoothed it into her bun.

"I intend to retire at the end of this year when I complete my term. If things don't work out here on the continent, you should consider coming back home and taking my place," she paused and her eyes grew glassy. "I always imagined that Mericus would ride my coattails and be elected as Premier by now. But that bastard took him from me."

Kallistê concealed her grimace by taking a sip from her glass.

"You flatter me, Premier. I appreciate your kind words and confidence in my abilities, but with all due respect, my hands are full with Llyr and my objective for the continent is far from complete."

Premier Eryx was the longest serving official in Kestramore's history. While Kallistê aspired to attain that type of longevity, she had no desire to be an elected leader like Eryx. The Premier answered to the masses—Kallistê ruled over her subjects with absolute authority. Though she loved Kestramore, her vision expanded beyond this small island.

Victory for Kallistê ended with the entire realm in the palm of her hands.

"Your friend, the blood mage. Haizea. How is she doing?"

"Quite some time has passed since we've spoken, but we left things on amicable terms."

The Premier placed her hand on Kallistê's.

"She got justice for my son. I'd love it if you could introduce us so that I can thank her properly."

"I'm sure you would. And I'd love to do that for you, but I think it should wait until things calm down in Olysseus. If Viltarin caught wind–"

"Viltarin, what a pleasure it is to see you again. You're here early," Premier Eryx interrupted as the door swung open.

The Premier finished off her wine and stood from her seat. The vitality swelled as she used her telekinesis to assist in moving her body. Eryx held the empty glass in her hand and another surge rippled through the air as she transformed the dish into a cane. The last time Kallistê had seen the Premier, she hadn't needed a walking aid, but she was in her seventies–an age where old and new ailments often caught up to people.

Viltarin strolled into the room, long dark locks cascading down his back. In addition to being a dignitary, he owned the largest bank on the island. He'd dressed accordingly—he wore a dark orange linen suit that matched the color of his eyes and complemented his terracotta skin. Numerous rings sparkled under the indoor lighting and a golden necklace hung loose around his neck. He took the Premier's outstretched hand and planted a light kiss.

"You look as wise as you are vibrant, Premier."

Kallistê nearly rolled her eyes. Unfortunately, etiquette required that she follow Premier Eryx's lead, so she pushed her chair back and deigned to offer Viltarin her hand. The amber gemstone in one of her rings glinted as he pressed his lips against her skin. He lingered for just a moment before he released her. She suppressed a shiver that trickled down her spine and retracted her hand.

"Our meetings are never without consequence, Kallistê. I must admit that I'm pleasantly surprised with your progress in Llyr."

Kallistê masked her bared teeth with a smile.

"I understand that you've had similar success in Arcelia. Unsurprising, given that you had no army to impede your efforts."

Viltarin quietly assessed her. He adjusted his sleeve cuffs, sending the scent of his cologne flowing toward her.

"We dignitaries thought it fitting to have another curse mage to replace Tarja's place so that your original plans could continue as intended."

"Tarja was one of the first acquaintances I made after moving to Kestramore. You may share her abilities, but a like-minded companion is not so easily replaced."

"Perhaps it is that like-mindedness that led to her death. Rather than take the helm into her own hands, Tarja allowed herself to be led by an outsider."

The barb stung more than Kallistê wanted to admit. She had not been born on the island, but she'd come as a young adult and subsequently spent many years here learning the ways of realmdrifting from the island's omens. In her heart, she was an islander and Kestramore was her home just as much as his.

She opened her mouth to reply, but the door burst open, halting her rebuttal. Lotus's ponytail flew behind her like a magenta flag as she stalked into the room. She paused on Kallistê for a brief moment, her gaze darting down her figure before she turned to the Premier.

"I apologize for my tardiness, Premier. An urgent situation arose at the last minute, which delayed my departure."

"No worries, Lotus, you're not late at all. We're all a little early," Premier Eryx cast a glance at Viltarin and Lotus responded with a slight nod. "The other dignitaries will be joining us soon."

Kallistê narrowed her eyes at Viltarin. She, Premier Eryx, and Lotus had planned to have a private discussion prior to the official meeting. Viltarin's presence made her suspect that he somehow had intercepted their letters.

He could have unveiled their plans in a plethora of ways. As a curse mage, he could wield the power over another's mind with a single word, a simple touch, or even through an innocuous seeming object. Kallistê kept her suspicions to herself but, as if he could read her thoughts, a faint irksome grin curled the Viltarin's lips.

The density of the vitality increased and Kallistê saw the approaching Souls of the other government officials, Quathir and Nehemias. They entered and seated themselves at the table, beginning the meeting.

"Lotus, I understand you called for this meeting," Nehemias said.

She nodded.

"Thank you, Nehemias. I had one of my assistants prepare an enchantment so that you can see the situation in Olysseus firsthand. I apologize for not getting it to you sooner," she pulled out a sheet of paper. Magic rolled off of it in waves.

Nehemias passed it over to Quathir without bothering to read the enchantment. He turned to Lotus.

"I'd rather see things for myself," he said.

Lotus winced as he pried open her mind.

Kallistê had experienced that pain for herself many years ago when she first arrived on Kestramore's shores. As she approached the island, she'd felt the faint tug of a seer reading her thoughts in real time. That sensation had intensified into blistering pain as they delved deeper into her memories to determine her origins.

"Nehemias, the enchantment is more than adequate. Continue delving into her mind without due cause, and I will personally see to it that your mouth and rectum trade places," Premier Eryx quipped.

Adding more weight to her threat, the skin on his lips began to bubble. Nehemias released his telepathic hold on Lotus. She gasped in relief.

"I've seen enough," he said with a shrug.

Quathir slid the paper to Kallistê, and the memory of the mage who enchanted it flowed into her.

Kallistê's mind teleported into a barricaded room. The wooden door quaked under pounding fists, accompanied by frightful shouts that begged to get in. Lotus lifted her hands and a wave of telekinetic magic bolstered the door against the bombardment.

Despite her efforts, the door groaned and fractured.

"Madam Lotus, if we stay they are going to kill us," the curse mage said.

"There's only one way out and it's through that realm's forsaken mob," Lotus hissed. "We're going to have to fight through them."

"Ma'am?"

"I'll lead the attack. You watch my back and take out any stragglers," Lotus said and tied her magenta locks into a ponytail.

Lotus curled her fingers and the door contorted and bent to her will. In a fraction of a second, she transmuted the wood into metal and used her magic to strap some pieces to her body, like armor. For the remainder she did not use, Lotus inhaled and her power amplified further, heating the metal until it became hundreds of molten shards.

The mob stormed into the room. Lotus flung the shards at them, blinding flashes of red streaking through the air. The first wave of attackers went down and the room itself vibrated from their cries of agony. A pulse of energy shoved the people to the side, creating a path for Lotus and her assistant. They made it to the end of the hall and sprinted down the steps. A group of mages stood waiting for them at the landing. They pushed back against her power, creating an invisible telekinetic wall to halt them in their tracks.

The omen aiding Lotus stepped forward.

"Rip off your own heads."

The vitality rippled under the weight of her command. In the blink of an eye, heads began to roll on the floor as the mages turned their own magic against themselves. Noting how some toward the back did not follow suit, the curse mage inhaled, ready to repeat her command once more—but she realized that those who still stood had stuffed their ears, rendering her words null.

They charged at the two women. Lotus did her best to protect both of them, but hundreds of people poured into the stairwell. A blade plunged into the curse mage's shoulder, and Lotus suffered a hit to the head. She grabbed Lotus and ran, commanding those who could hear her voice to move. The exertion left the curse mage exhausted as she pushed her power harder than she was used to doing. The mob gave chase, but they narrowly managed to escape.

As they fled, Lotus snapped her fingers and created a small fire. With a grunt of effort, she sent a blast toward the building, engulfing it in flames.

The enchantment released Kallistê's mind and her focus returned to the present. Lotus stood to her feet.

"The populace pushed us out of the Capital City of Vadronia several months ago in a similar fashion. This transpired in Zampus, roughly twenty miles to the east of the Capital. We've managed to set up a new station a bit farther south in Mariana City, but I'm going to need more forces to withstand the kingdom's sizable population that's attacking us. This isn't sustainable with the numbers I have now."

Quathir cleared his throat.

"Which is *precisely* why we were so resistant to this venture to begin with, need I remind you?"

"Dignitary Quathir, Arcelia and Llyr are decisively and firmly in our control, both of which are several times the size of our island. Olysseus is the only hold out. I do not think it is unreasonable to provide assistance with this," Kallistê said.

Quathir turned on her next.

"Perhaps rather than Lotus requesting that Kestramore expend further resources, you'd like to lend your friend a helping hand. Kallistê, you managed to subdue a kingdom *despite* its army. I find it difficult to understand why she's struggling."

"In the time leading up to the king's assassination, Llyr spent many months sending knights to fight against my Beasts. They suffered heavy losses by the time I took the throne. For those whom I could not appeal to with words, I instilled in them the fear of the Cosmos. But Lotus is operating under different circumstances and this course of action would not work for her."

"Well, given your and Viltarin's resounding successes, perhaps rather than a question of resources, this is a matter of whether or not Lotus is fit for the task," Nehemias said.

"It's only been a few months; this is far from a resounding failure, Nehemias. No need to salivate at the prospect of changing hands," Eryx chided, earning a scoff from the man.

"I'd be more than happy to swap places with Lotus. If she cannot subdue the masses with her transmutation, perhaps my curse magic is better suited for the job," Viltarin said.

"For realm's sake, I had a curse mage by my side," Lotus grated. "It wasn't enough. I need numbers. Bodies. Not a swap in responsibilities. Even with Cosmic magic, the issue is the weight of their magic against ours."

Viltarin leaned back in his seat.

"So what you're saying is that even with two omens, you can't accomplish what Kallistê managed to do alone," he said.

"Kallistê didn't work alone. She had the assistance of a blood mage, who wiped out an entire army. Because of that, you received the easiest assignment."

"If not for my vote turning the tide in favor of this endeavor, there'd be no assignment at all," Viltarin narrowed his eyes. "How about this: Tell me, Lotus, what is a blood mage's weapon?"

Lotus frowned.

"Blood," she said slowly.

"*Life*," he corrected. "You're a transmutation mage, Lotus. So what is your weapon?"

"Get to the point, Viltarin," she huffed.

"The world itself."

Viltarin looked across the table, his eyes momentarily locking with Premier Eryx, who, to Kallistê's surprise, nodded in agreement.

"With telekinesis and transmutation anything you can touch can be wielded with lethal force. Right before this meeting, Premier Eryx turned her glass into a cane. Hell, she threatened to transmute Nehemias himself. Yet when a mob attacks you, the most you do is transform a door? The uprisings in Olysseus aren't a question of numbers and forces, but of the objectively inefficient use of your magic. Why should we send assistance when you've proven you do not know how to utilize the resources available to you properly?"

Kallistê's brows rose. Lotus's mouth hung open for a beat in stunned silence before she flared with anger.

"Well, given your all-knowing wisdom and expertise, maybe we *should–*"

"Spoken with the arrogance of a man who did not have to fight for his position and can judge from the outside," Premier Eryx stepped in before Lotus could finish. "Lotus made perfectly judicious use of her abilities. Transforming human life draws more power from the Cosmic Realm, which means a more intense high that could have compromised her decision making during the escape. She handled the situation no differently than I would have."

Viltarin's smirk faded.

"Maybe we should extend this discussion beyond our closed doors. The people of Kestramore deserve to have their voices heard before the situation becomes untenable. If this blows back at us, they shouldn't be caught unawares," Quathir said.

Kallistê scoffed.

"Predictable that as soon as we hit a single block in the road, you all want to tuck your tails and run," her blue gaze darted between Quathir and Nehemias.

"Predictable that you would still wish to charge forward rather than think of the island's best interests. Our people have never concerned themselves with the continent's affairs. This venture was a mistake from the start and the risk of fallout could mean our island being wiped off the map in retaliation," Nehemias retorted.

"And the reward could be Kestramore expanding its influence across the entire realm. Every kingdom, every inch of the continent would be ruled by omens, bringing our world closer to the Cosmos."

"Then let's put it to a vote to the populace and see if that's what *they* want. Kestramore is engaged in a war across the ocean without their knowledge," Quathir quipped.

"It's going to take a few months to organize a referendum like that. By then, the situation might have resolved. Let's reconvene in three months' time. You all prepare the paperwork for a vote and if Lotus still doesn't have a firm grasp on the situation, then we can let the people decide," Viltarin said.

His words earned shocked looks from Nehemias and Quathir, but Viltarin shook his head. If the duo had further issues to raise, they remained silent.

Without yielding any positive results, the meeting disbanded shortly after. Premier Eryx pulled Lotus aside along with Kallistê.

"Are you certain you can't ask Haizea for assistance?" she asked.

Kallistê fluffed her hair, contemplating. Their alliance was based on mutual benefit–if Haizea was going to help them, she needed to get something out of the arrangement. Which would require more merrymaking than Kallistê currently had the patient for.

But perhaps the blood mage did not need to know she was acting on their behalf at all.

"Are you two familiar with the Treaty of Certain Demise?" Kallistê asked.

Lotus and Eryx shook their heads.

"It's an agreement between the Bruvian warriors of the Bayeux Mountain Range and the major kingdoms on the continent. No mountaineers can cross into any of the major kingdoms without permission. And anyone from the major kingdoms who crosses into the Bayeux Mountain Range without being granted passage is killed on sight. Furthermore, if they're discovered to be a part of a kingdom's throne, they will be taken as hostile actors initiating an act of war."

"Why are you telling us this, Kallistê?" Lotus asked. Beside her, Premier Eryx grinned in understanding and patted Lotus's shoulders.

"Because if *you* can't defeat the masses, then the mountaineers can. The treaty necessitates it. Think of the people as sheep, and the borders between your kingdom and the mountaineers as their pen. Rather than cull the flock like a wolf, we need to guide them toward greener pastures like a guard dog. I have the most splendid idea..."

Lotus stood in the center of a neighborhood block located in a small town just a few miles away from the border crossing–and far away from the rebel outpost in the Capital City of Vadronia. She rolled the sleeves of her shirt up so that they rested just above her elbows. Taking a deep breath, Lotus closed her eyes, held her arms out and sank into the vitality. When she opened her eyes again, they glowed and the world glimmered with a faint pinkish tint that matched the natural color of her irises. She could even make out the vitality of the inhabitants as they moved about within their homes.

She twisted the particles in the air, increasing the friction within them to create heat. With a snap of her fingers, flames ignited at her fingertips and enveloped her hands. Lotus raised her palms and, with a grunt of effort, sent fire bursting forth so that it encapsulated the homes within the vicinity. As the blaze spread down the block, she placed her palms on the ground, ignoring the panicked screams of the residents.

The paved road beneath her feet melted into molten rock. It spread in either direction, coinciding with the fire to act as a barricade. As people fled their homes, Lotus shot small bursts of flames at their front doors and windows so that they had no choice but to exit from the opposite end of the house. Her wall of fire effectively prevented the inhabitants from fleeing westward—and further into Olysseus—and forced them in one direction: eastward, toward the Bayeux Mountain Range.

Satisfied, Lotus extinguished the flames on her arms and returned to the steam powered trolley that would take her to the next town along the border. Her assistant waited for her in the passenger's seat. Lotus wove her telekinetic power into the engine, bringing it to life.

"That was much quicker than expected, Madam Lotus."

Lotus nodded.

"This is only one town. We've many more to go."

Chapter 5

Human Realm, Mount Illiniza, Windhaven Village

The soft thrum of Alastair's heart beat against Haizea's cheek. They lay on the bed in an entanglement of limbs with her head resting on his chest. She fell into a lull as he stroked his fingers up and down her back and had nearly dozed off when he shifted beneath her. Haizea lifted her head to see him staring at the ceiling, deep in thought. If she didn't know any better, she'd say that his cheeks looked like they lost a bit of their usual fullness. Not much, but just enough to notice. Maybe the dim lighting was obscuring her perspective.

Her heart dipped into her stomach. Or maybe it was something more than that.

Haizea quickly shook away the thought. She'd promised herself she wouldn't ask or pressure him in any way about using necromancy, and she'd stayed true to that. Not only had she seen first-hand how much the Soul Reaper terrified Alastair, but she'd once *felt* his fear in her own Soul. Alastair's magic tormented him in a way she would never be able to fully grasp as a healing mage.

He had already suffered so much. She wanted him to be happy. She just wished that him choosing his peace of mind didn't mean sacrificing his body in the process.

Something tugged against her magic and Alastair moved to sit upright. Haizea grimaced, realizing that he'd sensed her inner turmoil and she'd ruined their peaceful moment. He fiddled with his fingers, his brows knitting together.

~*I've started visiting the monastery.*~

Haizea blinked, taken by surprise.

~*I didn't think the monastery interested you. I would have shown you if I'd known. How did you like it?*~

He paused, contemplating his words.

~*I wouldn't say it* interests *me. A Soul guided me there. I spoke with some of the monks. Met a seer for the first time. It was a little...unsettling. But she introduced me to another necromancer. His name is Pamin.*~

Her expression remained even despite the hope threatening to take hold.

~*That's good. So he's teaching you necromancy?*~

~*We've mostly been meditating. He said that because I didn't go to mage school, my foundation with my medium magic is lacking and that I need to focus on that first.*~

Pamin's words aligned with what Haizea had told Alastair before. Given his lack of training and education, Alastair was an impeccable self-taught mage. But for as much power as he had, he lacked precision.

For someone like Haizea, precision meant the difference between healing an ailment and making a misdiagnosis that jeopardized someone's life. It meant recognizing when her blood magic posed a threat to Alastair and having the faculties to stop before she hurt him.

For Alastair, control over his magic meant that he no longer had his consciousness dragged to another realm against his will by various entities and beings. Quite some time had passed since his last fainting spell of that nature, but Haizea only knew the basics of medium magic and necromancy—just enough to wield it when she used her blood magic.

Only another medium would know the intricacies and could help Alastair bridge the gap between his power and his knowledge.

~Did you find it helpful, at least?~ she asked.

Alastair's mouth grew taut. He fixed his arms like he was about to sign but stopped short.

~You don't have to tell me anything specific. I just want to know if you feel like it's worth your time.~

~I think it's time well spent but...Pamin...he speaks of the Soul Reaper with this reverence. I can't tell if it's just because he's a monk or if all necromancers do. I don't get it.~

Haizea mulled that over.

~That's not so different from the Demon worshippers,~ she signed.

~You don't worship them.~

~Neither do you. But they returned magic to the realm, so I understand why people do. I'm guessing there must be some similar connection between the Soul Reaper and mediums for Pamin to respond that way.~

He shifted uncomfortably beside her. Haizea rested her hand on his leg.

~Pamin said that necromancers are children of the Soul Reaper. They look to him for protection. But I don't...~ Alastair stopped signing mid-sentence.

~You don't what?~

He searched her face for a long while.

~Everything the Soul Reaper does comes at a price. He told me that himself, and meeting Pamin reinforced it. The price he's asking for...I don't know if it's worth it.~

Haizea considered him silently. She tried not to think of the inevitable ending of where his continued hesitance would lead.

~All Cosmic magic comes at a price. It's up to each individual if they want to pay it. It's okay to feel uncertain. It's okay if you don't want to do it.~

~You want me—~

Haizea shook her head, cutting him off.

~I want you to make the choice you feel most comfortable with. No matter what it is. I'm sorry for what I said before about magical wasting–about leaving you behind. I was thinking about my own feelings, not yours.~

~You're not uncertain.~

~It didn't happen overnight. And not without great loss.~

Alastair's shoulders slumped.

~It would be easier if my magic could save people like yours does.~

~Your magic saved me, Alastair. You sent Rey to warn my grandfather. And I never would have been able to defeat King Rhys without your help.~

That seemed to get to him a little—he sat up straighter. Alastair cupped her face in his hands and pressed his lips against her forehead. It took her a beat to regain her train of thought.

~If you knew then what you know now about necromancy, would you have done things differently?~ she asked.

~I think I still would have tried to save Rey. Even now, a part of me hopes that somehow, someway, my magic can bring my family back. But I know it's futile. Necromancy would only turn them into pawns. It's not permanent.~

Her gut twisted into knots. He'd still have a family if not for her.

Their absence filled a vacuum that she would never be able to fill, but she owed it to them to care for Alastair. She would protect him with her very last breath if that's what it took. But she didn't know how to help with his magic. If she could take that choice away from him and carry the burden instead, she would do so in a heartbeat.

Much to her dismay, the choice was solely his.

One of Alastair's long locks fell into his face, and Haizea tucked it behind his ear.

~You never know, Alastair. A Soul guided you to the monastery, right? Maybe it's because the Soul Reaper is trying to tell you something.~

A long strand of white hair clung to Haizea's coat. She plucked it off, letting a gust of wind carry it away. Haizea did her best to push her conversation with Alastair that morning out of her mind and focus on the task at hand—she had received an assignment to patrol Stonecliff village alongside Shauni. It was part of the larger cluster that connected Windhaven to its neighbors.

They passed a construction area, where loggers had begun chopping down trees in the dense forest.

After much debate and deliberation, the residents decided to expand the ropeway system that connected the villages. In its current form, it followed a circular path, staying within the bounds of the village cluster at high elevation, but the expansion would add pylons that went further down the mountainside. The aim was to make ascending and descending the mountain much easier—and faster.

Grandfather Harzel's untimely demise helped spur on the change in part. Vendela and Shauni had traveled all the way down to the base, but it took many weeks, given that they resided at an elevation of 13,000 feet. While Haizea appreciated how the change honored her grandfather, she hoped that once they completed the ropeways, her people could better send resources to the villages at the base, who lived disconnected from the greater mountaineer community.

People at the base likely wouldn't send their children so far away to attend the mage academy, but maybe with enough resources, schools could be established near the bases. Trade routes could connect all mountaineers. They could look out for one another and provide in times of need. The ropeway construction project had only just begun and would take time to complete, but it was a step toward improvement.

"Any luck on identifying that person from the wolf attack?" Shauni asked.

Haizea nodded and kicked up a cloud of snow.

"The family was devastated to say the least. Fortunately, Vendela managed to smooth things over without getting any of the elders involved. How have things been going with you? Less eventful, I hope."

Shauni grinned lopsidedly.

"Well," she drawled. "I'm going to stop by and see Raquel after this. And then maybe Calin too."

Haize arched an eyebrow.

"Do they know about each other?"

"They know it's nothing more than a bit of fun," Shauni shrugged. Then, she paused.

Her lackadaisical expression shifted into a glare of concentration and her vitality surged around Haizea. The winds around them stilled. Haizea turned around just in time to see numerous knives barreling through the air. They came to an abrupt halt just a few inches from her face, one of the blades floating directly in front of her eye.

Before Haizea could fully register what was happening, Shauni's magic blasted outward and waves rippled across the ground, sending snow flying in every direction. Only then did Haizea see what had set Shauni off.

Further down the slope, Shauni had pinned someone down with her magic. They spat at her and, without lifting a finger, Shauni flung the wad back at his face.

"What's your problem, kid?"

"Murderer!" he cried.

"What?" Shauni asked.

"My father. All we get back is a pile of bones, and I'm supposed to believe a pack of wolves killed him?" He turned his glare on Haizea, his eyes as sharp as daggers. "Fuck you!"

Haizea closed the few feet of distance between herself and the young man and crouched down to his level. He shrank back and tried to inch away from her, but the vitality rippled as he writhed against Shauni's telekinetic grasp. Haizea opened her mouth to speak, to explain herself, to apologize, but every response she could have uttered rang hollow in her mind.

She waved at Shauni to let him go. The young man lunged at her, but Haizea side-stepped him with ease, and he lost his footing and tumbled into the snow. A cloud of white billowed upward when his body hit the ground.

He clenched his hands into fists as he got back on his feet, tears streaming down his cheeks.

"The wolves may have gotten to him first, but you finished the job. You're a healer. You could have helped him," he rasped. "It should have been you instead."

Shauni gripped his shoulder, eliciting a wince.

"How old are you, kid?"

"Seventeen."

She leaned in closer.

"I know you're having a rough time. And I'm sorry for that, truly. But attacking a warrior, or *any* other villager, is no small offense. If you have a problem with something we've done, you speak to the elders or to our leader. Do you understand?"

Haizea touched Shauni's arm.

"It's alright. Let him go."

He yanked his shoulder away from Shauni, giving them both a dirty look before running off.

"It's not alright. He's old enough to know better."

"His father went out one night and came back home as a pile of bones. I think he just needs some time to process what happened and had a lapse in judgment."

"He's just a teenager now, but he's still a mage. A year or two from now, he could very well be a fledgling omen with a grudge to match. It's foolish to overlook an act of aggression."

Haizea hummed.

"You sound like my mother," she murmured. Shauni's brows rose. "Really? The fearsome Ilmare?"

Haizea nodded, recalling the first time she ever witnessed another warrior challenge her mother for the leader's mantle. A challenge did not have to end in a fight to the death–the only rule was to leave your opponent in a condition where they could never fight again–but Ilmare never let any of her challengers live.

"Anyone who wishes to bring me harm does not deserve mercy," Haizea echoed her mother's cadence as she repeated her words of wisdom.

Shauni blinked.

"I may sound like Ilmare, but you *are* her. In any case, she wasn't wrong. We're warriors. We can't let an outburst like that go unchecked."

Haizea sighed, and her gaze fell to the footprints left behind by the boy.

"He's just a kid, Shauni. And every kid deserves a chance," she tightened her scarf around her neck. "Even if it's only one."

Chapter 6

Human Realm, Bayeux Mountain Range, Base of Mount Illiniza, Eaglestone Village

Sage brought her arm up to her forehead and wiped the sweat from her brow before it could drip into her eyes. The dirt splattered on her pale skin transferred to her forehead. Or at least, she told herself it was dirt as she drowned out the bleating goats running circles around her. Two of them geared up to ram their heads into one another. Not wanting to deal with another entanglement of horns, without raising a finger, she sent a wave of telekinesis to push them to opposite sides of the field.

She sighed and clucked her tongue against the roof of her mouth and frowned at the dryness. Sage reached into her satchel and brought the pig bladder containing water up to her lips. Unable to drink in earnest, she let it dribble into her mouth and tried very, very hard not to dry heave at the thought of what she was drinking from.

"Fucking pig piss," Felix hissed under his breath.

Sage looked over to see her brother watching her. Despite his eyes being a cool blue, they burned with a raging fire and the sneer he wore might as well have been permanently etched into his face. She tucked her pig bladder away.

"It's all they can afford to give us, Felix. We should be grateful."

"Grateful? *Grateful?* We are the crowned prince and princess of Arcelia. We belong in the Royal Palace. Pampered by servants. Eating until our bellies are full. Not subsisting on the leftover scraps some old rube throws our way out of pity. I thought the mountaineers were more sophisticated than this, given that it only took fucking *one* of them to kill an entire army and destroy my kingdom."

"*Miss Tamsyn* has given us a place to rest our heads and food to eat. Not to mention, she's agreed to teach you transmutation."

Felix scowled at her for a beat, his jaw moving as he ground his teeth the way Father often did…used to do. He kicked at one of the kids as it zipped between his legs. A moment later, the doe rammed her horns into his calf. Felix hissed in pain and used his telekinesis to fling her back by making a wide sweep of his arm. He turned back to Sage.

"While we're on the topic, we need to practice."

"Right now?" she groaned.

Felix looked around. At the moment, they stood in the middle of the barnyard shoveling manure for Miss Tamsyn, a goat farmer in the village they currently resided in. After a few coaching sessions with Felix, Sage had managed to act out their sob story well enough for her to provide them a place to stay for the time being. In exchange, they helped maintain her farm.

"Yes, right now. Never forget why we're here, Sage. Sooner or later, she's going to realize I'm no good at this, and the lessons will end. I need to teach you everything I can, while I can," Felix said.

Their original plan had been for Sage to learn transmutation because her magic was stronger, but Miss Tamsyn had refused, stating that she was too young for the Cosmic Arts. She did, however, agree to teach Felix, who then passed on what he learned to his sister in secret.

"We'll start with a refresher: transmutation is the art of changing an element from one form into another. It can be as simple as changing a solid to a liquid, or as complex as transforming a living being."

Sage nodded.

"Water is the easiest thing to do a transmutation with because it naturally takes up many forms: liquid, solid, and vapor. Show me what you remember so far," he said.

Sage used her magic to remove a small handful of water from her pig bladder and make it hover in the air. She focused intently on the liquid, attempting to home in on the small particles within. Sage wrapped an invisible hand around the puddle. She held an ironclad grip on the water, but she lacked the precision required to sense the minutiae of the vitality. It was like looking at a fuzzy portrait of a person, but she couldn't quite make out their face or other features.

Sage pushed forward to the next step and attempted to vibrate and accelerate the particles within the water so that it would boil. She strained and felt the beginnings of something trying to click but couldn't quite get that final push over the edge. Fatigued, the water splashed to the ground, wetting her boots. Felix let out an exasperated groan.

"At this rate, it'll take us years before you even come close to competency."

"Well, Miss Tamsyn said it takes mages years to master the Cosmic Arts. I'm not going to get it overnight. We haven't been here that long."

"Three months. It's been three months since we settled here and more than a year since that witch murdered Father and Mother. We cannot rest until we avenge them. We cannot afford complacency. If anyone here finds out where we're from, or worse, who we are–"

"I know, Felix. I know about the treaty," she sighed.

People of the kingdoms could not cross into the mountaineer territory without explicit permission. Anyone caught would be killed on sight–and trespassers with connections to the monarchy would be considered aggressors initiating an act of war. As the prince and princess of Arcelia, if discovered, the warriors would cut them down where they stood.

"Then you know we need to be able to defend ourselves from these mountaineer savages. If we cannot even do that, then we'll never be able to defeat *her*."

Sage started to wipe her face again, but she caught a whiff of her arm that smelled less like dirt and more like manure. Tired of her brother's lectures and exhausted from physical labor, she lost her patience.

"If I'm doing all of this work to learn the Cosmic Arts, the least you could do is learn how to sword fight properly," she quipped.

Felix stiffened, his jaw clenching and unclenching once again. She hit a sore spot by reminding of his embarrassment that fateful day in the bunker. He'd fought desperately to save their lives, only for his own clumsiness to best him.

They'd fled, leaving Mother and Jirina behind. The pungent scent of blood and innards tainted Sage's memories. Even now, her stomach churned at unearthly grunts and groans of undead bodies that had surrounded them.

It was only an act of divine intervention by the Angels themselves that she and Felix had escaped with their lives. Sage had never questioned the benevolence of the Angels before, but if they could act on her and Felix's behalf, then why couldn't they have done the same for her parents?

Sage looked down at the shovel in her hands. Calluses had begun to form on her once delicate fingers. Her legs ached from standing for hours on end, and sweat oozed from every orifice, making her blonde locks cling to her neck and forehead.

A bell chimed in the distance, signaling suppertime. Sage rested her shovel against the fence and trudged her way back to the house. She and Felix took off their dirt encrusted shoes and left them by the door before crossing the threshold to see Miss Tamsyn setting the table.

She had a head full of gray hair, and a short, plump build. Sage took her seat at the table. She dipped her chin in a prayer, silently asking the Angels protection and guidance and a sign that she and her brother were on the right path.

Sage scooped out a mouthful of the plain-looking stew and pretended it was a lavish dish of roasted pig and seasoned vegetables that she used to eat in the Royal Palace. She imagined her parents on either side of her, with her father's boisterous laugh filling the air. Felix sat down beside her and scowled as he ate.

"Thank you for the stew, Miss Tamsyn," Sage said once she finished her portion.

"You don't need to thank me at every meal, Serenity. You and Caspian are earning your keep here. I'm merely paying you all what I owe."

Felix's knuckles turned white as he scooped the soup into his mouth. Though she was not a seer, Sage could practically hear his thoughts plain as day:

A prince does not 'earn his keep'.

"How's that hole in the fence comin' along, Caspian?"

"It's nearly repaired and should be completed by tomorrow evening."

"Perfect. I appreciate your hard work. I stopped by the market earlier, apparently some of the villages higher up want to build a rope way to get us better connected. Could be a good thing for us down here. Sometimes our brothers and sisters up top forget about us."

Felix perked up.

"How long does something like that take?"

"Years, probably. We're right at the base, so we'll be the last to reap the benefits."

Sage got up to her feet and collected everyone's dishes, levitating them off the table with her magic. Miss Tamsyn and Felix discussed some more while she went off to wash the dishes and clean the kitchen.

Back home, she would be wrapping up her tutoring session with Grand Magister Ophelia around this time. She still had a few years of schooling left, but given the collapse of Arcelia's monarchy and army, most other kids her age back home had undoubtedly had their education cut short as well. She wondered how her friends were doing and if they'd managed to escape to safety.

Sage blinked against the sudden stinging in her eyes.

She wanted to go home. The mountains would never be her home—*could never* be her home. She couldn't even use her own name.

Due to the presence and influence of the invading omens, in addition to the risk of being recognized on the Arcelian side of the border, Felix had deemed it necessary to abandon their kingdom altogether. Like many other Arcelians, she and Felix had heard news of rebellion in Olysseus and used the mass exodus as a cover for their travels. However, her brother had no interest in joining them.

To him, the rebellion was a lost cause. A single omen had felled the Arcelian army. The Olyssean forces would not fare much better—the only way to defeat Cosmic magic was to combat it with the same. In either case, given that the rebels were fighting to push omens out of their kingdom, they would not take kindly to their plan for Sage to learn transmutation.

"I'm ready for that delivery, Miss Tamsyn."

Sage turned at the sound of Bose's voice. He stood in the middle of the dining area, grinning broadly.

Miss Tamsyn stood up and placed her hands on her hips.

"What did I tell ya 'bout realmdrifting into my house? There's a door for a reason."

"Invasion of privacy is part of the surcharge for my services," Bose said, floating toward the kitchen. He pushed his blue locks from his eyes. "Along with a healthy meal."

Bose poured some soup into his bowl and smacked his lips noisily. He wasn't nearly as old as Miss Tamsyn—at the age of twenty, he was just two years older than Felix, and five years older than Sage.

As Miss Tamsyn geared up to scold him, Bose pulled a heavy sack filled with coins from his satchel. Her mouth snapped shut, and she counted the money before sliding a small stack to him.

"There's a crate of fresh milk and cheese outback. We'll be butchering the next round of meat next week."

Bose tipped his bowl up and gulped loudly before letting the dish clatter back on the table. Sage quietly lifted it away using her magic. Felix joined her by the sink and positioned himself between their hosts and Sage, drying the dishes as she washed them. He strained for a moment, trying to use his magic to wipe the towel faster, but the movements were too unstable to be of any use, so he used his hands instead. Again, Sage could practically hear his thoughts despite his silence:

"Mountaineers savages. We use them, but we can never trust them," he would always say when they were alone.

Felix opened the overhead cabinets. As he and Sage began putting the dishes away, the entire house trembled. They stopped short and exchanged a glance. Shouting billowed in through the open window.

Bose vanished into thin air, leaving Miss Tamsyn behind as she clambered to her feet. Sage offered her a hand and led her outside. A massive crowd ran through the village, their clothes covered in filth and grime, and their eyes wide and wild.

Sage didn't recognize any of the people and Miss Tamsyn must not have either because her eyes narrowed on the crowd. The older woman put her hand up and a wave of her magic rushed forward. The people toward the front of the crowd ran into her invisible telekinetic wall.

"What's going on? Who are you?"

"Please, help us. They destroyed everything. We can't go back. There's nothing to go back to."

"Slow down. Who destroyed what?"

"The omens. That pink haired witch set fire to half the city in the middle of the night and walled us off. We had no choice but to run. For the sake of the realms, let us in."

The crowd began pushing against Miss Tamsyn's barrier. A group of telekinetic mages shoved their way toward the front and used their combined strength against the hers. To Sage's astonishment, Miss Tamsyn's brows drew together in concentration, but she otherwise didn't budge.

"I'm not sure I understand. Pink haired witch?"

"We have people with burns. Do you have a healer?" another person pleaded.

"We don't have anywhere else to go."

"There are children with us!"

Miss Tamsyn blinked a few times as the shouting voices blended into one another.

"I–"

"They aren't mountaineers. They're fleeing from one of the kingdom's cities and there are hundreds more headed this way."

The crowd fell silent at the sight of Bose materializing out of thin air. It wasn't a calm silence. Instead it vibrated–not heard but felt.

It lasted for only a single breath before they erupted into a frenzy.

A chunk of the group dispersed–parents took their small children by the hand, elderly individuals shuffled, and everyone else in between and fled in the opposite direction. Yet, to Sage's surprise, some of them remained. Their lips curled into sneers and they glared at them, eyes sharp as daggers.

"Realmdrifter!" they spat the word like a curse.

"Blue hair...?"

"They killed our Sovereign!" another person cried.

The vitality surged around Sage as they pressed forward. Miss Tamsyn braced herself, holding strong against four telekinetic mages.

"Stop," she rasped through gritted teeth.

The newcomers paid her no heed. Her wall did not yield, but a translucent shape shifted through it and entered her body. Not bound by the physical world, an astral projector forced their living Soul into hers. Miss Tamsyn clutched her head and sank to the ground. Her telekinetic barrier collapsed in kind.

The masses descended on them, and Sage reached forward to protect Miss Tamsyn, but Felix gripped her arm and dragged her away. Stumbling as she tried to keep up with Felix's footsteps, Sage peeked over her shoulder to see Bose maneuvering through the crowd.

He vanished once more and reappeared by Miss Tamsyn a few seconds later. Before he could get a solid grip on her, the mob pounced on him, forcing him back into the astral plane. Bose tried again and nearly succeeded, but he caught a punch to the face that sent him flying. Sage yanked free from Felix's grasp and turned around.

She focused her telekinesis on the mages around Miss Tamsyn. From this distance, her mind alone was not sufficient and she had to use her arms to guide her power. Like an invisible hand, her magic wrapped around their ankles and flipped them through their air, tossing them like rag dolls. That small reprieve gave Miss Tamsyn just enough time and space to get back on her feet.

Beads of sweat dripped down Miss Tamsyn's temples and she stared at the unfolding chaos with her lips ajar. Bose's cries of pain and the sound of flesh smacking against flesh as they assaulted him filled the air.

A wave of magic from the older woman sent many of them tumbling away from Bose, but people from the back of the mob rushed forward to take their place. Sage flinched with each blow that landed on him. Throat running dry, she found herself reaching for Miss Tamsyn.

Magical pressure intensified as the tips of Bose's fingers faded into obscurity as he tried to flee through the astral plane once more. The mob denied him the chance to fully latch onto his power—one person kicked him in the gut while another grabbed a handful of his hair.

"Miss Tamsyn!" He cried out.

"Serenity, step back," she said.

Sage's legs wobbled as she put more space between them.

The older woman stretched her hands and the air around Sage grew heavy and dense.

Sage could not see the changes in the vitality, but it rumbled deep within and tugged at her own magic. The people standing closest to Miss Tamsyn began to shift. Their skin rippled, wet, and loose. Their bodies shrank and twisted before they popped in a violent transformation from human to...Sage dry heaved at the sight of dozens of mice scurrying across the ground.

People in the crowd stumbled backward, screams of terror piercing the air. The goats bleated and sprinted about behind the enclosed fence. A flock of crows cawed overhead, their wings battering against the wind.

Father often told stories of how the connection to the vitality was strongest here in the mountains and how their magic often eclipsed those of the major kingdoms. Generations ago, when Demons returned magic to the realm, they did so in the mountain range–permanently restructuring the balance. The sight took Sage back to the bunker, surrounded by the dead and cornered by the blood mage whose very presence threatened to crush her from existence and she was too weak to do anything to stop it.

Miss Tamsyn limped toward Sage and her brother and grabbed their hands. Bose trailed behind them. Sage peered over her shoulder to see more people off in the distance—Bose had said this was just the first wave and more were coming. Eaglestone village barely had a hundred people itself. Sage didn't know if it could withstand such a swarm in numbers.

Miss Tamsyn ushered them inside the cabin but lingered out for a moment longer. Magic condensed around Sage once again. She peeked out of the window to see a cage of lightning surrounding their home. Miss Tamsyn limped inside and bolted the door shut. Only then did Sage see their injuries clearly.

Miss Tamsyn's right arm was bent at an odd angle and blood poured out of her nose. One of Bose's eyes was blackened and swollen shut. A blade protruded from his shoulder, staining his shirt red.

"Bose, drop the kids off back at your village. Get them away from here. Then, you have to get the warriors," Miss Tamsyn breathed.

Bose held his hand against his wound and blood seeped through his fingers.

"I can handle the kids, but I don't know if I can make it up the mountain, Miss Tamsyn. I've never drifted that far before."

"Just because you haven't doesn't mean you can't. You and I are the only omens here. I'm far too old to be fighting. I can stall them, but I can't hold off hundreds of kingdom dwellers forever. We need to nip this in the bud."

Bose nodded, his face growing pale. Felix put a hand on his shoulder.

"I can help put a bandage on the wound before we go. It might buy you more time. Sage, grab our things while I work on him."

"Bose lives a little ways up the slope. You'll be safe there for the time being," Miss Tamsyn said.

Sage absorbed that with a small frown. They couldn't leave Miss Tamsyn behind.

"Miss–"

"We're just a bunch of farmers. If the cities are running this way, they're going to overrun us without help. It's too dangerous."

"But—"

"Once this calms down, I'll send for you."

Sage's throat tightened. Miss Tamsyn patted her hand.

"You're a sweet girl, Serenity. Don't worry about me. I'll be fine. It's my job to protect you, not the other way around."

Sage nodded reluctantly. She went to her bedroom to gather her handful of belongings and items she thought Felix would want to take with him as well. She found her brother outside. She expected him to be bandaging Bose, but Sage was aghast to see Bose lying on the ground, with his skull cracked open and blood pooling on the ground beside him.

"Felix, you–"

Her brother formed a fist, and her mouth involuntarily clamped shut.

"Listen to me, Sage. We cannot afford for the warriors to come across us. What if Bose realmdrifted up top and brought...," Felix trailed off, his throat bobbing up and down. "We're not ready to face her yet. Your training has barely begun.

"Did you see what Old Lady T did? Once you master transmutation, that will be *you*, Sage. You'll be the princess who defeated the omens, who won our kingdom back. And I'll be the king who leads our people into a new era. If the Olysseans don't burn that fucking village to the ground tonight, when I'm on the throne, we'll come back and finish the job."

Sage swallowed heavily, her entire body shivering. Felix put his hands on her shoulders and leaned down to her eye level.

"We lost our homeland in a sea of blood. We'll have to drown our enemies in another to win it back. Never forget that, Sage. This nightmare won't end until we kill them all."

Sage glanced back at Bose's prone form on the ground, devoid of life. She prayed to the Angels for Bose's Soul to rest and find its home in the Soul Realm.

Death was as much of an end as it was a beginning—one's physical life ceased, but their Soul continued. Sometimes Souls remained in the Human Realm if they did not have peace.

As Bose's unseeing eyes bore into her, Sage could not help but think that Felix had nipped one problem in the bud, only to open another door for chaos to find them.

Chapter 7

Human Realm, Mount Illiniza, Shimmerpond Village

Heat from nearby torches warmed Alastair's skin. He sat crossed-legged on a small cushion with his eyes closed and his mind and Soul open.

Seated directly across from him, Pamin's Soul tugged the most forcefully on Alastair's vitality, but it didn't have the strength and vibrancy that he was used to with most people. It felt brittle by comparison.

Alastair branched out, venturing past other monks and parishioners in the temple. The outside world entered his perception. A small pinch bit inside of him as a hawk killed a mouse and the dead Soul passed through him. Alastair pushed that sensation to the back of his mind—not quite ignoring it but instead working around it.

He expanded his power further, stretching beyond the Human Realm and into the next. The vastness of the Cosmos surrounded him before the whispers from the Soul Realm filled the void. Emotions crashed into him like a raging river—fury blended with jubilance, grief meshed with contentment, hatred entangled with adoration. Alastair inhaled deeply to maintain his calm and refrain from being overwhelmed.

A familiar touch caressed his Soul. Woven deep within the call of the others was his family. Alastair could not resist picking them out of the crowd.

His mother's face appeared before him—brown skin, eyes a stormy gray, and a head full of tight curls. Alastair sprinted toward her, arms outstretched and his eyes welling with tears.

Mom, he called.

Just once, just one more time if he could hold her again, that's all he wanted.

Their fingertips brushed together. To his dismay, his mother's face contorted, and pain seared through him. Alastair halted in his tracks. He realized with a start that he hadn't been moving toward her but instead pulling her away from the Soul Realm and toward the realm of the living.

He didn't trust himself not to try to keep her here in the Human Realm—an act that would selfishly tear her away from the rest of their family. Heart fracturing, Alastair broke the connection and his mother's Soul faded from his perception.

Alastair wiped the dampness from his cheeks. He forced himself to refocus on the task Pamin had given him and pushed beyond the Soul Realm. The roar of the Beast Realm reverberated through him next.

The Beasts added a burden to his magic that he'd never experienced before. Alastair was accustomed to the Souls of other humans—even when he delved into the Soul Realm, those of his fellow man called to him most fiercely. There, it was easier to gloss over the dead Souls of other beings from the various realms, but by tuning his magic to the Beast Realm itself, he had no choice but to listen to their Souls.

They hovered over him, shrouding his body in a massive shadow. The strength of their vitality bore down on him with a frightfully crushing force. He gasped for air as his heart clambered in his chest. A cold sweat broke out across his body. His magic surged in tandem with his emotions and Alastair nearly broke off his connection with the Beast Realm until a memory surfaced.

He had faced the Soul Reaper—the entity watched him, even now. He'd stood up to a Demon and lived. The Beasts had great power, but it paled in comparison to them. The panic brewing within subsided. His vitality leveled out, making way for the emotions of the Beasts, which weren't much different from humans—fear, anger, distress, sadness, contentment and even something akin to love and concern.

Alastair sank into the Beast Realm, captivated by their Souls. However, his time there did not last as long as he'd intended—having never reached so far with his medium magic, his mind grew fatigued and his magic snapped back at him.

He opened his eyes and squinted against the firelight. A few moments passed before his vision cleared. Pamin smiled. Behind him stood an apparition of the Soul Reaper. Though his gaze was empty, satisfaction emanated from the entity.

Well done.

Alastair blinked. The image dissipated. He shook away the eeriness slithering down his spine and told Pamin everything he'd just experienced.

~Each realm has a path through the Cosmos. The Beast Realm is often what Spiritual mages experience first, given the similarities between our realms. Meditation is not only a powerful tool, but an essential skill for mediums. It helps us hone our ability to focus on the world around us, while simultaneously drowning out unnecessary information,~ Pamin signed.

He slid a small stack of books sitting beside him toward Alastair. One covered mindfulness and meditation, another was an encyclopedia of the various realms and the last was a guidebook geared toward mediums and necromancers.

Alastair stared at the titles for a moment, and a wistfulness overcame him. Were the types of books the mage academy offered to its students? Goldenleaf village didn't have resources like these, and even if they did, trying to figure out where the next meal would come from took priority over taking the time to teach magic. How different would he be if he'd had this type of access in his childhood?

~*True mastery is about control just as much as it is about power. Over time, you'll build the endurance required to sustain a connection to other realms for much longer. Diligent practice will make perfect,*~ Pamin signed.

Alastair shifted his weight back and forth to keep his legs from falling asleep.

~*I have a question. It's a little personal, but I think it's relevant,*~ Alastair signed. Pamin motioned for him to go ahead.

~*Your Soul felt feeble compared to the others. Is that because of your Cosmic magic?*~

~*Yes. The corruptive effects of using necromancy accumulate over time.*~

~*When we spoke before, you said that it's something that you 'allow' to happen.*~

Pamin pursed his lips and considered him before responding.

~*I can't stop the corruption, at least, not in the way you think. No necromancer can avoid it, which is why we wait until later in life to begin learning the Cosmic Arts. In turn, we use our powers freely until we sense that Souls are too frangible to continue. When that time comes, we send our Souls to the Soul Realm.*~

Alastair furrowed his brows.

~*So you...kill yourselves?*~

~*We consider it a farewell ceremony that ensures our Souls can continue on in the next realm. Our final sacrifice.*~

Sacrifice. Always, *always* sacrifice.

Only someone mad would willingly choose to be a necromancer if this was how their lives would end. Then again, maybe Alastair's perception was jaded.

Pamin had chosen this path with full knowledge of what it entailed and waited until he was ready. Alastair never had that opportunity.

What he once thought was a small accident, a mere moment of desperation, had permanently altered the trajectory of his life.

How many decades had he shaved off by a single decision made in ignorance?

~I'm sure this is a lot to digest. Especially for someone who was not raised in a community that properly educated you about the Cosmic Arts,~ Pamin said.

Alastair wrung his hands together in a fit of frustration. He tried to find something positive about this. Another path had opened for him—one where he didn't have to abandon his Cosmic magic and could still reunite with his family in the next realm. But that meant offering his Soul to the Soul Reaper when the time came.

~How much time do I have, Pamin?~

~You can stay for as long as you like. The monastery is always open.~

~No, I mean...how long do I have until my magic kills me?~

~Full Soul corruption can take between ten to twenty years to occur, depending on the mage.~

Alastair swallowed thickly. It was longer than he thought, but he wouldn't live past the age of forty.

~Death by magical wasting has a similar timeline, but since you've already suffered from it in the past, the disease will progress more swiftly if you allow it to take root a second time. Ten to twenty years will be slashed to five to ten.~

A year had already passed since he last used his necromancy. Signs of magical wasting had already begun inching its way back—evidenced by the way his shirt fit more loosely around his body. Ten years was probably more optimistic than realistic.

A haze skirted the edges of his vision and the room tilted as the gravity of the situation hit him. The vitality seemed determined to strip away every morsel of happiness he managed to find.

He had enough time to build a life only for it to be swept away. Alastair wanted a family and children of his own...but he didn't want to rush into it because of this, nor did he want to leave Haizea to raise them by herself. Acid burned his throat at the prospect of having this conversation with her.

His family awaited him in the Soul Realm but joining them meant leaving Haizea alone—she'd lost people she loved too. And despite everything, his one solace was that they had one another.

As much as he wanted to reunite with his loved ones, he didn't know if he could truly leave this realm peacefully if it meant leaving Haizea behind.

Alastair clasped his hands tightly in his lap, a pit forming in his stomach. Pamin allowed him stew without disturbing him. Several moments passed before Alastair mustered the will to get to his feet.

~You should take the time to read those texts. When you're ready, you should speak with the Soul Reaper on your own. By doing so, you'll understand your connection with him better and why we choose the path of necromancy despite the consequences,~ Pamin signed.

Alastair gathered the stack of books into his arms. He bid Pamin farewell with a nod and exited the temple. A ripple in the vitality cascaded in his wake.

Alastair had hoped that Pamin would have offered a secret loophole that would evade Soul corruption, and that this problem would solve itself. And for as much as he didn't want to involve Haizea in it, they had a life together. She needed to know.

Tonight, Alastair would tell Haizea about the reality of his magic.

Difficult conversations were best had over a meal, where food could serve as a distraction. He prepared supper as usual but took care to cook Haizea's favorite dishes—roasted elk with seasoned rice and miniature cakes with fruit fillings for dessert. His chest constricted as he set the table.

He didn't know how she would react.

Alastair wanted to live. He wanted a long, happy life with the people he loved. And then, when the time came, he found his place in the Soul Realm and was reunited with them once more.

But this...twenty years at best if he began using his Cosmic Power once more. A decade or less if he continued to abstain.

His hands trembled as he scooped a spoonful of rice from the pot. His knuckles appeared more prominent than usual, his fingers already slimming.

Gods, he wanted to *live*.

Filled to the brim with rice, the lid on the pot didn't shut properly. The elk meat was piled several inches high on the serving plate. Alastair sighed deeply. Back in Goldenleaf, he often ate whatever scraps he could find, and on the rare occasion that he did cook, he prepared a meal for his entire family. Growing up with a dozen people living in one house, he now struggled with portioning food for two people, but he remedied it by freezing portions to eat later.

The door swung open in his peripheral vision. Haizea walked in, followed by Shauni. A teen girl trailed behind them. She glanced around the house and rubbed at her arm.

Alastair pulled Haizea close and kissed her nose. Her lips curled upward ever so faintly. He smiled at the sight, but it quickly faded—the conversation he wanted to have with her would have to wait. Her Soul quivered and she studied him.

~*Everything okay?*~ she asked.

~*Yes, just surprised. I thought we'd have tonight to ourselves.*~

Haizea grimaced.

~*I'm sorry, it was last-minute,*~ she pivoted so that her back faced the others. ~*Vendela sent the younger warriors to shadow assignments but told Jassia she wasn't ready yet. We wanted to cheer her up.*~

Haizea introduced Jassia properly, who waved at him bashfully. Shauni greeted him with a light punch on the shoulder that stung a little more than he wanted to admit. She grinned as she looked down at the table.

~*You've cooked a feast, Alastair. If I got to eat like this every day, I'd race to head home too,*~ Shauni winked at Haizea, who blushed faintly, although her expression did not change.

Haizea's mouth moved as she said something to Jassia, who then sat down at the table. Her eyes never left the food plated in the center.

~*You first, Jassia,*~ Alastair signed before taking his seat.

She reached for the serving spoon and gingerly scooped a portion onto her plate. Shauni and Haizea followed, and Alastair went last.

~*It's been a while since I've seen you, Shauni. How have you been?*~ he asked.

~*You know how warriors' duties go. It's quiet until it isn't. But I recently took a short trip to the village cluster a little higher up from ours. There's a lake there called the Rushing Expanse and this time of year it freezes. Perfect for playing thundergoal.*~

~*Thundergoal?*~

Shauni grinned wickedly.

~*We set up goal posts on either side of the lake and, usually, people play by hitting a ball within those boundaries. Anyone can play, but when there's enough mages, we change the rules a bit. Rather than a post, we set up a wall of ice and use a rock instead of a ball. Whoever makes the wall shatter first wins. It sounds like a crack of thunder. You and Haizea should come play one of these times.*~

~*It sounds dangerous.*~ Alastair signed. Shauni shrugged.

~So is being a warrior.~

At the opposite end of the table, Jassia watched Shauni intently, but didn't speak much herself. She had, however, cleaned her plate.

~There's dessert too. Eat as much as you want,~ Alastair signed, and nudged the place with mini cakes toward her. Jassia brightened and reached over to take a few. She bit into one and practically danced in her seat.

~Haizea told me you're a warrior in training. She said you're an excellent swordswoman,~ Alastair signed. Her cheeks reddened and she sat up a little straighter.

~I'd like to take my mastery test in a few years. And maybe even be leader one day.~

~Well, you're in great hands,~ Alastair motioned to Haizea and Shauni.

Jassia grabbed another of the mini cakes.

~This is delicious, you made it all yourself?~

Alastair nodded.

~You should be a chef or open a dessert stand. People would pay good money for this. My dad would, at least. He has a big sweet tooth.~

Her expression wavered, and an emotion rippled through his magic. A melancholic longing.

~Sounds like you love him a lot,~ he signed. The disturbance in his magic intensified.

~I do. I...I miss him. He's a lumberjack working on the new ropeway construction,~ she glanced at Haizea and Shauni. *~He's stationed in Springbreach village, actually.~*

If Haizea had not been sitting directly beside him, he would have missed the way her nostrils flared and her shoulders stiffened.

~That's where our upcoming assignment is,~ she explained.

Alastair had never heard of the village, but he didn't get the chance to ask anything further, because Haizea turned her attention back to Jassia.

~Is everything alright with him?~ she asked.

Jassia hesitated for a beat before answering, her arms shaking as the words tumbled out of her.

~Well...he broke both of his legs when he was younger and he can't move around all that well anymore, but he keeps working because my mom has a heart condition that's gotten worse. She's housebound and has to see a healer every other day. My father is supposed to go once a week, but he's always busy with work. You two are going to Springbreach...and I haven't seen him in a few weeks...~

~It's too risky for you to tag along on an assignment like this, but we can check on him for you,~ Haizea signed.

~I understand,~ the teen's shoulders slumped. Alastair caught her eye.

~There's plenty of food to take home with you. You can freeze some for the next time you see him,~ he smiled when her expression brightened.

Haizea stood up to collect everyone's dishes. As her fingers grasped the plate closest to her, it floated in the air. It landed softly on the counter and one of the cabinets swung open. Shauni didn't move a muscle, but her magic spiked as she packed away the food. She left the dirty dishes in a neat stack by the sink.

After bidding Shauni and Jassia farewell, he and Haizea cleaned what little mess remained before sitting together by the fireplace. Alastair took a deep breath to steady himself, preparing to tell her about his magic, but just as he'd mustered up the resolve to make his arms move, Haizea began signing.

~For our new assignment, Springbeach is a ways down the slope. Depending on how it goes, I'll probably be gone for a week, maybe a little longer.~

Alastair's brows furrowed, caught off guard by the news. His own would have to wait. It wouldn't be fair to bring it up right before she left on an extended assignment.

~What was the call?~ he asked. Haizea shrugged.

~Vendela said they've had some villagers go missing, but not much else. There's no telling what we'll be walking into.~

~I want you to take some of my blood. Just in case.~

~Alastair, I'll be fine. Shauni will be with me. She's just as good a swordswoman as I am, and her telekinesis is unmatched.~

~But she's not an omen. At least this way, if you need help, you can send a Soul to me right away. It's faster than a messenger hawk. Besides, I'd rather you have it and not need it than regret not taking it.~

Haizea sobered, her light brown eyes flickering between his. A tidal wave of emotion crashed behind the dam of her even expression. The sensation clawed at his own Soul. Something about what he'd said must have struck a chord with her.

~Okay. Let me grab a vial. I'll wear it in my holster.~

She left and came back a few minutes later with a vial and her blade, and her holster. Alastair held out his palm. Haizea inhaled deeply before cutting his palm, and he flinched despite himself. As his blood poured into the vial, he noticed Haizea's chest did not move—as if she was holding her breath. She didn't exhale until she sealed the vial with a lid; a cool stream of air brushed against his arm. Haizea held his hand in hers and healed the wound shut.

~Could you do me a favor while I'm gone?~ she asked.

~Of course.~

~I don't have the time to do as many healing sessions as Jassia's parents need, but I'd like to at least help them with their medicine. I'm going to make a shopping list and leave instructions on how to prepare it. If you could drop it off to them, I'd appreciate it.~

~Consider it done.~

Nostalgia swelled within Alastair as he recalled their time together in Goldenleaf, where he briefly worked as her healer's assistant. He missed those quiet days when it was just the two of them. Here in Windhaven, Haizea's warrior duties kept her busy, and he couldn't help much with that.

Alastair rubbed his freshly healed palm. Maybe that wasn't true. His blood—his magic—was one of, if not the most valuable thing he could offer her. So long as life coursed through him, he could always help.

A week. He'd be alone for a week.

He nuzzled his nose against her braids and inhaled her scent before trailing his lips along the soft skin of her neck. When she shuddered at his touch, he grinned impishly and pulled her into a tight hug. They spent the remainder of the night in front of the fireplace, wrapped in one another's arms.

Chapter 8

Human Realm, Kingdom of Llyr, Capital City of Zemira

Kallistê snapped her fingers. Her *doyamas* jumped forward, ravaging the plate of raw meat she'd set on the ground. Chunks of flesh flew in every direction, and small growls rumbled deep in her Beasts' throats.

At the moment, their skin had a reptilian texture, but when alarmed or on a hunt, it became transparent and camouflaged with the environment—a peculiar adaptation given that they lacked eyes.

Wanting to try something new, Kallistê had taken it upon herself to train the Beasts rather than control them with her astral projection. The adults proved too resistant to following her commands, so she altered her approach by training younger, more malleable *doyamas*. She'd captured a few hatchlings and raised them herself. Now, they behaved more like oversized—yet incredibly loyal—dogs than wild Beasts.

One of them finished eating and began sniffing around the room. Roughly the size of an average horse, *doyamas* outweighed and outsized Kallistê with ease, but padded feet on three sets of limbs kept their footsteps silent as they moved about. It circled around Kallistê before shoving its nose into her hand and inhaling deeply. The retractable flaps of skin on the side of their heads open, unveiling their inner ear structures. When it opened its jaws, Kallistê knew the damned thing was about to scream.

They seldom vocalized, but when under duress, they unleashed a piercing, mind-shattering scream that paralyzed any and all living creatures within a half-mile radius.

"Stop," she commanded.

The Beast halted, mouth wide open. Saliva dripped down its dagger-like teeth. Hot breath fanned across Kallistê's face and neck. Behind it, the other *doyamas* stopped eating. They stood motionless, nostrils pointed toward her.

"Kneel."

All ten *doyamas* obliged, touching their noses to the floor. Their skin flaps retracted in tandem, and a moment later, a soft clink sounded behind Kallistê. Her Beasts growled in a warning but otherwise did not move. She turned to see one of her servants prostrated on the ground, with her forehead touching the floor and her scepter resting beside her.

"Not you, Ivor," Kallistê sighed.

"You've received a new missive from Lotus, Your Majesty," Ivor stood upright, her light green eyes meeting Kallistê's. She straightened her dress and patted her short dark tresses before handing over a letter.

Dearest Queen Kallistê,

I'm pleased to inform you that I've established a new stronghold near Olysseus's western border, based on your suggestion. I've managed to clear out an entire city and block their path toward the army's stronghold in Vadronia. They've been forced to flee toward the mountains.

Based on my observations, they've bombarded their way into one of the smaller villages at the base, but I don't think the situation is dire enough for the Olyssean army to dispatch soldiers quite yet. I'm cautiously optimistic about this strategy. I hope that once this is all over, I'll be able to welcome and thank you properly for your efforts.

Yours truly,

Lotus

Kallistê's lips curled upward deviously. She barely contained her chuckle.

This would wipe that smug smile right off of Vitarin's...Viltarin's...

Kallistê stared blankly at the letter before shaking her head to regain her thoughts. She cleared her throat.

"Prepare a gift basket for Lotus. Pack it with flowers and instruct the chef to bake sweets that can endure the trip," she said.

Ivor bowed deeply.

"Yes, your majesty."

Kallistê turned back to her *doyamas* and stood up straighter, holding her chin high. She clasped her hands in front of her, rubbing her fingers along the textures of her gemstones. With another snap of her fingers, her Beasts continued with their meal. The first *doyama* that had finished eating sat still, with its nose pointed toward her. She tapped its muzzle and it followed her.

Down the hall from her chambers was an incubation room, filled with eggs that would eventually hatch into more *doyamas*. Kallistê proceeded to the dining area, where her cook had prepared a meal for her. Her *doyama's* nostrils expanded and receded as its sensitive nose sniffed the air for poisons. The Beast emitted a small chirp, indicating her food was safe. Kallistê placed a napkin across her lap.

"Your Majesty."

Kallistê paused mid-spoonful. Ivor had returned.

"The cook is preparing tarts and I've put an order with the florist, as requested," Ivor said.

"Excellent. Have a plate, there's plenty," Kallistê said. She pushed her long blue hair back, flaunting the delicate skin of her neck and clavicles that her off-shoulder dress revealed. Ivor bowed before taking a seat, with a deep blush tinting her cheeks.

"I'd like for you to start compiling a list of mages you trust. Those whose loyalty is unquestionable and dedication absolute."

"As you wish, Your Majesty."

Kallistê arched an eyebrow in amusement.

"You're not going to ask me why?"

"Would you like for me to ask why, Your Majesty?"

"It's no fun if I have to tell you," Kallistê sighed.

"I'm going to take the list you give me and choose ten mages to serve as my Royal Guard. It's time I established an elite force to capitalize on the gains I've made this far, especially in light of Lotus's struggles. But I have no use for them if they don't have the drive–or if they lack the power–to learn the Cosmic Arts. People with families would be a good fit. Something we can hold over them. I'll send them to Kestramore for training over the next few years. Upon their successful completion, they'll live out their days on my court in an abundance of wealth. Because you've earned my trust, I want you to be among the first group. What do you think?"

"Thank you, Your Majesty. I think it's a great idea."

Kallistê rolled her eyes.

"Speak freely. I'm asking for your opinion as the queen's advisor."

Ivor tugged on her shirt sleeves.

"Well, the major kingdoms have long held a negative view of the Cosmic Arts, due to their believed connection to the Demons. The people here revere the Angels. The populace has grown accustomed to your presence as queen and submitted themselves to your rule, but witnessing the expansion of omens on your court may lead to the resurgence of riots that you've managed to suppress. Considering the revolt in Olysseus, that may also further add to them feeling emboldened."

"So you think it's a risk I shouldn't take?"

"I think this endeavor is something you should keep under wraps until you've reached a critical mass where any pushback from the populace is a non-factor."

Kallistê nodded thoughtfully.

"Then you can narrow the list down even further, to people who you know are discreet."

"As you wish, my queen."

Kallistê finished off her plate but was in no hurry to get up just yet.

"Another idea I'd like to bounce off of your mind. It's about Viltarin. I'm thinking about...," Kallistê paused and her gaze grew distant.

Ivor looked at her expectantly.

"Your Majesty?"

Kallistê blinked, disoriented. She looked down to see Ivor's hand hovering above hers—hesitant to touch without explicit permission. Kallistê cleared her throat lightly and fluffed her hair to compose herself. She winced at the sharp, piercing pain in her head.

"My apologies, Ivor. Could you fetch me a pain potion?"

Ivor jumped up from her seat and returned less than a minute later.

"Would you like for me to call the healer?" Ivor's gaze dated to her unfinished plate. "Should I fetch the chef as well?"

"No, that won't be necessary. It's not the food. I just have a headache coming on," Kallistê said as she downed the potion. It took a few minutes for the pain to subside.

"Provide me with that list within the next few days. I want to get started as soon as possible."

Kallistê stood up from the chair. She looked down at Ivor and frowned. She'd been about to ask her something but couldn't remember what. Kallistê walked the halls to clear her head, with her *doyama* in lock step behind her. Whatever her question was, surely it would come to her later. Until then, she had other tasks to tend to.

It would take years to fortify her forces and establish Llyr as the bastion of not only the Cosmic Arts, but the fortress of her empire. She had not a single moment to waste.

Chapter 9

Human Realm, Mount Illiniza, Nimba Forest

Two swords and a vial of Alastair's blood weighed down the leather holster wrapped around Haizea's waist. Her brows drew together as she tugged on the clasps and double checked its tightness. The first time she'd ever worn it was the day she'd slain King Rhys, her former comrades in the Royal Guard, and the Arcelian army in its entirety.

Thorns of regret rooted themselves in her chest. She inhaled a calming breath, but internal pressure left her winded instead.

If only she had a second chance, Haizea would have gripped her past self by the shoulders and screamed that the cost of her hesitation would be too high to bear.

"You look like you've got a stick up your ass," Shauni's voice sliced through her thoughts. She narrowed her eyes at Haizea and rubbed her chin. "More than usual."

Haizea rolled her eyes but tried to relax her demeanor. She tilted her head toward the sky and let Shauni's comment go unaddressed. They'd traveled well beyond the boundaries of the home village cluster and stood in the middle of the forest, at the halfway point of the village they'd been assigned to.

A pylon towered dozens of feet above them. The scraping sound of colliding tree branches grated against Haizea's ears, followed by a loud boom that shook the ground beneath her feet. She shifted her attention from her physical senses to her magical ones.

A dense pocket of vitality had concentrated just a little ways down the slope, in the same direction as the sound came. It glowed and glistened like a shining star.

"They're making good progress on the ropeway construction," Shauni said.

"Don't you ever wish you could see it?" Haizea asked.

"See it?"

"The vitality."

Shauni barked out a sharp laugh. Her magic expanded and she uprooted a tree a few feet away. She raised a hand and curled her fingers ever so slightly. The tree shattered into thousands of pieces, bark and dust littering the air.

"I told you before, however beautiful the vitality might be, I'll have to take your word for it. I'm not keen on being touched by the Cosmos. There's no going back once you do. Besides, I'm strong enough without it."

Shauni made a show of flexing her arm muscles and her fur coat bulged visibly. Haizea huffed out through her nose.

She paused. Her vitality ebbed and flowed before pulling taut. Frantic voices called in the distance, accompanied by a thunderous quake. Stillness followed.

"I think there's trouble," Haizea said.

With a sharp nod from Shauni, the duo pivoted, following the sound of the commotion.

They came upon a clearing where the lumberjacks had set up a station. Massive logs lay scattered across the forest floor, pinning a few workers. One man dangled precariously in a tree while some were on the ground. On the opposite end of the area, another was on their hands and knees, their face pale.

"Oh, thank Aaryn! We need a little help," one in the tree called down.

Energy ricocheted around Shauni in waves and her eyes glowed faintly. Logs levitated upward, freeing those on the ground. A lumberjack floated down from the tree, limbs flailing in every direction. He hit the ground with a soft thud and hissed as he rubbed his bottom, casting Shauni a sideways glance. He made haste in getting to his fellows and pressed his hands against them.

Another trickle ran through Haizea's magic and she arched her brow curiously at the sight. Beads of sweat formed as he worked and he gritted his teeth—scratches and bruises faded away and twisted limbs slowly returned to their normal orientation.

Haizea approached the fallen worker. She concentrated on her power—though tremors quaked through his lifeforce, it still pulsed strongly against her magic.

"He has a condition where he falls ill if he doesn't eat. He's a telekinetic mage and helps us move the timber. We wanted to wrap up this section before taking a break, but I guess we pushed a little too hard. He needs some sugar. There are snacks in his pack," one of the others said.

Haizea rummaged through the bag strapped around his waist and pulled out a few pieces of candy. The man chewed slowly and she helped him into a seated position. It took several moments, but his shaking began to ease.

"I'd give you a potion, but I don't have much supplies to craft one," Haizea said apologetically.

"It's fine. Mateo has it covered," he motioned toward a lumberjack walking toward them.

Mateo knelt beside them. His breath came heavy and laborious as he opened his pack, procuring a small bottle.

"So you *are* a healer," Haizea mused. He wiped moisture from his brow as he nodded.

"Rare to come across someone who shares the same power. Honestly, I'm surprised to see a healer working as a Bruvian warrior, but I can sense the weight of your magic. You're a blood mage," he said.

Despite herself, Haizea stiffened before answering.

"I am."

The other lumberjack drank the portion and clambered to his feet. When Mateo tried to assist him, he brushed him off, insisting that he was fine now.

"I thought about it—learning blood magic," Mateo murmured, watching as his fellow walked over to the rest of the group. "My magic has always taken a lot out of me, so I doubt my abilities are strong enough to pull the vitality from another person's body. That aside, I don't think I could bring myself to kill. Especially knowing I'd have to do it for the rest of my life. Healing's enough for me. At least you've found a way to put your blood magic to good use as a warrior."

Haizea brushed her fingers along her pendant.

"My grandfather taught me."

"Ah, so it's a family tradition," he pursed his lips. "Is it true what they say about the bloodlust? Pardon me if it's intrusive, I never get the chance to talk to other healers, let alone a blood mage," he asked.

"The bloodlust is always there. It ebbs and flows and spikes around stronger mages," Alastair's face came to mind as she spoke. "It's difficult at times, but nothing you can't control, so long as you want to control it."

Mateo tilted his head.

"Sometimes you don't want to control it." His words sounded more like a statement than a question.

Haizea's honey brown eyes met Mateo's, silent and arctic. He shrank back like a small rodent trapped in a cage and his pulse hammered against her magic. After a few beats, he cleared his throat, seeming to find his voice again.

"I've always been afraid of that. I don't want to..." Mateo trailed off. This time, Haizea acquiesced.

"Enjoy it?" she offered. Mateo nodded.

"Not every blood mage who experiences bloodlust delights in it. Based on what you've said, I doubt you would. My father was a blood mage, and he certainly didn't." Haizea paused and hummed to herself softly in an attempt to ease the newfound tightness in her chest.

"It feels like a significant gamble to make," he murmured.

"Looks like everyone else is fine. Do you need help?" Shauni sidled up beside her before she could respond.

"Yes, we were just finishing up," Haizea said quickly. She turned back to Mateo. "Take care of yourself."

"Likewise," he said, his face reddening as he rushed back to his group.

Shauni nudged her with her elbow as they left the area.

"If I didn't know any better, I'd say he has a little crush on you," she teased, earning an eyeroll from Haizea.

"Don't worry, I'm not trying to give Alastair competition. Not that I could," she added with a wink. "Besides, he's not your type anyway."

Haizea arched an eyebrow.

"What exactly *is* my type, Shauni?"

"I can sniff them out from a mile away. He ran off with his tail between his legs. It never works out when they're too shy. You like someone who is very sweet and mild-tempered, but assertive enough to put you through the mattress."

"Shauni—" Haizea coughed, nearly choking on her own saliva.

"Tell me I'm wrong."

When Haizea couldn't answer, Shauni grinned wickedly. Feeling her cheeks warm, Haizea grasped for a way to change the subject.

"You did some efficient work back there. Maybe it's time you went for the leader's mantle."

"I could ask you the same thing," Shauni countered.

"I haven't earned it. I left the mountains behind for two years."

"You left with Vendela's blessing and the understanding of the entire cohort. You're not some deserter. Besides, you know more about those kingdom dwellers than the average mountaineer does. That's important."

Haizea shrugged.

"There's nothing special about the kingdom dwellers. They're just people."

Shauni quirked an eyebrow.

"What?" Haizea said.

"They killed Mr. Harzel and tried to do the same to you. I just figured you'd feel differently."

"We mountaineers always say that the Cosmic Arts is only as vile as the mage who wields it. Each omen is responsible for their own actions. I'd be a hypocrite if I painted all kingdom dwellers with the same brush like they do to us…to people like me."

"I guess," Shauni shrugged.

Haizea rolled her shoulders as a companionable silence fell between them.

"How has your family been?"

"Every now and then I can convince my mother to have a sparring match. She's still got a bit of her old spark. My father—"

Shauni's footsteps faltered. Her violet eyes narrowed, and she twirled on her feet, looking behind them. Haizea reached for her swords, but Shauni shook her head and put her hand up.

Shauni shifted a little to her left and Haizea followed her line of sight. She squinted as something moved against the snowy backdrop. Shauni's magic rippled and curled her pointer finger in a 'come here' motion, creating a massive gust of wind. Haizea's cheeks stung as her braids whipped about. A fur-covered mass came flying toward them. Shauni flattened her palm, and the winds calmed, bringing the mass to a halt about a foot away from them.

Haizea frowned at the bundle of fur, confused until Shauni twirled her hand, revealing a person within. Upon seeing their face, Haizea and Shauni spat out a string of curses.

"Jassia, what the hell are you doing here?" Shauni said.

Jassia's copper eyes darted between them. The girl froze in place when she met Haizea's gaze, but Haizea made no effort to suppress the ferocity in her expression. She crouched down and put her hands on Jassia's shoulders.

"Vendela specifically did not give you an assignment for your own safety, Jassia. Do you understand the danger you've put yourself in?"

"I know, but...my dad's down this way working on the ropeways. Vendela said people are disappearing and I wanted to see if he's okay."

Steam practically poured out of Shauni's ears, her light brown skin reddening.

"Jassia, I understand your concern about your father, but you've directly disobeyed an order from the leader. Vendela would be well within her rights to ban you from continuing your warrior's training for this. Haizea and I now have to split our attention between protecting you and accomplishing the task we've been assigned. You're too young and not nearly far enough along in your training to be here," Shauni looked at Haizea. "Maybe we should turn around and take her back."

Haizea stood up to her full height. Both Jassia and Shauni craned their necks to maintain eye contact with her.

Given the reports of missing people, every moment mattered. They still didn't know what exactly they were walking into–the disappearances could be kidnappings or a string of murders.

It wasn't the place for a teenager. Young warriors worked their way up to the uglier aspect of their duties. But turning around meant delaying assistance to the villagers who needed help. It could mean more people snatched from their homes by the perpetrator—or worse, more blood spilled when they could have prevented it.

Haizea sighed when Jassia's bottom lip quivered.

"She managed to follow us all this way without being spotted until now. This is as much a slight on us as it is on her. I think we can manage it."

"I'm wearing the earth's smoke. Vendela said it makes it harder for mages to sense us and turns us into a blind spot." Jassia pushed back her coat, revealing wristbands.

Shauni's scowl faltered.

"Harder doesn't mean impossible. We may not be able to pinpoint you exactly, but I could guess your location. It also explains why I couldn't grab you directly and had to use the wind instead. You're not a mage, so it might be hard to understand," Shauni explained.

She raised her hand and a leaf floated toward her. A soft breeze made the leaf flutter in her palm.

"It's like feeling a breeze against your skin on a windy day, and for a brief moment, you stop feeling it when you walk past a big tree," she moved her free hand in front of the leaf, and its movements paused. "You can't see it, but you notice its absence."

Jassia nodded intently.

"Think of earth's smoke as a balancing act from the realm itself. It keeps mages from overrunning non-mages. A mage would know right away if they've been exposed, but non-mages can't sense it draining their vitality. Too much earth's smoke, even *once*, is lethal. You would drop dead and never know what happened," Haizea added.

"Didn't you get attacked with earth's smoke?" Jassia asked, finally getting to her feet.

"Yes, but I was very, very lucky. King Rhys turned it into a powder and it entered my body through my lungs, but I managed to get fresh air in enough time. When you're older and closer to mastering your weapon skills, you'll learn how to infuse the plant into your blades. A blade infused with earth's smoke is the most powerful weapon you'll ever wield. Once it's in your bloodstream, there's nothing anyone can do for you."

"Even for a blood mage, like you?" Jassia asked.

"Even for a blood mage."

Jassia fell silent, her eyes wide as she searched Haizea's face.

"Look at it this way: earth's smoke is a tool, no different from swords we carry. It's dangerous, but so long as you respect it, you'll be fine," Haizea said.

"Okay," Jassia said.

Shauni roughly clapped her on the shoulder.

"Now, with that out of the way, there's a village that needs our help. When we get there, the people won't see you as just a warrior in training. To them, you're a full-fledged Bruvian warrior. We've got your back, but you can't go sneaking off like you did today. Understand?"

Jassia nodded.

"Good. Now let's get into some trouble."

Chapter 10

Human Realm, Mount Illiniza, Springbreach Village

The stench of rotting flesh marked the warriors' arrival at their destination. Scrunching her nose at the putrid scent, Haizea affixed her skull mask.

"Jassia, you stick with Shauni," she said.

Keeping them at a distance would minimize the hazard her blood magic posed to her comrades. Shauni nudged Jassia behind her and the young warrior trailed behind, silent as a shadow. Haizea reached out with her healing magic to sense any signs of life nearby.

Her magic waxed and waned, but she struggled to pinpoint the source of the disturbance. Shauni and Jassia went to the left while Haizea searched toward the right. She ducked under a tree limb and stopped in her tracks at the sight of a body a few feet away. Frowning beneath her mask, she inched closer. The soft crunching of snow beneath her feet echoed in the stillness of the clearing.

The body lunged at her.

In one smooth motion, Haizea side-stepped its attack, unsheathed her swords, and decapitated it. As the head rolled on the ground, its shimmering eyes tracked her movement and the body gave chase. Haizea brought her knee up and planted her foot in its chest, sending it flying with a powerful kick.

"Shauni, it's a—"

Several pairs of hands grasped onto Haizea, cutting her warning short. Four more bodies tackled her. She hit the ground and slid, unable to regain her footing on the snow-covered slope. Her vision blurred in a cloud of white as she rolled down a hill–flashing between the sky above and the ground below. One of the bodies broke apart from the impact, and fluids splashed onto her. Haizea choked back a gag as the foul odor intensified and burned at her nostrils.

She managed to reorient herself on her hands and knees and skidded to a stop. Haizea tossed her coat to the side, just as more bodies entered the fray. Surrounded, she bit the inside of her cheek to draw blood. The vitality painted her world in a glistening vermillion hue.

Each undead body shone like a star in the nighttime sky, brimming with magic. Haizea gripped her swords and her muscles tensed, readying for her assault. Using the strength and speed of her Cosmic power, she tore through them with ease.

Up the hill, two glistening figures moved toward her. Shauni and Jassia's heads soon appeared.

"How the hell did you end up down there?" Shauni yelled.

"It's a necromancer," Haizea shouted back.

"Yeah, we noticed. We need to find the mage controlling them," Shauni held her hand out to the side and a pulse of magic ripped an approaching body into shreds.

With her friend on higher ground, Haizea turned in a full circle, observing every inch of her surroundings with her blood magic-fueled vision. Another beacon of vitality emanated further down the slope in an intense cluster of bright red light. Haizea said as much to Shauni, who nodded and turned to Jassia. The young warrior knelt. She rose again with an arrow nocked. A small ball dangled from the end.

Shauni unsheathed one of her swords and threw it like a spear. A thunderous crack reverberated through the air. Several paces down the slope, her blade pinned a body to a tree. A large fissure trailed down the trunk.

Beside her, Jassia unleashed a barrage of arrows. Haizea's brows rose as they hit their marks, piercing the heads and torsos of the undead. They rose higher when, a breath later, the balls on the end ignited. The explosions were contained enough to burn the putrified flesh without creating an inferno.

Haizea inched closer to the concentration of vitality. The call in her blood crescendoed with each step—the necromancer was close.

She pulled the vial of Alastair's blood from her holster and carefully poured a few drops into her palm. Her magical senses expanded and the Souls of the dead illuminated before her.

Shauni floated it down the slope, leaving Jassia in place up the hillside. They exchanged a glance.

"She's going to be an absolute terror when she outgrows her nervous streak," Shauni whispered with a smirk. Haizea nodded.

"The necromancer is in that cabin. People are hiding in some of the nearby homes, so stay clear of those. I'm counting about twenty more bodies between us and the omen," Haizea said.

Shauni outstretched her hand, recalling the sword she'd thrown. She unsheathed the other. Her glowing eyes glinted dangerously.

Haizea pulled out her blades and met Shauni's gaze, a silence passing between the duo before they broke out into a sprint. Their forms blurred as Haizea's blood magic and Shauni's telekinesis boosted their speed.

Shauni took a slight lead over Haizea, laughing behind her mask as she barreled down on five bodies. She leapt several feet into the air and threw her swords like daggers. Each blade hit their mark and impaled a body before she called them back.

Haizea faced the remaining of the dead. Her strength coincided with the power in the vitality she absorbed, and Alastair's power eclipsed that of the necromancer—she overwhelmed their hold over them with ease, unbinding the Souls from the bodies. They collapsed to the ground in a heap.

She charged toward the cabin where the necromancer hid and a massive wave crashed through the vitality before the door flew off the hinges–Shauni had assisted with her magic. As Haizea entered the house, the omen ran toward her.

He took two steps before he stumbled, caught in the vice tight grasp of her blood magic. The man clutched at his chest, right above the heart. His sparkling, diamond-like eyes met Haizea's brilliant red ones.

Blotches formed on his cheeks, and the vein in his throat bulged. The omen made a desperate choking sound and blood dripped out of his nose and slid over his upper lip before staining his shirt.

Pain pinched at her insides as his life slipped from him—the desires and within his Soul flowed into her. A pit formed in her stomach as she parsed through his emotions. She did not sense fear or regret or remorse.

Only relief.

He...he *wanted* this.

The realization stilled her, but only for a breath. She reached for her swords nonetheless and severed his head with a single blow. Before his body could even touch the ground, Haizea loosened the gate to her power, greedily consuming his vitality. His body shriveled before it burst into a cloud of dust. Haizea hissed quietly at the rush of ecstasy.

Her hands trembled as she resheathed her swords. A giggle bubbled up in her chest and spewed from her lips before she could swallow it back.

Again, a voice whispered in her ear.

"Everything okay?"

Haizea turned to see Shauni standing in the doorway. She dipped her chin in a stiff nod, and the room swirled from the movement. She took slow and deliberate steps to join her friend.

As they gathered the remains, Haizea frowned, deep in thought.

Why did his death bring him relief? Surely, he'd known that by killing so many people, he would pay for his actions with his life. Had this entire ordeal been an elaborate ploy to get the warriors' attention?

Her stomach churned as she recalled Alastair's words, ever hesitant about his magic.

Everything the Soul Reaper does comes at a price. The price he's asking for...I don't know if it's worth it.

The Soul Reaper wouldn't drive a necromancer to commit something so heinous, would he?

As she and Shauni placed the necromancer's head on a spike at the front of the village–a warning sign that the Bruvian warriors watched over and protected the area—her gut told her that he would.

An older woman approached them and introduced herself, pulling Haizea from her thoughts.

"I'm Lamiyah, one of the elders in this village. I sent the call for help," she said.

"I'm sorry we didn't make it sooner. We didn't realize how much the situation deteriorated after you sent the letter," Haizea said.

"We had a few disappearances over the last several weeks. It escalated when we identified the culprit. The bulk of the killings happened around the time we sent a messenger hawk."

"The important thing is that you all are safe now. Unfortunately, the fight caused a bit of structural damage to some of the homes. It's just the two of us, and we don't have much by way of supplies. We'll need to send a message back to get you more aid," Shauni said, but Lamiyah waved her off.

"Actually, we heard that some construction workers are nearby working on the ropeway. I think that might be quicker. If it's not out of your way, perhaps you could talk to them, send them our way?" Lamiyah said.

"My father is part of the crew helping install the pylon. Maybe he can help," Jassia piped in.

Shauni turned to Haizea.

"It's probably for the best to leave her with her father. Vendela will be marginally less upset about her sneaking off and us not sending her back immediately."

When Jassia pouted, Shauni patted her head.

"Isn't this what you tagged along for to begin with? Better a scolding from him than Vendela," Shauni said, earning a sigh of defeat from the young warrior.

Before departing, they helped the villagers gather supplies and for a funeral pyre. The necromancer had killed thirty people in total. They stepped back to give the surviving families space as they added bodies of their loved ones to the fire. For the bodies that had decomposed too much to handle directly, Shauni lifted them with her magic.

Lamiyah stood in front of the gathering crowd. The billowing smoke created a dark backdrop behind her.

"We lay our friends and family to rest, their lives stolen far too soon. May their Souls find peace and their final resting place in the Soul Realm. May Aaryn's blessing shine down upon our people," she said in a prayer.

With Spiritual vitality still coursing through her, Haizea watched the Souls depart. Each one offered a wistful farewell to the loved ones they left behind in the Human Realm. Their trio left shortly after, heading to the construction site to drop Jassia off to her father.

"Why didn't you talk to him first? Don't you want to know why he did it?" Jassia asked.

"Look at what he did to the villagers and how many people he killed. I don't think the 'why' matters," Shauni said.

Haizea hummed and pursed her lips.

"You know how Vendela said our job is to kill? Situations like this are what she meant. When a village reaches out to us for help, it's because they're at the end of their rope. There are always exceptions, but in this case, we're past the stage of trying to reason with him. It's why we call it a cull," Haizea said.

"When *would* you ask questions then?" Jassia asked.

"If we come across something on our own, we would investigate further. Or if a village has a problem, but they haven't narrowed down who the culprit is. There's always the rare occasion that someone sends us a false report. They might ask us to perform cull, but our instincts tell us something is off," Haizea answered.

"For the most part, when we have to perform a cull, it's because the villagers have asked us to do so. It's our duty to protect them, both from external threats and those that come from within," Shauni added.

Jassia nodded, falling silent for the remainder of their walk to the construction site. She brightened as the lumberjacks came into view and pointed to a man with copper eyes identical to her own.

Her father noticed them right away and made his way over to the trio. He walked with a noticeable limp. A small trinket hung from his belt loop, and as he got closer, Haizea realized it had Jassia's name engraved on it. He smiled but held a tightness in his eyes and lips that told Haizea he was likely in pain.

He pulled Jassia in a tight embrace and leaned back to look at her.

"Jassia, what are you doing all the way out here? Is your mother alright?"

"She's fine. Vendela handed out an assignment in Springbreach, and I wanted to see you."

Her father arched an eyebrow, and he glanced at Haizea and Shauni.

"Springbreach? I heard they've had a string of murders recently. Vendela sent *you* there?"

Jassia inched backward as if to hide behind Haizea and Shauni, but Shauni held her in place with a firm hand on the shoulder.

"Vendela did *not* send her with us. This little one is a master of stealth," she said.

"We're here to return her to you. The village also requested assistance with some of its damaged homes. We hoped you'd be able to help since you're close by."

Jassia's father flared his nostrils, but he agreed to pass the word along to the other lumberjacks.

"Since I'll be heading home sooner than expected, we'll take a look at it on our way back. I'm Jorah, by the way. Thank you for bringing her here."

They bid Jassia farewell, with the sounds of her father scolding her falling into the background.

Goosebumps prickled Haizea's skin as a cool breeze ran over her. She tugged at her coat with a small frown, but the chill rattled her bones. A light flickered in the corner of her eye.

She stilled, disturbed by the sudden, peculiar sensation that someone wanted her attention. She paused and looked over her shoulder before tilting her head toward the sky. A dim outline glimmered above—a man, a Soul, watched her intently.

Eaglestone village.

The unspoken words echoed within Haizea.

We were attacked by kingdom dwellers.

Her brows drew together.

"What happened? Why?"

They saw me realmdrift. Hundreds of them.

"Hundreds of kingdom dwellers?"

Please, they need help. Miss Tamsyn and Serenity. Caspian...I don't know why he...

At the mention of Caspian, hurt, grief, and betrayal threatened to drown Haizea. Shocked by the onslaught, it took a moment to regain her bearings.

"Eaglestone, right? We'll help them."

The anguish within the Soul eased, and the anchor that held it in this realm lifted. Before she could stop him or ask anything further, the man's Soul faded from sight. Haizea blinked a few times as her mind settled back into the physical world.

"Talking to yourself now?" Shauni arched an eyebrow.

Haizea shook her head, staring at where the Soul had just been.

She did not know the man's name, but she understood the calamity that befell him. Kingdom dwellers had invaded her homelands and killed him for no other reason than being an omen.

She gripped her swords. The handles groaned in protest.

The kingdoms could forbid the Cosmic Arts in their own territory, but they had no right to attack the mountaineers for embracing their magic and their culture.

She had already lost her grandfather due to their ignorance. She would not allow their influence to wreak havoc in the mountains.

"We're going to the base. There's a village we need to cull."

Chapter 11
Human Realm, Mount Illiniza, Village of Windhaven

An assortment of baked goods lay across Alastair's table at the marketplace–muffins, mini cakes, and cookies. Sweet aromas billowed toward him, and he inhaled, savoring the scent.

Jassia's suggestion about opening a dessert stand had stuck with him, and with Haizea gone on her assignment, he had more free time than usual.

Alastair smiled warmly as a man approached his stand. The man stopped and read his sign, which displayed his prices, as well as explained that he communicated via sign language. He perused the options available before ordering a dozen muffins.

They exchanged goods and money, but the man paused as he turned to leave and signed:

~I haven't seen you around here before.~

~Today is my first day selling here.~

~Ah. I suppose I'll see you more often then?~

Alastair paused, absorbing the way his expression brightened.

~I plan on selling two to three days a week to keep myself busy. But between you and me, I'm also doing this to save up for a special gift for my other half.~

The man's smile diminished faintly, but he nodded.

~Well, best wishes to you and your loved one,~ he signed before leaving.

Back in Goldenleaf, Alastair wedged the gap of his family's shortcomings through theft, but he no longer needed to do that in Windhaven. Haizea's income as a warrior supported both of them, and they lived in comfort. Although he didn't *need* the money from selling baked goods, he wanted to have something to call his own and that could contribute to their home.

Growing up, sweets like this were reserved for special occasions and even then, his family could only afford to make them from scratch. Yet with a stack of coins weighing down his pockets, the people of Windhaven purchased from him without a second thought.

They didn't have to worry about going to bed hungry or if they could afford to keep a roof over their heads. The children went off to school during the day and received a proper education.

How could life be so easy here while his own family had struggled to get by? Why did the vitality deem Windhaven more deserving than Goldenleaf?

Alastair blinked rapidly, his eyes afflicted with a sudden stinging. To distract himself, he counted the coins he'd collected so far—enough to purchase the medicine for Jassia's mother without having to dip into the stash Haizea had left for him. He gathered what was left of his baked goods and packed them away into his cart.

A rumble beneath his feet brought him to a halt.

He looked left and right, searching for the source. A commotion had broken out at the far end of the marketplace. Before Alastair could decide if it was worth getting a closer look, the crowd parted ways. People stumbled backward, looking over their shoulders as they dashed away from the area.

Two moose thrashed against one another. They reared back and charged forward, creating a cloud of snow in their wake. The two animals rivaled even Alastair in height—their shoulders were nearly at his eye level.

Wood splintered and food splattered across the ground as they crashed into the nearby stands. Shoppers and merchants scattered. One of the moose bucked wildly and sent the other tumbling away, leaving a cloud of snow in its wake.

It did not stop there—the bull gave chase, ramming its antlers into the others. Violent quakes tremored the ground as it stomped its hooves.

Blood coated the other's legs as it backed away. Its nostrils flared, and it swung its head wildly before charging into a nearby vending stall.

People's mouths contorted, undoubtedly screams, as the remaining bull continued its rampage. Alastair watched, mouth ajar.

Without consciously choosing to do so, he delved into the vitality and the world began to shimmer.

A handful of villagers encircled the bull and a sphere of luminescence surrounded them. Alastair frowned as he focused on the rampaging animal. Distortions trailed behind it—ripples and tears where there should have been stability. The distortions were minuscule, but it reminded him of what he'd seen while visiting the monastery.

The bull charged forward and the people surrounding it raised their hands. A wall of magic shoved it back. Together, the group levitated the animal into the air and carried it off.

As the dust settled, something pulled taut against Alastair's magic. The second bull remained on the ground, unmoving. His feet inched toward it, driven by an invisible force.

As he closed the distance, the animal began to strain. It tried to lift itself, but quickly tired, its chest heaving in the process. Alastair knelt. A cold breeze blew over his skin as he rested his hand on its side. The animal blinked slowly, and when its gaze met his, he felt a silent plea in his Soul.

Alastair glanced over his shoulder, looking for help, but the villagers were busy tending to one another. Warmth blew across his face as the moose huffed beneath him. More blood oozed from its wounds, and sharp pain pricked against Alastair's Soul in tandem. His magic couldn't heal the animal—and the other mountaineers would sooner butcher it for meat than tend to its wounds.

He sighed. If he could not save the animal, then maybe he could put an end to its suffering. Maybe that was why his magic had drawn him here.

Go in peace, he thought.

With a gentle nudge from his magic, its Soul departed from the Human Realm. Light faded from the bull's eyes and its head fell limp on the ground. The frantic pounding of its heart stilled beneath Alastair's fingers.

Something settled within Alastair and his magic stabilized. Several moments passed as he sat there, looking at its lifeless form.

Tightness in his throat choked him.

Why was it that he could ease this animal's transition to the next realm while his family had perished so violently and he'd been powerless to stop it?

Leg wobbling beneath him, Alastair climbed to his feet. He absorbed the aftermath as he returned to his cart. Nearly all of the shoppers had left and the remaining vendors were busy packing up their things.

Pressure pulsed behind his temples and a foreboding sensation slithered down in spine. A figure lurked at the edge of his consciousness. It observed him with a quiet detachment.

Eyes narrowing, Alastair looked over his shoulder. He knew he would not find the Soul Reaper, but still, a part of him expected something more–something concrete that the entity was the source behind the chaos just now.

Unable to prove his suspicions, Alastair shook the feeling away as best as he could and returned to the task at hand—he still needed to run the errands Haizea had asked of him.

He read over the list of plants to purchase from the herbalist. The primary ingredient was mirwort, which he remembered from helping Haizea create potions. A wistfulness swept over him at the memory. Working as a healer's assistant was the first time he felt like he'd contributed something toward the greater good.

He wished that they could go back to that—working together, just the two of them. Given his predicament with his magic, he wanted to spend the precious time he had left creating more memories with the people he loved. Tragedy had already struck his family like a bolt of lightning, lethal and without warning. Death took what it wanted when it so desired and tomorrow was not promised.

He hoped that Haizea returned home soon.

Soft tufts of snow landed on his coat and his coins thumped against his leg as he made his way to the shop. Alastair took his time perusing the inventory. His shoulders slumped when he found the available selections sparse. Worse yet, mirwort was out of stock entirely.

He turned to leave, and a woman passing by caught his eye. A few bushels full of mirwort poked out of her basket. Alastair altered his gait, leaning into his long and nimble stride, while minimizing any jostling motions to keep his coins from clanging around in his pockets. He closed the distance and fell in step behind the woman. In one smooth motion, he snagged the mirwort from her basket and placed it in his own. Oblivious, she continued onward to the shop's counter.

Alastair turned his back to the woman's anxious searching with a well-practiced ease. If she exclaimed or cried or questioned the shop owner, he would not see it. But he could not escape her Soul—her distress gnawed at his insides. He preoccupied himself with filling his basket with the other plants on the list. By the time he made his way to the counter, the woman had left.

Despite her absence, her anguish lingered on his Soul. A weight bore down on him, threatening to drag him under the tides of her despair. He closed his eyes in an effort to suppress the energy that trickled across his skin.

Alastair did not allow himself to wonder about what ailment she may have needed the plant for, or if it was to tend to someone she loved. Otherwise, the guilt would sink its claws in and refuse to let go. He let those persistent emotions slide off of him and pushed them to the back of his mind.

He didn't want for her to suffer, not truly. Maybe he didn't *need* to steal, and he knew it was wrong, but old habits die hard. Back in Goldenleaf, he'd made this choice on a daily basis. His family–the people he loved–always came first. Even if it meant depriving someone else of their needs.

He placed his items in front of the merchant, his cheeks stiff as he offered a small smile. The distant sensation of eyes watching him prickled across his skin and sent a shiver down his spine. His smile faded.

Why now?

Shaking his head, Alastair did his best to direct his attention away from the entity's presence. He grabbed the bundle of plants and returned home to prepare the potion.

The instructions Haizea left were straightforward. Alastair fell into a lull as he worked, taking his time and carefully mixing the ingredients together accordingly. He'd just finished the batch when the hairs on the back of his neck stood up. An invisible weight returned as the Soul Reaper hovered over his movements.

Alastair set down the plants and looked over his shoulder, expecting to see an apparition of the entity but only empty air greeted him.

What do you want from me?

He waited for an answer, but the entity did not grant him one. A sigh rumbled through his chest.

Alastair packed the potions away before heading for the door. Jassia's mother lived a few villages over, so he took the ropeways rather than walk.

Alastair rapped his knuckles on the door and waited. A woman opened it a few moments later. Her resemblance to Jassia was immediate—they shared the same curl pattern, though her tresses were longer and fell past her shoulders. When the woman's lips moved, Alastair signed that he was deaf and explained his presence at her doorstep.

~These are for you and your family.~

Jassia's mother took the package of potions and her gratitude flowed into his Soul.

~When you had Jassia over for dinner, she talked about it nonstop for at least a week. She's always running off with the warriors. I do wish she would sit still a little more sometimes. Kids, you know? Anyway, I appreciate you all watching over her.~

~She's a pleasure to be around. We're always happy to have her.~

Her mother's smile faltered. Her face paled and she patted her chest lightly while taking a deep breath. Alastair reached out to her, but she waved him off.

~I'm alright. Just got a weak heart, is all. Been this way my whole life, but it's gotten worse with age. Makes it hard to get around and even harder to keep up with a teenager,~ she looked at the potion with a wistful gleam in her eyes. ~Please, send Haizea my thanks as well.~

Alastair bid her farewell and walked toward the ropeways. The late afternoon sun painted the skies a rich orange and the wind nipped at him as he boarded the cable car. He leaned his head back against the seat and closed his eyes. After spending his day surrounded by people, the mere thought of returning home to a vacant house drained him.

Once he reached Windhaven, he began the long way to his cabin. Tension coiled in his shoulders, pressure bore down on his body and the faint pinch of a headache beginning to blister made him squint.

The whispers of the dead followed as he meandered toward his bedroom. Alastair curled into a ball and pulled the covers over his head, but sleep proved elusive—the Soul Reaper's presence cast a shadow in his every thought. He tossed and turned for what felt like hours before snatching the covers off and stomping to the living room. He lit the fireplace, pushed the furniture back, and set a blanket on the ground.

Alastair crossed his legs and closed his eyes. His magic rose and flowed until he touched the vastness of the Soul Realm. When the Soul Reaper appeared before him, he held his chin high and glared at the entity, making no effort to conceal his impatience.

Home alone and unable to sleep, every step of his path today seemed like a sign from the entity. Pamin had told him to seek out the Soul Reaper for answers. Now was as good a time as any.

What do you want from me? he demanded once again.

This time, the entity provided an answer. The Soul Reaper raised his hand and their surroundings shifted. A bright, golden gate towered over Alastair and clear blue skies filled the horizon.

I've been waiting for you to ask. I'll start from the beginning.

Chapter 12
Human Realm, Base of Mount Illiniza

Tufts of blonde locks blanketed Sage's boots. She sat on a tree stump with her hands clasped in her lap and her eyes squinted shut. Felix sheared away another bundle of her hair with his blade. A current of wind carried them away.

When she woke up this morning her tresses fell down to the middle of her back. Now her hair barely hung past her ears. Her brother smeared a thick paste that stained the little hair that remained into a much darker shade. She shivered as it settled onto her scalp.

"Given what happened to Eaglestone, we should start disguising ourselves properly. We don't want people recognizing us, not until we're ready," he explained.

Felix took the blade to his own head next. When he finished, his hair was so short he might as well have been bald. Sage wondered if it would bring more attention than if he'd have simply let it be.

Several days had passed since fleeing Eaglestone village. They'd assumed they'd have arrived at the next village by now, but hour upon hour of walking with only endless greenery and not a single sign of human habitation made them realize how spread out the mountain base's population was.

Sage's vision blurred as she looked up the mountain's slope, and she blinked slowly to dispel the dizziness. Her last genuine meal had been the bowl of soup Miss Tamsyn served for supper. Since then, they'd sustained themselves on a small fox Felix had managed to trap. Sage dearly regretted not properly savoring the food Miss Tamsyn had provided them. Watching the process of capturing, killing, and then roasting the animal over a fire made her squeamish. Sage had eaten as much of the fox as she could stomach, but they had no way to preserve the food for later.

Felix had much to say about that.

"Old Lady T started off with boiling and freezing water for a reason. It's simple, but practical. If you could learn to do just that, we could save these rations for later, but instead we have to throw it away. Keep practicing, Sage."

Felix recaptured her attention with a tap on her foot. He stood over her with his arms crossed.

"We need to get moving. We're vulnerable if we stay put for too long."

"Can't we rest a little while longer? Don't your feet hurt?"

"The sooner we get to the next village, the sooner we can get new shoes."

Sage's stomach growled audibly.

"And the sooner we can eat a real meal," he added.

Sage peeled herself off of the stool with a sigh. She ran her fingers through her shorn hair and cast a mournful look at the long flowing locks that now laid in the dirt. Felix waved her forward impatiently.

As they walked, he made her practice their cover story again. Their names had changed once more—Felix was now Fenton and Sage was his little brother, Julian.

An eagle flew overhead, its wingspan casting a shadow as long as she was tall. Her footsteps faltered. Sage couldn't tell if it was from the pain shooting through her soles, her empty stomach, or the memory the bird elicited.

Father's story had all started with something as innocuous as an eagle flying in the sky. It ended in unfathomable carnage committed by his best friend, Mericus. She prayed to the Angels that she would not end up like him.

The haze at the edges of her vision began to spread and Sage tripped over herself. Felix reached out to catch her but narrowly missed. His magic latched onto her body at the last moment, blunting her fall, though her bones still jostled from the impact.

Sage stood up and dusted herself off, but dirt stubbornly clung to her sweat-encrusted skin. She blinked, eyes stinging with tears that she fought to hold in. She longed for a warm bath and clean clothes and a proper bed to sleep in. Eaglestone may not have been home, but at least Miss Tamsyn had given them that.

Her throat went dry. How had the village fared against the Olysseans?

Sage's gaze fell to Felix with a frown, but she hurried to keep pace with him. Despite losing everything else, she still had her big brother. If the Angels had mercy, perhaps they would find their way home again.

Two days later, Felix managed to capture a squirrel for both of them. Sage bit into the rodent's roasted flesh and gagged. She closed her eyes and focused intently on keeping the bile from rising up her throat. Across from her, Felix chewed and swallowed so quickly that Sage doubted if he could even taste it. Maybe she should do the same. Sage took another bite and grimaced at the unfamiliar texture in her mouth. The only reason she didn't spit it back out was that it was the first thing she'd eaten in days.

After their meal—if you could call it that—they came upon a stream of running water. Sage rushed towards it. She crouched by the edge and willed the water closer without lifting a finger. She took a healthy drink before washing the grime from her face. Felix trailed behind her and waved his arms and gritted his teeth with effort as he did the same.

"I can help," she offered.

"My magic may not be the strongest, but it's not useless," he snapped. Sage retracted her hand.

"I–I didn't mean it that way, Felix."

He gulped down his water without another word before he stood up and stormed off. Sage did not follow him right away.

Back in Arcelia, she and her brother had never been particularly close. The strength of her magic eclipsing Felix's had always been a sore spot in their relationship. He undoubtedly would have taken up transmutation if their capabilities had been reversed. Sage chewed on her bottom lip.

Would Felix have left her behind if he did not see her magical prowess as a necessity?

Uncertain of what his answer would be and afraid she might push the only person she had left away, Sage did not dare utter her worries aloud. Instead, she decided to practice once more, as he always nagged her about. He wouldn't abandon her if she was useful.

She closed her eyes and raised a ball of water from the stream. She honed in closer, commanding the vitality to shift. According to Felix, in order to boil water, the particles need to accelerate. To freeze it, they needed to be motionless. The sensation of something trying and failing to snap in place returned–like flicking a match that wouldn't quite light. Sage did not break her focus. She continued pushing and pushing until finally, warmth billowed toward her.

Sage opened her eyes to see the ball of water steaming. It didn't roll and bubble in a boil, but it was progress nonetheless, and the first step of many toward a true transmutation. Her lips twitched upward with pride, but Sage suppressed her excitement. Felix's temperamental mood made it difficult to predict how he would react, especially while he smarted about his own magic.

With a gentle, smooth motion of her hand, water flowed into the stream. She turned around to see Felix watching her with his cold blue gaze. To her surprise, he dipped his chin in a faint nod. This time, Sage smiled in earnest.

Later that evening, a cloud of smoke in the distance led them to the next village. She followed behind her brother's determined footsteps, her gaze lingering on the hilt of a knife that protruded from his back pocket. He also carried all of the money they had—stolen from Bose's body before they fled Eaglestone.

They entered the next village, which seemed slightly less run-down than the previous one. Rather than dirt roads, these had clearly once been paved but rotted over from lack of upkeep. A towering field of crops stretched off to her right, while homes and buildings stood to her left. The houses appeared well maintained aside from looking a bit worn from age.

She halted in her tracks and read the nameplate: Snakewell Village. This was Bose's home village—where he would have taken them to if Felix had not killed him.

No, not killed. Murdered. Felix *murdered* Bose in cold blood. And they'd stumbled right into his home.

"Felix, maybe we should keep going until we find the next village. Bose lived here," she whispered. Her brother shrugged.

"You've been whining about wanting to stop and rest for days and now you say this? I eliminated a threat to our safety. Miss Tamsyn told him to get the warriors and as a realmdrifter, he could have brought them down the slope in mere minutes. You're not learning transmutation just to perform little circus tricks, Sage. His death was just the first of many."

Sage swallowed Felix's chastising tone, but she still could not shake the thought of how a murdered Soul may not find peace. A Soul without peace often lingered in the Human Realm. But demurring at the prospect of provoking her brother yet again, Sage kept silent.

They passed two meat and dairy merchants, both with empty stands and nothing to sell. On the opposite side of the marketplace, a long, bustling line curled around the fish merchant. The stark contrast between the vendors stilled Sage.

Bose made a living by using his realmdrifting abilities to transport food and goods quickly between the two villages. The village had already lost a portion of its food supply in the short time that had passed since his death.

Sage fell behind Felix's brisk pace, mouth ajar. For as long as she'd known him, Bose always made an effort to help the people around him. In his final moments, all he had wanted to do was protect Eaglestone from the attackers. And Felix...

Bile rose in Sage's throat at the memory of Bose's blood pooling on the ground.

A villager walked by, looking forlornly at the vacant section of the market. They carried two baskets, one of them empty.

Was their mission so important that it should have cost his life? Surely, this community didn't deserve the hardship they'd brought upon them.

She didn't know if the Angels would forgive them for the blood that stained their hands.

Felix's magic wrapped around her and tugged her forward, ripping her attention away.

"This is a new village and we don't know these people. Stay close," he whispered harshly.

They stumbled upon a small shop that sold warm soup. After days of eating burnt wildlife, Sage welcomed the change. The duo seated themselves at a small table. A young man who looked around Felix's age approached them barely a moment later.

"Mind if I sit here?" he asked. He took the seat before they could answer.

Sage's chair shifted beneath her as Felix pulled her closer. He narrowed his eyes on the newcomer.

"Yes, I do mind."

The newcomer shrugged. His gaze turned away from Felix and toward Sage, offering a bright smile.

"What's your name?"

"Sa-Julian," the answer tumbled out of her.

"Julian," he drew the name out. "What city are you from?"

A tingling sensation vibrated through her as he spoke. She opened her mouth to answer, but Felix balled his fist, using his magic to snap it shut. She shrank away from his glare. Then his eyes narrowed and turned on the young man.

"We're from Eaglestone *village*. Not a city," Felix's calm tone did not match the ferocity in his expression.

The young man sized him up.

"That disguise is obvious from a mile away. You're kingdom dwellers," he said matter-of-factly.

Felix's fists clenched.

"What is your problem?"

"*I* don't have a problem, I just have a feeling that you might. Julian? Give me a break. Botched haircut aside, I know a lie when I hear one."

Sage touched her head and tried not to pout.

"Anyway, I've seen a lot of you city folk coming through here the last few months. If I can spot you so easily, then bet your ass the warriors will."

Sage and Felix exchanged a glance. Her brother crossed his arms and sneered at the stranger in a way that reminded her of their father.

"Say we *are* kingdom dwellers. What does us possibly getting spotted have to do with you?"

The young man smiled impishly.

"I'm an enchanter. Boosting disguises with magic is easy money, especially when it's for a bunch of desperate city folk."

"How much?" Felix asked.

"For both of you, it'll be fifty coins."

Felix studied him.

"Disguise her first. If I like it, I'll pay you. If not, no deal."

"Oh. I see you're confused about how this all works. Either you pay me, or I'll send word to the warriors about your being here. It's not optional."

"I can scalp you without even lifting a finger," Felix said. His bowl of soup elevated from the table.

"*So can I.*"

A jolt snatched the air from Sage's lungs. Her vitality thrummed to the tune of the enchanter's voice. A dare. A threat.

Felix leaned back in his seat. He must have decided that the odds were against him with a Mental mage because he pushed the coins toward the enchanter. The young man pulled a necklace from a small bag and handed it to her. Her magic pulsed faintly at its touch. Sage put it on and looked at her brother.

"How...how do I..." she trailed off and touched her neck, stunned by the sound of her own voice.

The enchantment changed her intonation, giving her voice a wispy quality that she normally did not have. Felix considered her.

"You look like a distant cousin," he said and paid the enchanter.

When Felix donned his own wristband, Sage saw what he meant by his comment. They still looked related, but the enchantment gave them subtle changes to their face shape, a slight alteration to the distance of their eyes and nose that made him look less like Felix and more like a distant relative. His naturally dark hair lightened, just a few shades away from Sage's blonde locks.

The enchanter walked away, chuckling to himself and counting the coins Felix had given him. Finally alone, Sage whispered to her brother.

"Do you think the warriors will really come here?"

Felix stared at the mage's retreating form.

"They have no choice but to come. Not only did those people overrun that village, but they were kingdom dwellers. Imagine if it were Arcelia and the mountaineers attacked us. Father would have sent his forces to clear them out. Made an example of them..." he trailed off, a newfound glassiness in his eyes. Sage's hand hung in the air, hesitating before she held his hand. To her surprise, Felix squeezed her back lightly. "We should be fine. But as useful as these enchantments are, I don't trust that guy as far as I can see him. We'll stay for a little while and see if they have another transmuting mage to learn from. And try to find a way to get rid of that guy."

"Felix, killing him is a surefire way to break the enchantment."

He cursed under his breath.

"You're right. Okay, you're right," he raised his hands in surrender. "This just means that we have to leave at the first sign of trouble. A swindler like that is sure to lord these enchantments over us and sell us out as soon as it benefits him."

Sage's shoulders relaxed, and the tension in her chest eased. Felix opened his mouth like he wanted to say something, then paused, likely deciding against it.

"Hurry up and eat. We need to find a place to rest our heads."

Chapter 13

Beast Realm

Three newly hatched *doyamas* clung to Kallistê's body—two rested on her arms and one curled over the back of her neck. Her older *doyamas* stalked close behind, with their ear flaps open wide and their nostrils flaring periodically as they breathed in the various scents around them.

One of the larger ones pressed its damp, cold nose into her hand. A deep growl rumbled low in its throat. Kallistê nudged it away, rolling her eyes as she readjusted her rings. Her Beast's reptilian skin turned transparent, rendering it invisible to any onlookers—although here in the Beast Realm, there would be no other human observers.

A gust of wind lifted her long, blue hair off her shoulders. Tall azure grasses brushed against her calf in kind. She hummed a note and her Beasts sprang to attention, leaping off her body. They maintained their transparent camouflage, so she hummed a note higher in pitch. Her Beasts altered their skin accordingly. Kallistê performed a series of snaps and her *doyamas* darted off into the distance.

She'd taken advantage of the Beast's impeccable hearing by teaching them to respond to different sounds—like a snap of her fingers or stamping her feet. If she were ever in a position where she could not speak, then she could use her hands, and if she could not use her hands, then she could hum a note in the back of her throat.

Kallistê had not risen to power by chance and she would not so easily leave herself vulnerable to any who wished to unseat her.

Bringing her Beasts to their natural habitat gave them time to run and hunt to release any pent up energy from living in the Palace. It also provided the opportunity for her older, fully trained *doyamas* to teach the younger ones to follow her command by example.

As her Beasts played and hunted in the sanctity of their home realm, Viltarin's face popped into her mind. Kallistê stood up a little straighter, as it jogged her memory. That's what she wanted to talk to Ivor about.

She needed to check on his doings in Arcelia and keep tabs on anything he may have up his sleeve. Once she finished her work here, she would slip into Arcelia and–

A piercing sensation ripped through Kallistê so forcefully that she cried out. A handful of her Beasts returned in a flash. Their growls sent forth another shockwave of pain. Her vision clouded over and she clutched her forehead. Several dizzying moments passed before she managed to reorient herself, but the pounding in her head remained.

A group of trees shuddered down the hillside and a flying Beast broke through the foliage. Kallistê did not have a chance to prepare herself for the mind-shattering cry that followed.

Her body seized and she collapsed back into the grass. Vibrations rocked through her, rumbling deep in her ears before racing down her spine. She could only manage to move her eyes–she could not muster the ability to move her arms and cover her ears.

In the distance, the flying Beast seized in the sky before plummeting toward the ground. Two *doyamas* leapt several feet in the air and bit down on each end–one ripping into the head while the other caught the tail. Limbs and blood went flying, and her doyama's long teeth shredded into its flesh.

The piercing scream ceased. Several moments ticked by before Kallistê was able to move again. She rubbed her temples and squinted her eyes. Arms trembling, she sat down in the grass and the rings on her fingers glinted under the sunlight.

A golden ring with an amber gemstone caught her eye, and she twirled it, brows drawing together. She'd worn it as a tribute to Aaryn for her visit with Premier Eryx and Kestramore's dignitaries.

Kallistê stilled.

With a slow deliberateness, she tugged at the amber ring. Flames scorched her mind, and she doubled over in agony. She gritted her teeth through the pain, but her hand refused to do what her mind willed. Her fingers trembled in place, trying and failing to grasp onto the cursed object. Breathing out a string of curses, Kallistê let go.

As if it sensed her agony, one of her *doyamas* skulked toward her. It emitted a high-pitched chirp and lay its head in her lap, pressing its nose against her hand. Her Beast growled and nipped at the ring, its throat vibrating against her legs. A warning.

Viltarin, you bastard.

She wanted to scream the words aloud, but her throbbing head wouldn't allow it.

When he'd kissed her hand at the meeting, Viltarin must have used his magic on her ring right in front of her, without saying a word. The pain that crippled her when she tried to think of him was the hallmark sign of a curse over an enchantment. She could see Viltarin's smug face now. When she found him, she would banish him to the Cosm—

Kallistê doubled over, assaulted by the sensation of dozens of daggers impaling her flesh. Her breaths came raggedly as she waited for it to pass.

Although she did not know the specifics of the curse, at the very least, one component of it evidently prevented her from taking actions to bring Viltarin harm. It also stopped her from removing the ring. Given that the most straightforward way to get rid of the curse would be to either take off the ring finger or to kill Viltarin, he'd put her into a vice-tight bind.

What an absolute nuisance to deal with.

Still, the mind was a complex thing to subjugate. Even the most ironclad, seemingly unbreakable curses contained vulnerabilities—nooks and crannies that could be exploited. Kallistê could circumvent this curse, but she faced an uphill battle in finding the pathway to do so.

She laid back on the grass and burst into a fit of laughter. Conquering the realm just got that much harder, but she welcomed the challenge. She needed to approach this situation with caution and decipher what she could and could not do within the curse's boundaries. One step at a time.

Kallistê smirked to herself with a newfound determination. She wouldn't just kill Viltarin. He would suffer for defiling her in such a manner. Every instance of pain she endured would be repaid tenfold.

Kallistê recalled her *doyamas*. It was time to return home.

Sand prickled against Kallistê's feet as her body rematerialized in the Human Realm. Ocean waves splashed behind her as she stood on Kestramore's shores.

With the cursed ring weighing heavy on her finger, a visit to the island seemed in order.

Ivor had delivered promptly on the list of mages Kallistê requested. With Premier Eryx's permission, she'd sent ten mages to Kestramore to learn the Cosmic Arts—six telekinetics, two mediums, an enchanter and Ivor, a clairvoyant. Although she'd sent her mages a few weeks ago, Kallistê would not bear the fruits of her investment so soon.

Not only did full mastery and control over the Cosmic Arts take a few years of dedication, but realistically, only half of them would possess the strength necessary to successfully complete their training. In either case, five fully realized omens was a move in the right direction.

Of the mages she'd sent, she hoped that Ivor persevered. Having a trusted seer on her court could wedge this newfound gap in her defenses.

Kallistê whistled and the air rippled before her as one of her pets unveiled itself from its camouflage. She weaved her Soul with the doyama's and entered the astral plane.

Premier Eryx's Soul called out to her from within one of the temples, where the islanders paid obeisance to the Demons. Kallistê's lips twitched upward involuntarily. She covered her mouth with one hand in an attempt to muffle the laughter bubbling up inside of her chest. Despite her efforts, she cackled out loud, giggling until tears blurred her vision.

The invisible hand of Cosmic Realm wrapped around her, its vastness threatening to engulf her where she stood. She rested her hand on the temple's facade and closed her eyes to ground herself.

Flash.

Her ears buzzed from the deafening roar of a *tri-vialis*. Tall cerulean grasses tickled her skin.

Flash.

A shadow blackened the sunlight and the ground quaked beneath her feet. A Titan passed overhead, its massive foot narrowly missing her.

Kallistê gritted her teeth. Inhale. Exhale. Several moments ticked by before she finally grounded her body and her Soul firmly in the Human Realm.

A faint buzz tremored through Kallistê as she walked through the temple's long entrance, which had columns on each side of the walkway. A handful of statues towered inside of the main room.

Aaryn's golden skin glimmered even in the natural lighting. Two statues stood on either side of her—a light gray Demon with charcoal colored wings and another with rich bronze skin and white wings adorned with bronze flecks.

The other two Demons bore little significance to Kallistê. None of Kestramore's records contained any information about them beyond the fact that they'd accompanied Aaryn when she returned magic to the realm. They were probably nothing more than mere servants—eager to please with little ambition.

Premier Eryx stood in the center of the room with her head bowed and her eyes closed. Kallistê lingered by the door, silently watching the foolish, but well-intentioned effort. Humanity held just as much worth as the Demons. They could tap into the power of the Cosmos all the same—they stood on equal footing. A queen would never bend the knee before another queen, so Kallistê saw no sense in bowing her head in prayer.

A few minutes later, Premier Eryx raised her head. She turned around and offered Kallistê a small smile.

"I wasn't expecting you Kallistê. What brings you all the way to Kestramore?"

Viltarin and his nuisance of a power, Kallistê wanted to say, but daggers raking through her skull suffocated the words before she could breathe life into them.

"I'm here because I've given your proposition regarding your retirement further consideration. I still don't want to turn my back on Llyr. But my vision has always included prosperity for Kestramore. I'd like to see someone take your place who has a similar mindset. If not myself then someone trustworthy who you believe will be amenable to my plans."

"Someone obedient," the Premier countered.

Kallistê flipped her hair over her shoulder.

"Someone who is an asset rather than an obstacle."

Eryx pursed her lips contemplatively.

"Walk with me, Kallistê."

She followed the Premier outside of the temple. Her *doyama* trailed behind, invisible to the naked eye and undetectable to human ears.

"I'm certain this goes without saying, but your approach to Kestramore will have to be much different from the continent. You're a gifted realmdrifter and your command over the Beasts is admirable, but when facing people born and raised by the Cosmic Arts, it's going to take more maneuvering to make them bend."

"Of course, Premier."

"Expect significant pushback from Quathir and Nehemias as usual. I have no doubt they'll be vying for my position once I step down. You're the only person I've told, but I'm sure they suspect it's coming sooner rather than later. I'm not as young as I used to be and it's quite obvious."

Premier Eryx led her through a back passageway, away from the busy roads where the islanders congregated. The leaves on nearby palm trees ruffled from a gust of wind and Kallistê's hair blew behind her in a long sapphire streak. The sun beamed down on them from high above and she basked in the heat spreading on her skin.

"I know that being a realmdrifter means you can travel far and wide in the blink of an eye, but it's still impossible to be in two places at once. What do you think of Lotus?"

"If you think she's fit for the position, I'm content with her. But who will rule over Olysseus?" Kallistê said.

"You, my dear. Let Lotus continue doing the work of bringing them into submission. By the time I step down, the kingdom will be primed for the taking. Annex them into Llyr."

Kallistê nodded, satisfied with the proposal. Because Kallistê was a Spiritual mage, transmutation magic didn't cause as much of a nuisance for her compared to curse magic. Her ability to realmdrift removed the chains that bound her to the physical world, giving her an edge over the Physical class.

The Mental Class, however, was quite a vexing magic for her to deal with. Realmdrifting provided no protection to her mind—the cursed ring on her finger was a testament to that.

Kallistê snapped at her *doyama* and it unveiled itself.

"And what might this be?" Premier Eryx arched a brow as the *doyama* ventured closer and sniffed her.

Kallistê waited before answering, watching intently to see if anything set her pet off in the way that her cursed ring did. When the Beast did not growl, Kallistê felt a wave of relief. Though far from foolproof, it was the only way she could think of to determine if a curse afflicted the Premier. By the looks of things, Viltarin had not taken such measures with Eryx, but Kallistê would not let her guard down entirely.

If she had to guess, he likely anticipated the Premier's upcoming retirement—as she'd said before, her advancing age did not go unnoticed. Not to mention, considering the Premier's popularity among the islanders–she'd served for many decades for a reason–cursing her posed both a personal and political risk for Viltarin. It made no sense for him to take such measures if the Premier would soon remove herself from the equation entirely.

"This is for your safety. I do not trust...," Kallistê tried and failed to speak Viltarin's name. She relented with a sneer. If she pushed too hard, the curse would interfere with her thought processes.

"Not everyone on the court shares our viewpoints. We have many friends, but enemies always lurk in the shadows. What better than a Beast that can do the same? Could you lend me your hand?" Kallistê said, choosing her words more carefully. The curse did not kick back at her this time—it appeared to rebuff direct thoughts toward Viltarin, but a meandering path did not elicit such a reaction.

Eryx obliged and she placed her palm on her *doyama's* nose. Kallistê leaned in and whispered softly, so that only her Beast could hear her.

"*Friend. Guard,*" she commanded.

Her *doyama* stood behind the Premier.

"I raised and trained it myself," Kallistê explained. She told Eryx a handful of verbal commands. One that would instruct the Beast to conceal or reveal itself. Another to attack or stand down.

"How resourceful," Eryx said. She fell silent for a stretch before speaking again. "After my son was murdered, I prayed for justice. I think the realm sent you to me in response. Not to replace Mericus, no one could ever do that. But because of you, my prayers were answered and King Rhys is finally dead. I will forever be grateful to you for that, Kallistê. And I continue to beseech the Demons for your prosperity."

"Thank you, Premier," she smiled in earnest.

Premier Eryx patted the *doyama's* muzzle and sighed.

"I'm curious. How many of these do you have?" she asked.

"Ten that are fully trained. Three new hatchlings and another seven eggs are incubating. I intend to breed more in the coming months."

The Premier arched an eyebrow.

"Twenty Beasts, bred and trained by hand. And ten mages sent across the ocean to train in the Cosmic Arts?"

Before she could answer, her Beast blinked out of sight. It emitted a low whine that Kallistê quickly cut off with a soft hum.

Down the shoreline, she saw Viltarin. He walked with a man on his arm, smiling gently. The man had chestnut skin, similar to Viltarin's, but his tresses trended closer to dark brown than black.

Through the crinkle in his eyes, their gazes met and the smile on Viltarin's lips turned taunting.

Her visit had been impromptu, but his appearance did not feel like a coincidence. How many spies did he have crawling over this island for him to cross paths with her so quickly?

How many more would she need to employ to root them out?

She turned to the Premier.

"V-V," Viltarin's name refused to form on her lips, a fog beginning to skirt the edge of her thoughts.

"What was that?" Eryx asked.

Kallistê glanced down the coast again, but Viltarin and the man had practically disappeared from sight, their retreating forms mere dots in the backdrop. It had happened so quickly that she doubted if she'd seen them to begin with—but what her eyes could not detect, her magic filled in the gaps.

Kallistê locked the touch of their Souls into her mind.

"Never mind," she sighed. "In the meantime, if anything pertinent arises, I'll let you know. We never know what may prove useful in boosting Lotus when she campaigns."

"Always planning the next step, aren't you?" the Premier murmured.

"A wise woman once told me that it's one thing to usurp a throne, but it is an entirely different undertaking to maintain that power."

"You make a fine pupil," Eryx said, eyes crinkling.

Kallistê smirked. The rhythmic clashes of the ocean's waves rolled in the backdrop.

"I learned from the best."

Chapter 14

Human Realm, Mount Illiniza, Deerkeep Village

Rays of sunlight beamed down from the center of the sky and the snow cover faded from sight as Haizea and Shauni neared the mountain's base. At their current pace, they would arrive at their destination by the end of the day.

Shauni inhaled deeply.

"You can't appreciate how thin the air is up top until you're at the base," she commented.

They walked past a fenced off wheat field. The plants came up to Haizea's eyes while Shauni's head barely grazed the top of their height. A group of villagers tilled the land. One of them noticed the two warriors and waved.

"You two down here for that village that got attacked, aren't ya?" they asked, resting their arms on the fence.

"Yes, Eaglestone. Have you heard any new information from them?" Haizea asked.

The farm worker shook their head.

"Eaglestone had some meat and dairy farmers who traded with us for our crops, but that's dried up recently. With the influx of people who got chased out over the last few weeks, food's a little harder to come by. We're managing for now, but folks are feeling a little uncertain."

"We'll clear the kingdom dwellers out. The villagers will be able to return home soon," Shauni assured them.

"How well did you know the people in Eaglestone? The person who contacted us was a realmdrifter, but he'd already passed away and came to us as a Soul," Haizea said.

The farmer's face fell.

"Bose was the only realmdrifter 'round these parts. He lived here in Deerkeep and transported goods between our two villages. He'd just gone to Eaglestone to bring back a delivery when the attack happened. He's been missing since then. I figured something bad must have happened, but I still hoped...he's really dead?" glassiness glinted in their eyes.

Haizea nodded somberly.

"Even in death, Bose wanted to protect his people. There's nothing more becoming of a mountaineer than that. Did he have any family? We want to notify them."

The farmer shook his head.

"Sickness ran through our village when he was young. Took his parents and a lot of other good folks. We were his family," he wiped a tear from his eye. A moment passed before he spoke again.

"You all must be hungry. We'll feed ya before you go on your way."

"The situation in Eagleston could be dire, so we should eat while we can. Might be our last meal for a little while," Shauni murmured as they followed the farmworker.

"I think we should do our due diligence here, too. Make sure all the newcomers are actually who they say they are. Otherwise, we might clean up Eaglestone just to find another mess in Deerkeep on our return trip," she said.

Shauni shrugged.

"I don't disagree, but I think without a seer to weed them all out, it might be a wasted time and effort. I take it you all don't have one that lives nearby?" She turned to the farm worker, who shook their head.

"As far as Mental mages go, we've got a few enchanters, but that's it. No seers."

"Enchanters are useful, but it's not foolproof like reading minds," Shauni pursed her lips and sighed. "Things are calm right now in this village, so it's probably not worth the delay it would cause."

"We can assess the damage in Eaglestone first. Then we'll have a better idea of what type of presence we warriors might need to have going forward," Haizea agreed.

The farm worker led them to the village's marketplace, where a long line had formed. When Haizea realized they were skipping to the front, she opened her mouth to speak up, but Shauni elbowed her in the ribs, and a sharp pain silenced her. Haizea glared down at her friend, but Shauni's violet irises had darkened so much that they nearly blended with her pupils. Her words died in her throat.

"It's either this or, by the looks of things, be stuck here all day. There are people who need us and will be worse off if we wait."

The harshness in Haizea's expression dulled.

"You always know just the right thing to say, don't you?" she grumbled, prompting a lopsided grin from Shauni.

"Doesn't hurt that I'm starving either," Shauni added. Haizea rolled her eyes.

The farm worker spoke to some of the people toward the front of the soup line, and they made space for them. Shauni cracked her knuckles and readjusted her mask, which hung from her holster. Her vitality simmered. Haizea's magic spiked in response, her irises flickering between honey brown and a rich mahogany. She closed her eyes briefly to focus on quelling the embers within.

"We'll be alright. We took down a necromancer, no problem. We can handle them," Haizea said. What little light remained in Shauni's eyes dimmed.

"That's what I thought the last time I descended the mountain. A Soul came and told us a mountaineer needed our help. I *knew* I'd be able to save Mr. Harzel and protect him for you. But I failed…I…" Shauni clenched her hand into a fist.

Haizea placed a hand on her shoulder. She paused, contemplating her words, when a pulse in her magic stopped her short. Her gaze drifted in the direction of the source and landed on the next line over, where a teenage girl stood. She but quickly shook it off.

"Your efforts weren't fruitless—you gave my grandfather hope in his final moments. And given how he died, how violently his life was taken from him, that small moment of relief was worth its weight in gold. What happened to my grandfather was King Rhys's doing and my own failure to see the warning signs until it was too late. You did everything that you could, and I'll forever be in your debt."

The teen girl's attention snapped to Haizea as she spoke. For some reason, she could not shake a nagging sense of familiarity. Nothing about the girl's appearance sparked recognition–she had dark hair and eyes. But there was a delicate, yet regal nature to her mannerisms–she stood her shoulders poised and her chin raised high. Distantly familiar.

Brows furrowed in concentration, their gazes met, and the girl's face blanched into a ghostly white. In fact, she began trembling so violently that her knees visibly knocked together. Not even a blink later, she bolted from her spot in line, dropping her bowl of soup. The food splattered on the ground and the dishes broke into pieces.

The people nearby fell silent and watched the girl run. Only Shauni looked at Haizea.

"What was that about?" she asked.

"I don't know, I just looked at her, that's all."

Shauni snorted and patted her arm.

"With you, that's all it takes. If I didn't know any better, I'd say the poor girl pissed herself."'

The girl's retreating form faded into the village streets. Though the call in Haizea's blood diminished with distance, she clung to the way the girl's fluttering pulse plucked the cords of her magic.

Thump thump. *Thump* thump.

Thump thump. *Thump* thump.

Sage's heart slammed painfully against her rib cage, desperate to break free. A white haze blurred the edges of her vision. Her footsteps pounded on the ground and she choked back a sob. She could still feel the blood mage's eyes on her, like a hawk circling over its prey.

Sage had felt her presence before she'd seen her. The vitality had crashed in massive waves when two newcomers jumped to the front of the line, escorted by one of the farmhands. Her eyes had glued themselves to the towering warrior with honey blonde hair. Then the woman spoke and mentioned Father by name.

They're here to kill us. She's going to finish the job.

Tears welled in her eyes with each step. She ran face-first into her brother's back. Felix cursed in surprise.

"I thought you were getting us food. Did they run out?" he asked.

Sage opened her mouth to respond, but her voice eluded her. Her brother frowned.

"What's wrong? Did something happen?"

She shook her head weakly. Felix exhaled a long sigh. His expression landed somewhere between concerned and annoyed.

"For the love of the realms, *speak,* Sage. I can't do anything if you won't tell me what's wrong with you."

Sage opened her mouth to respond but only managed a small croak. Her brother placed a hand on her back.

"Nothing happened, but you're scared speechless. You saw something..." he trailed off, stiffening beside her.

Thump thump. *Thump* thump.

Another disturbance sent shockwaves through the vitality. Magical pressure bore down on Sage's body and she collapsed to her knees, hands doubling before her.

"That fucking witch is here," Felix hissed.

He shrugged out of his coat and threw it over her.

"Keep your hood up and *walk* this time. When you panic, you draw unnecessary attention. You saw her, but did she see you?"

When Sage nodded, Felix spat out a string of curses.

"Did she recognize you?"

"I...I don't know."

Felix looked over his shoulder again, where the disturbance in the vitality emanated. His jaw moved back and forth, grinding his teeth.

"If she did, she would have followed. There's a chance she might suspect something–these enchantments aren't exactly a professional job. But no way in the seven realms would she recognize you and let you walk away. We're probably fine."

Sage clenched her trembling hands into fists.

"It's always because she *'lets'* us. Felix, we're going to die. She's going to find out who we are and figure out why we're here, and she's going to kill us the same way she did our parents. I-I..." she trailed off.

He wrapped his hands around her fists.

"I know you're scared. But you have to feel the fear and push through it. I was terrified that day in the bunker, but I still fought back. We can't just roll over and let this happen. We can't lose sight of what's important."

"Felix, why...?" Sage trailed off.

"Why what?"

"Why is it always about fighting? Miss Tamsyn treated us well. After months on the run, she fed us and gave us a solid roof over our heads. I'd rather that than this."

The blue oceans in Felix's eyes froze into glaciers.

"Old Lady T had us drinking from a fucking pig bladder from realm's sake. Every single person we've come across in the mountain range would kill us if they found out who we really are. That's why the warriors are down here to begin with. They're going to slaughter the Olysseans back in Eaglestone."

Sage stared at her hands.

"How do you suppose they found out, Felix? Didn't you kill Bose to prevent exactly that from happening?" she demanded. Her brother crossed his arms over his chest.

"Someone else must have sent a letter. Obviously."

"Or Bose's murdered Soul persisted rather than pass on to the Soul Realm because you killed him in cold blood."

Felix flared his nostrils.

"Not every Soul that feels wronged remains in the Human Realm; otherwise, they would constantly haunt us. You're jumping to the worst conclusion possible."

Sage bit her tongue—a rebuttal would only devolve further into an argument. Still, his swift dismissal stung. She had listened to him all this time since their parents had died, but it felt like that trust only went in one direction.

Her brother was wrong, woefully so. Bose's Soul persisting in the Human Realm *wasn't* the worst conclusion. Felix had glossed over the fact that the blood mage herself had answered Bose's call—the very thing he'd wanted to avoid.

They hadn't survived the witch's onslaught because Felix fought back in the bunker. They survived because they'd been spared, granted mercy—their lives hinged on a mere whim.

Sage did not want to gamble on whether the winds of luck would blow in their favor a second time.

"It's not safe to stay here any longer. We must leave now. Before...*she* can think twice about what she saw," Sage locked her legs to stop her knees from wobbling.

Felix nodded. At least on that front, they agreed. They gathered the few belongings they had, just enough to fit in a small satchel. Tension wrapped around Sage's temples. The blood mage's vitality still blanketed the air, the weight of it dragging down her movements. She cast a sorrowful glance over her shoulder and, for just a breath, a faint shimmer flickered in the distance.

Chapter 15
Celestial Realm

Golden rays of light danced on the ground, reflecting off the massive gate that stretched toward the heavens. Although the Sun warmed his skin, an inexplicable and intense wave of sadness and longing chilled Alastair's Soul. He peered up at the skies and could not shake the odd sensation that the Sun returned his gaze, aware of his presence.

~What is this? Where are we?~ he turned to the Soul Reaper.

This is the Celestial Realm. Once home of the Angels.

Alastair rotated in a slow circle. He expected to see the celestial beings flying high above, but only empty skies greeted him. When he turned his attention toward the ground, he gasped.

Heaping piles of rubble littered the land, as far as his eyes could see. Even more disturbing was the stillness in Alastair's magic. It did not push and pull like it did back in the Human Realm. He closed his eyes, evened his breathing, and cleared his mind, stretching his power just as Pamin had taught him. The hairs on the back of his neck stood up.

For the first time in his life, Alastair called, but a Soul did not answer.

An internal nudge from the Soul Reaper prompted him to turn toward the entity once more.

The Angels are dead. The Demons wiped them out thousands of years ago.

Alastair swallowed thickly.

~All of them?~

All of them, the Soul Reaper answered.

Alastair gazed upon the Celestial Sun. Anguish and grief seeped into his Soul.

The Celestial Sun is sentient. Long ago, it gave life to the Angels. Today, it mourns the loss of its children; the entity's words echoed within.

~Why...?~ Alastair trailed off, unable to wrap his mind around an entire realm—an entire people being annihilated.

In answer, the Soul Reaper crouched down and pressed his bony hand against Alastair's forehead. The scenery around them transformed and the destroyed architecture rebuilt itself anew.

An Angel materialized before Alastair and the Soul Reaper. His skin, eyes, hair, and wings glimmered a crisp gold. The Angel flapped his wings and flew down a long pathway leading to a temple. Statues lined the route, each with a word transcribed on it: Light, Awareness, Purification, Truth, or Spirit.

The Angel's feet nimbly touched the ground, his eyes lingering on the temple's entrance. A wave of power cascaded through the air as he formed an orb of Light in his hands.

The Light began to warp and shift before darkening. A bond buried deep within the Angel snapped in two. Its Soul separated from its body, leaving a void. The power of the Darkness in his hands eclipsed the presence of the Light before blanketing the temple.

The Demon's breath hitched in fascination as the vitality in the world around him blossomed before his eyes, each particle sparkling like a star in the night. He'd never witnessed such a sight before or beheld the source of his power in this manner.

How foolish his brethren were.

He turned his back on the temple and flew away.
"All I wanted was freedom."

As the vision faded, Alastair saw that he no longer stood in front of the gate but instead in front of the temple. Though broken and battered, one of the statues still stood–an Angel wielding the power of Light. The Soul Reaper went on to explain:

Halloran, the first Demon, tapped into the Cosmos and pushed beyond the boundaries of his Light Affinity to create Darkness. He used that power to birth the Demon Realm with his own hands. He went on to have many offspring and cultivated many followers, who similarly relinquished their Souls for power and enlightenment. The Angels viewed the defection as a betrayal and responded with force, but they were at a disadvantage.

Alastair inclined his head. It felt like an eternity ago when one of his fainting spells brought him to the Soul Reaper, and the entity mentioned that Angels had unchained themselves from their Souls. He'd never known of the relationship that existed between their Souls and their power.

~*What do you mean by disadvantage?*~ he asked.

For an Angel, their Souls are the chains that bind their power. They can live without a Soul because the Celestial Sun is what breathes life into them. When the Demons broke that chain, they were no longer restricted to the five Affinities. Instead, their Affinities transformed to reflect who they were as a person. For Halloran—who once could wield the Light of the Celestial Sun—his Darkness gave him the ability to mold the Cosmos in an unprecedented act of Creation. The Angels and their five Affinities—Light, Awareness, Truth, Purification, and Spirit—paled in comparison to the Demons. So they searched for a power that could even the scales.

Realization dawned on Alastair.

~The Human Realm.~

Yes. The Angels stole magic from humanity. And they nearly succeeded in wiping out their own brethren.

Alastair stared contemplatively at the temple's ruins. These piles of rubble had once been massive halls that carried countless untold stories. The Angels had come here to worship and congregate, no different than his visits to the monastery.

They had witnessed the power of the Cosmos and rejected it to protect their Souls from destruction.

Yet here Alastair stood. Despite the heavy toll the Cosmos extracted and his frustrations with the Soul Reaper, for some reason, he still had not run from it. He sought to understand it.

Maybe Halloran and his followers had felt similarly. Unlike Alastair, abandoning their Souls did not mean forfeiting their lives, but it isolated them from the ones they cared about. That rift ultimately created a wedge so deep that the two sides annihilated one another, eliminating any chances of reconciliation.

~I suppose I get why they went so far. But I don't understand how. Their abilities sound very different from ours.~

The Soul Reaper waved his hands and ten swords appeared before them. Vibrations rocked Alastair's body, and shockwaves ripped through his magic.

They forged these blades. The materials in them have special properties that allow it to absorb the vitality. By bonding their Souls to them, it enabled the Angels to not only take humanity's but also wield it as a weapon. They hunted down Halloran, his followers, and his offspring. They only spared those who were smart enough to hide or too young to pose any real threat.

Afraid and paranoid about retaliation, the Angels held onto the swords and did not relinquish the magic they had acquired from humanity. Instead, they stood guard over the Human Realm and prevented the Demons from leaving their home realm. They also Purified the Titans in an attempt to rid them of their bloodlust, which they feared would make them sympathetic to the Demons' cause.

~So the Demons destroyed the Celestial Realm in retaliation,~ Alastair signed.

In response, an unmistakable sensation of affirmation poured into his Soul. Their surroundings shifted once more.

Alastair would never forget Aaryn's face for as long as he lived. She floated before them, her massive white wings flapping in a slow, rhythmic motion. With golden skin and shimmering amber eyes, she resembled her forefather, Halloran. She shot forward, lithely weaving through the thick foliage of the Beast Realm as she hunted an enormous Beast with three heads. In one fell swoop, she ripped its Soul straight from its body. Afterward, she brought it to the Soul Realm and laid it to rest, but Aaryn did not encounter the Soul Reaper.

The wheels of time accelerated and Aaryn continued her ritual with Souls over many years. The number ticked well into the hundreds before the Soul Reaper finally turned his attention to her. Initially, the Demon and the entity did not speak—she would merely meet his empty gaze and stood silently for a moment before flying off. But eventually, Aaryn broke her silence.

"One day, I'll be strong enough to Steal the Soul of an Angel. One day, my realm and my people will be free. We'll be able to explore the Cosmos and wield our Affinities as we see fit."

Decades passed, and the number of Souls Aaryn collected inched its way into the thousands. Her years of solitude came to an end when she befriended another Demon by the name of Gadriel. With light gray skin, and hair and wings the color of charcoal, he seemed to exist in Aaryn's golden shadow. It was here that Alastair learned that Aaryn could do much more than Steal a Soul.

Gadriel created a fire on his fingertips. His Inferno burned with sweltering heat, but it did not create Light—the fire was pitch black and teemed with Darkness. Aaryn's amber eyes glistened with glee and she fixated on him, deep in concentration. A moment later, she had copied his ability, though her flames did not match the potency of his. Gadriel's vitality carried more power than hers, but he followed Aaryn's lead, a kinship forming between them after she told him of her dream for their realm.

As time went on, Aaryn and Gadriel gained a following, much like their forefather, Halloran. The Demons slowly reunited, all invigorated by Aaryn's dreams and ambitions. She forged an alliance with the Titans, who long held resentment toward the Angels for Purifying them. Even as her influence grew, Aaryn never abandoned her pastime of collecting Souls. One day, the entity presented her with an offering she could not refuse.

"You've brought tens of thousands of Souls to me. It is time I pay you back and balance the scales."

The Soul Reaper pressed his hand against Aaryn's forehead, and ensuing the wave of power nearly knocked Alastair out of the vision. Aaryn threw her head back, her golden strands of hair glinting in the dim light as she cackled furiously with maniacal glee. She turned and perched her wings to fly but paused.

"Thank you, Soul Reaper. With this, my people will be free. You were...you were my first friend."

The Soul Reaper returned Alastair to the present.

Aaryn and Gadriel had shared a fondness he never imagined that Demons were capable of. Even the gratitude she'd shown the Soul Reaper caught him by surprise.

It took him back to the time Aaryn had called him to the Soul Realm and how the Soul Reaper had chastised her. At the time, Alastair thought that his power had caught her attention, but what if his bond with the Soul Reaper had drawn her out instead?

The Angels had left a vacuum devoid of life in their wake and Aaryn had grown up in the aftermath of that destruction. She had rebuilt her home from the ground up. Demons did not have Souls, so Alastair could not sense her emotions. If he could, he imagined that he'd feel the delicate warmth of companionship, the icy loneliness that stemmed from its loss, and the bitter rage that fueled her vengeance and paved the way for the Celestial Realm's destruction.

Odd, how her journey felt so human.

With another wave of power from the Soul Reaper, the Celestial Realm disappeared and another one replaced it. This new realm teemed with life. Massive domiciles made of stone filled the landscape and the air churned as a Demon flapped its wings overhead. They were smaller than what Aaryn or Gadriel and their vitality similarly did not carry the same weight. Though Alastair did not verbalize his question, the Soul Reaper answered him:

Because Angels with Light could directly manipulate the power of the Celestial Sun, they were the strongest of their kind. As such, they became stronger Demons. Other Affinities were naturally weaker, therefore when those Angels became Demons, their power reflected that.

The events of their attack unfolded before Alastair.

Aaryn, Gadriel, and their followers returned to the Celestial Realm to avenge their forefather. The Angels fought back with the same swords that felled Halloran, but the Soul Reaper's gift to Aaryn amplified her powers—no longer did she mimic others, but she stole the affinities of those weaker than herself. The swords did not have sufficient power to fully balance the scales.

Aaryn bested every Angel, save for Zephon, the mightiest Angel in the Celestial Realm. But Zephon was prideful to a fault. He grew to resent the innate weakness of his own kind, who could not defeat the Demons with their own strength, but only with stolen power. Aaryn cultivated and fed into those feelings. Eventually, his resentment grew into hatred. Zephon relinquished his Soul, becoming a Demon himself and following in Halloran's footsteps. That was the final nail in the Celestial Realm's coffin. With his defection and betrayal, the Demons brought ruin to the Angels, destroyed the swords, and in doing so, returned magic humanity.

Alastair digested the new information and fiddled his fingers together. Aaryn received all of the credit and admiration, but she did not achieve those feats alone. She'd had help—Gadriel, Zephon…and the Soul Reaper.

He turned to the entity.

~*You gave Aaryn power as repayment–because she brought Souls to you. And in your realm, Souls are currency.*~

Yes.

Alastair stewed for a few moments longer.

~*If…if I brought you Souls, would you stop corrupting mine?*~

All it takes for your Soul corruption to cease, is to avoid using necromancy. Soul corruption is a condition of drawing power from here. That will not change.

~*If I stopped using necromancy, would you do nothing to halt the magical wasting then?*~ he asked.

The Cosmos itself has set that price. I will not interfere with its decision.

Alastair clenched his fists. '*Will not*' and '*cannot*' meant two completely different things. With each death, with each Soul laid to rest in the Soul Realm, the Soul Reaper gained power. Alastair supposed that his premature death made no difference to the entity–power was all the same to him.

Something within Alastair's Soul ruffled. An unexpected emotion flickered from the Soul Reaper—sympathy, not the apathy he'd expected.

The sensation gave him pause. He tilted his head upward to meet the entity's gaze. The value in his demise was easy to see, but what did his life mean to the God of Death? What did *he* mean?

Alastair didn't know the answer, but he struggled to see the point in the entity's sympathies if he couldn't fix this.

A band of tension tightened around his head and a sigh of frustration bubbled forth, but Alastair swallowed to contain it and find his calm once more.

The Soul Reaper had shown him these visions for a reason—he'd even guided Alastair to the monastery and effectively introduced him to Pamin, who had taken Alastair under his wing and taught him more about his magic. It felt like the entity wanted to help him in its own cryptic way.

Something useful had to be woven inside all of this. He just wished that every realmsforsaken answer didn't have to be broken into a puzzle that he had to piece back together.

Alastair swayed where he stood as the strain on his power from the Soul Reaper's presence began to burden his body. He wanted nothing more than to go home and welcome the sleep that had eluded him earlier in the night. Maybe he could forget all of this had happened. Maybe with rest, he would see the answers.

He did not communicate his desires, but his Soul spoke in his stead. The Soul Reaper's power cocooned his body and lifted him off his feet. In the span of a blink, Alastair's consciousness returned to the Human Realm. The Soul Reaper's presence faded, but the entity's parting words persisted:

All power necessitates sacrifice.

Chapter 16

Human Realm, Base of Mount Illiniza, Eaglestone Village

Collapsed roofs, broken windows, and scattered debris marked Haizea and Shauni's arrival to Eaglestone Village. They concealed themselves in nearby foliage to further survey the situation. Haizea closed her eyes and reached forward with her healing magic.

"There are injured people here. I can sense them, but I can't pinpoint their exact locations yet," she said.

"We'll find them. We just need to root out the weeds first," Shauni said.

"As soon as they see us, they'll try to flee."

"*Try*, but they won't," Shauni's magic flared and she cracked her knuckles.

Haizea rolled her shoulders and suppressed her Cosmic power to lay dormant beneath the surface. Best to avoid the high and keep her senses—for now, at least. The duo walked past the worn-out welcome sign and entered the village.

The faint tug in Haizea's healing magic sharpened and intensified with each step, rapid heartbeats drumming against her own. She followed the sensation. Wordlessly, she raised her hand and motioned for Shauni to follow her to a small cabin. Once inside, they found a small family huddled in a closet–a young mother with a baby on her bosom and a toddler at her side.

When the woman darted out and ran toward them, Haizea breathed a sigh of relief—only a fellow mountaineer would have such a welcoming response to the warriors' presence.

"Thank Aaryn, you're here. Those kingdom dwellers ran through here like a herd of bulls. We managed to hold them off at first. We've got a handful of mages, but the sheer numbers...," the woman trailed off.

"Numbers won't matter tonight. Do you know where the rest of your villagers are hiding?" Shauni asked.

"Everyone else either fled or died fighting. What's left of us gathered in this group of six cabins. Miss Tamsyn managed to secure this area of the village. She's a transmuting mage. I think she scared 'em good because the kingdom dwellers haven't bothered us. But no one has seen her since. I fear she's in bad shape...or worse."

"Do you happen to have a clairvoyant mage among the survivors? It will be helpful in tracking her down. And also making sure we don't cull the wrong people," Haizea said.

"Yes, actually, in the next cabin over. But they're young, just a teenager. I'm not sure how much control they have over their abilities."

"That's fine, all I need is a bit of their blood."

The woman's brows arched high.

"You're a blood mage?"

"Yes."

"Haizea, right? Haizea Ambrose?" the woman asked, patting her baby on the back when it began to fuss.

Haizea stiffened but answered with a tight nod.

"They call you the Destroyer of Armies. The Harbinger of Death. They say that you single-handedly crushed Arcelia. That you drained the blood of their soldiers and set their very corpses against the king."

Haizea frowned behind her mask. She shouldn't have been surprised that word of the massacre had spread, but for a complete stranger to know her name, and only because of bloodshed...a chill slithered down her spine.

The woman watched her expectantly. Haizea cleared her throat.

"I had some help, but yes."

The young mother's expression darkened.

"Those kingdom dwellers trampled over us like we don't belong here, but this is *our* home. You two are our warriors, our protectors. Remind them exactly why the treaty exists. We should have never let them forget."

"We'll keep you safe," Haizea assured her. "Just make sure the other villagers don't leave this area. If they wander after the fighting starts, we won't be able to differentiate between friend and foe."

The woman nodded and led the duo out of the house. She introduced them to the young clairvoyant mage who offered Haizea some of their blood. As the warriors approached the section of the village that the kingdom dwellers had taken over, a pocket of vitality radiated like a beacon. It drew Haizea in with each breath she took, pulling her to the opposite end of the village.

She found an older woman lying on her side with her hands and feet bound and her body bloodied and beaten. Haizea crouched down and pressed a healing hand against her wounds.

"Miss Tamsyn?" she murmured.

The woman coughed, and blood spewed from her mouth. She had several broken and missing teeth. When she tried to speak, a hoarse, raspy noise crackled from her throat. All she managed was a feeble head nod. Haizea sat her up properly, and Shauni came around and cut the ties around her wrists and ankles. The woman sagged against Haizea as she tended to her injuries.

Haizea's hands roamed over Miss Tamsyn's skin—weaving together her broken ribs, a fractured arm, and a sprain in one of her ankles. A welt protruded from her forehead. A large bruise covered half of her abdomen in a way that alarmed Haizea—some of the woman's bleeding was internal. Haizea healed the worst of it, but due to her advanced age and the extent of her injuries, Miss Tamsyn needed several healing sessions and a variety of potions to fully recover. Haizea frowned at her chapped lips and sunken cheeks—signs of dehydration.

They moved Miss Tamsyn off the walkway and onto the porch of a nearby house.

"We'll be back," Haizea promised, but the longer she looked at her, the more she feared that when they returned, Miss Tamsyn may have already departed this realm. "We met a young woman with a small baby and a toddler. She told us about you and what you did to protect the village. Your people are waiting for your safe return. Just hold on a little longer."

Hopefully, her words of encouragement would help Miss Tamsyn maintain her grasp on the world of the living. The older woman's mouth moved, and she whispered so faintly that Haizea strained to hear her clearly. She could only make out one word:

"Serenity."

"We'll find her," she said. As Haizea left her behind, a quiet rage settled deep in the pit of her stomach.

Miss Tamsyn had borne the brunt of the violence to protect her fellow villagers. In turn, the kingdom dwellers had left her to rot because she was an omen.

Haizea bristled at the uncomfortable familiarity of it all.

She unsheathed her swords, cold metal slicing through the air. Magic twisted around her as Shauni created an invisible barrier around the area's perimeter to cage the kingdom dwellers inside. One by one, she dragged them out of the homes with her telekinesis. Some of them attempted to flee, but Shauni's unbreakable grasp rendered those efforts futile.

Haizea poured a few drops of the clairvoyant blood into her palm. The people in front of her stiffened into stone as her eyes brightened into brilliant rubies through her skull mask.

Her mind opened to the world around her. Haizea could not read their thoughts, but she gained a sense of even the smallest actions—each fidget, every angry yet frightened grumble under a person's breath, the rapid acceleration in the rise and fall of their chests. Nothing escaped her perception. Haizea walked up to the nearest person.

"Where are you from?" she asked.

The man's throat bobbed up and down.

"We fled from a nearby village."

The vitality rippled and distorted–he'd spoken a falsehood. Haizea did not call him out on it. Instead, she remained in place and turned her head toward the person standing beside him.

"Where are you from?"

This person glanced between her and the first man, their eyes wide and their hands trembling.

"Oniosea. It's a city in Olysseus, a few miles away from the border crossing."

Despite the tremors running through him, the vitality remained stable. When it came to understanding a person's intentions, clairvoyance was not foolproof by any means, but it tipped the scales and helped lead a mage to a particular conclusion. Haizea turned back to the first man.

"You know why we're here, correct?"

"Y-yes."

"Then you understand what's about to happen," she said.

He turned on his heels and ran. At least, he tried to.

Haizea latched onto every ounce of his vitality and pulled. The man sagged to his knees and clutched at his chest. He wheezed and screeched a terrible groan as his heart stuttered and strained against the force of her blood magic.

She watched him struggle with an idle curiosity, like a cat who'd caught a mouse by the tail. Obscured by her skull mask, a grin played on her lips as the Cosmic high emerged and pulsed against her temples. Without releasing even a modicum of her grip on the man, Haizea spoke to the rest of the group.

"When you lie, this is what happens. You've already done enough damage by taking lives and destroying the homes of the people who live here. Speak the truth, and your death will be quick. Waste my time with falsehood—even so much as a half-truth—and I'll drag it out until I'm tired of hearing your screams. Do you understand?"

The man's choked moans punctuated her words. Red blotches covered his cheeks, and Haizea pierced his flesh with her blade. She drew on his life force with a deliberate slowness. His body shriveled into a brittle, dry looking husk before it burst into a cloud of dust.

She leveled her gaze on the crowd. Those towards the front inched backward, beads of sweat dripping down their foreheads and their heartbeats quickening against her power.

Only a breath passed before another person foolishly broke rank and ran. Shauni caught them with her telekinesis. Their head and limbs twisted in opposite directions before their body burst from the torsion, blood spraying like a water spout. The kingdom dwellers cried out, arms covering their heads.

Haizea's magic quaked within and she suppressed a shudder. The faint grin on her lips deepened into a smile behind her mask. Her eyes lingered on the blood pooling on the ground before her. Its sparkling radiance drew her in and everything else blurred into the background. Her fingers curled into claws as she prepared to consume the last dredges of his lifeforce.

"Why did you come here?" Shauni asked, pulling her away from the sight.

With great effort, Haizea clenched her hands into fists and swallowed the laugh burgeoning in her chest to stabilize herself—she could not indulge in his vitality now. She needed to maintain her wits.

No one answered Shauni at first. After a few moments, a man stepped forward hesitantly.

"A transmutation mage attacked our city and set fire to our homes. When we tried to run, but the witch boxed us in with a wall of flame. It kept us from going eastward. Our only options were to run toward the mountains or burn," he said.

The vitality remained calm as he spoke, implying veracity in his statement.

"This omen, what did they look like?" Shauni asked.

"I only caught a glimpse of her, but she had a head of pink hair and eyes of the same shade."

"Doesn't sound like anyone we know," Shauni whispered.

Haizea shook her head.

"No, but this entire situation reeks of Kallistê," she muttered.

Haizea hadn't spoken to Kallistê in over a year–not since she'd killed King Rhys. Kallistê's had made it no secret regarding her desires for a world ruled by omens—sending a transmutation mage to weed out the populace seemed par for the course for the realmdrifter, especially given that she'd done something similar with Beasts to destabilize Llyr.

Haizea stared at the kingdom dwellers, deep in thought. She'd resolved not to interfere in the kingdoms' affairs again, but now their matters had begun to bleed into her homelands.

Once she returned home she'd investigate if the realmdrifter had any involvement—best to nip this in the bud before it escalated further. She and Kallistê had parted ways in fairly amicable terms but Haizea did not trust her as far as she could see her. Any semblance of an alliance began and ended with the safety and integrity of the mountaineers and their borders. Haizea would not stand for anything less.

A woman limped forward. Shauni inhaled sharply beside her and Haizea grimaced. Welts and blisters covered the woman's skin and half of her head was bald, while the hair that remained hung in straggles.

"The flames swallowed my home and consumed my husband as we tried to escape. I...I hear his screams every night. I don't know when or if the omens will come back again. I played no role in the violence that transpired here–I can barely walk as it is. We all just wanted a safe place for refuge," she whispered.

Neither warrior spoke initially, though Haizea could sense a subtle acceleration in Shauni's heartbeat. They exchanged a glance before Shauni turned to the woman.

"You say you played no role. Which home do you reside in? Did the residents invite you to stay?"

"No, but—"

A swell of magic clamped the woman's mouth shut.

"Then you're just as guilty as those who spilled blood."

The woman's voice muffled beneath Shauni's power. When she finally fell silent, Shauni lessened her telekinetic grasp.

"They're just a bunch of omens," the woman rasped, spitting the last word like a curse. "They're no different than the witch who did this to me. Your *kind* did this," she hissed, raising a charred arm.

She paused, fixing her glare on Haizea.

"And *you*–"

Haizea felt the woman's death more so than saw it—the snapping of her vertebra ricocheted through her magic. The woman's body dropped to the ground, motionless. Shauni shook her head, so faint that Haizea nearly missed it, but her grip visibly tightened on her swords.

They continued questioning down the line until they felt reasonably certain about who belonged here and who didn't. She separated one mountaineer, who had been unable to escape and hide with the rest of the natives. Haizea also pulled aside a child.

"Please, don't hurt him," his father reached for them.

Without a word, Haizea ushered the young boy toward Shauni. As she settled him by a tree several yards away, he called out for his father. Shauni turned the boy around to face the opposite direction. Haizea worked to ignore the way her chest tightened.

"We have nowhere else to go. I'm all he has. If you kill me, he won't have anyone to look after him," he pleaded.

Haizea paused, her gaze flickering between man and son. A bitter taste twinged her tongue. She couldn't think of him that way—as a father who loved his son. She drew a mental line to keep herself in check. Mountaineer and kingdom dweller. Those who belonged versus those who invaded her homelands.

A threat to her people and her duty to eliminate it.

Her resolve hardened into steel. The air surrounding her simmered with energy, held back by only a thread. Sweat began to trickle down the man's temples.

"You're asking me for a level of consideration you didn't bother to offer when you forcibly displaced these villagers. It's fine when it's someone else's child, but now that it's yours, you expect mercy?"

He opened his mouth to reply but only managed a croak as Haizea's vermillion gaze bore into him.

"Children are not shields. I won't overlook the violence you inflicted upon this village," The man's fleeting heartbeat pulsed against her magic. "But we will not harm your son."

A streak of silver flashed in the night. His head rolled off his shoulders and tumbled to the ground before he could utter a response.

Haizea and Shauni moved in unison to cull the rest. Shauni's telekinesis prevented them from attempting to flee again while Haizea struck them down.

Once the dust settled, they gathered the villagers and assured them it was safe to come out. To Haizea's surprise and relief, when they returned to Miss Tamsyn, some of the villagers had helped move her into a nearby cabin. Haizea made a potion from the little supplies they had available and offered it to her.

She and Shauni placed a few of the kingdom dwellers' heads on stakes to deter anyone outsiders from approaching the village. If Haizea's suspicions were correct, they would need it.

They built funeral pyres—one for the kingdom dwellers and another for the mountaineers who had perished. Some of the villagers came forward and knelt before the flames. Shauni did not kneel but instead bowed her head. On the opposite side of the pyre, Haizea caught sight of the young mother from earlier.

She now had three children in tow: her infant, her toddler, and the young boy whose father they'd culled. Other villagers had gathered around her, harsh whispers carrying over the crackling flames.

"–him back to where he came from."

"–a kid–not his fault."

"He's still a kingdom dweller. –doesn't belong–"

"Let the boy grieve–out the rest later."

The mother bent down and spoke into the boy's ear but he jerked away and ran into the distance.

Haizea pursed her lips. She wondered how he would fare going forward. Would the village eventually accept him or send him to fend for himself? Would he come to understand the harm his father and the kingdom dwellers had caused? If only his father hadn't dragged him into this so that she would not have had to make such a decision to begin with.

She silently shifted her attention toward the blaze.

"May Aaryn guide their Souls to the next realm," one of the villagers prayed.

"How long will you be with us?" another asked.

"We need to get word back to our leader and tell her what we've learned. Given what happened here, I think we should stay until we get a response," Shauni answered. Haizea nodded in agreement.

"We'll bring you a messenger hawk."

The answer to their hawk arrived a few weeks later, while Haizea and Shauni were seated at a table, eating their midday meal. Soft clanks of silverware scraping against their dishes filled the space between them.

Several yards off to their right was the village entrance—precisely where the stakes displayed the heads of the kingdom dwellers to any others who might approach.

"I'm all he has."

The kingdom dweller's last words had lodged in her thoughts, like a splinter in her skin. She could still see the bag under his eyes and the lines on his face. His fear had been as palpable as the plate in front of her. Haizea nudged what remained of her food to the edge of her plate, her appetite now absent.

Shauni's boot knocked against her foot. She looked up to see her friend's dark eyes studying her.

"You're still thinking about them," Shauni said, motioning to the village entrance.

"They were seeking refuge. They had injured people and children. It doesn't excuse what they did to this village. But I still can't help but to think about how they had nowhere else to go."

Shauni took a bite from her plate.

"I don't know what it's like to grow up in a place where Cosmic magic is stigmatized so severely that the mere sight of an omen incites violence. On the other hand, if a transmuting mage burned me out of my home, I'd want retribution. Their anger was justified but misdirected. The villagers needed our protection. It was our responsibility to step in," she said.

The twisting in Haizea's belly eased somewhat—it was their duty to defend the mountains. Still, that voice nagged at her, quiet yet pervasive. She hummed softly, hoping to silence it.

"When protecting the people under our charge means hurting people that are in dire straits, sometimes it's difficult to reconcile. Even if I know that they didn't deserve leniency," Haizea said. Shauni pursed her lips.

"You spent years with the kingdom dwellers, so I see why it can be difficult for you not to see their humanity. But they certainly didn't see ours. As far as I'm concerned, that's all that mattered in this case."

"I—"

"Haizea. Shauni," a voice called, interrupting their conversation.

The duo turned to see two warriors approaching their table.

"Vendela sent us to take your place. Until the situation in Olysseus settles, she wants to maintain a constant presence at the base," they explained.

Haizea and Shauni finished off their meals before making their leave. As they began their ascent, Haizea looked up at the sky, bright and blue with the sun shining overhead. Feeling warm, she doffed her fur coat. What was supposed to have been a one to two week trip had turned into a several week long trek to the base.

She never intended to leave Alastair alone for so long. Most days, he seemed fine, but she could tell he still struggled more than he was willing to let on. Her pace quickened, and she found herself pushing ahead of Shauni.

After seeing the broken families here in Eaglestone, she couldn't return to her own fast enough.

Chapter 17

Human Realm, Kingdom of Olysseus, Oniosea

The astral plane cloaked Kallistê's floating form as she drifted through the skies, ten of her *doyamas* in tow. Her blue tresses flowed behind her like a waterfall and her eyes mirrored the delicate clouds above.

Though tranquility reigned over the heavens, devastation marred the earth below. Broken bricks and felled trees littered the landscape. A vulture rode a thermal before swooping down and perching on unmoving form. It snapped its head forward before rearing back, gulping down a chunk of flesh.

She nodded to herself. Lotus had followed her instructions to the letter.

Kallistê continued onward, passing over the wreckage until she reached at the western border of Oniosea, where the pristine brick buildings still stood, whole and untouched. She landed gently on the ground and her Beasts materialized behind her.

Crisp winds whipped against her body and the dull brown grasses slumped over, but small buds bulged on the trees–a sign that the end of the winter season neared. Stone roads lined the neighborhood streets, and the only sign that something might have been awry were the abandoned carriages and steam-powered trolleys along the way.

Not all of the people had fled–as Kallistê realmdrifted, she could see the vitality of many of the inhabitants within her homes. A satisfied grin crept across her face at the way their Souls quaked and trembled. A pliant populace best suited her endeavors.

She traveled down one of the roads to a sizable house in the middle of a residential block where Lotus had set up a base.

"You've managed to establish your roots and expand your reach," Kallistê said.

If Kallistê's sudden emergence out of thin air surprised Lotus, she made no show of it. Instead, the transmuting mage greeted her with a warm embrace.

"It's lovely to see you again, Kallistê. Your advice was well-informed. I've heard whispers that the mountaineers confronted those who fled. They 'culled' them, as they like to call it."

Kallistê fiddled idly with her jewelry. Her fingers lingered over the cursed golden ring. In the months since her last meeting with the dignitaries, she'd failed to remove it successfully. Keenly aware of her heightened stress levels, one of her *doyamas* brushed against her, invisible to the naked eye. A part of her hoped that Lotus would take notice as well, but her fellow omen did not–toying with her jewelry was a long-held habit of hers and as such, Lotus paid her no mind.

"Regarding the Olyssean army, have you received any further information on the strength of their forces?" Kallistê asked.

"Yes, they sent a platoon our way–not their entire force, of course, given that they don't want to risk losing their stronghold on Vadronia. The acquisition of these cities has fired them up a bit, but a small wave was much more manageable than what we endured when they snatched the Capital City from our grasp. We subdued them with ease."

"Excellent," Kallistê smiled broadly. "They're mere mice running into a trap."

"So, what's next after this? Now that we have a winning strategy, it's just a matter of time before Olysseus is ours," Lotus said.

Kallistê paused, her blue eyes twinkling with mischief.

"Our goal is to bring more omens into this realm—people who embrace the power that the Cosmos bestows upon us. You'll need to consider how you'll inflict consequences for disobedience on a broader scale and how you'll balance that with gaining loyalists. Offer amnesty to the people who worked in Sovereign Jasver's court; they'll guide you in how to navigate the land. It will give you more sway over the populace," she continued.

"I must apologize. I haven't managed to make things go as smoothly as you'd hoped. You and Viltarin make it look so easy," Lotus sighed.

Kallistê rested a hand on hers. A vile curse settled on her lips at the mention of Viltarin, but even now, a fog edged her thoughts and she couldn't quite get the words out. Instead, she offered Lotus a soft, yet alluring smile. A gasp caught in Lotus's throat and she leaned forward ever so slightly.

"I did not take Llyr's throne without obstacles and major losses. Viltarin had Arcelia handed to him on a silver platter—not only was their king slain, but their entire army. The hard work was already done for him in advance. If I'd had it my way, I'd rather you have taken Arcelia, but the dignitaries voted otherwise. Having setbacks is a foregone conclusion. What matters is how we adapt in the aftermath."

"You're right. This is just a small bump in the road," Lotus's magenta eyes searched hers and she gave Kallistê's hand a light squeeze.

"Thank you for visiting me. It's difficult being so far from home. The island is so warm and full of life compared to this place. The continent's stance on the Cosmic Arts is so unusual. How can you stand it? Don't you ever feel homesick?"

Kallistê's old life in The Three Corners came to mind. How, despite leaving it all behind, as soon as she'd returned to the continent, a part of her had still felt compelled to check on her parents.

She wasn't entirely certain if her actions stemmed from curiosity or genuine longing…but perhaps some small part of her still cared about them in some capacity for her to even think about their well-being at all. In either case, it hadn't been enough for her to change course.

If Kallistê had settled for inheriting their shoe shop, she would have never overthrown Llyr's monarchy and ruled over the kingdom. And her aspirations did not end here—eventually, her reach would expand to the entire realm.

She turned back to Lotus.

"Sometimes I do. But that's why we're here to begin with. The people here are narrow-minded and weak. With your help, I'm going to change that."

Lotus chuckled softly.

"The mountaineers do not seem weak in the slightest. Especially given how you've utilized them to forward your cause," she said.

Kallistê shrugged, blue tresses glinting under the light.

"They're a valuable resource."

"I thought they were an ally."

"One in the same as far as I'm concerned."

Lotus inclined her head.

"Allies are *people*. Resources are *things*."

"And both are utilized to our benefit. The end result is the same. You're arguing about semantics," Kallistê rebutted.

"Resources don't have thoughts and feelings. Allies do. I just wonder how they might react if they realize we're intentionally pushing conflict toward their borders, even if we aren't infiltrating directly.

You're a bit further away from the range in Llyr, but Olysseus is right next door. They'll be looking right at me."

"People naturally flee violence. It's a byproduct of conflict," Kallistê paused, absorbing the worried look on Lotus's face. "Should that happen, Haizea would come to me, not you. I'm the only face she knows."

"She only speaks for one out of the five major peaks in the mountain range. It may not be her that arrives at my doorstep."

"And that's why, for the time being, your efforts are purposefully focused on Illiniza. Why are you so worried, Lotus?"

"The woman wiped out an entire army in a single night. Meanwhile, I've struggled to accomplish the same over the span of a few months. From what you've told me about the treaty, these people are unforgiving. Not to mention, we never uncovered how King Rhys was able to kill Cyrus so easily."

Cyrus had died a humiliating death at the hands of the king—decapitated in front of an entire coliseum. While Cyrus's demise didn't keep her up at night, the unsolved mystery did float around in the back of Kallistê's mind from time to time. She'd never learn the king's secret to how he'd bested transmutation with his mere telekinesis.

"The mountaineers–specifically the warriors–take no prisoners, but they never attack without due cause. Things will only escalate if you or anyone who holds a position in your court crosses their borders. With civilians, they handle them and keep moving."

Lotus grimaced.

"Just...have a plan, Kallistê. What happened with Tarja and Cyrus is proof that even the most well thought out plans can get derailed–through no fault of your own. Your relations could similarly turn sour."

"Rest assured, I have a plan. What you're doing here in Olysseus is a key part of it and I wouldn't put you in danger," Kallistê held her gaze. "Your concerns are not unfounded, but your focus is in the wrong direction," she paused, fingers brushing her ring. "Some of our enemies lurk closer than you realize."

Viltarin came to visit Kallistê a week later—unannounced and uninvited. Knowing she had no real choice over the matter, she instructed her servant to allow him in. She greeted him with a smile plastered on her face and led him to her throne room.

He sauntered over to her chair and sat down.

"*Kneel.*"

Her body moved on its own accord, long blue locks wading around her face as her forehead kissed the cool flooring. She strained to right herself, but her arms locked in place.

"Do you mind fetching us some tea?" Viltarin asked one of her servants.

Kallistê bristled. One of her *doyamas* pressed against her, but she did not react outwardly to its invisible presence. She felt the Beast move between herself and Viltarin. Then, she heard a slight intake of breath that signified it was preparing to emit its piercing howl. Kallistê hummed, halting it in its tracks–the howl would incapacitate Viltarin, but in such close quarters, it would leave her useless as well.

"Kallistê, how have you been faring? Well, I hope."

When she did not dignify him with an answer, he added:

"*Look at me when I speak to you.*"

Her head jerked upward. A cloudy white flickered in her irises, replacing her rich blue gaze. She gritted her teeth as she reached for the Cosmos, intent on dragging him away and leaving him to wallow in its depths but buckled as pain exploded behind her temples.

"How do you think, Viltarin?" she asked between shuddering breaths.

Soft clicks sounded behind her, followed by the clattering of dishes. Kallistê glanced over to see her servant walking past her. They cast her a bemused look and faltered when they caught her gaze.

"*Leave us,*" Viltarin commanded.

Her servant turned on their heels and promptly exited. Viltarin took a sip of his tea with a soft chuckle. The sound grated her ears.

"I find it quite amusing to see that Queen of the Beasts has been leashed. I know you must find it infuriating how easily I bested you."

Kallistê imagined throwing that hot tea on him, but even that brought on daggers stabbing in her head. His smirk widened.

"Don't worry, I have no intention of harming you. And I'll spare you from having to ask why I've done it. You're useful. I admire what you've done on the continent. But you have a reckless ambition and an unquenchable thirst for power, which means you're a danger to a civilized society like Kestramore," Kallistê's brows rose incredulously. "No one else had the will to rein you in. Not the Premier. Certainly not Lotus. Neither Quathir nor Nehemias have the ability to, so it came down to me."

"Is *that* what you're telling yourself? That this is some altruistic act to protect the island and not to further your own interests? From the man who owns Kestramore's largest bank...really, Viltarin?"

"My financial ties are a reflection of my efforts to increase the island's prosperity. What's good for me, is good for the people."

Kallistê barked out a laugh.

"How *noble* of you."

Viltarin studied her.

"Despite what you think, my position is genuine. The way you've embraced the ways of the Cosmic Arts is admirable, but I won't let my homelands slip into the hands of an outsider. If Kestramore is to expand its borders, it should be under the helm of someone whose blood runs deep with the island's history. You're no islander, not truly."

Kallistê rolled her eyes.

Kestramore was her home just as much as his. Not by blood, but certainly by choice.

"Let's stop the charade and get on with it. You're here for a reason."

Viltarin set down his teacup.

"Very well then. I'm sure you're aware that Premier Eryx's current term will be her last. Who does she plan on endorsing to take her place?" Viltarin infused his magic into his words, compelling her to answer.

"Lotus," Kallistê said.

His eyes narrowed.

"Not you?"

"Initially, yes. But I told her Llyr is my priority," Kallistê could not lie, so she told the truth while offering as little information as possible.

Viltarin rubbed his chin.

"Lotus has been around for a while. She's a native to the island, unlike you. I suppose that's an acceptable choice."

"I heard that the Premier has been walking around with a new gift, courtesy of you. Stand," he added with a wave of his hand.

Kallistê rose to her feet and brushed off her dress.

"I've found a new toy to play with and wanted to share. Especially given my…predicament."

"And what all can your 'toys' do?"

"They can turn invisible. They can unleash a mind-piercing scream that renders you motionless. I've trained them to my liking."

"Is that so?" He arched an eyebrow. "How about a demonstration?"

Compelled by the curse, Kallistê obliged and beckoned her Beasts. Her *doyamas* uncloaked themselves, revealing that they already surrounded Viltarin. If the sight of their bared teeth struck fear into the curse mage, he did not show it.

One of her *doyamas* sauntered closer to her and growled. It pointed its nose toward Viltarin, poised to strike. A distant part of her yearned for her pets to rip through Viltarin's flesh, but she could barely formulate the thought, much less vocalize that desire.

"Fascinating. This is why I say you're useful. I can't bring Beasts to our realm and train them, but I can command you to do so with ease," he stated matter-of-factly.

"I have less control over them than you think," Kallistê sneered.

He contemplated her for a moment.

"I know you want to kill me. Unfortunately for you, I've rendered you incapable of doing so. You can't even think about hurting me. You can't remove the ring and you can't ask anyone else to do so. You're bound until I say otherwise, Kallistê. Which brings me to my next point," he began.

"What?"

"The blood mage. You're going to invite her to Premier Eryx's farewell party when she retires six months from now. I'm going to leash her just like I've done you so that when you inevitably ruin that situation, she won't set her sights on our island," Viltarin stood up from his seat and put his hand on her shoulder. Her eyes fell to the tattoo that tinted his middle finger–the islander's tradition for betrothal.

"And if your attempts to do so fail, and *you* attract her anger instead?"

"After what she did to Arcelia, Kestramore is better off with her dead if she can't be brought into the fold. The threat she poses is much too great to think otherwise."

Kallistê opened her mouth to speak, but Viltarin raised his hand, silencing her.

"In the same vein, just to be clear, you're useful, but not entirely indispensable. If I have even the slightest suspicion or the faintest whiff that you've warned her in any way, I'll make you slit your own—"

A loud crack snapped through the air as one of her *doyamas* lunged at Viltarin. His eyes widened, and he leaned back, barely managing to avoid the attack. Its jaws snapped shut just a few millimeters from his face.

How unfortunate.

"Tell them to stand down," A small tremor quivered in his voice.

Unable to refuse, Kallistê bent to his will. Her Beasts vanished from sight, but they didn't fully obey her command—she could still sense their Souls in the immediate vicinity. They'd merely adopted a new tactic to stalk their prey. Viltarin opened his mouth, ready to say something, but glanced around the room with narrowed eyes. He turned on his heels and walked toward the door.

"Do you know how Cyrus died, Viltarin?" Kallistê asked as his hand touched the knob. He paused but didn't respond.

"He foolishly brought his family with him to Arcelia because he thought victory was inevitable. When that arrogance ultimately made him slip, King Rhys killed him and his children. A mere telekinetic mage bested an omen," she said.

Viltarin met her statement with silence.

"Just some food for thought," she added with a shrug and tossed her hair over her shoulders. The door clicked shut.

She hummed a note, beckoning her *doyamas*. Kallistê held her hand out as they sniffed her fingers. She fetched a few treats and fed them.

"My darlings," she purred. "You did so well. Next time...next time..." she trailed off as the curse prevented her from giving voice to the violence brewing within.

Next time, she wouldn't let him catch her off guard.

Next time, her Beasts wouldn't hold back.

Next time...next...t-time, she would erase Viltarin from existence.

Chapter 18

Human Realm, Mount Illiniza, Village of Windhaven

Alastair jutted upright, gasping for air. His vision blurred and it took several moments and a few deep breaths for his world to stabilize. Heat from the fireplace warmed his skin and sunlight peeked through the curtains. Alastair's arms and legs wobbled as he pushed himself off the floor.

He did a double-take at the sight of Pamin sitting on the couch behind him.

~Welcome back,~ he signed.

Alastair blinked.

~How long have you been sitting there?~

~I've stopped by once a day for a few hours for the last two weeks.~

Alastair rubbed his hands over his cheeks to wake himself up.

~Two weeks? I just sat down to meditate last night. It's morning now.~

Pamin shook his head.

~I got worried when I hadn't seen you at the monastery. Diora saw you meditating, so I came to check on you. That was two weeks ago. Given your lengthy absence, I'd say you've been sitting here for at least three or four.~

Nearly a month had passed? Impossible. Alastair frowned. Haizea had told him she'd only be gone for a week. If that much time had passed, *she* should be here, not Pamin.

As if he'd read Alastair's mind, Pamin picked up a letter from the table and handed it to him.

~This was sitting by the front door.~

Alastair ripped open the envelope and unfolded the sheet of paper within. He immediately recognized Haizea's handwriting.

As he read over her letter, his throat tightened. Their original assignment had more or less gone according to plan, but after receiving a message from a village down at the base, she and Shauni had extended their trip to assist them.

Pamin tapped his shoulder.

~*Diora checked on your partner as well. She's fine. She's making her way back home as we speak.*~

Alastair absorbed the information with a nod, working to calm his pounding heart. The news worsened his already frayed nerves from his time with the Soul Reaper. He rubbed his forehead as white spots speckled his vision. Alastair slowly reached his hand out to brace himself as he sat down on the couch.

~*She's alright?*~ he asked.

Pamin nodded.

~*And Shauni's with her?*~

~*Yes, she's traveling with her comrade.*~

Alastair ran his fingers through his hair. So long as she wasn't by herself. Pamin considered him, the wrinkles in his forehead deepening.

~*Given that your magic is strong enough to sense the Souls throughout the various realms, you should easily be able to sense another person right here in the Human Realm. Unlike Diora, you won't be able to see the happenings going on around her, but if you focus, you'll feel the pulse of life in her Soul.*~

Hesitantly, Alastair reached for his magic. A band of tension wrapped around his head and the accompanying fatigue quickly halted his efforts. Using his magic for such a long stretch of time extracted a toll on his vitality. But despite his exhaustion, he wouldn't be able to rest properly until he checked on Haizea for himself.

Alastair closed his eyes and cleared his mind. The tendrils of his magic stretched outward in search of Haizea's Soul. A bead of sweat dripped down his forehead. After several laborious moments, the burning flame of her essence entered his perception. A similarly vibrant cluster of vitality concentrated next to her—undoubtedly Shauni. He was only able to observe them for a few seconds before his connection severed.

He opened his eyes to see Pamin still standing in front of him. Alastair stumbled a little as he got to his feet. He held onto the arm of the couch to keep himself righted.

~*I'm being quite an inhospitable host. Would you like a cup of tea?*~ he asked.

~*You've been in a trance for several weeks, so I wouldn't go so far as to say that. Though I must admit, I would enjoy some tea.*~

Alastair managed a small grin. He started a fire on the hearth and placed a kettle over it to boil. Surprisingly, he didn't particularly desire food, but he still rummaged through the cabinets for something edible that hadn't spoiled during his...absence. The most he could find were some nuts and dried fruits. All the bread had grown moldy, and he'd have to let any meat thaw before he could cook it–not that he had the energy for that.

~*I assume that your time away was a result of your reaching out to the Soul Reaper?*~ Pamin asked.

~*I sat down to meditate last ni—a few weeks ago. I asked him a few questions. He answered by showing me what happened between the Angels and the Demons.*~

Pamin inclined his head.

~*What did you learn?*~

~*He confirmed the legends about Angels stealing magic from humanity and the Demons returning it. I learned that he granted Aaryn power in exchange for Souls,*~ Alastair paused. ~*He also told me that the Cosmos* sets the price with magical wasting, and that he will not intervene to stop it. I don't get why he'd show me all of that if, in the end, he won't help me with the one thing I need the most.~

~Your frustration is justified. But I think you're viewing this too narrowly.~

Alastair flared his nostrils and his chest vibrated as he huffed out noise.

~How the hell is not wanting to die young 'viewing this too narrowly'?~

Pamin started to sign, but he stopped short and glanced at the hearth. Only then did Alastair notice the steam pouring out of the kettle. He measured out the tea leaves and set them to steep in the hot water.

~The Soul Reaper is the first child of the Cosmos. I think to better understand him, we must understand the power that the Cosmic Realm bestows upon us all.~

Alastair furrowed his brows but nodded.

~As omens, from the moment we first wield Cosmic power, we are forever bound to it. We must maintain balance by replenishing the corrupted vitality within. And we both know what happens if we fail to do so.~

Alastair ran his fingers over his knuckles. They looked slimmer than he remembered. With each passing day, his magic consumed his body, wasting it away.

~The Soul Reaper follows a similar framework in his rules. He holds steadfast in one in particular—the scales of power must always be balanced. Regarding us necromancers, whatever we take from the Soul Realm, the Soul Reaper takes from us in kind.~

Pamin paused, leveling his gaze at Alastair.

~And whatever we add to the Soul Realm, the Soul Reaper will bless us in return.~

Alastair blinked.

~Why do you think he told you about Aaryn?~ Pamin prompted.

~She paid for her power in blood.~

~More specifically, she paid in Souls.~

Alastair wrung his hands together to keep his fingers from trembling.

~Aaryn killed thousands of Beasts. She slaughtered the entire Celestial Realm.~

~And as a result, she restored balance to the Human Realm. That is the price of humanity's magic and the consequence of the Angel's sins,~ Pamin signed.

Alastair rubbed the sweat from his palms onto his pants.

~If the Soul Reaper gifted Aaryn power by heightening her Affinity, does that mean he's done something for necromancers in the past?~

Pamin pursed his lips.

~I've never experienced it myself—only heard whispers of those who have. Tales passed down from necromancer to necromancer.~

~And what do these 'tales' claim that he has done for them?~

~Anything that they desire, so long as they offer a sacrifice of adequate value.~

Alastair reached over and focused intently as he filled their cups with tea. Assuming the tales were true, how much blood did other necromancers shed to receive the Soul Reaper's so-called blessing?

Alastair's gut churned and his eyes landed on the pictures on the mantle. For a fleeting moment, the flame of hope flickered within. Could the Soul Reaper grant the one thing he wanted most—to bring his family back? Could he undo the violence that had been inflicted upon them?

His magic trickled across his skin, responding to the call of their lost Souls. He felt his baby cousin, Amiri. His parents. Even now, Alina's Soul whispered to him from the far corners of the Soul Realm.

Weeks...they'd spent weeks chasing after her and it was all for naught.

If his village were still intact, Alastair would trade their lives in a heartbeat. But the Bruvian warriors had already delivered justice on that front—they'd killed everyone responsible for his family's murder and laid his family to rest.

He touched his belly, empty yet without hunger, even though he hadn't eaten in a few weeks. Though his shirt clung to his form loosely, it still fit the same as when he first sat down to meditate. If he had to guess, the Soul Reaper probably had sustained him during their time together.

Surely, if the entity could do something like that, then he could restore a life and rebuild a body anew.

Just as he dared to latch onto hope, a dreadful, pessimistic wind blew his wishes away. He was getting ahead of himself. *Could* wasn't the right word. *Would* the entity do such a thing?

The Soul Reaper thrived and sustained himself on death by absorbing the Souls of beings across the realms. Resurrecting a single person—let alone an entire family—seemed diametrically opposed to the Soul Reaper's interests. And on the slim chance that the Soul Reaper agreed, Aaryn had killed thousands for a single gift from the entity—how many more lives would Alastair have to sacrifice for his family?

His shoulders slumped. As much as he longed for them to be alive, he didn't think he had it in him to harm innocents for something like that. More than a year had passed since their deaths. Did he have the right to disrupt their existence in the Soul Realm? Would they forgive him for doing such a thing?

Yet, despite his doubts, Alastair could not fully cast away the idea of bartering with the Soul Reaper for power. It felt like he'd barely broken the surface of better understanding his magic.

If what Pamin said was true, if he could somehow take the reins over death itself and undo the calamity it brought about...even if helping his family was out of reach, he still had people dear to him in the Human Realm. Maybe he could prevent the same thing from ever happening again.

Alastair tucked the information away in the back of his mind, stashing it for later use like a sack of coins.

Pamin scooped out a handful of nuts and dried fruits from the bowl between them.

~I think I understand why mediums willingly risked magical wasting and Soul corruption by learning necromancy,~ Alastair stated after a while.

~The vitality has blessed you and as a result, you have the Soul Reaper's favor, Alastair. Very few necromancers can call upon him at will as easily as you do. Even fewer have the benefit of him offering direct guidance. You have the power of a god by your side. Don't let that go to waste.~

Alastair sipped his tea. The air shimmered and rippled around his hands. Even Pamin had a slight glow about him. When he set his cup back down, the table vibrated beneath his palm.

~I suppose I'll be spending a lot more time at the monastery.~

Pamin smiled at him, deepening the faint wrinkles around his eyes and mouth. His gaze widened as something over Alastair's head caught his attention. The magical pressure shifted, intensifying as two phantom, bone-shaped hands rested on his shoulders. Energy condensed around Alastair. He sank into it with a newfound confidence.

Pamin's jaw fell slack and several seconds passed before he finally blinked.

~I suppose you will.~

Chapter 19

Human Realm, Mount Illiniza, Windhaven Village

Alastair stood in the kitchen with his back turned to the front door as he began rolling dough to prepare baked goods for his trip market. An intense, yet familiar surge in magical pressure brought him to a halt.

He turned to see Haizea standing in the doorway. She'd taken her braids down at some point during her trip–the style had stretched her dense coils so that her mane of hair hung in waves down her back.

The distance between them vanished in an instant and he pulled her into a tight embrace. They spun around once before he set her back down–he didn't have the strength for anything more than that. Haizea's chest vibrated against his and her lips moved. He didn't know what she'd said, but he perfectly understood the blush blooming across her cheeks and the way her gaze darted between his eyes and lips.

He cupped her face in his hands and showered her with affection–her eyebrows, her cheeks, her nose, and when he went for her lips, she gripped his collar and tugged him closer. She wrapped her arms around his neck and answered his gentle kisses with insatiable ones of her own.

His shirt eased its way over his head and she planted a trail of kisses down his body as her fingers worked their way past his belt. Alastair's breath hitched at the feel of her mouth against him. Long blonde coils obscured her face and he pushed her tresses back to get a better view. When her light brown eyes met his, a shudder of release trickled down his spine.

He coaxed her upward and situated himself between her legs as she sat on the counter. She rolled her hips against his tongue while raking her fingers through his hair. Her satisfaction culminated within him as if it were his own, sending a jolt through his magic.

He brought his lips to hers and she hooked her legs around his waist, pulling him closer. They fell into a rhythm, intense yet familiar. He grazed his teeth against her neck and another pulse rippled within. When she unraveled in his arms, her pleasure pushed him toward his peak. He brushed his thumb across her bottom lip and grinned lopsidedly.

~*If I didn't know any better, I'd say you missed me,*~ he teased.

She flared her nostrils, but her lips flickered upward ever so slightly.

~*Just a little.*~

~*A little?*~ he arched an eyebrow.

~*A lot,*~ she admitted.

~*I'm sorry for being gone for so long,*~ Haizea added. ~*Things didn't go as planned. How have you been? Did you get my letter?*~

~*I did. I'm glad you're safe.*~

She cupped his cheek with her hand, a frown on her lips.

~*Are you feeling alright?*~

The blood drained from his cheeks. Her attention trailed down his face, as if she were following its flow.

~*I'm fine. Better now that you're here.*~

Haizea's honey brown eyes bored holes through him. Alastair tried to keep his expression even, but he grimaced as something within her Soul barbed against his vitality.

~You seem a little paler than normal, that's all. And your clothes look a little big on you.~

A knot formed in his stomach.

~I feel fine,~ he insisted. ~I—~ his hand hung suspended in the air as he caught on his words. He had every intention of telling her, but she'd just returned home from her long trip and looked like she could use a good rest. Now didn't feel like the right time. ~I take it that you and Shauni got everything under control,~ he signed, changing the subject.

Haizea pursed her lips, still studying him. A moment passed before she finally nodded.

~I'm glad you were so insistent about me taking your blood. I'd have never heard the Soul calling for help otherwise. We culled the kingdom dwellers.~

~They beat an elderly woman and left her hogtied in the middle of a street. Forced so many families from their homes. The first people we found were a mother and her small children. When we rounded up the outsiders, a man...a father...he asked for mercy. For his son's sake.~

~Did you spare him?~

Alastair already knew the answer, but he asked her anyway, wanting to share her burden. A shadow fell over her face.

~His head is on a stake at the village entrance. We left his son. Some of the others didn't seem too keen about taking him in, but one of the villagers stepped in—the young mother that we found.~ She paused, faint tremors running through her fingers.

~You did what was necessary,~ he signed.

Haizea's frown deepened.

~Sometimes doing the right thing means watching the people you care about get hurt. Maybe it's not right to leave a young child fatherless. But you did it to protect the villagers. You fulfilled your duty. That's what matters most,~ he added.

~When you put it that way, I guess I can't disagree,~ her chest heaved up and down. ~The kingdom dwellers claimed they'd been attacked by a transmuting mage who put up a wall of fire that forced them out of their homes. Given that they'd just run from an omen, encountering more of them in the village set them off. It's a reason, but not an excuse. Vendela's going to expand our patrol routes down to the base to keep an eye on things. She's giving Shauni and me a long break since we were gone for so long.~

Alastair perked up at the last part.

~So you'll be home?~

She nodded.

~I'll still hit the training grounds, but I won't have any assignments for a few weeks.~

He beamed at her, unable to conceal his excitement. Haizea glanced toward the kitchen. Particularly, the mess he'd left behind on the countertop—bowls and spoons, the bag of flour he'd just opened, a jar of sugar, fresh fruits he still needed to cut.

~Cooking up a feast again?~ she asked.

~Actually, I started selling baked goods at the market. I was just starting when you walked in.~

Her brows rose.

~I hope this means that Windhaven is feeling a little more like home to you.~

~It's home because you're here.~

She studied him for a moment, her expression indecipherable.

~In that case, give me some time to freshen up so that I can help you.~

He grinned.

~I'll join you.~

***

A sack of coins plopped onto the table. Haizea's arm brushed against Alastair's as she packed up half a dozen muffins and passed a man his order. As he looked between Alastair and Haizea, Alastair recognized him from before.

~This must be your other half?~ the man asked.

Alastair nodded. To his relief, the man smiled.

~I see why you work so hard. And I'm glad to see you've returned. I was worried that you would go out of business as soon as you got started.~

Haizea inclined her head.

~I spent some time with Pamin,~ Alastair signed as the man walked away, answering the question plainly written in her face.

And the Soul Reaper, too, he added internally.

He still needed to talk to her about his magic, but it felt like no time was the right time for a conversation like this. Telling her before her assignment would have been insensitive and now that she'd returned, he wanted to enjoy their time together.

Alastair sighed. If he didn't force himself to create the opportunity to talk, he knew he'd continue avoiding it.

~I learned quite a bit while you were gone. I'll tell you more about it once we get home. There are some things you should know about.~

Haizea started to nod, but her attention shifted off to the right, where a woman approached them. She faltered in her footsteps, meeting Haizea's impassive stare with a timid one of her own. Alastair waved at the woman and put on his winning smile. The tension in the woman's shoulders eased, and she came up to the table.

~What would you like to order?~ he asked.

~I'll have half a dozen fruit tarts.~

She handed Alastair a handful of coins. As he counted them, Haizea wrapped the treats and placed them into a bag.

~Pleasure doing business,~ Alastair signed. The woman blushed as she turned away.

~We've only got a few muffins left. You're really popular,~ Haizea commented. ~Still, I can tell I'm scaring some of them off.~

~What? Of course not.~

Haizea rolled her eyes.

~You don't have to flatter me. You're a charmer, Alastair. You draw people in. Next time, I think I should just help with the baking and leave the selling to you. This work suits you.~

~I don't care how much or how little I sell. I always want to spend time with you.~

Her brown eyes softened on his, light and sweet, like pools of honey.

He kissed her on the cheek and began packing up what little baked goods remained. The midday sun shone bright up above, and coins weighed down his change purse.

~I think we deserve a good meal after all our hard work. My treat.~

Chapter 20

Human Realm, Mount Illiniza, Windhaven Village

With a belly stuffed with roasted elk and potatoes, Haizea yawned, ready for a much-needed nap. Alastair sighed as they entered the cabin and she thought he was tired too, but he wrung his fingers together. She pursed her lips at the motion. He held her hand and led her to the couch, his touch sending waves of energy from her fingertips to her shoulder.

~I wanted to talk to you about this before you left, but the timing didn't feel right. You should know what I've been learning from Pamin. And, more importantly, the conversation I had with the Soul Reaper this,~ he signed.

Haizea blinked. Alastair had communicated with Soul Reaper again?

The only time she'd ever seen the entity was back when she'd employed Kallistê to help get his magic under control. A shiver ran down her spine at the memory. For as much as the Soul Reaper unsettled her, he had struck so much terror into Alastair that the encounter made her regret ever pushing him to learn necromancy. If he was reaching out to the Soul Reaper on his own, perhaps he overcame his fears. Maybe this meant he would embrace his magic after all.

Hope budding, Haizea gave him her undivided attention.

~I can contact the Soul Reaper at will now. Actually...I spent the last few weeks in the Soul Realm talking to him.~

~Weeks?~ she asked, her brows arching high. Alastair chewed on his bottom lip.

~He taught me quite a bit. For necromancers, there is more to Cosmic magic than magical wasting. Because our abilities pull power from the Soul Realm, each time we necromancy, the Soul Reaper takes a portion of our Souls as repayment. It's...~ his hands trembled. *~It's fatal.~*

Haizea stilled, brows drawing together.

~I'd hoped that by learning from Pamin, I could find a way to avoid Soul corruption. But the Soul Reaper told me that he would not undo it. He said the price is set. He will not bend his rules for my sake.~

His words slammed into her heart like a hammer. A crack split it down the middle as it threatened to break in two.

~He told me the story of the Demons and the Angels,~ Alastair went on to recount the story of Aaryn's origins and the return of humanity's magic in great detail. *~When I woke up, Pamin was here. And after discussing it with him, I think the Soul Reaper wanted me to know that it works both ways. Aaryn brought him Souls and he amplified her power. But I don't see how it's of any use to me when, no matter what I do, my magic is going to cut my life short.~*

The room began to spin as she tried to make sense of Alastair's words.

Fatal. Embracing necromancy was as lethal as abandoning it.

This realm had already taken so much from him. Hadn't he suffered through enough?

The corners of her mouth tightened and her eyes hardened. Time stretched on as she stared blankly at the fireplace, frozen where she sat. When she finally did move, she pulled Alastair into a tight embrace. His warmth enveloped her, and although his vitality tugged on hers, the call in her blood felt hollow in that moment.

"You don't deserve this," she whispered into his hair and he leaned into her as her voice sent vibrations between them.

~All this time, I thought I was helping you by telling you to pursue necromancy. I had no idea it was a double-edged sword. I'm sorry, Alastair,~ she signed once they pulled apart.

Why did peril keep befalling the people she loved?

Just once...Alastair was the *one* person she had resolved herself not to fail. Yet, despite everything he'd endured, the realm seemed determined to deny him every semblance of peace and happiness.

The gravity of his magic settled on her chest like a boulder, suffocating her. Her nudges for him to accept his power had actually been putting him in harm's way. Worse yet, she'd added more pain to an already agonizing choice and he'd suffered in silence. He'd begun visiting the monastery to try to find a resolution, which meant he'd known about Soul corruption for much longer than she realized.

She concealed a sniffle by wiping her nose. Haizea didn't know what hurt more—that she couldn't even begin to fathom how to protect Alastair from this, or that he'd kept this from her all this time.

Alastair tapped her hand to regain her attention.

~It's not your fault,~ he signed. ~I opened the gates to necromancy long before we ever met. I don't think there's a way around it. Pamin said that magical wasting will progress much faster if I allow it to set in a second time. If I keep using my necromancy, we'll have more time together, but...~ Alastair trailed off.

~But what?~

~But it means that I have to send my Soul to the Soul Realm before it's completely corrupted. If corruption takes over, it will destroy my Soul. And without a Soul to offer the Soul Reaper upon death, there'll be no place for me in the Soul Realm.~

Haizea's eyes flickered between his.

~You'll die if you do that.~

Alastair tore his eyes away and didn't respond. She put a hand on his knee.

~What did Pamin have to say about this?~

~Necromancers typically work around this by training in the Cosmic Arts much later in life. By the time their Souls become brittle, their better years are behind them. For me, I'd have until I'm forty before that happens, at best. Many don't even begin training until then.~

Mediums spent their entire lives connected with the dead. The Cosmos always extracted a heavy toll, but for their own magic to bar them from such an intrinsic part of their identities seemed an especially cruel fate.

She stroked her fingers through his long locks and vibrations palpated her skin as her magic responded to his. The strength in his magic had not faded, but as she cupped his cheek with her hand, she could not help but to note how they'd lost some of their fullness. The implications made her stomach sink, but Haizea had to be strong–for the both of them.

~We'll get through this, Alastair. Together.~

Later that night, Haizea crept out of bed, gently maneuvering around Alastair's sleeping form. She made her way to the living room, sat on the couch, and wept. There was nothing she could have done to prevent his predicament, but she could not shake the intense guilt that cleaved her heart in two.

Alastair often said that he felt like the loss of his family was a balancing act from the realm itself–an atonement for his days as a pickpocket. Usually, Haizea would refute that sentiment, but now she wondered if Alastair's fate was her *own* form of punishment. Maybe this was her family's curse–her father had failed to save her mother and her grandfather had watched his only child die. Ironic, given that healing magic ran in her family.

A stone settled in the pit of her stomach. Between her blood mage training with Grandfather Harzel and her time as a knight in Arcelia, having a family of her own wasn't something she had previously given much consideration. But with Alastair here in Windhaven, she welcomed the idea. Now it felt like a dream that existed just out of arm's reach.

Haizea stood up with a sigh and went into the kitchen—that thought reminded her that she hadn't drunk her hormone potion since leaving for her assignment.

The potion kept her from bleeding each month, which she appreciated. Unfortunately, she hated the taste. As the plants steeped, the bitter smell coated her throat before a single drop had even touched her tongue.

She washed it down with a glass of water, but the room seemed to close in around her. Thunder pounded in her head and dryness scratched at her throat. Maybe some fresh air would help clear her mind.

As she put on her coat, her eyes landed on her swords resting by the front door. A small bulge in the holster caught her attention. She never removed the vial she'd taken with her on her assignment. Haizea opened the pocket and pulled it out, surprised to see that a few drops of Alastair's blood remained. She strained her ears, checking if he had stirred from his slumber. Reassured by his light snores, she left the house and closed the front door softly behind her so that the vibrations would not rouse him.

Haizea walked aimlessly, without any particular destination in mind. But a little while later, when she arrived at Grandfather Harzel's old cabin, she realized that her heart had been leading her instead. She placed her hand on the doorknob, but more than a year after his death, she still could not bring herself to enter. The front steps groaned under her weight as she sat down.

Moonlight illuminated her hands as she pulled out the vial and poured its contents into her palm. She closed her eyes, Grandfather Harzel's face at the forefront of her mind.

A Soul answered her call. Upon its arrival, her jaw fell slack.

Haizea, you've grown up so much.

Haizea blinked, absorbing his honey blonde coils and youthful brown eyes. It was not Grandfather Harzel that stood before her, but her father.

She opened her mouth to speak, but her voice eluded her and for the second time tonight, Haizea burst into tears. She hadn't seen her father's gentle smile or heard his soothing voice in seven years, much less sensed his Soul. He sat down beside her and rested his hand on her leg. Her Soul breathed life into the words that filled her heart.

"It's good to see you again, Father."

It's good to see you too, sweetheart. I know you were expecting your grandfather.

Haizea never imagined she'd speak with her father again, not in this realm at least. And she always assumed that once they reunited in the Soul Realm, she'd be met with his intense disappointment at the path that she'd taken–from becoming a blood mage, to slaying Arcelia's army and toppling their kingdom.

Haizea, I do wish you'd chosen differently. I wanted you to be better than me and to rise above our family's bloody history, but I'm in no position to judge.

Her brows creased.

"Father, you dedicated your life as a healer and spent every day helping people. You were a good, honorable man. You did rise above."

A wave of sadness and regret emanated from her father's Soul.

No, I didn't. When your mother fell ill and my healing couldn't help her...I got desperate. I discarded every principle I thought I held and did the one thing I'd vowed never to do.

"You reached for your blood magic."

I killed people, Haizea. My last act of consequence was to take the lives of innocent people. They had hopes and dreams—no different than you, me, or your mother. I sacrificed them for your mother's sake...I would have done the same if it were you. Even now, my only regret is that it didn't work and that I left you behind when you needed me.

Haizea stared at her hands, clasped in her lap. She worked to keep her expression neutral, but her internal frustrations still seeped out through her Soul.

I don't think that our worst moments define us. However, I do believe that what we choose to do when our backs are against the wall speaks more to who we truly are than during times of ease and serenity. We're all responsible for our own choices, but some things are nature just as much as they are nurture. What you did in Arcelia and your current path now–the part of you that chooses violence, you get it from me just as much as you do from your mother. You've put me on a pedestal I don't deserve to stand on.

Memories clouded her vision. The weight of her father's blood magic bearing down on her when he entered their home, threatening to crush her out of existence. How he'd rested his hands on her mother's, and it was as if they traded places. Her mother regaining strength while her father weakened, frail and thin...like Alastair had once been. She shuddered. Haizea turned to her father.

"I remember watching you that first night. Your magic wasn't weak. You reversed *the flow of your blood magic*," she said in a daze.

I did.

"Grandfather never taught me to do that. Is that something he taught you?" she asked.

No, I figured it out on my own. Although when he realized what I planned, he fought me every step of the way. Said I wouldn't be able to resist the pull of my magic and was more likely to kill your mother than save her. And if I didn't kill her, I'd deplete my own vitality to the point of no return.

But every ounce of her vitality was desecrated and giving her some of my own was the only thing I could think of that might work.

Haizea sat up straighter, absorbing the information.

"Father, I owe you an apology. All this time, I thought you failed Mother. I thought you died because you were too weak and refused to embrace your magic. But you're stronger than I ever imagined."

He offered a wry smile.

Well, you weren't entirely wrong. Magical wasting took its toll. Your mother might have lived if I wasn't out of practice.

Her father's form began to fade.

I can't tell you what to do or what not to do. I'm in no position to judge. Just know that I've loved you with all of my heart in this realm and the next, and I always will. And I know—probably more than you'll ever realize—how that can lead to the highest acts of kindness to the lowest acts of depravity. Love is a redemption just as much as it is a corruptive force.

His voice grew fainter.

The vitality has given you a gift that's as precious as it is monstrous. I think that's why healers originally embraced blood magic. They sought not to harm, but to alleviate the pain of those they cared about. It just came at the expense of their own principles—to save one life, they had to sacrifice another, he wrapped his arm over her shoulder. *I think you're capable of succeeding where I once failed.*

Before she could respond, her father vanished into thin air. Haizea sat on the steps, her eyes glued to where he'd just been sitting. Her hands trembled in her lap. Already, her heart ached after him. She'd lost both her parents as a teenager. Their conversation made her realize that even as an adult, she still needed them—their guidance, their support, their love. Hundreds of questions lingered at the tip of her tongue, but she would have to make do with what she'd been given.

With the blood of Alastair's family on her hands, she'd promised herself she would do whatever it took to keep him safe. She never imagined that meant protecting his Soul from the god of death himself. Haizea didn't know if she could even do such a thing.

But she'd be damned if she didn't try.

Chapter 21

Human Realm, Mount Illiniza, Windhaven Village

Battle cries and the clash of colliding blades echoed in through the air. Haizea followed the sound as she climbed the hill leading to the training area. She had nearly reached the top of the curve when a disturbance in the vitality made her falter. Kallistê materialized in front of her a blink later.

The realmdrifter wore a long blue coat that fell down to her ankles with feathers decorating the collar and cuffs. Despite her shorter stature, her cloudy eyes still somehow managed to peer down her nose at Haizea.

"Haizea. I'm pleased to see you're in good health."

Startled, Haizea met Kallistê's bright smile with a glare of her own.

"What brings you here, Kallistê?"

"It's been a while. I'd hate for you to forget about your friend and ally in Llyr."

"You use the word friend loosely," Haizea muttered. "You're here for a reason. What is it?"

Kallistê twirled the jewelry on her fingers. Haizea thought she saw the woman tug on one ring a bit harder than the rest—it was golden with an amber gemstone. It clashed against the rest of her attire's blue and silver scheme. Peculiar, given how the realmdrifter took such pristine care of her appearance.

"The Premier is nearing the end of her term and plans to retire. She's the longest-serving official in the island's history, so her farewell party will be a rather lavish event. I'm here to extend an invitation."

"I'm not exactly familiar with the workings of the island's government. The Premier is what you all call a king?" Haizea inquired.

"The Premier is an elected leader, chosen by a majority vote amongst the inhabitants. There are dignitaries who are also elected, who act to balance the Premier's power. Back when you and Alastair stayed in Llyr, the dignitaries were who I had to convince regarding assistance for my endeavors. But Premier Eryx is a longtime friend of mine and extended to me her eager endorsement."

Haizea silently glowered at Kallistê, mentally parsing through what the realmdrifter did and—more importantly—did *not* say.

"So Kestramore as a whole doesn't fully support what you're doing. And the one person who does is stepping down from power."

Kallistê's smile tightened.

"Premier Eryx's long-standing popularity means that she will continue to hold influence in the government even after the end of her tenure. She already has a name picked for who she'll endorse in the upcoming election."

"Let me guess: you?"

To Haizea's surprise, Kallistê shook her head, her sleek blue tendrils glistening with the movement.

"No, I'm a bit preoccupied with Llyr and the happenings on the continent. But I fully trust the person who will be running to take Premier Eryx's place. I'm doing everything in my power to ensure that they win–including inviting the blood mage who leveled an entire army and assisted in my endeavors. You're notorious back home, Haizea. Don't tell anyone I said this, but it's that exact display of power that made the dignitaries so hesitant to help," Kallistê threw her head back and laughed. Haizea's expression remained neutral, not remotely amused.

"Speaking of the continent, I spent some time down at the base recently to investigate reports of a village that Olysseans had overrun. According to the kingdom dwellers, omens attacked their city and forced them to flee. If you're going to make a mess, at least keep it contained within your borders, Kallistê."

"My sincerest apologies. When mice go scurrying, it's quite difficult to catch them all."

Haizea's eyes narrowed into slits. Kallistê neither denied her accusation nor did she even pretend like she'd concern herself with fixing the problem. The realmdrifter cleared her throat.

"All of that aside, I'd greatly appreciate it if you accept my invitation. You and Premier Eryx each share a personal history with King Rhys," her eyes darted to Haizea's hands as she clenched them into fists. "But I'll let her tell her own story. She's asked me many times to introduce you two and I think it would be a fitting farewell gift for her."

Something in Kallistê's tone piqued Haizea's curiosity. If she didn't know any better, she might have gotten the impression that Kallistê cared about the Premier.

She stood silently and chewed over the invitation. It could be a trap, but again, even in this case, the mountaineers knew very little about Kestramore. She didn't think she should pass up the opportunity to learn more about the small island of omens across the ocean, especially with conflict brewing at the base.

There was an advantage to keeping your enemies close—the more she knew, the better.

"Alright. I'll go," Haizea said.

"Fabulous. I'll send you the details once event planning is finalized. It's always a pleasure, Haizea."

Kallistê smiled radiantly before she vanished from sight. In her absence, a band of tension tightened around Haizea's head. Between her conversation with Alastair, the following discussion she'd had with her father's Soul, and now this new task of gathering information about Kestramore, it felt like a massive boulder had settled on her shoulders.

Diplomacy didn't particularly hold her interest, but the realmdrifter's request seemed genuine. Still, she didn't quite trust it. Even if she did not say it, Kallistê always had a motive, usually to benefit herself in some way. When she'd offered a helping hand while King Rhys chased Haizea and Alastair across the continent, it wasn't out of benevolence—Kallistê had wanted her to kill the king.

If Kestramore's leaders feared Haizea's power, and if some of them presented an obstacle to Kallistê's plans, perhaps this was more about flexing her muscles than a gift to an old friend as the realmdrifter claimed. She would have to approach the visit accordingly.

Haizea continued onward to the warriors' training grounds. Vendela had paired off the young warriors in training for sparring. She briefly scanned over the crowd but didn't see Jassia. A familiar, boisterous laugh carried over the grunts and shouts of effort from the cohort. Haizea followed the sound to Shauni, where she and the other warriors were in the midst of setting up training dummies.

The dummies were meticulously designed to mimic human anatomy. A false skeleton and internal organs made up the interior, which gave them a dense weightiness. Haizea chose a half-sized dummy that was only a head and torso on a stick. Some of the other warriors had opted to work with the full-bodied ones. Shauni gave her a light punch.

"Not like you to be late," she paused, violet eyes assessing. "You feeling okay?"

Haizea huffed through her nose.

"I just need to blow off some steam."

"Well, you're in the right place."

It had been a while since she'd had traditional hand-to-hand combat practice, so Haizea started with a series of strikes with her dummy. She aimed precisely at vulnerable weak spots—the sternum, the collar bone, and the orbital area.

Haizea unleashed a relentless barrage of punches on the dummy's sternum. When it began to feel brittle against her knuckles, she moved onto the rib cage and traded her fists with her powerful legs. It only took two hits before the dummy began to sag to the side–the synthetic bones within had shattered and compromised the internal integrity.

To her left, Shauni drove her sword into her dummy's chest, directly into the heart. Her friend stepped back and wiped her forehead as she exhaled from the exertion.

"Hard to impale the heart without using my magic," Shauni said.

Haizea inspected the dummy and shook her head.

"Hard, but not impossible. My mother wasn't a mage and she could do it. She taught me how. Made it look easy."

"You miss her," Shauni mused.

Haizea stood a little taller. The conversation with her father's Soul clung to the tip of her tongue, but that would inevitably lead into Alastair's magic and how no matter what he did...

She blinked away the budding moisture in her eyes. Not now.

"Kallistê came to visit me on my way here," she said, and explained who and what the Premier was and why Kallistê had invited her to the farewell party.

"So it'd be like if Vendela stepped down and we had a big gathering to celebrate."

"Yes, exactly."

Shauni rubbed her chin and nodded.

"Alright. I'm coming with you."

"Shauni, they're an island of omens."

"Which is *precisely* why you need me by your side. I'm not letting you go to a strange land by yourself. Not again."

Shauni's violet eyes darkened and her fingers tightened around the hilt of her sword—a painful reminder that she was yet another person who Haizea had scarred by her decision to leave the mountains behind.

"If I know him as well as I think I do, Alastair will want to go too. He's a powerful mage and he would never let anything happen to you if he can help it, but he's not a warrior. If I'm there, it's another set of eyes. Besides, warriors travel in twos. I'm not taking no for an answer," Shauni said.

"You're right," Haizea acquiesced.

Shauni's brows rose—she'd probably expected more pushback.

"Of course I am," she grinned. "Another thing, while I'm at it: you mentioned they're an island of omens. It's a risk. They already know you're a blood mage, so you should take precautions if you can."

Haizea rubbed at her pendant, an idea forming.

"I will."

Movement caught her eye—Jassia tossed her school bags down and sprinted over to where the younger warriors sparred. She joined in the large circle and her usual sparring partner, Covy, quickly took her aside. Vendela frowned at the disruption but didn't intervene.

The two teens quickly began their sparring drills, with Covy starting on the offense. Jassia met Covy blow for blow with a look of determination.

She deftly blocked one of Covy's swings with her wooden swords before answering with a strike of her own. Covy narrowly avoided the hit and managed to knock one of Jassia's swords loose with a kick. Haizea thought she was about to witness another swift defeat, but Jassia dropped to the ground and spun in a sweeping kick. Covy lost her balance and hit the dirt. Jassia had nearly settled on top of her when Covy scrambled to regain the upper hand.

Haizea learned forward in anticipation when Covy went for Jassia's wristbands, but Jassia unsheathed her daggers and managed to land a swipe against Covy's wrist. Vendela walked by without a word, but she monitored the fight through the corner of her eye. This type of training seemed to suit Jassia better—where the entire group practiced at once and no particular person was the center of attention.

Jassia jabbed one of her daggers toward Coby's abdomen, but the other girl twisted out of the way. She grasped onto Jassia's outstretched wrist and wrenched her dagger away. Jassia's expression darkened. Using her free hand, she jammed her other dagger against Covy's chest just as Covy did the same–each girl aimed right at the heart in a killing blow, ending the match.

Jassia helped Covy to her feet and each girl smiled widely at the other. Covy caught Haizea's eye and whispered in Jassia's ear. When Jassia turned toward her and beamed, a muted smile toyed at Haizea's lips.

Vendela came up behind the two girls and their attention snapped back toward the leader. Haizea couldn't hear her, but she knew that Vendela was coaching them on what they could improve on.

Haizea went back to sparring with Shauni for a little while longer before Vendela called everyone together to hand out assignments. She established a rotating schedule for trips down to the base to support Eaglestone village as well as keep guard over any more possible attacks. Haizea and Shauni still had a while before their turn came up, but they were back to running patrols again.

The warrior's new activities had not gone unnoticed by the villagers and as word spread, construction for the ropeways picked up considerably. The first section had been completed, but they planned to build several more.

After much discussion, they deemed it necessary to have designated stopping points for people to acclimate as the air thinned. For people who lived their entire lives at the base, a direct trip to the summit would cause severe altitude sickness. Under the right circumstances, it could quickly turn fatal.

Ultimately, the mountaineers hoped to take what currently was a week's long trip and reduce it by as much as they possibly could. Until the situation at the base settled, the warriors would set up stations at each of the pylons' stopping points in case kingdom dwellers tried to ride them.

As the younger warriors dispersed for the evening, Jassia ran laps around the camp–Vendela's punishment for sneaking off the way she did. It had been unwise on the teen's part, but in the grand scheme of things, she'd come back better for it. Jassia had gone on her first mission, partook in her first cull, and based on her recent performance in her sparring match, she had learned and grown as a fighter from that experience.

Haizea still had some steam left so she and Shauni teamed up against another pair, Yelena and Faryz, for more sparring matches. Yelena was shorter than Haizea, but taller than the others. She kept her dark brown tresses contained in a braided ponytail while Faryz's red curls hung around her ears.

After a few grueling duels, they packed up their supplies in the storage area and she noticed Covy lingering at the edge of the training grounds. Vendela called Jassia over as she completed her final lap. Haizea caught part of their conversation as she and the others took their leave.

"Jassia, I don't know what's gotten into you lately. First, you directly disobeyed my orders, and now you're showing up late to training?"

"I'm sorry, Vendela."

"I'm not saying it for you to apologize. I'm concerned. Is everything alright?" Vendela rested a hand on her shoulder.

Jassia opened her mouth, her eyes glassy as she started to answer, but stopped short.

"It won't happen again," she said.

Covy tapped Haizea's arm as she and Shauni walked by.

"Her mom's not doing well," she whispered. "She had a fainting spell a few days ago. Jassia's been running home to check on her between the academy and training."

That didn't surprise Haizea. Jassia's mother already had a dedicated healer who visited her numerous times throughout the week—anyone needing such close supervision was definitely worse for wear. She'd tasked Alastair with delivering a potion while she was on her assignment, but maybe she could check in on the woman herself.

Haizea sighed, noting the faint circles under Jassia's eyes. She knew all too well what it felt like to watch her mother deteriorate while her father worked himself to an early grave.

"Thanks for letting me know, Covy. You're a good friend," she said.

Her gaze fell to an unraveling, blood-stained bandage around Covy's arm. The girl put a hand over it.

"Training accident," she said quickly.

"A wooden weapon wouldn't make a cut like that," Shauni said.

"I may or may not have gotten a hold of my mother's swords," she admitted, rubbing the back of her head.

"Let me take a look at it," Haizea said.

Shauni crossed her arms.

"Swords are nothing to play with. She should sport her wounds." Haizea sighed.

"At the very least, I can show you how to bandage it properly."

Haizea unwound Covy's bandage and examined the injury. A long cut extended down the length of her upper arm. It was inflamed and a little bloody but otherwise looked fine.

"You cleaned it pretty well, which is good. That's always the first step. You're going to want to put ointment on it to aid in the healing. Mirwort is the best."

She rummaged through her pack and pulled out a fresh wrap.

"The bandage should be tight enough to compress the wound, but loose enough to allow blood flow," she said as she wrapped it around Covy's arm. "For deeper cuts, you'd make a tourniquet instead. Put it just a few inches above the wound. Like this."

Haizea placed a bandage on her other arm. A shape in the corner of her eye caught her attention. Jassia had joined them.

"Shauni, can you–"

A small stick floated into her palms.

"Already on it."

"The stick not only holds the bandage in place, but it's the only way to get it tight enough to bring the bleeding to a stop. You need enough pressure to get to the vessels that are deeper in the body. Twist it until the bleeding stops. Then you'll use another bandage to hold it in place so it won't unwind," she explained as she demonstrated.

"Hopefully, you'll never need to do something like this. But it's a good skill to have. Many warriors in training take a few basic healing courses in their final years at the mage academy."

"I took an anatomy class and a first aid course," Shauni added. "Anatomy, because it helps you identify weak points to strike. First aid, because nine times out of ten, there won't be a healer around if you get injured."

Haizea untied the tourniquet, and Covy shook her arm. She went over to Jassia, who had a muted smile on her face.

"What's got you in a good mood?"

"Vendela said she's going to let me shadow my first assignment."

Covy snorted.

"Technically, you've already done that."

"My first *official* assignment. She said I've improved but wants to keep a close eye on my performance. We're going to run a patrol together."

"You've already completed a cull. A patrol is nothing."

"I hope so."

Covy slipped her bag over her arm and the duo began walking away.

"Thanks for the bandage," Covy hollered over her shoulder. Jassia offered a shy wave.

Shauni clapped Haizea on the back.

"At this rate, you'll be taking Vendela's place soon enough."

Haizea scrunched her nose.

"We've been over this, Shauni. A challenge isn't on the table."

"That's not what I mean. She's not getting any younger. It's something you should start thinking about."

Vendela had to juggle training the younger warriors and coordinating assignments with the rest of the cohort while also keeping open communication with the nearby villages for any conflicts that needed addressing. It made Haizea wonder how her mother had managed being the cohort's leader while raising a family. Being the type of leader who truly deserved the title required a high amount of personal investment and responsibility.

"I don't envy her position. The cohort deserves someone who wants it."

Shauni shrugged.

"I'd say that's a good thing. It means you have a level head."

"You're more than qualified," Haizea rebutted.

"The entire cohort looked up to your mother. We look up to you too. And not just because of Ilmare—the entire mountain knows your name because of what you did to Arcelia."

"They call you the Destroyer of Armies."

Haizea suppressed a shudder. The woman hadn't said it out of fear or reproach, but instead with respect and fascination. The Bruvian warriors were the mountains' sword and shield. They committed to a life covered in the blood of others so that their people would not have to. By slaying thousands in the span of a single night—by annihilating an entire army—Haizea displayed a level of fortitude few warriors ever got the chance to prove they had.

Despite the reputation that preceded her, she hadn't proved her worth yet. Not to herself.

"Vendela still has a few good years left. We should appreciate it while she's still here."

Chapter 22

Human Realm, Mount Illiniza

Sage put all of her focus into her transmutation efforts after the near miss with the blood mage. Days blended into weeks, filled with training. A month came to pass before she finally broke the dam to her magic and successfully made a container of water boil. It took her two weeks after that to successfully freeze it into ice.

The best part of it all was the smile on Felix's face. She could not remember the last time her brother had looked genuinely happy.

"This is just the first step in our long road toward reclaiming what's rightfully mine," he said.

Sage had cackled and a peculiar glee vibrated through her. She still had quite a ways to go before fully realizing her abilities as a transmuting mage, but Felix was right–this *was* only the beginning. She had accomplished all the skills that Miss Tamsyn had taught Felix.

They spent a few more weeks asking various villagers for more information–they'd learned that mountaineers kept written records on the Cosmic Arts. She and Felix managed to swipe some of the books pertaining to transmutation and made themselves scarce before anyone noticed. Now, they were situated somewhere between the previous village and the next.

They sat on a dead log and read over the texts.

"'The true hallmark of mastery in the Cosmic Arts is not the strength of one's power, but of an omen's ability to utilize their magic without losing themselves to the lure of the Cosmos.'"

Sage drowned out her brother's voice as she looked over the words in her own passage.

The first step in transmutation is to familiarize oneself with the vitality of the world around you. Note the calmness of a pond of water compared to the volatility to a ball of fire. Memorize the smoothness of a silk fabric versus the roughness of a rock. Take advantage of the ability to see the vitality and visualize these differences.

Sage flipped to the next page, which showed a series of drawings. The first image was of a glistening orb.

The Cosmic Arts brings us closer to the power that birthed us all. To open one's eyes to the vitality is to open one's eyes to the Cosmos. To be touched by the vitality is to be touched by the Cosmos. To wield the vitality is to wield the Cosmos.

The next image depicted a variety of objects with a description of what the vitality within them felt like and the minute differences an omen could detect visually. At the bottom of the page was a description of air and fire. It explained that transmuting one into another required altering the properties of the vitality—flames teemed with heat and energy, whereas air had a more subtle presence.

Sage squinted her eyes against a sudden tingling that buzzed in her temples. She took a deep breath and combed over the instructions before following them step by step.

She held her hand out in front of her face and closed her eyes. She concentrated on firmly grasping the wispy vitality that made up the air around her. Imagining as if she were striking a match, Sage snapped her fingers. A searing heat ripped across her skin, earning a pained hiss–but no fire. She shook her hand in an attempt to alleviate the pain.

A sudden light-headedness overcame her and her eyes began to droop.

"Sage," Felix's voice was a distant echo.

Sage snapped again. Her hand recoiled from the heat, but her lips curved upward. An oddly pleasant buzz radiated from her fingertips to the rest of her body. She chased after that feeling.

Snap.

She climbed higher, higher, higher.

"Sage."

Snap.

More. She wanted–*needed* more.

"Sage."

She gazed forward, not looking at anything in particular, and yet seeing everything. The world around her glowed in a way she'd never seen before. The air itself sparkled, and the vibrancy of the light intensified at her fingertips.

Snap.

"Sage!"

Something shook her shoulders. Sage blinked. Felix's form swam in her vision. He stared at her for several long moments, frowning.

"I feel...I feel...," Sage trailed off.

"You're feeling the high," Felix said. "It means you're on the right track. What was that you were trying to do just now?"

"It s-said I can...turn air into fire."

Felix glanced at her hand. The skin on her fingers burned a bright red and a blister was already forming. His eyes darkened, but a satisfied grin cemented itself on his face.

"This is exactly what we need. The power to turn anything you can touch a weapon–even the very air we breathe. Eventually, you'll be able to do what Old Lady T did to the Olysseans," her brother paced back and forth.

"We'll be able to return home and I'll take my rightful place on the throne. I'll do what Father failed to do. We'll rid the realm of the omens, one by one, village by village, house by house if we have to. Those abominations will die by the hands of one of their own kind. Starting with that witch who took everything from me."

The deep-seething hatred permeated Felix's voice and settled in Sage's bones.

Abominations...one of their own kind...?

She shifted and shoved her quivering hands beneath her bottom. The movement made her slump over and she barely caught herself—it felt like a lead weight was weighing her down.

The omens that had trampled over their kingdom were undeniably horrific. But they'd met more since they'd left Arcelia. Miss Tamsyn had shown them kindness and opened her home to them when they had nowhere else to go. And Bose...

Sage squeezed her eyes shut, pushing away the gruesome memory. She placed a hand over her galloping heart. Did Felix think of *her* as an abomination too? What did that mean once they finally went home...once things went back to normal?

No. Arcelia was *both* of their homes. He wouldn't treat her like the rest of them. Sage wasn't just any omen. Felix was her brother—the only family she had left. He'd urged her to take up transmutation to begin with. They'd started this journey together and it would end just the same.

Felix turned to face her. His expression chilled her to the bone.

"You'll be Arcelia's sword, Sage. And I'll be the king who wields it."

Sage lost track of time as she continued her training. Before she knew it, weeks had turned into months, and her sixteenth birthday was upon her.

She bit her quivering lips. Yet another birthday without her parents. Nearly two years had passed since their deaths. She'd never have the chance to celebrate with them again.

Felix rested his arm on her shoulder. She quickly wiped away the moisture budding in her eyes and looked at him expectantly.

"We ought to put that flame of yours to good use. You need to learn how to properly use it in a fight. Once we face the blood mage, there'll be no room for error."

Her shoulder slumped. Perhaps he'd lost track of the date.

"I don't know if I'm ready," she said, fiddling with the hem of her shirt. "Today is–"

"That's why we're here to practice," Felix waved his hand at the welcome sign as they crossed into the next village.

"Practice?" she drew out the word. A sudden cramp twisted her stomach and she grimaced.

"That witch wiped out an entire army. She killed Father, despite the fact that he had the anti-magical plant. Don't be so delusional as to think you can defeat her if you've never spilled blood before."

Sage blanched.

"Felix–"

"I see the perfect target."

He pointed to a woman entering a tavern. The raucous sound of laughter and chatter carried through the air as the door swung open and closed shut behind her.

"We can't go around picking off random innocent people for 'practice'," she hissed.

He squeezed her shoulder. She winced.

"You can't even bring yourself to say the word. You have one sole, singular purpose, Sage. And it's to *kill*. Not 'pick off'. Not 'eliminate'. Your purpose is to kill anyone who obstructs our path to the throne. You can't think of them as people. They're mountaineer savages. Ignorant rubes that aren't even worth the pot they piss in."

A lump in Sage's throat choked her.

"If we turn back now, it means living in fear and looking over our shoulders for the rest of our lives. It means you've befouled your magic for nothing. We're nearly halfway up the mountain now. We've come this far. We can't let our efforts be for naught."

Felix pulled her into the tavern called the Broken Cauldron. The warm, sweet smell of powdered sugar drew her gaze to the right. An elderly woman sat at a table and enjoyed a massive slice of cake. Sage's eyes watered at the sight.

Back home, the servants would have brought her a twelve-layer lemon cake with frosting for her birthday. Father would have pulled her aside in his study to offer her some arcane piece of wisdom that went over her head. Mother would have fussed over her dress and pushed the servants aside so that she could brush her hair properly.

The old woman caught Sage looking and smiled at her. Something about the way her eyes crinkled reminded her of Miss Tamsyn. Sage wondered how she was faring.

They found an open booth toward the back of the tavern. As Sage slid into her seat, her magic sprang to life. Her body tensed, craving the rush that came from using her transmuting abilities.

Snap.

A small flame ignited at the tips of her fingers, scratching the internal itch. Sage sank into the world of the vitality. A glass of water on a nearby table shimmered. The wooden floor beneath her feet glowed faintly. And the people—they *brimmed* with vitality. Each person illuminated the tavern like a star in the sky. Sage looked down at her hands, mesmerized by how her body shone brighter than her brother's.

Another bout of pain brought her observations to a halt. Sage tried to ignore it, but the longer she sat, the more her gut twisted. She excused herself to the restroom.

Her footsteps felt heavy as she walked through the tavern. Sage gently locked the door behind her and sat down. She gasped.

Blood stained her underwear red.

Mother had taught her about this years ago, but the sight still caught her off guard. Sage had yet to bleed until now and with her travels with Felix filling her days, it wasn't something she gave much thought about preparing for. She didn't have any hygiene products or clean garments to change into.

Sage did her best with the tissue and washed as well as she could at the sink. When she exited the restroom, a woman was standing outside waiting.

Luminance nearly blinded Sage—the woman radiated so dazzlingly that it brought tears to her eyes.

The princess stared at the woman, captivated. Voluminous red hair framed her face and her eyes were the color of topaz. She smiled gently at Sage. The vitality concentrated most intensely around her head, rippling and writhing. Something pinched deep in Sage's mind a moment later.

The woman reached into her purse and handed Sage a handful of small packets. When Sage hesitated, she nudged her.

"It's for you. Do you need help with it?" she said.

"I—thank you," Sage said.

She hurried back inside. When Sage came out again, the woman had returned to her table. She sat with two other women, shining like a small sun.

Understanding dawned on Sage as she made her way back to Felix. She had read about this before in one of their books.

"I think that woman over there can read minds," she whispered. She glanced at the table again to see the woman laughing at one of her friends.

Felix raised his head from the menu, eyes narrowing.

"Are you certain?"

Sage shrank back at his tone.

"No, I just..." she trailed off. Her vision faded in and out and she struggled to focus.

He leaned across the table.

"Sage, what's the *one* type of magic that can see through an enchantment?"

Sage blinked. Up until now, they had never crossed paths with a seer. The threat of exposure that came with that particular magical subtype never crossed her mind. An enchantment was nothing more than a flimsy veil for a seer who could circumvent it entirely by reading one's thoughts.

"Exactly. Which means that we need to get rid of her before she can tell anyone else."

Sage clenched onto her napkin.

"We don't know if she knows anything. Besides, she helped me just now. When I—"

"Killing one pest will make eliminating the rest that much easier," he said grimly, his eyes darkening and his hands balling into fists.

Sage gripped onto his arm and dug her fingernails in. As she parted her lips to admonish him for his rashness, a bright flash caught her attention. A swell of magic came hurtling toward her brother and he crumpled to the ground.

She followed the blast to the source. When her eyes met the seer's, she froze in place. Though they sat too far to overhear one another's conversations, the distance did not impede the omen's ability to pick up on their thoughts–Felix's plan to kill the woman had undoubtedly played out before the omen's eyes.

The seer's display of power chilled Sage to the bone. This was precisely what Felix wanted her to do to the omens invading their homelands—exert complete control over their enemies and destroy them from within.

That nagging feeling returned. They would win back their home—and then what? Felix concluded that the woman needed to die in the span of a breath. What if he ended up doing the same toward her?

In the background, her brother cried out and pressed his palms into his forehead.

"Sage," Felix sputtered out, still paralyzed by the seer's grasp.

Her brother groaned, writhing and clutching his head–earning a few sideways glances from nearby patrons. The omen made her way toward them, the vitality encasing her in light. Sage squinted against her shimmering form and the urge to run nearly overwhelmed her.

"Sage," her brother's voice clawed at her insides.

"Please stop," Sage whispered.

Her words went unheeded–the seer closed the distance on Felix.

"We won't hurt anyone. Just let us leave and we won't come back," Sage pleaded.

The woman cast her a quick glance, something in her gaze softening before it sharpened on her brother.

Sage's vision swam and the scene shifted before her.

She no longer stood in a tavern, but inside the bunker. Mother's face overlaid Felix's and she cried out in pain as a sword pierced her flesh and impaled her into the wall. She sobbed as Jirina pulled the sword to free her. Felix confronted the blood mage, but the omen overpowered him with ease. Her magic latched onto his blood and he sagged to his knees.

Dying. Her brother was dying and all she could do was watch. They were powerless against the blood mage's power. They could not defeat an omen.

Sage didn't know what she intended when she raised her hand in the direction of the seer, only that she wanted her brother's agonizing cries to stop. Flames birthed on her fingertips, growing wildly as it fed on air. Searing heat singed her skin and a burning ball went hurdling toward the omen. The seer barely breathed a word of warning to her friends before the fire swallowed them.

Bile rose in Sage's throat at the sight, and yet a giggle bubbled on her lips. Part of her tried to pull her power back, but another sector of her mind forced her to chase after the rush.

Snap.

The tavern transformed into an inferno as flames shot from her palms. Her giggles turned into full-blown hysterical laughter, so intense that it made her belly hurt. It drowned out the cries of the people around her. It masked the smell of scorched skin and incinerated clothes. Her sparkling vision turned white and tremors raced through her.

More. She needed more.

Sage pressed her fingers together again, but something warm wrapped around her arm, halting her. She looked down to see Felix's hand on her. She coughed against the black and arid smoke. Felix steadied himself as he got to his feet.

"That's enough, Sage," he said.

Sage laughed, even as she burst into tears.

"You did well. This is exactly what you've been training for. This power is exactly what we need to defeat her."

Felix patted her head and shushed her.

"This is the only way we can return home," he whispered.

Sage clung to her brother as he led her out of the burning tavern.

Mericus, is this what you felt?

Father said his childhood friend had been evil. Or had his power driven him mad?

Blazing forms rolled on the ground in an attempt to extinguish the flames. Sage squeezed her eyes shut and turned away from the sight, but screams of agony followed their footsteps.

If the result was carnage like this, she didn't know if it made a difference.

Chapter 23

Human Realm, Mount Illiniza, Crow's Peak Village

"How long are you going to give me the silent treatment?"

The crunch of stiff grasses beneath Sage's shoes filled the space between them.

"She was a *seer*, for realm's sake. She knew our real identities. She could have outed us to the warriors. What then, Sage?"

Sage sniffed, the scent of burning flesh still lingering in her nostrils. She'd never hurt another person before, let alone taken a life. And now not only did the seer's blood stain her hands, but the entire tavern—people who had nothing to do with their goal. That wasn't even the worst part.

The part that horrified her–that made her stomach threaten to heave–was that she'd enjoyed every second of it.

Snap.

Frost formed at her fingertips, accompanied by a rush of euphoria that made her shudder.

"The higher we ascend on the mountain, the closer we get to the blood mage. The closer we get to the blood mage, the more people we'll have to silence to cover our tracks," Felix continued.

Sage sped past her brother. When he tried to catch up to her, she shoved him back with her magic without even a glance in his direction.

"If you can't handle something like this, we'll die long before we're able to kill her."

"I wish she had," she muttered.

"What?"

Sage spun on her heels.

"I said I wish she'd have killed us. I'd rather be in the Soul Realm with our parents than be stuck here with you. You keep saying 'we', but we both know that when the time comes—*if* the time comes—it'll be *me* who risks my life and faces the blood mage while you keep a safe distance. You're too weak to do anything else."

Felix recoiled as if he'd been slapped.

"The mountains aren't my home, Felix. I don't want to be here anymore. I don't want to fight. I don't want to hurt anyone," Sage toyed with the hem of her shirt. "I wish we had never left Miss Tamsyn's farm. I wish Mama and Papa were alive. I wish we'd never survived that day in the bunker. At least then, I would've died before I became a monster," she wiped away the stream of tears flowing down her cheeks.

When Felix reached out to her, she smacked his hand away with a wave of telekinesis.

"Sage, you're not—"

"Don't lie to me, Felix. You're just like Papa with the way you talk about omens. I'm the one who has to become one while you sit back and watch, unscathed and uncorrupted," she fell silent and stared off into the distance. Frost expanded from her fingertips to her wrists. "You're probably just going to have me executed as soon as you're on the throne. It's what you'll do to the other omens. Why should I expect anything different? You didn't even care enough to..."

Sage's words caught in her throat. Her birthday came and went and Felix hadn't even bothered to acknowledge it. When he opened his mouth to respond, she clenched her fists, denying him the ability.

"Only a monster could do what I did in that tavern. I don't want to be that. I don't want to end up like Mericus. If you want the throne so badly, then fight for it yourself."

Felix bucked against her telekinetic wall and, to her surprise, broke free. He rested his hands on her shoulders.

"Sage..." he trailed off. "Okay, you're right. Let's forget about the blood mage for just a second. Let's forget about the throne. *You* are the crowned princess of Arcelia. It is your home. *Our* home. Father fought to his very last breath to protect it. Maybe I do sound like him. So what? His legacy continues with us. His *fight* continues with us. Is that really how you want it to end? By rolling over and letting them win?"

Sage bit her trembling lips. She shook her head.

"Omens and their traitorous sycophants have invaded our home and installed a false monarch. If we go back now and abandon our pursuit of the blood mage, we still have a battle on our hands. We will still have to shed blood, even for something as simple as having a place to rest our heads."

He squeezed her shoulders.

"What you're feeling now is exactly what I was talking about before. It's your conscience trying to convince you that you've done something wrong. That voice is lying to you, Sage. They invaded our kingdom, forcibly pushed us out, and any Arcelians who remain have been made secondhand citizens in their own homelands. They took it by force—they will not give it back if we ask nicely. The people we cross paths with may seem like innocent bystanders, but their very existence is an assault on ours. The people in the tavern were no different."

"It feels different," she murmured.

"Eventually, it won't," Felix released her. "You mentioned Mericus. Father loved him. Mericus was his best friend, and yet he killed him. I'm sure that ate away at him, but Father never wavered. Imagine how much worse things would have turned out if he'd allowed Mericus to live. This is about more than just *us*, Sage. It's about our kingdom and our way of life. The people of Arcelia need us."

Sage twiddled her thumbs. The sun beamed down on her and warmed her skin, yet a cool breeze kept the brunt of the summer heat at bay.

"What happens to me, Felix?"

"What do you mean?"

"If we succeed, what happens to me?"

"*When* we succeed, our people will hail us as heroes."

She searched her brother's face. That same fire blazed in his ice blue eyes. She wished she could find the same in her own–maybe then she'd be able to discern if her brother's ambition kept him from giving a fully honest answer to her question. She didn't know why she'd bothered asking–he would be foolish to say anything different.

Sage clenched her fists.

Maybe that didn't matter. Maybe Felix had a point—that this was bigger than them. Bigger than the blood mage. She had more than just the throne to fight for. If they did not wrest control from the omens, then her people would continue suffering. And given what had happened in Eaglestone, the mountains may not always have peace either.

If she allowed this injustice to take root, it would continue to spread.

For Arcelia, she thought. *For home.*

"What next?" she asked.

"We're only halfway up the mountain. We'll take our time climbing so that we can get a lay of the land and figure out an escape plan along the way. We're deep in enemy territory. We'll have to run after we strike. You should focus on training. In terms of raw power, I don't know if you'll ever be able to match the witch. But you still need to be competent enough to put up a fight. Our best bet is to catch her off guard. She'll hesitate when she sees you. That will be your opening."

Sage grimaced.

"How can you be so certain that's what she'll do?"

"Because it's what happened in the bunker."

Her frown deepened.

"There's no way to know if she'll react the same way again."

Her brother scoffed.

"She's always had a soft spot for you. None of the other knights bothered themselves with watching our telekinetic lessons, and yet, she consistently found time to observe. She always made sure you saw her nods of encouragement," his tone developed a biting edge. "She didn't even flinch when I hurt myself fighting her. Mother's cries for help fell on deaf ears. She only stopped because of you."

"Two years have passed since then. A lot can change during that time. We certainly have. It's foolish to believe she hasn't too. Your plan's success hinges on putting ourselves at the whims of her mercy yet again."

"It's called a calculated risk. Much as I hate to admit it, the witch has a heart. When every other effort to bring her back failed, that's how Father finally pierced her armor. She evaded his mercenaries. Overwhelming her with numbers didn't work. She only bent to his will after he used her grandfather as bait. As much as we need to learn from his errors, we should copy his successes as well."

A cold sweat broke out across her body.

"Sparing us will be the witch's undoing. Once we take her out, it will be *our* names who strike fear in the hearts of men."

Felix raised his fist into the air, nostrils flared and jaw clenched.

"We will lay waste to everyone and everything that stands in our path to reclaiming Arcelia. Once I reclaim my throne, we will sail across the ocean and unleash hell on those abominable islanders. We will wipe them from the face of the earth for what they've done to my kingdom."

His blue eyes landed on hers, wild with untamed, feral rage. Oddly, Sage thought his skin looked a little paler than normal.

"You can transform the air itself into water and fire. I think it's time you learned how to transmute a living being."

A bird screed overhead. Sage looked up to see a golden eagle gliding through the air, its wings spread outward as it scanned the ground below. Her stomach twisted into knots.

Felix pulled a dagger from his waistband.

"Let's set up a trap now, shall we?"

Moonlight illuminated the red undertones of the blood-stained dirt, and a small blade rested in tufts of fur and clumps of bone. Dampness cooled Sage's thighs as she wiped her palms on her pants. She rolled her neck to loosen the band tension wrapped around her head and shoulders.

Sage picked up the blade and examined it. She'd done as Felix had asked of her—transforming the body of a living being into a weapon. A hollowness left her feeling empty.

This time it had just been a squirrel, but eventually, as they continued down this path, she would have to do the same to another person. She squeezed her hands, now slick with sweat. The blazing flames of the tavern scathed her memories. Their blood-curdling howls of pain still grated against her ears.

The inferno had consumed them all indiscriminately. No...no *the* inferno—*her* inferno.

Every extinguished life had been by her hand. And they'd done nothing to deserve it. She and Felix had entered the establishment and wreaked havoc on people simply going about their lives. They weren't any different than the omens that had usurped their throne.

Sage frowned. She didn't know how they were supposed to reclaim their home without harming the people they were supposed to protect.

She tore her gaze away from the remnants of the small rodent, her eyes falling on her brother, whose light snores filled the night. He lay just a few feet away with his back toward her.

Sage slumped over on her side and covered her mouth with her hand as she tried and failed to choke back a giggle. Felix stirred but did not move.

Tremors raced up her arms as Sage forced herself upright. Despite the darkness of the night, her world shimmered and sparkled. Felix glowed like a beacon, more brilliant than the gentle moonlight. Without consciously deciding to do so, she raised her hand, spurred on by a sudden indescribable need.

She curled her fingers. The vitality around her brother shifted. Just a little more and she could—

A loud crash and the ground shaking beneath her feet broke her concentration. Felix rolled over.

"What the–you're still at it?" he groggily rubbed his eyes.

Sage shoved her hands into her lap.

"J-just getting some training in. Like you s-said," her words slurred together.

Felix crossed his arms and frowned. He picked up the blade.

"You made this? From that tiny little squirrel?" he asked, examining the metal. Her head bobbed up and down in response.

"The blade's a bit dull. And it took you a few hours to complete. You should strive to be like Old Lady T when she took out that mob. It needs to be instantaneous."

To her surprise, he patted her head.

"But, for a first try, this is decent."

Despite the tension in her chest, she managed a small smile. Another boom quaked in the distance, along with shouting voices.

"W-what was that?" It felt as if fur coated her tongue.

Felix's vitality surged and their handful of belongings slowly levitated into their respective satchels.

"Let's go find out," he said.

She trailed close behind him and they followed the sound of the commotion. A shape peeked over the tops of the massive trees that filled the mountain slope. Sage squinted and thought she saw people on it, though it was much too far to be certain. They looked like ants compared to the tower's size, especially with the darkness of the night shrouding them.

It took a few minutes to close the distance and get a better view. Dozens of people worked on the tower. A massive piece of metal floated in their air as telekinetic mages moved supplies to and fro. At the top of the structure, people had attached themselves to it with harnesses as they installed thickly braided metal ropes.

Felix stumbled and Sage caught him with her magic.

"Watch your step," she whispered.

They inched closer. Sage had to crane her neck to look up the tower's height and still couldn't see the top.

"What in the realms are they doing?" Felix grumbled, rubbing his forehead.

"Are you feeling alright?" she asked.

"I'm fine," he whispered, waving her off.

Shimmering figures approached from the right. Sage grabbed Felix and pulled him into the foliage. A trio of men passed by each carrying lumber. A woman wearing face paint and two swords on her hips followed a few paces behind. Sage blanched.

Darkness encapsulated the warrior—she didn't glow in Sage's vision like the men did. Sage couldn't sense even the faintest whiff of her vitality. She cast a worried glance at her brother.

"Looks like they're hanging a massive carriage on that tower. I think we've caught up to the ropeways Old Lady T mentioned. This is good," he said.

"A warrior is with them. I don't see how this is good."

"It's perfect. It means we're close enough to their regular stomping grounds that we can track their patterns."

Sage frowned at the woman's retreating form.

"I can't see her vitality. I can see yours and the men's. But not hers."

"Can't sense her vitality...," he rubbed his chin. "That plant that Father used, it cut off a mage's ability to sense magic. He said he found it in the mountains, back when his parents tried to strengthen diplomatic ties with the warriors. I wonder if she's carrying it with her."

She studied her brother's face. The gears turned with each passing second.

"Father tried to snuff out the blood mage's magic and that wasn't enough to subdue her," she cautioned.

"That may be so, but there may be ways the warriors utilize it that he was never aware of. I doubt his means of deploying it were the most efficient. Plus, we need to think ahead about our return to Arcelia. Aside from the blood mage, it worked on other omens. At the very least, we can use it against the island invaders."

"So you think we can steal it from a warrior? That sounds reckless. Fatally so."

"So does killing a blood mage. And yet, that's precisely why we're here to begin with."

Sage looked at her feet.

"It just seems like an unnecessary risk on top of everything else."

"It's riskier to face her when you haven't prepared yourself to do what it takes. You lack grit, Sage. If I had your power, I'd...," he trailed off. "We're too deep in mountaineer territory for any slip-ups. We'll start off with simple reconnaissance. And when the moment is right, we'll strike. Alright?"

"Alright," Sage sighed.

"Good," Felix yawned. "Now that we know what the commotion is, I'm going back to sleep."

He pulled his blanket from his bag and unrolled it on the grass. Sage followed suit but couldn't bring herself to lay down. She sat with her knees huddled to her chest and gazed toward the nighttime sky. A constellation of stars twinkled overhead. She imagined herself back in Arcelia, where her castle bedroom had a similar view. She would sit on her bed while Mother brushed her hair before going to sleep.

A tear slid down Sage's cheek. She'd become the living embodiment of everything her parents despised.

If she and Felix saved Arcelia, if they freed their people from the omens, then Father and Mother would overlook her transgressions.

Wouldn't they?

Sage lay on her side and closed her eyes to keep the dam from bursting. She sent another silent prayer to the Angels, asking for guidance and protection and most importantly, forgiveness. She'd already committed many sins, and for what her and her brother planned to accomplish, many more lay in the path ahead.

Chapter 24

Human Realm, Mount Illiniza, Windhaven Village

A rat's high pitched chirps filled the air as the trap door shut behind it. Haizea crouched down in front of the tiny cage and its beady eyes met hers. It gnawed on the bars, trying to escape. In one swift motion, she unlatched the door and caught the rodent by the base of its tail before it could flee.

She unsheathed the blade strapped to her ankle and made a small cut in its flesh. Blood bubbled forth. Haizea closed her eyes and steadied herself as she concentrated on the rat's vitality.

Pull.

Its life force flowed into her. She worked to keep the brunt of her magic at bay to keep from draining it entirely. Slow. Steady. Controlled.

Haizea commanded each individual particle of vitality and closely monitored the levels within the rat. Its body condition diminished little by little. When the balance began to tilt toward the point of no return, she paused, took a deep breath, and focused.

Push.

A wall of resistance blunted her efforts. Haizea pushed harder, and it felt like she was trying to roll a boulder up a hill. She lost her footing and went tumbling under its massive weight, gravity bearing down on her.

The rat squealed as she inadvertently absorbed more of its vitality. Its body shriveled further. A bead of sweat trickled down her forehead. Haizea rolled up her sleeves and exhaled.

Slow. Steady. Controlled.

She groaned in frustration after a few moments—she couldn't quite build the momentum to reverse the flow of her magic. She frowned at the animal. The sun's light beamed down on her, warming her skin.

An idea formed. Haizea flicked open her blade and dragged it along her palm. She pressed it against the rat.

Movement. Slow as molasses, but her vitality obeyed her command. Bit by bit, the rat's body condition returned to normal. Haizea sank back and rested on her haunches, astonished.

It worked. It actually worked.

Haizea suppressed the fleeting beat of her heart. She couldn't let herself get carried away—one lone rat was a far cry from a human being. It did not lure her in nearly as strongly and yet she'd nearly killed it. For what she intended to do, she couldn't afford any mistakes. A single slip in her concentration, even for a moment, and she'd do something irreversible.

But it was a first step. A means to an end. She would practice the technique. Master it. Just like Grandfather taught her—first the animals, and then her fellow man.

Wanting to observe how it fared over time, she moved the rat into a small enclosure that was more suitable for habitation than her trap.

Resting on the ground beside the rat's cage were her pendant, one of her father's rings, and three empty vials, stained red with blood. Her fingers pulsed as she gathered her belongings, which radiated with energy. She stumbled as she rose—a faintness nearly overwhelmed her. But rather than the giddiness of the Cosmic high, she felt drained.

She waited a few seconds to reorient herself before making her way back inside the cabin. Her body swayed and her feet hit the ground heavier than normal.

The letter Kallistê had sent regarding their trip to Kestramore had been sitting on the counter for weeks now. The time for the visit was nearly upon them.

My dearest friend Haizea,

I'm certain my letter will find you well. Your mountaineer garb won't be suitable for the island's tropical climate, so I'll personally curate your wardrobe—just send me your measurements.

This is a historic moment for the island—we've not had a foreign visitor step foot on our shores for several decades. Though my people prefer to keep to themselves, as a fellow omen, I'm certain you'll find yourself right at home. I'm excited for you to see everything Kestramore has to offer. With this, my quest for a united coalition of omens throughout the realm will be one step closer to being fulfilled.

Best wishes,

Queen Kallistê

As Haizea set the letter down, static filled her vision and the room swirled around her. She rubbed her temples to fend off the wave of lightheadedness.

A handful of pastries rested on the counter—Alastair had left earlier in the morning to set up his stand at the marketplace. He wouldn't return until late in the evening, as he planned to visit the monastery—he'd started spending even more time there after learning about Kallistê's invitation to Kestramore. Haizea bit into one of the tarts and the sweet taste of apples and cinnamon greeted her. Though she hoped to replenish some of her energy, faint tremors ran up and down her arms.

The portraits above the mantel caught her eye and her delighted hum turned into a wistful sigh. She picked one up, her throat tightening at Alastair's dimpled smile. He looked so healthy and–despite everything that had happened to him–happy.

Alastair would not meet his end that way. He *could not*.

The rat's chirps flowed in through the open window. Haizea set the portrait down and leaned on the sill to get a better view. She stilled.

The animal's body condition had already deteriorated. In just that short time span, it already looked noticeably smaller and slightly hunched. Haizea's brows drew together. She didn't know what to make of the rat's sudden afflictions.

She'd used her power with careful precision, yet somehow she had still erred. Tightness coiled in her belly as the cost of failure loomed over her head. What if this happened with Alastair? What if her attempts to remedy his illness ended up exacerbating it instead? Or worse.

Sweat slicked Haizea's palms, but her body moved with a deceptive calmness as she made her way back outside. Gentle chirps of nearby birds filled the backdrop as she set up another trap. This time she had failed, but she would practice and try again until she perfected her technique.

She had no other choice not to.

"This realmdrifter, Kallistê, she seems a bit pompous. I know she offered you protection from the bounty during your time in Arcelia, but jog my memory about her again," Vendela said.

The trio sat around Vendela's dining room table. Shauni had turned one of the chairs around and sat with her arms resting on the back.

"The most dangerous thing about her isn't her magic–it's her charm. For a little while, Alastair and I stayed in her castle, she had her servants wrapped around her finger. It's not like it was a secret that she'd assassinated their rulers either–they didn't care. I'd think she was an enchantress if I hadn't seen her realmdrift with my own eyes."

"Ah. You think she'll try to swoon me too?" Shauni arched an eyebrow.

"She'll do anything if you allow her to."

"Beautiful *and* ruthless. I'll be sure to stay on my toes then."

"What else should we know?" Vendela asked.

Haizea hummed and pursed her lips.

"From what I can tell, not everyone on Kestramore agrees with her actions on the continent. Right now, her focus seems to just be on the major kingdoms and the island, but I don't trust her as far as I can see her."

"So the day may come when she sets her sights on our homelands. It sounds like she only extends her respect towards omens," Vendela said.

"We're more than a bunch of omens. They need to respect us as mountaineers as a whole, not just for our magic," Shauni said.

"Which is why it's a good thing that you're going. I think you have a solid plan of action...but I also think it's incredibly dangerous. The last time one of my warriors ventured so far from home, things didn't go so well."

Haizea's cold visage hardened into a deep grimace. Shauni punched her shoulder.

"That's because she went alone. Warriors always travel in twos. We'll make light work of those islanders if they give us any trouble."

Haizea's pendant brushed against her skin, eliciting a rush through her magic. With it came the sound of her mother's voice.

"Anyone who wishes to bring me harm does not deserve mercy. It doesn't matter how long we've known each other."

"It won't be like last time," she said, clenching the jewelry in her fist.

Vendela's deep blue gaze softened. She surprised Haizea when she reached across the table and squeezed her other hand.

"Have you gotten started on the preparations?"

"Yes. I took care of everything earlier this morning. We're ready."

"Good. And you're certain Alastair is up for the task?"

"He's the reason I was able to destroy an entire army. Not to mention, one of the monks at the monastery has taken him under their wing over the last several months. He's always been a powerful mage, but he now has the control to match. He can...," Haizea trailed off, still in disbelief about it all. "He's learned how to contact the Soul Reaper at will. Rest assured, Alastair can handle himself."

Vendela and Shauni's eyebrows rose in unison.

"Mediums can *do* that?" Shauni asked.

"Trust me, if I hadn't seen it for myself, I'd say it wasn't possible."

"This is as much about gathering knowledge as it is about putting on a strong front for us mountaineers. Reveal only as much information as necessary, while gleaning as much as possible. Be safe, but more importantly, be smart. Look out for one another," Vendela said.

Shauni's violet gaze darkened.

"Always."

Haizea nodded.

"Shauni, I'm nearly finished with forging the items you'll need. Haizea, if the realmdrifter contacts you again, let me know right away."

"Of course," Haizea said.

Shauni stood up and flipped her chair around before pushing it back under the table. She squeezed their leader's shoulder with a broad grin. Vendela offered her a pinched smile and gently uncurled Shauni's fingers from her body.

"I know I don't say it as often as I should, especially to fully fledged warriors like yourselves, but I'm proud of you both," the crows' feet around Vendela's eyes revealed themselves.

"Thank you, Vendela," Haizea said. Shauni nodded beside her.

The door closed behind them, and the duo strolled down the walkway. Haizea stretched, popping her shoulders and twisting her back.

"Do you want to come over for dinner?" she asked.

"Do I want a free meal? Hell yes."

"Good. Because I'll need your help cooking it."

Shauni snorted.

"I usually cook when Alastair is out all day. I set aside some goat meat this morning. It should be thawed by now. I'm going to make stew with it, so there'll be plenty to go around. If you chop everything up, I'll take care of the rest."

Shauni chuckled. Her ankle knives began floating in the air and she twirled them around her head with her magic.

"I am pretty good with a blade. I guess I can help."

Chapter 25

Human Realm, Mount Illiniza, Heaven's Breath Village

Thunder clapped in Sage's head and her expression crumpled with pain. Felix lagged behind her, wheezing as he struggled to keep up. An inexplicable fatigue had afflicted them over the last few days and it only worsened the higher they climbed.

Felix stumbled into a tree and sank to the ground. Sage crouched down in front of him and pressed her hand against his forehead. He didn't have a fever, but his skin was pale and blue tinted the tips of his fingers.

"Felix?" she asked.

His head lulled to the side.

She stood upright only to lose her balance from a dizzy spell of her own. She took one step forward and narrowly caught herself on the tree when her knees buckled beneath her.

Sage squinted against the brilliant rays of sunlight beaming down on her. Trees surrounded them as far as the eye could see. They were between villages once again, but unlike before, a paved walkway provided a path for them to follow. If she kept going, she should be able to reach the next village and get help. But that meant leaving Felix behind.

Her fingers dug into the bark and she frowned, hesitating where she stood.

Sage tried lifting him with her magic, hoping to carry him with her, but her vision flashed with white at the effort and her brother's body slipped from her grasp.

She patted his cheek. All she could see were the whites of his eyes.

"Felix, I'm going to get help. Just stay there until I get back. Alright?"

No response. Sage rummaged through her satchel and draped her blanket over his shoulders. One of Felix's knives caught her eye. Her heart thudded in her chest as she rested her hand on the handle. He would tell her to take it.

She let it go.

Sage continued down the walkway without Felix or his blade. For the first time in two years, she didn't hear the heavy thump of his footsteps, or the constant mutterings under his breath, or the way he ground his teeth in frustration. It was just her, alone on the mountain.

She shivered—that all too familiar itch that she could not physically scratch reemerged.

Snap.

Frost dusted her fingertips. The action did not offer nearly as much relief as it did before. She yearned for the rush she'd felt with the squirrel, from transmuting life itself.

She shook her head. The warriors patrolled this part of the mountain and chances of running into them again were much higher now. She couldn't afford to lose focus. Sage shoved her hands into her pockets to quell her desires.

Follow the path. Find help. Return to Felix.

Sage kept walking.

Log cabins and loud voices led Sage to the next village. Towering over the massive trees, a pylon lined the sky. The ground shook beneath her feet, accompanied by a distantly familiar clopping sound. She jumped out of the way as a horse trotted by, with a man on its saddle. The animal had a cart attached to it with multiple carcasses lying on top.

Sage stared at him as he stepped down. He wore a quiver on his back that held at least a dozen arrows.

A cool breeze brushed against her skin, spiking her magic yet again. Sage pulled her jacket from her satchel and slipped it over her arms. The temperature had plummeted as they'd ascended the slope. It felt as if they'd passed some invisible tipping point over the last week or so.

Her legs wobbled as she moved closer to read one of the signs by the walkway. The letters blurred together and it took her a few breaths to reorient herself.

Arrows on the sign pointed toward the marketplace, public toilets, a monastery, and various other locations. Felix would benefit from a healer, but nothing on the sign indicated where she could find one—and that was assuming the village had one to begin with. Due to the magical subtype's rarity, healers were hard to come by.

Sweat trickled down her neck. Sage knew of only one healing mage who lived in Illiniza. What if she asked for a healer and the villagers brought *her* here?

A potion. Anyone could craft a potion. She may not be able to diagnose an ailment like a healer could, but even a non-mage could throw plants and herbs together.

She'd go to the marketplace and see what she could find.

An herbalist's shop was located toward the center of the shopping center. Sage hesitated by the door. She didn't even know what sort of plants Felix might need.

A man approached one of the shelves and picked up a plant. He walked with a noticeable limp, but, strangely, a large ax hung from a strap on his waist. The scent of timber trailed behind him.

She crept closer to get a better look. The label identified it as mirwort. She'd seen that before, in the Royal Palace. Sage put a bundle in her basket.

"You look a little uncertain," the man commented.

She gripped her basket and shifted her weight.

"I..." she trailed off.

A white tint furled in the corners of her vision and with it, a faintness that nearly made her knees buckle. She blinked, struggling to focus.

"My brother's not feeling well. He needs a potion, but I'm not sure what to get him."

The man rubbed his chin.

"Well, the bad news is, this village doesn't have a healer. The good news is, I've seen a healer often enough back in Windhaven that I've got a good idea of which plants do what. If you tell me what's wrong with him, I might be able to help."

"We...our village was attacked a few months ago. So we've been traveling up the mountain to find a safe place to call home. He was fine up until recently. He passed out."

He frowned.

"You came all the way from the base?"

Sage nodded.

"Sounds like mountain sickness. Your bodies haven't adjusted to the thinner air. You look a bit pale yourself."

"Mountain sickness," the words felt frothy on her tongue. "How do we treat it?"

The man motioned for her to follow as he picked up a variety of plants.

"Now, again, I'm no healer. A potion *should* stave off the worst of it. But until you acclimate, I wouldn't suggest traveling any further. The air only gets thinner the higher you go. Worst case scenario, you have to go back down the slope to an elevation your body can tolerate," he explained.

Sage pursed her lips, imagining Felix's inevitable conniption fit upon hearing this.

She followed the man to the shop counter. To her surprise, he paid for the items and handed her the bundle of plants and herbs.

"Now with this potion, it's a little different than what you're probably used to. It works best if you boil it so that you can inhale the plant's vapors."

"Thank you, sir," she said.

"You can call me Jorah."

"I'm...I'm Sienna."

He huffed a quiet laugh.

"It's a pleasure to meet you, Sienna. I hope your brother feels better. If you need anything else, I'm working on the pylon construction. You can't miss it."

The man limped away. Sage started to do the same, but she couldn't remember which direction she came from. She paused and read a nearby sign. The words jumbled together. Nausea roiled in her belly.

She didn't know how to get back to Felix.

Her legs buckled beneath her and she hit the dirt face first. The white haze obscuring the corners of her vision overtook her entirely.

"—me move her."

Warm hands pressed against Sage's skin as they set her upright. The world spun around her.

"—fire started—hand me—."

A tangy scent wafted into Sage's nose. She breathed. Several minutes ticked by before the dizziness subsided, but a faint buzz replaced it. A desire that made her vitality pulse. Her fingers rubbed together subconsciously but she managed to stop herself. Sage opened her eyes. Unfamiliar faces surrounded her, brows upturned and eyes wide with concern.

"Thank Aaryn," one of them breathed.

Sage stiffened. A Demon. They'd uttered a Demon's name—*thanked* them. She tried to shift away from them but her back hit something hard. A rough texture grated against her fingers. Tree bark.

Trapped. She was surrounded on all sides like a rat in a lion's den.

The man–Jorah–was amongst the strangers. He held the potion to her nose. Something in his expression gave her pause. She couldn't pinpoint it. Mistrust? Suspicion? In either case it added to her rising panic.

Pressure built behind her temples, replacing the lightheadedness from before. Her limbs tingled with pins and needles as energy built within. Just as she pressed her fingers together again a breeze brushed against her skin. Her hands flew to her neck.

Her enchanted choker wasn't there.

"You must be looking for this," one of the strangers said. "Thought it would be easier to breathe without it. It broke when we took it off."

She snatched the jewelry back and shrank back against the tree. Her eyes locked with Jorah. He knew her face. Her *real* face. This high up the mountain, how likely was it that he would cross paths with the blood mage?

Her breath hitched in her throat.

The seer. A tavern full of people burned in her wake. Felix would tell her to add these men to the pile to cover her tracks.

"The people we cross paths with may seem like innocent bystanders, but their very existence is an assault on ours."

Wrong. Felix was wrong. Miss Tamsyn, Bose—they'd helped them.

"That voice is lying to you, Sage."

Stars flickered in and out of her vision. Her body tingled. She curled her hands into fists, suppressing the urge, fighting the itch.

Sage wheezed. She couldn't breathe. Couldn't think. She squeezed her eyes shut and clutched her pounding temples. She clenched her teeth, desperately trying to contain the energy coiling within.

She would always be running, always be hiding. It would never end.

Her magic ignited.

Jorah's head twisted inside out. His mouth migrated to his throat and his nose receded into his face. His eyes vanished entirely, replaced by a pinkish looking flesh that oozed from his orbitals. He dropped to the ground, motionless.

Sage's laughter punctuated the ensuing screams.

Fire and ice burst forth with each breath, engulfing those before her. Unsatiated, her magic fanned outward and their bodies warped in tandem. Their intestines fell to the ground as their innards swapped places with their skin. The odious stench of bile burned her throat.

Sage buckled under the weight of her magic and vomited, cackling still, even between retches. The soil gave way beneath her fingers, caving to her power. Only once her stomach emptied it its entirety did her magic calm.

She sat on her haunches and balked as the full brunt of the grotesque scene looked her in the eye. Blood stained the grass beneath her feet. Limbs twisted and curled in unnatural directions.

Bones jutted from broken bodies with peculiar protrusions on the surface–hair, skin, scales, even feathers. Sage dry heaved, but nothing came out.

The container with the potion rested on the ground. Right. Felix needed it. Sage picked it up in a daze. Although she walked with purpose, her mind floated into the clouds. Another giggle bubbled forth.

She wanted–she didn't mean to—she'd never–

Sage clutched her head with trembling hands. Her power had done this. *She* had done this. Tears streamed down her cheeks as her laughter pierced through the night.

Chapter 26

Human Realm, Island of Kestramore, Khisfire Province

The fabric of Alastair's shirt clung to his skin, drenched with sweat. Heat rolled off the ground in visible waves and his feet cooked inside his shoes.

~*How the hell do they live like this?*~ Shauni signed as beads of moisture dripped down her forehead.

Having realmdrifted the three of them to Kestramore, Haizea's eyes blazed like a fire and her magic burned against his Soul. She fanned herself by tugging at her collar a few times.

They'd done their best to prepare by leaving their coats at home and wearing thinner clothing, but even a warm day in the mountains paled in comparison to the island's sweltering heat.

Kallistê threw her head back in what looked like a hearty chuckle, her sleek blue tresses shining under the sunlight. She turned her beaming smile on Shauni.

~*You have a lovely sense of humor,*~ her signing was still slow, but smoother than it had been the last time Alastair had crossed paths with her.

Shauni's dark eyes trained on the realmdrifter. She didn't have a hard stare like Haizea did–her expression was neither warm nor cold, but she did not seem particularly amused with Kallistê. Alastair couldn't be certain though–Shauni had adorned the earth's smoke shortly after arriving here, which cut off his ability to sense her emotions. She'd transported it in a dense metal tin that sealed its effects until they arrived.

Kallistê patted down her dress—with its thin fabrics, she showed no signs of overheating like their trio. She fiddled with one of the rings on her fingers and a wave of anger emanated from the realmdrifter, putting Alastair on high alert. It took him a moment to realize it was more intense than just anger—it was hatred.

His eyes narrowed on Kallistê, but she did as she always did and flashed a bright, unperturbed smile. He hooked his finger through Haizea's and tugged her a little closer. Unable to sense Shauni's Soul, he made it a point to keep her in his line of sight.

Kallistê led them around a mansion—smaller than the castle in Llyr, but much larger than the average cabin back home in Windhaven. They passed the front entrance altogether and entered via a back door. Kallistê's lips moved, and she fumbled a little as she signed, so Haizea stepped in to translate.

~*Your attendance is a surprise so you'll be quartered in this wing rather than the main one. The Premier's estate spreads across five acres of land. After the current Premier retires, the newly elected successor will move in. I spent all day yesterday decorating for tonight,*~ she explained.

The farewell ball did not begin for several more hours, but Kallistê had asked them to come earlier to give them enough time to prepare with hair, make-up, and the like.

~*Each Premier has their portrait taken at the beginning of their term. Premier Eryx is the longest-serving government official in Kestramore's history. Her portrait is much more youthful than what she looks like today.*~

The ceiling towered high above and a long line of portraits hung on both walls in the hallway. The last portrait on the wall was of a young woman. She had brown skin with a distinct red undertone and thick jet black hair. A nameplate identifying her as Eryx was placed below.

~All of Kestramore's leaders are Cosmic Arts practitioners. Premier Eryx is a transmuting mage. When I left the Three Corners to learn the secrets of realmdrifting, she took me under her wing and helped me get connected with a teacher. She'll be elated to find out that you've come, Haizea. You have my sincerest appreciation for doing me this favor.~

For once, Alastair detected a hint of candor from the realmdrifter. She lingered in front of Eryx's portrait, her expression somber. When she turned to face them, a faint gleam lit in her eyes.

Kallistê led them down a hallway with several rooms and numerous servants running about.

~Take your pick,~ she signed.

Although experience told him that Kallistê was a hospitable host, she had political motivations for inviting them. Not to mention, Alastair knew nothing of the rest of the islanders. To say that things had gone awry the last time he'd been caught in the middle of political disarray would be an understatement.

Back then, Haizea constantly had to protect him, but things had changed since then. *He* had changed. He'd spent months under Pamin's wing—and the Soul Reaper's. The entity's presence persisted in the back of his mind, even now. If this visit turned sour, Alastair would not let his training go to waste.

He would protect Haizea, just as she had protected him.

Alastair and Haizea took one room while Shauni went to the one directly across from them. They'd barely crossed the threshold before servants began pouring in. Some of them carried food and refreshments while others held garments in their hands. One of them spoke to Haizea as they showed her a pallet with a variety of rainbow colors. Haizea combed over them before pointing at a few. The servant dipped their chin and scurried off.

Alastair grabbed an overflowing handful of the snacks they provided–a wide array of fruits he'd never seen before. They ranged from tart to sweet and from juicy to dry. As he munched on them, he took note of the clothing items the servants had hung in the room. They'd given them each matching sets to choose from—one was jet black while the other was a bright red.

His outfits were more or less the same outside of the change in color—a soft, short sleeved shirt with a pair of pants made of breathable material. For Haizea, the red outfit was a long dress with a plunging neckline. The black outfit was a two-piece skirt set with a thigh-high slit on each side and a bra-like top.

Haizea stood beside him and scrunched her nose.

~*You don't like it,*~ he signed.

~*Kallistê expects me to squeeze into this?*~

Alastair grinned as her ever-present scowl deepened on her full lips.

~*It suits the climate. Much more so than what we're wearing now.*~

He grabbed the dress and guided her in front of the mirror. Alastair held it in front of her for a few moments before Haizea took it from his hands.

~*Red makes your skin glow. The dress suits you.*~

Her eyes met his in the mirror's reflection and the harshness in her expression eased. She hung the garment back on the rack.

~*I'm a sweaty mess. I should bathe before I try it on,*~ she looked him up and down. ~*You should too.*~

Alastair shrugged out of his sweat-soaked clothes while Haizea sat on the edge of the tub and turned the faucet. As it filled, she tied up her hair to keep it from getting wet—she donned fresh braids for the occasion. They both eased into the water. The tub was massive, much larger than what they had at home. Not quite enough room to fully stretch his legs, but enough that they could both sit comfortably.

~*I think this might be even more extravagant than Llyr's Royal Palace,*~ he signed.

~Kallistê never does anything halfway, I'll give her that.~

He rubbed his thumb along the ring on his finger and the jewelry sent soft vibrations rolling across his skin. Haizea had given him the ring to wear for the duration of their trip. She'd instructed him not to take it off for any reason. Not even for a second.

Alastair grabbed the container of shampoo and lathered his hair. Haizea motioned for him to come closer and took over, massaging her fingers against scalp before rinsing it away. After she finished, neither of them made haste to leave—he leaned back against her and she wrapped her arms around him. The water chilled against his skin, keeping him cool despite their intertwined forms.

He closed his eyes and let the tendrils of his magic fan outward. Haizea's Soul burned against his, brilliant with an undercurrent of ferocity. Just outside of their room, the Souls of servants flitted to and fro. Alastair counted at least a hundred more within the mansion's vicinity.

Not all of them were of this realm. One Soul had a barely contained savagery to it. Too wild to be an animal. A Beast, maybe? Without the guide Pamin had given him to reference, he couldn't be certain, but it carried similar traces to what he'd sensed before in his meditation sessions.

Alastair's brows drew together. Was the Beast's presence simply a peculiar custom among the islanders? Or did Kallistê have something up her sleeve?

Haizea pressed her lips against his temple, pulling his focus back to the physical world. The call of Souls faded, but the Soul Reaper's presence dwelled in the background.

Always watching. Always waiting.

Only a moment away if Alastair needed him.

He caressed his thumb along the back of Haizea's hand before getting out of the tub. He helped her slip into her dress before putting on his own outfit.

~*How do I look?*~ she asked.

Haizea had been right about one thing—it was much more form-fitting than it had even looked on the hanger. It accentuated her curves while simultaneously highlighting the strength in her physique. He could make out the musculature in her legs and the hard lines of her abdomen.

~*Beautiful. And a little terrifying. Like always.*~

Her lips flickered, almost smiling, but not quite. Despite her muted outward reaction, warmth filled Alastair from within, latching onto his Soul. He found himself offering her a beaming smile of his own. For just a breath, Haizea returned it.

She quickly sobered.

~*After what happened with Grandfather, I told myself I'd never get involved with the kingdom's affairs again. Now I'm here on a strange island, inserting myself into foreign matters yet again,*~ she shook her head.

~*When King Rhys was chasing after you, you tried to do everything by yourself. Whatever happens tonight, you're not alone,*~ Alastair signed.

Haizea searched his gaze.

~*That's what worries me the most.*~

Her attention snapped toward the door. Haizea opened it and the servants from earlier entered. Their mouths moved and a moment later, they were wrapping a long robe over her dress and sitting her down in a chair. Then, they proceeded to paint her face with glittering gold eyeshadow, vibrant crimson lipstick, and a full contour with blush.

A few came over to him and dusted his face—nothing as eye-catching as Haizea's, just a light contour. After the servants left, he crouched down and helped her put on her shoes—wedge sandals that nearly made her height match his. He held out his arm and Haizea looped her hand in the crook of his elbow. They crossed the hall to fetch Shauni.

Their friend emerged wearing a sheer black top and pants with heavy jewelry to match.

A mischievous grin spread across her lips.

~Let's go see what these islanders are about.~

Kallistê stood atop the balcony, watching as guests rolled into the Premier's mansion. Her eyes narrowed when Viltarin entered with a man on his arm–the same one she'd seen him walking on the beach with. They each sported a tattoo on their middle finger. Though she couldn't be absolutely certain from this distance, they looked identical. Viltarin's gaze met hers and he sent the man away before making his way up the stairs.

"What a lovely party you've put together," he put a hand on her shoulder. "I presume your friend accepted the invitation?"

Kallistê didn't respond right away, her eyes tracking Viltarin's guest. He squeezed her shoulder and she suppressed a wince as small pinpricks assaulted her.

"I know what you're thinking. And *you* know that you'll be long dead before you can touch him. Now, I believe I asked you a question that still needs answering. I'm sure you'd hate for me to make you grovel in front of a crowd, but if you continue to test my patience, I'll have no choice."

Kallistê's sapphire eyes hardened as she turned to the curse mage.

"Be my guest."

"Excuse me?"

"Do it, Viltarin. You've been threatening me for months now. *Make me.* I wonder what all these witnesses would have to say about you treating their host in such a denigrating manner."

Viltarin blinked. He opened his mouth to speak but stopped short as the magical pressure in the room intensified. Behind him, Haizea, Alastair, and Shauni entered the fray.

"There's your new pet. What was it you were saying about a leash?" A few people passing by looked up at Kallistê's raised voice.

"If you're nice, I'm sure she won't bite," she whispered into Viltarin's ear as the trio closed the distance.

I hope she drains you where you stand, but if not, the satisfaction of your undoing will be mine, she thought.

The weight of Haizea's magic pressed against their bodies. With Alastair in lockstep behind her, it was impossible to tell where hers ended and his began. A woman with violet eyes joined last–a non-mage based on the way the vitality did not shift with her presence. Kallistê tilted her head curiously.

She'd seen how the blood mage prepared for her battle against King Rhys. There wasn't a way in the seven realms that she'd come to the island without some sort of contingency in place. But bringing a non-mage here–to an island of omens–was a peculiar choice beyond Kallistê's comprehension.

"You all look fabulous," Kallistê said.

"Well, you took great lengths to ensure it," Haizea spoke and signed simultaneously.

"Viltarin was just saying how he hoped I'd introduce the two of you," Kallistê motioned toward the curse mage.

Haizea's cold gaze fell to Viltarin, whom she towered over in her sandals. Her irises flickered between light brown and a rich mahogany, the threat of her blood magic on full display.

"I'm eager to put a face to a name that has so much notoriety," he spoke evenly, though his weight shifted ever so slightly.

Viltarin started to hold out his hand but startled when non-mage barked out a laugh. Only then did Viltarin seem to notice the woman with violet eyes.

"So I've heard. Viltarin, is it?" The blood mage looked him up and down. "I'm Haizea, this is Alastair and Shauni. I've much to learn of Kestramore's practices, but I assume that you're one of the dignitaries?"

Viltarin dusted off his top.

"Yes, I represent the people of the Kaladis Province."

"Then I suppose we have common ground that will help us all come to an understanding. We're here to represent the Bayeux Mountain Range."

"I—"

"I'm afraid that's all we have time for right now, Viltarin. We mustn't keep the Premier waiting. She is the guest of honor, after all. There'll be plenty of time and opportunity to catch up later," Kallistê cut Viltarin off with a dismissive wave of her hand.

She twirled the cursed ring on her finger, watching as he returned to his lover. Viltarin wouldn't retaliate so openly, but he would undoubtedly make her pay dearly for her antics. At least, he would try. Kallistê had no intention of allowing that to happen. Before the night was over, one way or another, she would bring the curse mage to ruins.

Chapter 27

Human Realm, Island of Kestramore, Khisfire Province

The mountaineer trio followed Kallistê's floating form through the halls to Premier Eryx's quarters. Shauni picked up her pace and sidled up beside the realmdrifter. It was odd for Haizea to not be able to sense her vitality, but the absence of her magic was the very thing keeping her safe on this island full of omens.

"So, the man we just met, Viltarin. He said he's a dignitary of a...province, you call them? How many of them are there?" Shauni asked.

"There are four: Khisfire, Kaladis, Kastellor and Kyrenia."

"And the dignitaries that rule over each of them?"

Kallistê nodded.

"Yes. There's Viltarin, whom you just met. And also Quatthir, Nehemias, and Lotus."

"And where do you fit into all of this?"

"Aside from ruling over Llyr? I'd consider myself an ambassador. A liaison between the continent and our small island."

"What exactly are you hoping to facilitate?"

Kallistê inclined her head, scrutinizing.

"The island defers to the voice of the populace by allowing them to elect our leaders. Though I find that notion misguided. People are fickle creatures. Easy to persuade and herd like cattle. I see no reason why we should bend to the will of the masses. They should be bending to us."

Alastair tapped on Haizea's hand, pulling her attention away from the conversation.

~Everyone seems nice enough on the surface, but the man we just met...I don't like the looks of him.~

~Frankly, I don't think Kallistê does either. And I don't know how much that should concern me.~

Alastair's periwinkle eyes met hers, stern and without a hint of his usual humor.

~I felt his Soul. I don't like him,~ he reiterated.

Haizea nodded. Alastair could read people in a way she couldn't.

~We'll keep tabs on him then.~

"—two-hundred thousand people on the island. Roughly a quarter of them are Cosmic Arts practitioners. Kestramore's court is constituted entirely of omens."

Haizea perked up that information and relayed it to Alastair.

"What about non-mages?" Shauni asked.

Kallistê chuckled softly.

"That *would* concern you, wouldn't it?"

She stopped at a massive door and pushed it open.

"Here we are," she said.

Inside, a woman sat in a lounge chair. Premier Eryx still had the same reddish brown tone as her younger portrait, but her skin had lost a bit of its elasticity and wrinkles lined her eyes, forehead, and neck. Yet, fascinatingly, her vitality brimmed with energy.

Grandfather Harzel's frail form resurfaced at the sight.

Had she not injured him all those years ago during her training, he would have been just like the Eryx—old and feeble, but with magic just as strong as his youth. His magic would have been strong enough to fend off King Rhys's forces before they cornered him with the earth's smoke.

Haizea's eyes stung, but she maintained a neutral expression.

Alastair's hand pressed against the small of her back. She welcomed the distraction when her magic flared at his touch.

The Premier finished off the drink in her hand before transforming the cup into a cane. She steadied herself on the walking stick and got to her feet.

"Is this her?" Eryx asked. Kallistê nodded and introduced the trio. The Premier greeted each of them with a tight hug, but she smiled more broadly at Haizea.

"It's such a pleasure to finally be able to meet you. I prayed to Aaryn every day for more than twenty years to make King Rhys pay for killing my son. You are my answered prayers."

Shauni took over interpreting while Haizea spoke.

"Thank you for your kind words, Premier. I'm sorry to hear that about your son. I wish things could have been different."

"Me too, my dear. Have a seat. And a glass of wine while we're at it."

Once they were all situated on the various chairs and couches, the Premier reverted her cane back into a glass. Kallistê refilled it for her.

"Tell me more about yourselves. I know you're a blood mage. I can sense that Alastair here is an omen. And Shauni...I don't sense any vitality from you," the Premier's eyes crinkled as she smirked. "Brave of a non-mage to come to an island of omens."

Shauni snorted.

"Oh, believe me, Premier. I'm not trapped here with you. You all are caged here with me."

Eryx's brows arched higher and her mouth slackened. Shauni's violet eyes danced as her lips curved into a wicked grin.

"I've grown up around the Cosmic Arts my entire life. My best friend is a blood mage. The fact that you and your people are omens bears little significance to me."

"That is…an interesting take, to say the least. We've much to learn about you mountaineers."

Haizea met Shauni's eyes and gave a slight nod. This was a good start. They wanted Kestramore to see them not as omens, but to respect them as mountaineers as a whole.

"Haizea and Shauni are a part of a group called the Bruvian warriors, who protect the mountain range's territory," Kallistê said.

"So you act as the mountains' military force?"

"In a sense, yes," Haizea answered.

"Ah. I must assume your presence here is much more than just a favor to Kallistê. This is a diplomatic meeting between the island of Kestramore and the Bayeux Mountain Range."

"Your assumption would be correct."

"Well, as you all know, I'm retiring from my position as Premier. So while I'm happy to address and accommodate any concerns you may have, please know that my power and influence will be limited in the near future."

Haizea hummed.

"I do recall Kallistê getting the runaround from your court back when we first met. So while I may not have knowledge of all of the intricacies, I do understand that no single person makes decisions here. That's a similarity between our homelands and yours. Back in the mountains, power flows between the villagers and the warriors."

"It's good to know we share some common ground. I'm sure you have some topics you'd like to discuss. Please, speak your mind," Premier Eryx said.

Haizea looked between the realmdrifter and Kestramore's top leader.

"There's really only one thing to discuss, which is the treaty that exists between the Bayeux Mountain Range and the neighboring kingdoms. Although leadership in the kingdoms has changed hands, our stance has not. Mountaineers do not take kindly to having our people or our lands trampled on, and in recent months, there have been skirmishes at the base with kingdom dwellers doing precisely that.

"I'd like for relations to remain peaceful between us, but my diplomacy begins and ends with the safety and well-being of my people. As it stands, the Treaty of Certain Demise calls for us warriors to kill any trespassers found in mountaineer territory on sight. If said trespassers are found in any way to be connected to the kingdom's throne, we will take it as an initiation of an act of war. Given the current rulers' ties to the island, Kestramore would also be implicated should such a situation arise," Haizea held the Premier's gaze and she leaned forward, her voice even.

"The mountaineers and the major kingdoms have coexisted peacefully for generations. So long as you abide by the treaty, that peace will continue," Shauni added.

Premier Eryx sat up a little straighter and studied them. Kallistê leaned over and whispered in Eryx's ear and the older woman sighed deeply.

"I will do everything in my power to ensure that my successor respects your borders while staying true to Kestramore's newest endeavors."

Haizea nodded. Things were on the right track, but it almost felt too easy. Alastair must have thought the same—he rested his hand on her leg and shook his head infinitesimally. He stared intently at the far corner of the room, his eyes narrowed. Based on the way his vitality waxed and waned, he was seeing something she could not see. Haizea squeezed his hand in acknowledgment before returning her attention to the Premier.

"You mentioned that King Rhys killed your son. I presume this is because he was an omen?" Haizea probed.

Eryx cleared her throat.

"Decades ago, King Rhys's father approached our island and claimed he desired to warm up relations between our peoples. Personally, I was ambivalent to the endeavor, but my son, Mericus, took a liking to Arcelia's crowned prince. I foolishly allowed Mericus to attend mage school in Arcelia. Years went by without incident, but the night of King Rhys's coronation, his brother went missing. According to the king, they found his mangled body shortly after. He accused Mericus of killing him with transmutation, but Mericus had not begun his formal training.

"Here on the island, we don't even begin to teach the Cosmic Arts until adulthood. They were barely of age. And I made sure that Mericus knew the dangers of attempting transmutation before his time. He was a well-behaved boy. I don't believe Mericus committed those heinous acts, but all I've ever had were King Rhys words to go by. He executed my son without so much as a fair trial."

As Premier Eryx dabbed at her eyes, a weight dropped into Haizea's lap. For the first time in the two years since Grandfather Harzel's death, she felt a flicker of understanding.

It wasn't difficult to imagine a teenage boy ignoring his mother's warnings about engaging in Cosmic magic before he was of age. The high was difficult enough to resist as an adult—how much easier would it overwhelm a young person's mind? It happened occasionally in the mountains, not often, but seeing it just once was enough.

If King Rhys's accusations were true, if his best friend truly killed his brother because he couldn't resist the Cosmic high, then he never would have listened to anything Haizea had to say after the attack in Llyr. His stance on forbidding Cosmic Arts had nothing to do with culture—it was personal. Haizea already had a long list of regrets in how she'd handled the situation, but had she known how deep his grudge went and *why*...

She shook her head, dispelling that thought. She couldn't turn back the wheels of time. The damage had been done. Imagining 'what if' would only bring more anguish.

"No parent should ever know what it feels like to lose a child. I'm sorry that happened to you."

"I hope that you never experience it," Premier Eryx pursed her lips. "Did King Rhys have children of his own?"

"He had a son and a daughter."

"And did they share their father's fate?"

Her throat went dry. Alastair caressed his thumb across her thigh.

"No. They shouldn't have to pay for their father's actions."

"And yet your grandfather paid for yours," Eryx took a sip of her drink. "I understand why your conscience barred you from doing such a thing, but from my vantage point you've left two loose ends. You killed their father and left their kingdom in shambles. They know your face and, presumably, your origins in the mountains. Perhaps they did not inherit their father's narrow-minded, violent disposition. But I doubt it."

A fracture inched its way down the side of the glass.

Eryx's words teleported Haizea back to the bunker, suppressed memories resurfacing. Felix's desperate, yet futile attempts to stop her. Sage, cowering in the corner, frozen by fear. Haizea thrusting them into Alastair's army of the dead to get them out of harm's way. It spared them from the sight of their own mother's death, but they knew what fate befell the queen all the same.

Eryx probably came the closest to understanding what she felt toward King Rhys—if not more. King Rhys had killed her son. For as much as Haizea loved her grandfather, it paled in comparison to the precious and irreplaceable bond between a mother and her child.

Irrespective of Mericus's guilt, Eryx had undoubtedly endured unspeakable anguish all these years.

The Premier placed her drink on the table. She clasped her hands together and smiled, but a tightness surrounded her eyes and lips.

"That's enough serious talk for now. This is a party. You three should go back out and enjoy yourself. I'll catch up with you all in a moment. Kallistê, dear, if you don't mind helping me with a few last-minute tasks before I make my official appearance."

With that, the mountaineers had been dismissed.

As Haizea stood to her feet, a pit settled in her stomach. She didn't want to think of children as loose ends, but the question had been gnawing at her since that fateful day in the bunker.

And what disturbed Haizea the most was that the more she stewed over the Premier's words, the more her instincts told her that the older woman was right.

Chapter 28

Human Realm, Mount Illiniza, Windhaven Village

"I've upped the dosage in her potions to help ease her pain. Aside from that, the best thing for her right now is some much needed rest."

Jassia nodded as the healer handed her several bottles. She set them down on the table and handed him a sack of coins. The fabric stretched, threatening to burst at the seams under the currency's weight.

The healer had long stopped charging her family for the hours he spent in their home for her mother's healing sessions, but he purchased the plants and herbs that made the potions and had to balance the cost somehow. Although his prices were fair, a higher dose meant yet another increase in their payments.

Papa was home even less now. The pylon construction project paid well, so he couldn't pass it up. Food filled their pantry. Jassia had brand new clothes for the academy. And, most importantly, they had plenty of money for the healer. But as Jassia looked at her mother's ashen face, her father's absence was much more palpable than the money he'd left behind for them.

"Jassia, training starts soon. You should go," Mama murmured, her voice hollow as she struggled to catch her breath.

Jassia nodded but didn't move.

"I'll be fine. You heard the healer; all I need is a bit of rest. There's no point in staying here and hovering."

Reluctantly, Jassia grabbed her swords. Her skin still had welts and blisters from forging the weapons with her own hands. Now at the age of fourteen, Vendela had finally given her and the other girls in her group permission to train with real blades. As they proved their competency, eventually, Vendela would show the non-mages how to infuse their weapons with earth's smoke.

Jassia paused in the doorway, watching as her mother downed one of her potions.

"Go, Jassia," Mama pressed.

She locked the door shut behind her. Jassia sprinted toward the training grounds, clear on the opposite side of the village. She arrived, sweaty and gasping for air. But at least she made it on time. Covy waved at her and Jassia took her place beside her.

"I heard today's another strength training day," Covy whispered.

Jassia hung her head and sighed, knowing she'd woefully regret sprinting all the way here. She set her weapons down in the storage area and removed her coat. Her muscles coiled with the movement. Over the last year, her body had evolved and grown denser from constant training. Covy watched her as she returned to her spot, a faint blush on her cheeks.

At Vendela's instruction, the young warriors lined up at the bottom of the hill so that they could run drills up and down its incline. They each strapped packs over their shoulders, adding about fifteen pounds to their weight. Jassia's legs burned at the thought alone, but when Vendela whistled, she still gave it her all.

Running cleared her mind. The only thing she could focus on was the exertion it took to keep pace with the rest of the cohort. For the time being, her worries about her parents fell to the background. Covy pulled ahead of her by a few paces. Jassia pumped her legs harder, determined not to fall behind.

She fell into a trance at the sound of her own footsteps and pounding heart, so much so that she didn't notice the falcon swoop down from the sky with a message strapped to its back right away. It took several laps before she realized that Vendela had stopped watching them altogether.

"Yelena and Faryz, a moment please," she called.

She held a letter in her hands. Vendela's lips tightened into a thin line as the two warriors ran over. Jassia struggled to eavesdrop over the sound of her own heavy breathing and the other girls around her.

"–from Heavensbreath village."

Jassia's footsteps faltered. Papa was in Heavensbreath, half way down the mountain. She strained to hear more but couldn't make out the words and started to fall behind. She pushed harder to catch up to Covy and the others.

Vendela walked off and Faryz took her place in watching over the drill while Yelena trailed behind the leader. They went to the storage area and emerged a few moments later with weapons in tow. In addition to dual swords, Vendela sported a bow and arrow. As a mage, Yelena did not retrieve any additional weapons.

They left the training grounds without a word or explanation. The swiftness of their departure made Jassia's stomach churn.

Faryz instructed them to repeat the drill before letting them take a break. Jassia drank a swig of water and pulled Covy aside.

"Vendela bolted," she whispered.

Covy nodded, wiping sweat from her brow.

"Something must have happened. Usually, she sends someone else out. Last time she raced out of here like that was a few years ago, when Haizea sent a letter for help."

"They said something about Heavensbreath village, but I didn't catch anything else. My father's there working on the pylons," Jassia bit her lip.

Covy put her hand on hers.

"If Vendela's going, I'm sure whatever's wrong will be taken care of quickly."

"There are already warriors out there patrolling the project's perimeter. Why didn't they come back themselves?"

"I heard a tavern burned down a while ago. A lot of people died. They never found the culprit, but rumor has it that a mage did it. If something happened in another village, maybe they think it's connected. Probably better for the villagers if they keep a close eye on things until they hear back from Vendela," Covy said.

"The letter is still over there. I...if you could just tell me what it says. I can't go over there without being noticed, but you can. Please."

Covy frowned but nodded and closed her eyes. Jassia silently wished could emulate friend's astral projecting power, but the vitality had not blessed her in such a way. With her brows knitted together in concentration and her eyes still shut, Covy spoke.

"There's been an incident in Heavensbreath village. They found four mangled bodies but can't identify them due to extreme disfigurement. Some of them had axes so at least some of them were lumberjacks. They think a transmutation mage did it due to the nature of the injuries."

Jassia swallowed heavily and wrung her hands together. Four dead bodies. Her father might be fine, but she had no way of knowing. Covy's eyes snapped open and she covered Jassia's hands with her own.

"I wouldn't worry too much until Vendela gets back. They'll confirm everything once they get there. And whoever is responsible will certainly be culled."

Her nails dug into her palms. She tried to respond, but her voice caught in her throat. Faryz instructed them to line up again, bringing their rest period to an end.

The rest of training went by in a daze. Muscles she didn't even realize she had ached. Her arms protested as she packed away her weapons.

"Me and some of the other girls are going to go to the lake tomorrow, since the academy won't be in session. You should come with us," Covy said.

"I..." Jassia trailed off. "I appreciate it, but maybe next time," she said, twiddling her fingers.

"Okay," Covy sighed. "I'll bring something back for you then."

Jassia offered a faint smile. Preoccupied.

"Thanks Covy."

She left the training grounds with the other girls. As they splintered off to head home, Jassia circled back. She concealed herself in the foliage, waiting until the older warriors finally departed. Once the area was clear, she went to the storage area. She slipped a bow and quiver over her shoulders and grabbed a pair of daggers.

As Jassia reached the edge of the training grounds, she paused and glanced behind her. Maybe Covy was right–she should wait and see what news Vendela brings back. She'd already run off once and while she got away with a slap on the wrist, it probably wouldn't go over so well if she did it again.

Still, her mother's pale skin and labored breathing echoed in her mind. She always seemed to be in higher spirits when her father was home. The last time they'd spent some quality time together as a family was the last time she'd snuck off.

Jassia gripped her blades and shook her head. She held her head high, doing her best to block out the way her heart galloped in her chest.

She walked through the village until she reached the pylon. With the first section of the rope way complete, it would take her a little more than halfway to her father. Jassia seated herself in one of the empty cars. All alone, she sent a silent prayer to Aaryn to keep him safe.

Sage fiddled with her fingernails, picking away at the dried blood caked underneath them.

She sat in front of her brother, watching his face intently. His chest rose and fell, but blue tinged the tips of his fingers. The potion container rested on the ground, empty. She had used the last of it the day before, but Felix still had not roused. Only now did he begin to stir, but his return to normal was sluggish.

Most of the potion it had spilled onto the dirt in her haste to escape. There hadn't been much left to properly treat her brother. Maybe if he'd had more, his condition wouldn't still be so poor. Another misstep in a long series of errors.

Felix shifted and she propped him up against a tree trunk to help him sit properly. He groaned as his eyes fluttered open.

"Sage?" he murmured.

"It's me."

"My head is pounding. What in the realms happened?" his words slurred together.

"You passed out. I went to the nearest village to get help and—"

Jorah's head twisted inside out. The stench of blood invaded her nostrils as brain matter oozed from his eye sockets.

Sage swallowed the rising bile in her throat.

"And?" Felix prompted.

"I found an herbalist. They gave me this potion."

Felix rubbed his forehead, and his eyes unfocused. A long stretch of silence passed before he spoke.

"What did you tell them?"

Four broken bodies splayed out before her. Twisted. Defiled. Deformed. Reptilian-like scales replaced flesh. Bone exchanged places with skin.

Sage's magic fluxed. An inexplicable want, a *need*, clawed at her. Desire pulsed within, building pressure behind her temples.

"I told them the truth. We're traveling up the mountain because our village was attacked. They told me that we have mountain sickness and that our bodies are struggling to adjust to the thinner air."

"You seem fine," Felix grunted. "For the most part."

A glazed look still clouded his eyes, but they narrowed ever so slightly.

"I think it hit you much harder than it did me," Sage said.

Felix struggled to his feet. He rested his hand on the tree and clutched his head before sagging back down to the ground.

"I feel like someone's hit me with a trolley and reversed it back over me," he sighed.

"They said it's best to avoid climbing higher until we acclimate. I think we should rest here. If either of us passes out again, it leaves us vulnerable."

"Did they say how long it takes to recover?"

Sage shrugged.

"A few days. A few weeks. Some people never get better and have to go back down."

Felix shook his head.

"That's not an option. We're not going anywhere until we kill the witch."

"Well we certainly can't do anything if we can't even breathe well enough to remain conscious."

"Would probably be a good idea to get some more of that potion then."

Sage stiffened. A small gust of wind tousled her shirt and the scent of decay billowed into her nostrils.

"What?" Felix asked. "Something happened in the village, didn't it?"

Her voice caught in her throat. If she told him what happened, that made it real. It would transform the images in her mind from abstract to tangible.

"No. They were just...low on the plants I needed for the potion. I took the last of what they had."

He stared at her, a slight frown on his lips. Then he closed his eyes and shook his head before resting it against the tree.

"Then we'll wait for them to restock. I can't function like this."

Sage fell quiet as she absorbed that.

"Okay," she whispered.

Felix's chest heaved up and down. When he spoke, his words came hollow and breathless.

"If you can, try to scope out the warrior's routes. See if you can get the plant off of them."

She blinked several times, batting away the tears welling up. She'd have to go back to the village. After...after...

Sage couldn't bear the weight of finishing the thought.

"I will."

Chapter 29

Human Realm, Island of Kestramore, Khisfire Province

Outside of Premier Eryx's quarters, the party was in full swing. Music filled the halls, the melodious tune greeting Haizea as she descended the steps. A band had set up in the forum and played a variety of instruments—drums, trumpets, flutes, and strings. Alastair reached the bottom of the staircase first and held his hand out for her. Unused to wearing heels that added about four inches to her height, Haizea took it gratefully.

Shauni's head swiveled as she took stock of the islanders in attendance. People close by glanced in their direction, their eyes glazing right over Shauni and landing on Haizea and Alastair. Haizea purposefully made no effort to suppress her vitality's presence and neither did Alastair. If not for the earth's smoke concealing her, even Shauni's magical prowess would have been comparable to the omens here.

"That went better than expected," Haizea said.

"The night's not over yet," Shauni muttered.

Haizea turned to Alastair. He was scanning the crowd just like Shauni did a moment before. Her shoulders relaxed as the tension she didn't realize she'd been holding eased. By joining her on this venture, Alastair and Shauni had put themselves at risk, but not being alone did have its benefits.

Alastair met her gaze, having missed their brief exchange, his eyes darted back and forth between her and Shauni.

~What did you think?~ Haizea asked.

~I think they're placating us. I don't believe a word they say. I also think Kallistê was acting strange.~

~How so?~

~Her Soul keeps bombarding me with a wave of anger. It spiked near Viltarin. There's also a Beast lurking in the Premier's quarters~

~That's what you were staring at,~ she mused.

Alastair nodded.

~I could see its Soul plain as day, but not the Beast itself. Pamin gave me a guide to identifying various Beasts. There are many that can camouflage themselves in plain sight. But without the guide or visual confirmation, I have no way of knowing it for certain.~

Haizea hummed to herself as she mulled it over. She'd never found the realmdrifter to be trustworthy to begin with. This could be a trap, but it was such an obvious one that she doubted Kallistê would do something so reckless. The other islanders, however, were another story.

~It could be subterfuge, but it also might be a cultural practice here on the island. Just keep me abreast if you detect any more.~

"I'm going to go scope out the land. And see if they have any good food and drinks," Shauni said.

Before Haizea could respond, she disappeared into the crowd. Alastair's magic spiked beside her and his eyes shimmered like diamonds.

~I can't see her Soul, but I do see a blind spot shifting in my vision. It's like a shadow moving through the crowd. I'll keep an eye on her.~

~Thank you,~ Haizea signed.

Alastair grasped her hands in his and led her closer to the band.

He stopped directly in front of the bass player—a petite woman dwarfed by the large instrument. He twirled her around before pulling her in closer and resting his hands on her waist. Haizea placed her hands on his shoulders and they swayed back and forth in sync with the baseline. It was only then that she realized she could feel the vibrations humming against her body as the musician plucked the strings.

The song came to an end and they separated. Alastair's eyes combed over her, pausing on her lips and drinking in the plunging neckline of her dress. He laughed, his smile deepening so that his cheeks dimpled in the most delightful way. He let her go so that he could sign.

~You know, I may not be a seer, but I can tell exactly what you're thinking.~

~Really? Do tell.~

Alastair made to respond, but he stopped short, his eyes glazing over. Haizea recognized his expression—a Soul was communicating with him. She waited patiently and a few moments later, his attention refocused on her.

Before she could ask what the Soul had said, Alastair guided her a few steps away. He turned her so that they stood side by side, but he positioned himself slightly toward the front. Not even a breath later, Viltarin appeared. This time, he had another man on his arm.

"Our introduction was quite brief earlier. I was hoping that I'd have the opportunity to get to know you a little better before you left. This is my partner, Milo, we're soon to be wed," he said, holding out his hand.

Viltarin reached for Haizea, but Alastair shook his hand instead. Viltarin smiled and offered his hand again afterward, but Alastair squeezed her waist. Despite her shock, she upheld an impassive expression and heeded his subtle cue. Viltarin's smile tightened and he dropped his hand.

"It's a pleasure to meet you both," Milo said.

"Likewise," Haizea said, signing at the same time.

Viltarin was looking pointedly at Alastair now. His eyes locked onto the ring on Alastair's finger before flickering to Haizea's pendant that hung low on her chest. She cleared her throat.

"I was just admiring your jewelry. That's such a beautiful necklace. I've never seen anything like it."

Haizea blinked. Something about his words rang familiar.

"In the mountains, all Bruvian warriors receive a pendant after they pass their mastery test. Mine is an heirloom that's been passed down for generations. My mother gave it to me when I was sixteen years old. One day, if I have a daughter and she chooses to become a warrior, I'll pass this one to her."

"Fascinating. It sounds like all...Bruvian...?" Viltarin dragged out the word. Haizea nodded. "warriors are women?"

"Is there any particular reason for that?"

"Hundreds of years ago, before magic returned to the realm and the mountains and kingdoms went to war as a result, it used to be more equal. In fact, warriors were traditionally non-mages. But a cultural shift occurred during the war, when a woman named Saimira Bruvia rose to the top and led the mountaineers to victory. Her actions inspired many women to follow in her footsteps."

As Haizea spoke, memories of The Festival of Olysseus rose to the surface.

She stood in front of the enchantress's booth, with Zander and Jirina at her side. The woman's emerald green eyes absorbed her pendant.

"That's a beautiful necklace," she said.

Understanding downed on her—Viltarin was a curse mage.

Back then, had she known that the enchantress was the curse mage, she could have killed her before the assassination attempt...before she revealed her secret, King Rhys...before he set his sights on Grandfather Harzel.

Here she stood yet again, facing another curse mage in the midst of festivities. Back then, she had unknowingly lost the chance to end the conflict before it even began.

She kicked herself internally—the signs had been obvious and she nearly missed it.

Haizea's vision flickered red. Her magic flared as her power rose to the surface—a silent threat.

The men inched backward, but a smug grin cemented itself on Vilatrin's face.

Alastair's grip tightened around her waist. She paused. Breathed. Found her calm. Far away from home, on an island filled with omens, attacking would be reckless. They had come here to learn and observe. Haizea did not come here to start a fight–only to finish one. Besides, she'd anticipated and prepared for such a scenario.

Based on Viltarin's insistence in shaking her hand, he most likely wanted to clandestinely place a curse on her through physical touch. Thus far, his antics had failed. She'd weaved her own protective curse into her pendant and Alastair's ring. In addition to that, Shauni's earth's smoke made her impervious to magic. As a result, she'd rendered Viltarin's magic useless.

Haizea glared at him, making no effort to hide her souring opinion of them. Behind Viltarin's smiling visage, his pulse accelerated. That was the thing about arrogance–his body's instincts told him that he should be afraid, but overconfidence prevented him from heeding those cues.

"I suppose your pet, the non-mage, is a warrior as well, given her pendant. I'm a bit intrigued as to why she would want to come to an island of omens," he said.

"Her name is Shauni and she's my friend."

"Shauni. Right. You let her wander off by herself. Even for a warrior, it's a bit reckless if you ask me."

"You don't know Shauni."

Viltarin's brow furrowed in a dubious, if not bewildered expression. He shrugged.

"Well, I was hoping that we could have a candid conversation. Omen to omen. I think there's much to discuss regarding what Kestramore's future looks like with our friends from across the ocean."

"We've already spoken with the Premier. It's my understanding that Kestramore has four dignitaries. It would make sense to speak to the rest of you before we depart. The three of us."

Haizea flinched when wetness touched her hand and her magic spiked in response. She glanced down to see Alastair's bleeding finger pressed against her skin.

Her body absorbed his vitality, enveloping it within her own before the wound sealed shut. As her eyes opened to the Spiritual world, her honey brown eyes shifted into a gleaming crimson. The distinct tug of death slammed into her almost instantly—at least a dozen Souls barreled toward her and Alastair.

Applause erupted around them and Haizea squinted as it sent waves of energy rolling through her blood magic-fueled vision. The Premier had officially entered the party. She stood at the top of the landing and rested her hands on the railing. She smiled down at the crowd, poised yet calculated—and completely unaware of the death that surrounded them.

Movement on the other side of the room caught Haizea's eye. Her jaw dropped.

Shauni appeared in the doorway with her hands and arms covered in blood and her dark eyes beseeching violence.

The alcohol ran through Shauni and her bladder threatened to burst. Not that the islanders seemed to give a damn if she made a mess of herself. She tapped the shoulder of the nearest woman.

"Excuse me, could you tell me where the bathroom is?"

The woman looked her up and down, her eyes a bright turquoise.

"Oh good, a servant. Could you refill my glass? I'm low on wine."

When the woman tried to pass the glass off, Shauni didn't bother reaching for it. The woman obliviously let it go as she turned back to her conversation and the glass clattered to the ground and broke into pieces. She looked back to Shauni, her mouth agape.

"Didn't you hear me? I said I need another glass of wine. Now clean this mess up."

Shauni's violet eyes darkened.

"I heard you just fine."

"Do you realize what you are and who you're speaking to? As a non-mage, you should be careful of the way you speak to omens. Now, as I said, clean this mess up."

Shauni snorted out a laugh and instantly regretted it as her bladder protested. She hurried off to find the bathroom on her own and left the woman sputtering where she stood. A hushed hiss followed behind her:

"That's the blood mage's pet! Viltarin told us about her."

Shauni kept moving, tabling that information for later. She sighed as the bathroom came into view just down the hall. As she relieved herself, footsteps thudded against the floor and the door clicked shut. Shauni emerged from the stall. Roughly a dozen people had crammed inside. She walked to the sink, but none of the newcomers moved toward the toilet. Shauni calmly dried her hands off with a towel and discarded it in the trash bin. The omens gathered in front of the door.

"Excuse me."

They didn't budge. Shauni's chuckle concealed her agitation. She'd already heard and seen enough throughout the night—unless you were an omen, your place in Kestramore was at the bottom of the food chain.

It was a complete departure from the major kingdoms, but an over correction as far as Shauni was concerned. In the mountains, mages, omens, and non-mages all stood on equal footing because what the vitality gifted, it could also take away. The earth's smoke melded into her wristbands and pendant was proof of that.

These people did not understand the importance of balance.

Shauni stretched one of her arms across her chest to loosen up your muscles.

"Here's how this is going to go," she paused and switched to the other arm. "You all are going to step aside and let me exit. If you don't, I'm going to assume that this is not only an act of imprisonment, but an attempt on my life and respond accordingly."

As expected, no one moved. Shauni's lips turned upward into a grin, but her eyes told another story. The violet in her irises blended in with her pupils, so that her eyes appeared pitch black.

"Shameful how Kestramore treats their guests. Don't say I didn't warn you."

Shauni cracked her knuckles and balled her hands into fists. When she attacked, she could not muster the same speed as when she had access to magic, but she still moved at a breakneck pace. She went for the nearest mage, who put their hand up as if to stop her with telekinesis. With the earth's smoke on her body, Shauni could not sense the vitality, but she knew the ways of her magical Class like the back of her own hand.

Shrouded by the plant's anti-magical properties, she barreled through the invisible telekinetic barrier and landed a punch directly on their windpipe, collapsing it. As they gasped for breath, she landed another blow to their head. Their body hit the floor in a motionless heap. She turned on the remaining omens and continued her assault without hesitation.

Shauni flipped the nearest person through the air before slamming them into the ground with a satisfying crack. Blood leaked out from their ears and pooled around their prone form.

She absorbed the sight in her peripheral vision, keeping the center of her attention on the others. A small voice wondered if she should have exercised more restraint. Her instincts swiftly quashed it.

These people had waited until she was completely isolated to corner her. That alone was indication enough of their intent to harm. So far from home and heavily outnumbered, holding back meant gambling on her safety, if not her life.

A hardness settled in Shauni's chest. If protecting herself meant spilling their blood, so be it.

"Stop," one of the omens commanded.

Shauni's footstep stumbled and she waved her arms out to regain her balance.

"See, that's all it takes," the mage shrugged flippantly.

The curse mage patted the top of Shauni's head as if she were a dog. She stopped pretending like their magic had any effect on her. Shauni grabbed their hand, purposefully placing her fingers on their pressure points and twisted until their bones snapped from the torsion. They opened their mouth in a soundless scream, the pain having stolen the breath from their lungs.

Something flickered in the corner of her eye—another telekinetic mage gearing up to attack. Shauni positioned the curse mage in front of her so that they caught the wave of magic intended for her instead. The curse mage's body crumpled—their bones ground together and their internal organs sloshed audibly as the transmutation mage turned them into a mouse. Its body crunched under the weight of Shauni's heel.

Telekinesis was the most prevalent across all mage Classes, so it was probably safe to assume that at least half of the omens standing here were transmuting mages, if not more. While Shauni did not practice the Cosmic Arts, she'd grown up around omens and telekinesis was the basis of transmutation magic.

Shauni knew precisely how the mages would think and act. Their every action played out before her before they even moved.

The transmuting mage touched the trash bin and transformed it from a simple container to a long spear. A smirk crept across her lips.

What a shame it would be to die by a weapon made by their own hands.

Shauni charged toward the transmuting mage and two other omens lunged to intercept her. She slid to the ground and evaded them in a smooth sweep. The transmuting mage struck at her, but Shauni rolled back onto her feet and twisted to avoid the spear. She wrenched it from their grasp, flipped it around, and impaled it in their chest.

The others inched backward, their eyes widening. Shauni positioned herself between them and the door, making eye contact with each and every one of them before she spoke.

Her laughter bounced off the walls.

"I gave you the chance to run."

Chapter 30

Human Realm, Island of Kestramore, Khisfire Province

"Come on out, Ivor," Premier Eryx said once the door shut behind the mountaineer trio.

Kallistê's brows rose as her advisor emerged from one of the doors on the far side of the room.

"Your Majesty," Ivor bowed deeply.

"It's been several months since you sent her to the island for training. Ivor has made admirable progress. I thought the gala would be the perfect opportunity for you two to catch up."

"It's a pleasure to see you, Ivor. Please, show me what you've learned so far," Kallistê said.

"I still haven't learned how to pick up internal musings, but I can see thoughts in the form of images. It works best when I make physical contact. If I may?" she said.

Kallistê nodded. Ivor placed her hand on either side of her face, balmy fingers trembling against her cheeks.

"Now, I just need you to picture something in your head. And I'll describe it to you."

Kallistê closed her eyes and let her mind wander. Ivor's vitality whirled. Though it did not carry the oppressive weight of a fully realized omen, Kallistê could taste faint hints of its twisted flavor. Something within her coiled and she perched forward on the edge of her seat—this would be her first glimpse into whether her investment would pay off.

She settled on the vision of a Soul.

"I see something bright and sparkling. It's rife with vitality," Ivor whispered.

"A Soul," Kallistê answered.

She opened her eyes.

"You can see mine. And the Premier's…and there's a Beast in the corner behind me. A *doyama*."

It was the Beast she'd gifted the Premier. She'd wanted to protect her from–

A whip cracked Kallistê's skull open. Ivor's expression pinched in kind, but her thoughts traveled onward and a memory resurfaced:

One of her doyamas lunged at Viltarin, its jaws snapping shut just a few millimeters from his face.

They broke apart, each gasping for air.

"What happened?" Premier Eryx asked.

Ivor's lips parted as her light green eyes searched Kallistê's gaze. Kallistê willed herself to speak, but the curse choked the words in her throat before she could utter them.

"I think something's wrong. I saw a man in her thoughts, one of the dignitaries. A *doyama* attacked him," Ivor said.

Eryx turned to Kallistê. She pressed her lips together in a thin line, her dark eyes scrutinizing.

"Which dignitary?" she asked.

Again, the answer rose in Kallistê's throat, but the words did not form.

"Viltarin," Ivor said.

The Premier studied Kallistê, a frown deepening the wrinkles on her face.

"That underhanded bastard. She's been cursed."

Ivor's brows rose high.

"Cursed?"

"Yes. He'd never get away with doing something of this nature against the other dignitaries. We have measures in place against it. But Kallistê does not serve in Kestramore's government in an official capacity. She's a foreign ally—fair game as far as our laws are concerned," Premier Eryx sighed.

"Ivor, I realize your abilities are still developing, but your magic is best suited for determining how he planted the curse. It appears he has rendered Kallistê incapable of doing so."

"I'm not quite sure how to go about doing that, Premier."

"You'll need to delve into her memories. It will be difficult given your lack of experience, but not impossible. The memory you just saw is a solid starting point."

Doubt colored Ivor's expression as she looked at Kallistê, but she followed the Premier's instructions and pressed her hands against her face once more.

Kallistê doubled over and mental blades sliced through her as images flashed before her eyes: Viltarin's shit-eating grin, her *doyamas* attacking him, her fingers tugging at her ring.

Ivor broke contact and stumbled backward. Kallistê and the Premier exchanged a glance as the seer sank to her knees in a fit of laughter.

"The...," she cut off, her breath ragged. "The ring. It's the ring," she wheezed.

The older woman's vitality amplified and the golden ring slid down Kallistê's finger. It floated in the air between them and the mental fog lifted, but the pain from Ivor's delving persisted. The Premier put a hand on her shoulder.

"The effects of an inchoate omen. I don't suggest you use your Cosmic magic anymore tonight, Ivor. As a seer, it's essential that you protect your mind. Not only are you susceptible to the Cosmic high, but the thoughts of others can infiltrate your own and drive you mad. Moderation is key to prevention and it's a habit best formed early on."

"Y-yes, Premier," Ivor stammered.

The band of skin where Kallistê's ring had once been was a few shades lighter than the rest of her hand.

"Words cannot fully express my gratitude toward both of you. You have my sincerest thanks," Kallistê whispered, still reeling.

"There'll be time for sentimentality later," Premier Eryx said. "I doubt this was the only arm of Viltarin's scheme. He's bound to have something up his sleeve for tonight."

"He specifically commanded me to invite Haizea so that he could curse her in a similar fashion. For all that talk about bringing her ire onto this island, he's playing with fire," Kallistê hissed.

"Frankly, her choice to bring her non-mage friend is a bit bewildering. She looks sharp, but she must realize she's parading her own weakness by doing such a thing."

Kallistê shook her head.

"Even if it seems foolish on the surface, she wouldn't come here without some sort of contingency in place. I agree that the non-mage is peculiar, but that's the least of our worries. It won't matter if Viltarin fails in his efforts—it's the very attempt itself that's dangerous. My alliance with the Haizea has always been delicate. Anything could tip the scales at any moment. I'll have to smooth things over with her and clean up his mess to avoid any fallout."

"She may be a blood mage, Kallistê, and it's right to respect that power, but you're a gifted realmdrifter. Your ability to control the Beasts is unparalleled. If this goes awry, your loss is not a foregone conclusion. The alliance is useful, but it is not paramount to your success."

Kallistê fell silent, absorbing the Premier's words. Ivor had gathered herself in those few moments and struggled to her feet. She sat down in a nearby chair and held her head in her hands.

"Someone's coming," she whispered. Paused. "Downstairs. Something's... something's..."

The doorknob jiggled. When it didn't budge, whoever was on the other side began pounding instead.

"Open it. I told Lotus to join us," Premier Eryx said. "But, just to be safe," she held up her hand and lightning sparked across her fingertips.

Kallistê answered the door. Lotus breezed inside, a river of magenta trailing behind her. She waved her hand and a swell of magic locked the door shut. Her eyes locked on the Premier's hands.

"Is there a reason you're aiming bolts of lightning at me?" she asked.

"We've just learned that Kallistê has been walking around cursed, right under our noses. If she opened the door and you happened to be the person responsible, I would have responded accordingly," the Premier said, her hands dimming.

"A curse?" Lotus's brows rose. "Viltarin," she hissed.

"Bathroom. Fight in the...bathroom," Ivor murmured.

Kallistê turned to the Premier.

"My other mages? How has their training progressed as of late?"

A year had passed since she'd sent them to Kestramore—enough time to accurately discern who truly had the potential to succeed in this endeavor.

"Two have unlocked the gate to their Cosmic power and are making steady progress. The third is still in limbo. She's close but can't quite cross the threshold. It's probably best to send her back to the continent at this point," Eryx said.

Kallistê nodded. She'd known that the return on investment would be low. Neither the medium nor enchanting mage had been able to overcome the initial hurdle of tapping into the Cosmos to unlock their power. Cosmic Arts training had whittled her ten mages down to three—two transmuting mages and one seer. And they all still had a very long way to go before they could be considered masters of their craft.

Her gaze fell to Ivor, whose eyes glazed over. She muttered under her breath, taken by the high. Useless for the time being. Given what had transpired with Viltarin's curse, it would probably be best to arrange for Ivor to continue her training on the continent. Kallistê would benefit the most from a Mental mage by her side.

"We'll deal with Viltarin accordingly, but there's no time for it right now. It's nearly time for me to make my entrance. Lotus, I want you behind me while I give my speech. I'll introduce you near the end."

The door shut behind Eryx. A moment later, cheers erupted from the crowd, so loud that it made Kallistê's ears buzz. It took a few minutes for it to die down.

Kallistê sat beside Ivor as the Premier began her speech. She poured herself a glass of wine.

Her retaliation against Viltarin would be as swift as it was cautious—if she acted carelessly, he could curse her again. Right now, his focus was on the blood mage, but should his efforts fail on that front, Kallistê did not put it past him to target the non-mage to use as leverage.

Ivor gripped Kallistê's hand.

"I think he's...he's already started," her words slurred together.

Kallistê frowned.

"You saw something?"

Ivor nodded.

"A f-fight in the bathroom. But there's a blind spot. I can't...see everything."

Kallistê leaned back against her chair. Ivor hadn't been babbling incoherently—the Cosmic high had hindered her ability to communicate her warnings.

"I'll be right back."

She vanished into the astral plane and drifted through the door. Shouting voices traveled up the steps. Kallistê paused at the top of the landing and scanned the crowd.

Viltarin stood in close quarters with Haizea and Alastair. A few feet away, the non-mage rapidly closed the distance, her arms covered in blood. Kallistê's eyes widened, balking at the sight. Viltarin's mouth moved, and although she could not hear his words, she saw the effects. Those in his immediate vicinity set their sights on the mountaineers.

Haizea nudged Alastair. He reached into his pocket and poured a vial of blood into her palm. She raised her hand and her vitality whipped outward, wild, and violent and heavy, like an ocean wave. An invisible force twisted the limbs of their attackers, going against the grain until the appendages tore from their bodies.

The blood hit the air like a spark to a flame. Haizea did more than merely drain them—she *unmade* them, reducing their bodies into a cloud of dust. The omens under Viltarin's control positioned themselves between him and the blood mage. He used the unfolding chaos as cover and tried to bolt from the scene.

Shauni stood between Viltarin and the door. Kallistê narrowed her eyes. Even a non-mage should have *some* luminescence, though fainter than mages and omens. Yet Shauni did not shimmer at all in Kallistê's vision.

Odd. How very odd.

Viltarin hissed something at Shauni and a ripple tore through the vitality as he infused his words with his magic.

Shauni walked onward, unfazed, and unaffected. Viltarin faltered, repeated his efforts. This time, Kallistê could faintly make out the timbre of his voice, but the individual words still blended in with the background.

The non-mage continued forward and Kallistê blinked in astonishment. Shauni had most definitely heard him. And yet she seemed entirely unbothered by Viltarin's magic. In fact, the woman was grinning.

For once, Viltarin's own smug grin evaporated. He shouted something again and dozens of people jumped between him and Shauni. He turned on his heels and darted in the direction of a different exit. As he reached the door, he glanced back once. Somehow, his eyes found Kallistê.

She raised her bare finger, both as a rude gesture and to display the absence of her cursed ring. Viltarin sneered before he turned on his heels and ran.

Lotus was already escorting Premier Eryx away from the ruckus and headed back toward her quarters. Kallistê drifted back to the room and unlocked the door to give them entrance. Her lighthearted laugh broke the silence.

"What's so funny?" Lotus asked.

Freedom. It had been so long since she savored its sweet taste.

"I'm afraid I have to run. Would one of you be a darling and create a pair of earplugs for me?" Kallistê asked.

Finally, gloriously, Viltarin would meet his end.

Lotus grabbed a napkin and the magical pressure intensified as it twisted and turned, warping under her power. She placed two small pieces in the palm of her hands.

"Premier Eryx, please make arrangements with Ivor's tutor to continue her training on the continent."

The older woman nodded.

"We'll clean things up here. You get a handle on him," she said.

Kallistê drifted into the astral plane once more. Viltarin was smart enough to know that he needed to run, but for a realmdrifter like her, there was no place in this realm or the next where she could not find him.

Chapter 31

Human Realm, Island of Kestramore, Khisfire Province

A shimmering cloud of dust settled at Haizea's feet. She barely suppressed the smirk tugging on her lips from the influx of power. An array of abilities now teemed at her fingertips—telekinesis and transmutation, mediumship, and necromancy, and, as thoughts began to pour into her mind, clairvoyance, and telepathy.

Her irises brightened, the taste of their terror caressing her tongue.

A moment ago, the fear in the room had merely been something she perceived through facial expressions and body language, but now she experienced every hushed whisper, panicked glance, and accelerating heartbeat firsthand.

She'll kill us all.

Run, run as far away as you can, run!

Another new viewpoint entered her perception. She saw Shauni's side profile, grinning and soaked with blood. Viltarin stood across from her. The chaos muffled his words, but Haizea caught enough.

Come here, now, he commanded.

Shauni did not move, but the dozens of people around them fell under Viltarin's spell.

Viltarin's skin paled, his jaw slack. His throat bobbed up and down as he swallowed thickly. Shani met his bewildered expression with a grin of her own. The curse mage doubled down on his efforts, this time a vein protruded from his neck as he shouted.

Haizea strained against the internal onslaught as Viltarin's Mental magic clashed with hers. Years had passed since she last held the power of a seer—not since her training with Grandfather Harzel.

She could practically hear his voice now and feel the warmth of his hand on her shoulder.

"Sense the traces of the vitality and follow its path to the source, just like you would with an injury. Controlling the power of sight is no different from healing or blood magic. Breathe, clear your mind, and focus."

The cacophony faded into soft whispers. She followed the traces of magic, visualizing the connecting points between the people before her. A thick line led to Viltarin, with numerous branches linking to those under his curse. Dozens of them stood in her immediate vicinity while several more were interspersed throughout the mansion.

Trails of vitality led to Kallistê and the Premier upstairs, but the distance muted her ability to hear their thoughts. Clairvoyance, on the other hand, gave her an exterior bird's eye view. Kallistê and her lot made a swift exit, escaping the unfolding chaos altogether.

Viltarin followed suit. With numerous mages under his control surrounding their trio, it provided him the opportunity to flee.

Shauni shouted as omens pressed closer. Even without her telekinesis, her movements blended together, difficult to follow. She bobbed and weaved their attacks and beat them back with a flurry of punches and kicks. But for each enemy she downed, another three sprang up behind them.

Haizea outstretched her palm toward Shauni's direction and curled her fingers. Her healing magic sputtered when their spines bent backwards, snapping in half like a twig. Their eyes met and Shauni dipped her chin in a nod.

Of all the people here, Shauni was the only one completely impervious to any magical attacks because the earth's smoke acted as a barrier between her and the vitality. The same could not be said for Alastair, who stood beside Haizea. She filed his essence away in a corner of her mind to wall him off from her power. Then she cracked her knuckles. Outside of those two, she did not discriminate.

Although Viltarin's curse affected some of the attacking mages, many of them were not under his spell—they'd only seen the ongoing fight between their fellow islanders and the mountaineer trio and stepped in to intervene. Many of them had no idea their own people had incited the ongoing clash by attacking Shauni first. But given the broken bodies that littered the ground, that did not matter–their people were dead nonetheless, killed by outsiders.

The vitality bent to Haizea's will. Twisting and turning, multiplying and dividing.

Blinding light sprang to life on her fingertips, accompanied by a thunderous boom that made the walls of the building shake. She pointed to the incoming attackers and released the energy coiled in her hands, directing it with ironclad control.

Lightning streaked across the dance floor. Bodies crumbled to ash, incinerated where they stood. Scorch marks marred the ground and tendrils of black and caustic smoke wafted off the pile of remains.

To any onlookers, they died in silence, unable to scream. But even in that split second, each individual life flashed before Haizea's eyes. Parents, siblings, children. Tender moments. Joyous occasions. Grief and heartbreak. She saw all of it—the things that gave their life purpose. And she'd erased it in the span of a breath.

Tremors raced up and down her arms as Haizea concentrated her power once again. Sparks simmered in her hands–lightning daring to strike again. Her vision blurred and the people around her doubled. She blinked in an attempt to ground herself, but instead stumbled forward, a smile on her lips and a giggle threatening to bubble forth.

Warmth enveloped her–Alastair wrapped his arm around her waist, steadying her wavering form. Her blazing red eyes locked with his shimmering diamond ones. Although his touch created more shockwaves that rocked through her body, she leaned against him.

Alastair pointed and she followed the motion—a realmdrifter weaved through the astral plane. With both Alastair's medium magic and a seer's vitality pumping through her, Haizea could not only sense their Soul but track the realmdrifter via their thoughts. They planned to catch her from behind. As she braced for their attack, the vitality rippled as more omens converged around her and Alastair.

She gritted her teeth in an effort to resist the growing buzz that vibrated through her temples and put up a telekinetic wall against their onslaught. More thoughts infiltrated her mind: one of the mages catapulted themselves in the air while another two flanked her from the left and right, pulling her attention in three different directions. Haizea hummed, faintly amused.

When the first mage flew into the air, she focused the whole of her transmutation on them.

Pop.

The omen buckled under the weight of her magic, its body caving in on itself before transforming into a sword.

She aimed the blade at the omen flanking her left, piercing through their heart. Then she whipped a wave of telekinesis at the omen to her right, their bones shattering from the invisible wall of energy. Haizea recalled the sword once more before tossing it toward Shauni. Her friend laughed heartily, even as she proceeded to impale the nearest person.

Ecstasy flooded into Haizea. Her legs wobbled and a haze blurred the corners of her vision, but Alastair's steady hand tightened around her, keeping her upright. She'd absorbed more than just human life or the power of other mages, but that of other *omens*—the corrupted nature of their vitality amplified to the intensity of the Cosmic high tenfold.

Killing intent laced her thoughts as another omen closed in. A realmdrifter materialized in thin air. They wrapped their hands around Alastair's wrist and intertwined their Soul with his.

I'm going to drag you to the Cosmos and leave you to rot.

Haizea's body reacted on pure instinct. She clenched her hand into a fist, calling upon the combined power of blood magic and transmutation. Their heart burst open inside of their chest and rivulets of blood poured from the realmdrifter's mouth. Their form began to fade as they attempted to retreat into the astral plane, but the damage had been done. They rematerialized and dropped to the ground, unmoving.

Two more realmdrifters took their place, flanking Haizea and Alastair. No, more than just two. A third Soul joined them. Large and wild and untamed.

Haizea froze where she stood.

Two massive nostrils and a muzzle spawned before them. Hot, malodorous air fanned across Haizea's face. As the creature's head emerged, it opened its jaws wide, revealing rows upon rows of sharp, canine teeth. A beam of reddish orange light ignited in the back of its throat.

The world ground to a halt. Alastair coaxed her behind him. Her legs moved, but her mind lagged—seeing the threat but not fully grasping it. Somewhere, Shauni screamed. Distant and yet somehow right beside her.

A Beast, she realized, much too slowly. The realmdrifters had brought a Beast. It inhaled once more and the embers within surged, ready to incinerate them where they stood. She needed to absorb the power of one of the realmdrifters to wrest control of the creature—at the moment, she only had the ability to wield telepathy, necromancy, and transmutation.

Haizea tried to stand properly and push in front of Alastair, but she only managed to slump forward, her head landing on his back.

This was how the two people she loved the most would die. On an island far away from home, by the hands of an enraged Beast. Coming here had been her idea. Tears streamed down her cheeks as an intoxicated laugh tumbled from her lips.

Alastair rested his hand on hers and squeezed. His mind and Soul remained calm despite the impending blaze. He closed his eyes and reached forward with his free hand, placing his palm on the Beast's muzzle.

Something snapped deep within and the Beast's Soul. Its eyes glazed over and the overwhelming heat receded.

She stiffened as the creature's death pulled her magic tight. Alastair's long locks of hair waded in and out of focus as she tried to look at him properly. He had never done that before.

His thoughts came to her much differently than everyone else. Alastair thought in signs and images, feelings, and desires. But she understood, clear as day.

A silent plea. A prayer.

Soul Reaper, please help us.

Somewhere, deep in the shadows of the Soul Realm, the entity turned its head.

Chapter 32

Human Realm, Mount Illiniza, Heavensbreak Village

Sage stood at the entrance to the marketplace. She had managed to obtain more plants to make another potion, but dizzy spells continued to afflict Felix and he didn't have the energy to move around much. Until his condition improved, they were stuck here.

The market bustled with activity—people flitted to and fro, carrying baskets and tugging carts filled with packaged meat and bundles of fresh produce. Her mouth watered at the spicy aromas wafting from the nearby eateries.

Her magic roiled. She shoved her trembling hands into her pockets in an attempt to suppress it, but the pressure merely intensified. Her arms tingled, accompanied by this burning, insatiable ache. Sage's fingers pressed together, having a mind of their own.

Snap.

One of the torches that lined the walkway bent at an angle and its flames sputtered out, leaving behind a cloud of smoke.

Sage stumbled forward and fell to her hands and knees. The blades of grass between her fingers blended with one another. A laugh fought its way up her throat and she clenched her teeth, desperate to hold it back.

Haggard breaths fell from her lips as she fought to cling to her composure. Even now, the rush she felt paled in comparison to the squirrel she'd transmuted. Nothing like the men she'd—

She buckled and sank face-first into the dirt, blinded by the tears collecting in the corners of her eyes.

"That voice is lying to you, Sage."

Something warm touched her shoulder.

"Are you alright?"

Sage looked up to see a girl beside her. She had warm copper eyes, rich tan skin, and short, loose curls. She looked close to her age, maybe a year or two younger.

Despite the girl's slight stature, she practically lifted Sage off the ground as she helped her to her feet. Sage blinked. She swayed back and forth, barely maintaining her balance. The girl held her arm to keep her upright.

"You don't look too good," the girl said.

"M-mountain sickness," Sage mumbled.

The girl tilted her head.

"I've heard of that before. They say people from the base get it. You're not from here then?"

Sage shook her head. Everything around her sparkled and shimmered, rife with vitality...except for the girl, who stood cast in a shadow. She rubbed her temples.

"You're carrying a lot of weapons," Sage commented.

Armaments loaded down the girl's small frame—two swords on her hips, a bow and arrow strapped to her back, daggers around her ankles. The girl shifted and something in her copper gaze stilled Sage.

"I'm a warrior in training."

Felix's voice nagged at her. Something about the warriors. Getting a plant from them.

"That's why I can't see you," Sage murmured.

The girl frowned.

"You can't see me?"

"I'm...," Sage trailed off. A vague instinct warned her not to answer.

Wind whipped against her bare neck. This was the first time in a year that she had gone out without her enchanted choker. She hadn't been able to find the tools to repair the broken chain after...after...

Sage swallowed thickly and shook her head.

How many false names had she used over the last two years? How many lies had she told? Couldn't she be herself, just this once? Just for a moment?

"I'm Sage. What's your name?" she said.

"Jassia."

She smiled at Sage. Muted, yet kind. Sage's lips quivered, not quite able to return it. As she opened her mouth to speak, her growling stomach cut her off and she grimaced.

"I'm sorry, I haven't had supper."

"Me neither. I was in such a rush to get here that I forgot to eat."

Sage dug through her pockets and pulled out a handful of coins. Between buying potions and Felix falling ill, they hadn't been able to replenish their stash. She and Felix had begun splitting their meals to get by lately. She only had enough money left for one more portion.

She looked at Jassia, still intrigued by how darkness shrouded her form in the glimmering world around her. Felix's voice whispered in her ear, telling her not to let the girl leave with the plant. He would say that if Sage couldn't do something this simple, how could she possibly defeat the blood mage?

"I've got enough for both of us. There's a soup stand nearby that's pretty good."

Jassia gazed into the distance. Sage followed her line of sight to the pylon.

"Jassia?" she nudged. The girl blinked and turned back to her.

"It's very kind of you, but I don't have much of an appetite right now," Jassia paused, frowning. "You haven't heard anything about the people who died here recently, have you?" she asked.

"No," Sage answered a little too quickly. She wiped clammy palms against her pants. "Is that why you're here?"

Jassia nodded.

"My father is one of the lumberjacks working on the pylon. I just want to make sure he's okay."

A cold sweat broke out across Sage's forehead and her heart clambered in her chest. Damn the plant, every cell in her body told her to walk away now. If Jassia's father was a lumberjack, she didn't want to know. She didn't want to face yet another person she'd hurt.

Sage readied herself to leave, but something in Jassia's expression gave her pause. When she spoke, her own words surprised her.

"I...If you want, I can go with you."

Jassia didn't answer right away. Then she sighed.

"The other warriors don't know I'm here. I just want to get in and out before anyone sees me. I don't want to cause any trouble."

"Well, it sounds like you could use help. If you're worried about being spotted, I can check for you," Sage offered.

"Alright. He's pretty easy to spot. He broke both of his legs when he was younger so he has a bad limp."

Sage's breath hitched as she and Jassia walked to the pylon. Lumberjacks ascended and descended the massive structure, timber in tow. To her relief, Sage didn't see any warriors nearby. As they closed the distance, there was an area roped off just a ways away from the actual construction site. The bodies were long gone, but blood still stained the grass.

Jassia rushed over and pushed past the rope. She picked up a small trinket lying in the grass. Although Sage could not see what it was, Jassia's knees buckled and she sagged to the ground.

Sage squeezed her eyes shut to block out the gut-wrenching sobs from the girl in front of her.

This was her reckoning. The realm itself had sent this girl, intent on retribution. Just like it had with Bose.

But this time, *she* had done this. Not at Felix's command, but her own. She had left a trail of destruction and death in her wake. Worse yet, Jassia's cries mirrored her own. Sage had taken that wound of losing a parent and brandished it onto someone else.

"Jassia?" a voice called.

Both she and Sage jumped at the sound—a few of the lumberjacks had spotted them. Her world tilted as they made their way toward them. One of them sped up, jogging to close the distance. He knelt down beside Jassia.

"He—he," she hiccupped, holding up the trinket she'd found. At this angle, Sage got a better view. It had Jassia's name engraved in it.

"I'm so sorry. You weren't supposed to find out like this," he rubbed her back. The rest of them gathered. Several yards away, more people turned to the commotion—a handful of villagers and...Sage blanched.

A woman with face paint was amongst them.

Sage's frayed nerves pulled taut against her magic and the earth roiled beneath her feet. Ice crept across the paved walkway, slicking the ground.

Jassia sniffed, eyes widening. She wiped her cheeks.

"Did you see that?" she whispered.

Jassia's voice flowed into one ear and out the other as the high resurged with a vengeance. Sage doubled over and belched out fire. The wave of energy made the ground quake once more.

"Transmutation," Jassia whispered. She inched backward, her hands resting on the hilts of her swords. Surprised murmurs raced through the other villagers as they looked to and fro, but the young warrior's copper gaze locked onto her.

"It's you, isn't it? The lumberjacks...the-the burning tavern a few weeks ago...you killed them."

Sage tried to respond, but only a laugh came out, unfiltered and uncontrolled. Jassia's hand slipped lower to her ankle and unsheathed one of the daggers there. It emanated an intense blackness in the sea of light that made up her glistening vision.

The plant.

Felix wanted it. She'd left him, all alone back at camp. She needed to get back to him. In a daze, Sage reached for the plant with quivering fingers. Her magic whipped outward and the vitality exploded before her eyes.

Bone crunched audibly as they bent and twisted in unnatural directions. Bodies collapsed in on themselves before bursting open, some of them splattering innards on the ground, others transforming into various elements, orbs of flame and water taking their place.

"No, no, no, no," Sage's hands flew to her mouth.

A deep groan rumbled overhead. The last thing Sage saw was the pylon's metal legs buckling inward before darkness swept over her.

The realm itself collapsed around Jassia. The pylon came tumbling down and with it, thousands of pounds of metal, wood, snow, and bodies.

Jassia thought she would be crushed to death and sent to the Soul Realm in an instant, but instead, the rumbling seemed never-ending. She rolled and slid, and the force of the avalanche knocked the wind out of her lungs. By the time the dust settled, Jassia still wasn't entirely certain if she was alive.

She lay there, her chest heaving as she gasped to catch her breath. Her vision swirled, and the ringing in her ears drowned out any sound. Jassia squeezed her eyes shut to quell the dizziness, letting the darkness swallow her. She lost track of time before she mustered the strength to open them again.

A metal pole dangled a few feet above, and snow and debris covered her body. Jassia tried to wipe her face, but her arm would not move—the rubble pinned it in place. Blood seeped out from beneath the debris, slicking her skin.

A piercing pain sliced through her forearm with each movement. The handle of her dagger jutted out from the rubble, stained red. Her heart stopped.

At some point, she'd lost her grip on her earth's smoke-laced blade.

She blinked. Surely, her eyes were deceiving her. This was just some sort of vivid nightmare that she would soon wake from.

But the pain did not lessen. The image of the limbs tearing away from torsos and bodies twisting in unnatural directions continued to assault her. She could still see Papa's blood-stained trinket lying on the grass, clear as day. It felt real. All too real.

The blade was still there.

Jassia unbuttoned her coat with one hand and tore at her shirt underneath with a panicked desperation. It didn't budge. She looked around and saw a sharp piece of metal within arm's reach. Jassia let out a mangled cry when she stretched and jostled her trapped arm, but she managed to reach it. She used the jagged piece like a knife and cut through her top once. Then, she bit down on her shirt collar and cut again, creating a strip of fabric in the center.

Jassia twisted and tucked the fabric under her injured arm, right below the shoulder. She looped it around and used her teeth and hand to tie a knot, tugging until her arm screamed in protest.

A shaky exhale expelled from her lips. Each heartbeat felt like a slow march to her death. She had no way of knowing if she'd stopped the spread or simply delayed the inevitable.

The rubble shifted overhead and dirt rained down upon her face. Jassia coughed. If the earth's smoke did not kill her, eventually this pile would when it collapsed.

Her father had died here. Soon, her Soul would join him.

"Papa...," she sobbed.

"Jassia?!"

She hiccupped.

"Vendela?"

"Oh thank Aaryn, you're alright. What are you doing here? Never mind that, keep talking, I'm coming toward you."

"I'm stuck," her voice wavered.

"I'll get you out. Just stay put."

After what felt like an eternity, Vendela's face appeared through the debris above. Blood trickled down her forehead and one of her eyes was swollen shut. Vendela cursed as she began moving the pile on top of her, bit by bit. A few moments later, Jassia heard her talking, but her voice sounded muffled, like maybe she'd turned away or walked off. The sound of several footsteps and multiple voices came closer.

"One, two, three!"

The entire pile lifted off of Jassia at once and her body floated into the air before being placed gently on top of the snow. Someone helped her sit up properly. Jassia suppressed a cry as they jostled her injured arm.

"I'm sorry."

The evening sun illuminated the remnants of the pylon—massive piles of wood and metal littered the area. Peculiar shaped masses protruded from those piles, covered in red and pink. Though they were too mangled to form a recognizable shape, deep down, Jassia knew that they were remains.

She swallowed thickly. Death surrounded her. And with each painful throb in her arm, it sunk its claws that much deeper, hoping to snatch her away as well.

Vendela hobbled into her line of sight. Jassia's heart stuttered at her appearance–a jagged piece of wood protruded from her side, blood trickling from the injury. Her leader winced as she stepped closer.

"Your dagger," Vendela breathed. As she examined it closely and her face blanched. "You took this from the supply area," her words came out as a statement rather than a question.

"You were right to tie it off, but it's only slowed the spread–it hasn't stopped it. The earth's smoke is potent. The only way to completely eliminate the possibility of it spreading is to cut off the arm."

"Vendela, I–"

"Once it spreads to your vital organs, there's nothing we can do. This is not a gamble you want to make, Jassia. Not one I will *allow* you to make."

More blood oozed from Vendela's wound. It soaked her shirt, pants, and boots. Droplets splashed onto the snow. Vendela waved one of the workers over.

"She's been poisoned. We have to cut off the arm before it spreads. We need a telekinetic mage. If you have a healer, all for the better, but if not, an enchanter will help."

"Are you crazy? She's...she's just a girl, you can't do something like that."

"She'll be a *dead* girl if we don't. We're warriors–our weapons are laced."

When the worker hesitated, Vendela grabbed them by the shoulders.

"Time is of the essence. If you won't help, send someone who will," she hissed.

A few people stepped forward and volunteered.

"We don't have any healers, but I'm an enchanter, I can help. Tell me what you need."

"Block out her pain as much as you can," Vendela said.

They laid Jassia on her back and the enchanter placed their hands on her head. A telekinetic mage came around and knelt on the ground by her right arm. Jassia's stomach churned.

"Sleep, Jassia," the enchanter whispered. Her eyes began to droop.

"Aaryn, if you're listening, if you don't answer any other prayer then answer this one: Let this work," Vendela whispered.

The last thing Jassia saw was Vendela's bruised face hovering over her before the world faded to black.

Chapter 33

Human Realm, Mount Illiniza, Windhaven Village

The Soul Reaper only had a few rules. They were simple, yet absolute.

The first: he did not give freely. The second: to him, Souls were currency.

After spending years running away from the nature of his magic, Alastair finally understood his connection with the entity. As a medium, he could freely commune with the Soul Reaper without limitation. But if he wanted something tangible, if he wanted the entity to use his hand to alter the tides of reality, to offer his *power*, then it necessitated sacrifice.

A strange calmness washed over him. He closed his eyes to block out the unfolding chaos. Alastair presented his offering.

Rather than bind the Souls of the dead to an empty vessel like he did with necromancy, he did the opposite. His Spiritual power overwhelmed the realmdrifters and severed their Souls from their bodies before thrusting them toward the Soul Realm. The Beast suffered the same fate.

The Soul Reaper inched closer but did not intervene on their behalf. Alastair's offering had not satisfied him. Of course, three Souls would not suffice.

Haizea stood behind him. Her hand shivered in his and vibrations rumbled along his back. He couldn't see her face, but he knew the sensation was her laughter. Her magic burned against his, bursting at the seams as the Cosmic high overtook her.

Shauni was still fighting on the other side of the dance floor. At least a dozen bodies lay at her feet, limp and unmoving. Their Souls had not yet traversed to the Soul Realm, but instead they floated in the astral plane and watched the battle unfold. Alastair honed his focus on those wayward Souls. They bent to his will like leaves in the wind. One by one, he presented them to the Soul Reaper.

An apparition of the entity's hand overlaid Alastair's. It was faint and barely visible to the naked eye, but unmistakable nonetheless.

Pins and needles raked through his mind. His own thoughts replayed before him. Haizea's vitality intensified and she reached outward with her free hand. Some part of her must have still been aware because the omens around Shauni seized where they stood.

She did not absorb their vitality—that would have undoubtedly tipped her into oblivion and she already danced perilously to the edge. Her fingers curled into a fist, tightening around the omens in an invisible telekinetic grasp.

Blood oozed from their eyes, noses, and mouths as their skulls caved inward. Their chests collapsed and their torsos twisted and snapped at unnatural angles. They gasped for air, but even that was a futile effort under Haizea's power. The resulting smell assaulted Alastair's nostrils—not only did blood pool on the ground, but their bowels emptied before their bodies collapsed in on themselves under the immense pressure.

He suppressed a gag. He'd seen Haizea kill before—and he'd taken lives himself as well. But experience did not make witnessing their violent demise any easier. Each death ripped through his magic and his expression pinched in discomfort.

Alastair swallowed to dispel the queasiness. Better these strangers than the people dear to him.

He took control of their Souls and pushed them to the Soul Realm. The Soul Reaper's attention grew pointed, but still the entity did not intervene. More islanders converged on them. They circled around him and Haizea, their magic at the ready.

Shauni was clutching her arm now. Blood stained her fingers. At some point in the fight, the omens must have realized that they couldn't attack her directly with their magic and had taken other measures. Transmuting mages held a variety of elements between their hands—fire, ice, gusts of wind, twisted metals that they'd formed into blades. Realmdrifters weaved through the astral plane, ready to snatch them away.

How many? How many more do you need? Is this not enough? Alastair shouted in his mind.

Alastair could only guess as to how many Souls the entity desired. He went for the next wave of realmdrifters first, as they presented the greatest danger. His eyes flashed, bright and clear, like diamonds. As he prepared to take command over their Souls, a bone-chilling cold froze him in place.

The apparition of the Soul Reaper solidified. First his bone hand, then the long sleeves of his garments, and finally his skull face.

The entity's vacant eyes met Alastair's before turning to the floor, where onlookers fell to their knees. Even Shauni stopped and stared. Not even the earth's smoke cloud blind her to the oppressive weight of the Soul Reaper's presence.

You called, the entity stated.

Alastair's bones protested against Haizea's tightening grip on his hand. She could not safely transport them back to Windhaven in her current condition. His own vision grew fuzzier by the second and a faint smile curled hips lips as the high began to set in. At this rate, they would both lose themselves to the Cosmos before they could escape.

He absorbed the scene around him. Tonight, the people of Kestramore had put on their best for the occasion. They wore extravagant clothing and decadent jewelry and brilliant makeup. The power of the Cosmos emanated from them—power that, one way or another, would inevitably belong to the Soul Reaper. For the dozens of islanders who had perished in the fight, Alastair had pushed up the timeline of their eventual demise.

A paltry number, the Soul Reaper said.

Alastair's stomach dropped at his words. Everything happened in a fraction of a second.

The entity outstretched his hands and his power blanketed the room, suffocating the people inside. He consumed more than just the Souls of those that had already been slain but devoured those of the terrified islanders standing before him. One by one, each death slammed into Alastair like a hammer on a nail.

Shauni vanished from across the room and appeared beside him. Alastair barely had time to register her stunned expression before a veil of darkness enveloped them.

Alastair floated through the Cosmos in suspended animation. It suffocated him. It breathed life into him. It glistened and sparkled with the brightness of a thousand suns. It obscured him in the deepest depths of its vast oceans. It disintegrated his body and Soul. It rebuilt him anew.

He waded through its waters, aided by a guiding hand pushing him forward. Its ancient, arcane power seeped into his veins, making blistering pain twine with ecstasy.

An eternity passed. A moment passed. Alastair's eyes fluttered open. His vision blurred, and it took several moments for him to get his bearings.

Overhead, a soft white cloud drifted through the clear blue sky. Thin blades of grass pricked his skin and he shivered as a cold breeze flew over him. Alastair sat upright and barely caught himself when he tipped back over. Haizea lay on the ground to his left. In spite of his wobbling legs, he bent down and helped her stand upright.

He straightened her clothes and she brushed his hair with her fingers. Their eyes met. Although neither of them signed, they both nodded before embracing one another.

Off to his right, Shauni climbed to her feet. She rested a hand on a nearby tree and clutched her head. Her lips moved and, going by her facial expression, it was a string of curses. She removed the earth's smoke from her body and the light of her Soul returned, her vitality fanning outward in rolling waves.

Haizea went over to Shauni and addressed her injuries. The blood oozing from her broken skin slowed to a stop. The discoloration from deep bruises faded into her normal light brown tone. Her shoulders slackened and the tension in her expression eased.

Shauni's lips moved and Haizea shook her head. They both turned to him.

Alastair had long learned how to decipher the different meanings behind Haizea's ever present scowl. He gauged it in subtle cues—the tightness in the corners of her mouth, the way she flared her nostrils, how her brows cast a shadow over her eyes. The more she hardened her expression, the deeper the emotion she was trying to hide.

And right now, she'd practically turned into a statue.

Still, emotions eked through her stony exterior—fear, confusion, and anger, each laced with an undercurrent of bloodlust. Her eyes still shined a brilliant crimson. The flames of her magic flickered toward him, threatening to engulf him. A shiver raced down his spine at the sensation.

~*Do you know where the Soul Reaper brought us?*~ she asked, her arms tremoring as she signed.

Before Alastair could answer, something tugged at his magic. A shadow fell over them as a flock of birds filled the sky. They scattered in every direction, wings flapping erratically. A soft breeze against the back of his neck prompted him to turn around.

The earth rumbled beneath his feet and a gang of elk galloped by, their hooves kicking up dirt. Alastair lost count at twenty. The group splintered as a pack of wolves nipped at their heels. Foaming saliva dripped from their jowls. Some of them paused and turned their frenzied gazes toward their trio. One of them bared its teeth at Alastair and, before he could react, it flung itself into the air.

He barely had time to brace himself for impact—before he could even blink, hot breath fanned across his face as the wolf's teeth grazed the tip of Alastair's nose. But, to his surprise, it never clamped its jaws shut—the canine came to an abrupt halt mid-lunge. The animal jerked backward and its nose and muzzle smashed inward, like it had hit an invisible wall. When a few other wolves tried to follow suit, they were beaten back in a similar fashion.

Alastair's gaze flickered to Shauni. She had not moved a muscle, but her magic snapped about like a whip and shimmered and glistened around her. In fact, the air itself rippled in long waves. She fended off the wild wolves with another telekinetic shove. Again the air distorted from her power.

His brows furrowed—he'd seen a similar disturbance before, but only at the monastery. Alastair took a closer look at his surroundings. Foliage spanned as far as the eyes could see. He didn't recognize the area, but Alastair usually traveled to the monastery from the east since he came from the village cluster. A densely wooded area lined the western side—maybe the Soul Reaper had left them on that end instead.

He tapped Haizea on the shoulder and signed as much to her. They followed his lead. As they walked, more fauna raced by them in a frenzy—mice scurried over their feet and squirrels leapt from tree to tree. When he looked at Haizea and Shauni, their bewildered expressions mirrored his own.

Several minutes later, they emerged from the woods and, as he predicted, the back side of the monastery came into view. It gleamed so brightly that Alastair couldn't look at it directly for more than a few seconds. Haizea raised her hand to cast a shadow over her eyes. Shauni stood motionless with her jaw slackened.

~*The atmosphere feels heavy. Like someone's put a giant boulder on my shoulders.*~ she signed.

~*It's because the vitality is more concentrated here. More people. More mages and omens.*~

And, undoubtedly, the Soul Reaper's presence had tipped the scales even further. The entity had faded, but he never fully disappeared from Alastair's perception. He still lingered in the background, ever watchful.

Even more unnerving was the entity's satisfaction. A hundred Souls. That was the price for the Soul Reaper's intervention on their behalf.

The pain of their deaths clung to Alastair like a second skin.

He'd killed before—an entire army, in fact. But something about this felt different. It was one thing to die and for a wandering Soul to find their home in the Soul Realm. Alastair had taken control over their Souls and fed them to the God of Death himself.

One moment, they'd lived and breathed. The next, the spark of life had been extinguished from within. No, it was more than that—*he* had blown out the flame.

Their open mouths, twisted into silent screams as their Souls severed from their bodies, still played before his eyes.

Alastair wrung his hands together, palms clammy. He couldn't think of it that way. If he did, then guilt would eat him alive. He'd acted to protect Shauni and Haizea. They were his family and family always came first.

He refused to allow anyone else he loved to meet their demise in such a violent way ever again. Even if it meant someone else suffered...even if it meant someone else perished.

Haizea searched his face and took his hand in hers, squeezing it lightly. Based on the way another prickle raked through his skull, her sight must not have worn off yet.

Up ahead, two robed figures stood outside of the monastery. Alastair recognized Pamin and Diora's Souls, even though he couldn't make out their faces just yet.

His back stiffened. Alastair didn't know if he was ready to face them. Not so soon after what had just happened...after what he'd done.

As they closed the distance, Pamin and Diora's grave demeanor further gave him pause. Diora locked eyes with Haizea's. Although Haizea's expression did not change, her hand trembled in his grasp and the fangs of her anxiety sank into his Soul.

Pamin stepped forward.

~We've been waiting for you. Something terrible has happened.~

Chapter 34

Human Realm, Mount Illiniza, Heavensbreath Village

The cable car swayed from side to side as it traveled down the ropeway. Trees flashed by in the viewing window, creating streaks of brown and green. From this high off the ground, Haizea could see the curvature of the mountainside. Under normal circumstances, she would have admired the sight, but right now she couldn't expend the energy to properly appreciate it.

A pit settled in her stomach. Diora had seen a vision of a pylon collapsing about halfway down the mountain's slope. It all happened in the span of a breath. Massive chunks of metal rained down from the sky, crushing anyone unfortunate enough to be standing in its path.

Given how the timing worked out when they arrived in Windhaven, Haizea suspected that the Soul Reaper might have weighed his hand in the manner.

She'd known Alastair could communicate with the Soul Reaper. But she never expected him to call on the entity in the way that he did—by sacrificing the Souls of so many islanders. His intervention helped them escape, but all of Kestramore's leaders had been in attendance. The mound of corpses left in their wake would certainly result in calls for retribution.

Unfortunately, it was a problem she would have to table for later. One that she needed to discuss with Vendela—assuming that she had survived after the collapse.

Haizea clenched and unclenched her fists.

Why was Vendela down the slope to begin with? She didn't mention going on an assignment down there.

Haizea turned at the sound of Shauni's voice, but her friend was staring out of the window with her brows casting a dark shadow over her eyes. She frowned to herself—the telepathic power in her blood had not faded yet.

"Something must have happened while we were gone," Haizea said while signing simultaneously. Shauni arched an eyebrow but quickly shrugged it off.

"A fucking lot happened," she huffed. "First the islanders, and now this. Not to mention animals losing their minds. I've never seen anything like that before."

~*The Soul Reaper's presence probably had something to do with that. Animals are more sensitive to the vitality than we often think,*~ Alastair offered.

Haizea turned toward the window again and the memory of the man, eaten by wolves resurfaced–the animals had fled after she flared her power. Her brows drew together. Perhaps their behavior had been influenced less by animal instinct and more by an unseen force agitating them.

The cable car slowed as it reached their destination. They'd have to walk the rest of the way to Heavensbreak village because the next section of the ropeway was still under construction. Haizea's satchel hung heavily on her shoulder—numerous containers filled with a variety of plants weighed it down. Given the likelihood of grave injuries, she would need to make potions to aid in her healing.

It took another half day to reach Heavensbreath. Her healing magic waxed and waned as they drew closer. Beside her, Alastair stiffened.

They found the source of the disturbance rather quickly. A mound of mangled metal littered the construction site. The villagers had removed many of the bodies and lined them up a little ways away. People came by and added to a stack of wood that would soon become the pyre.

Haizea scanned the crowd, but she didn't see Vendela. Shauni whistled, high-pitched and loud, so that it made her ears vibrate. Some of the people moving about turned their heads. Only then did Haizea see Yelena amongst them. She jogged over to their trio.

"Thank the realms you're here. I didn't think you all would be back from the island so quickly," she looked them over. "What the hell happened?"

"It's a long story. A hell of a story, actually. We can talk more over a stiff drink," Shauni said.

"One of the monks at the monastery told us about the pylon collapsing after we returned. We came straight here," Haizea added.

Yelena sighed.

"It's not pretty. As I'm sure you can see, quite a few of the lumberjacks died in the collapse. And for those that survived, there wasn't a healer nearby that could help. We had to make do with what we had," she paused, grimacing. "Apparently, Jassia was here too. Her father was working on the pylon."

Haizea turned to stone.

"Vendela and I left in the middle of training. I think she caught wind of it then and followed us. She got her hands on a blade infused with earth's smoke. When the pylon collapsed, it lodged into her arm. We had no choice but to cut it off and without a healer..." Yelena trailed off. "Of the survivors, she's fared the worst. I don't know how much you can do for her, but I don't think she has much time left."

Alastair rested his hand against her back. Haizea didn't look at him—she couldn't. If she met his soft gaze, she would crumble where she stood. But the warmth of his touch gave her strength. When she spoke, the bravado in her tone did not betray the way her heart stuttered in her chest.

"Take me to her."

The villagers had sequestered the injured in a cabin not too far away from the construction site. Vendela entered Haizea's sights first. She was sitting in a chair beside a cot. A pool of blood settled at her feet. She held her left arm at an odd angle, her hand falling limp. Her once faint wrinkles had deepened into hard lines on her forehead and around her mouth.

Haizea touched Vendela's shoulder. Her eyes widened before she jumped up from her seat.

"Thank the realms," she whispered.

Jassia's small form was lying in the cot. Only a bloody stump remained of her arm—they'd chopped it off at the elbow.

Vendela's chest rattled against Haizea's magic with each breath she took. The vitality in her chest was dim and warped, but she knew that Vendela would rebuff any attempts to address her wounds until she healed Jassia.

Haizea held her breath as she unwrapped the blood-soaked bandage. More seeped from the wound. She carefully cleaned it off and pressed her hand against the stub of Jassia's arm. It sealed shut at a sluggish pace—Jassia's vitality lacked its normal density. Haizea encountered numerous voids and there was very little vitality for her magic to mend and weave.

She pressed down on Jassia's fingertips. The skin under her nails paled and the color did not return. Jassia had lost a lot of blood. Her chest rose and fell in shallow breaths and her brows knitted together, as if in pain despite her slumber.

As she touched Jassia's skin, faint images flickered before her eyes: Jassia's parents. Covy. Vendela. Herself.

Jassia traveling down the mountainside and running into a girl with blonde and blue eyes.

"We put an enchantment on her. It's the only option we had to mollify the pain," Vendela rested a hand on her leg. "How bad is she? Did we get the earth's smoke in time?"

Vendela's voice faded into a distant echo. Haizea stared blankly at Jassia's face.

"Haizea," Vendela prompted.

She blinked.

"I—" she cleared her throat. Shook her head.

"It's not the earth's smoke. If it were still within her, I wouldn't be able to sense her vitality. She's in bad shape because of the blood loss. I can heal her, but healing magic has limitations. I can seal a wound shut. I can take the vitality from a robust area in the body and move it to a spot with insufficient amounts. Jassia has lost so much blood and has so little vitality left in her body…it's like trying to sew a hole in a shirt without enough thread. That's why her arm is still raw despite my efforts."

"So there's nothing you can do?"

"Her body needs to replenish the vitality it's lost," Haizea opened her satchel and pulled out its contents. She mixed the plants into a topical cream and massaged it onto Jassia's wounds. "This treatment will help supplement, but it's a process that takes time. Time I'm not sure she has."

A few tufts of gray hair sprouted along Vendela's hairline. She frowned and studied Haizea's face for a long moment.

"You're thinking of something. What is it?" Vendela asked.

Haizea hummed, stewing over her words.

"Healing magic may not be sufficient, but I might be able to do it with blood magic."

Vendela's grimace deepened.

"How?"

"Healing mends and weaves. It neither adds nor subtracts. But blood magic does."

"I'm no omen, but even I know that blood magic subtracts from *others* and adds to the *user*," Vendela said. She narrowed her eyes. "Are you really telling me you can do the opposite?"

"Blood magic taps into the power of the Cosmos. By nature, it bends the rules. Absorbing the vitality is what's most natural for blood mages. But we can also reverse the flow. It goes against the grain, but it's possible."

"You can do it for Jassia," she stated, her voice low and even.

"Conceptually, yes. In practice, I don't know if it's truly feasible. I've yet to try it on a person. My father is the only person I know of who has. When my mother fell ill and normal healing didn't work, it's what he did to save her. Or, at least he tried to. We both know how that turned out."

Vendela sobered and rested her hand on Jassia's leg.

"She's hanging on by a thread and she'll die if we don't. I want you to try it."

"Vendela—"

"I should have kept a better eye on her. I got careless. And now one of my warriors is on death's doorstep. She still has a mother and many warrior sisters waiting for her back in Windhaven. If you say blood magic will help her, then do it."

Haizea made to move but hesitated in place. If her control slipped for even a fraction of a second, she would reduce Jassia to ash. There was no room for error. On top of that, she'd only tested this ability on a rat before—and it had deteriorated within minutes. She didn't know if it was truly possible.

"You won't hurt her," Vendela insisted, as if she'd read her thoughts.

"You don't know that. You've never experienced its pull."

"Your magic may tempt you, but your heart would never allow such a thing to happen."

A lump formed in Haizea's throat as she met Vendela's gaze. She steeled herself and unsheathed her ankle blade. She made a small cut in her palm before repeating the same with Jassia. As she cupped her hands around Jassia's, a nostalgia settled within.

Her father had held her mother the same way. He'd brought her from the brink of death, but she'd succumbed to her illness, wasting away further each time they thought his efforts had been successful.

Haizea stopped short. Suddenly, it all clicked together. Wasted—her mother had *wasted* away. Her father was an omen with corrupted vitality. What if by passing his vitality onto her mother, his efforts exacerbated her illness by adding on the extra burden of magical wasting?

It's something he may not have considered—and if he did, years of nonuse undoubtedly dulled his senses and precision. He would not have been able to filter through the particles and differentiate them effectively.

It explained why the rat she'd tested perished so quickly.

"I can't use my own vitality. Jassia isn't an omen," Haizea said after a moment.

"I'll do it," Shauni offered. Haizea shook her head.

"You're a mage. It might be fine, but it might not. There's no room for error here."

"Use me," Vendela said.

"She needs a substantial amount and you're injured. You might not survive it."

"How about me?" Yelena said.

"Absolutely not," Vendela said. "It's a warrior's duty to protect the mountains. It's a leader's duty to protect those underneath them—that includes all of you."

"Vendela—" A sharp look from their leader cut Shauni off.

"I'm replaceable. You all aren't. You still have most of your lives to live."

Still, Haizea hesitated, but Vendela took her blade and sliced her own palm.

"Help her. Before it's too late," she insisted.

Haizea sighed and held Vendela's and Jassia's hands in her own. She drew upon Vendela's life force, first taking a small, cautious amount. Not only did she have to ensure she did not push her own vitality toward Jassia, but she had to move quickly enough that her body did not absorb Vendela's vitality in the process—corrupting it as a result. She shifted through each particle with precision.

Then, Haizea went against her every instinct as a blood mage: rather than pull, she pushed.

The vitality inched its way outward. Haizea grunted and pushed a bit more, her eyes glued on Jassia's face. Her control *absolutely* could not slip. Not even for a second, because that was all it took for her to reduce a human body to a pile of dust. Her magic stretched like a rubber band, pulling taut so that it threatened to snap back despite her best efforts.

Still, Jassia looked all too pale and her heart pumped much too weakly.

Haizea gritted her teeth, *pulling* from Vendela and *pushing* into Jassia.

Delayed, she realized she was shivering. Exhaustion hit her like a brick wall, but the fruits of her efforts began to bloom: a soft pink blush tinted Jassia's cheeks and her chest rose and fell much more evenly. Vendela's hand fell limp in her grasp and felt cold as ice. Haizea turned toward her, but violent tremors wracked through her body and she swayed. An invisible force caught her before she hit the ground.

Shauni crouched down beside her.

"I think that's enough," she whispered.

Another set of hands pressed against her and her magic jolted in response. Vision swimming, she leaned into Alastair. They only made it a few steps before her stomach lurched. She sagged to her hands and knees and vomited.

Alastair helped her right herself, keeping a steadying hand on her back.

Haizea could hear Shauni and Yelena behind her. They called Vendela's name a few times, but as far as she could tell, they received no response. Tears welled in her eyes as Alastair ushered her away to the far side of the site. He sat her down on a tree stump and knelt in front of her, cupping her cheek in his hand.

Haizea hated the way he looked at her in the moment—the way the light in his eyes dimmed. How his fingers quivered against her skin. The frown puckering his lips.

She took a deep breath to steel herself and mustered the strength to sign.

~I know who did this.~

Chapter 35

Human Realm, Island of Kestramore

Viltarin tiptoed across the threshold of his home. The floorboards creaked under his weight despite his efforts to move stealthily. His eyes darted in every direction, searching for the slightest movement or disturbance.

He'd managed to slip away from the gala tonight unscathed, but with his curse no longer impeding Kallistê, she would undoubtedly hunt him down. Still, Viltarin made no efforts to hide—the realmdrifter could scour every inch of the seven realms, much less their small island. It made more sense to hold up the fort at home.

So long as he did not allow her to catch him unawares, he could simply curse her again. Though the realmdrifter frustrated him, she was not worthy of his fear, not in the slightest. But the mountaineers...

The mountaineers disturbed him.

It was one thing to nullify a curse by removing or destroying an object or killing the mage who cast it. It was another thing entirely for Viltarin to infuse the weight of a curse into his words, and it had no discernible effect. The violet-eyed woman hadn't even been a mage, much less an omen. Yet she remained completely unfazed by his magic. In fact, she'd found his failed efforts humorous.

By the realms, what the fuck was happening?

Viltarin ushered Milo into their bedroom and locked the door. As a seer, Milo would hear the realmdrifter's thoughts as she approached and alert him accordingly. Once she entered his range of attack, Viltarin would simply utter a few words to bring her to heel. A straightforward, two-step plan. It only required that they stayed diligent and alert.

Milo entered the room first and did a careful sweep with his telepathy. He held up his hand before turning to Viltarin.

"I—"

Wetness splattered across Viltarin's face. He flinched and wiped his eyes. A Beast materialized out of thin air and now had its jaws clamped down on Milo's neck. It growled, a low rumble deep in its chest. A massive chunk of flesh smacked against the wall. Milo dropped to the ground in a heap, a gaping hole in his throat and blood pooling beneath his motionless form.

A cry swelled in Viltarin's throat as he gaped at the sight of his body. He traced over the tattoo on his finger—he and Milo had gotten matching ones a few years ago, after they got engaged. Now his beloved lay before him, his vacant eyes staring at him. A sneer crept across Viltarin's face and he turned on his heels.

"Kall—"

The Beast emitted a piercing, mind-splintering howl that brought him to his knees. The windows shattered and thousands of shards rained down on him. Blood trickled from his ears.

A pair of high heels and carefully manicured toes appeared before him.

A kick to the head sent his gaze upward. He met Kallistê's cloudy gaze and she smiled down at him with an angelic radiance. Some sort of substance poked out of her ears. Given how the Beast's howl seemed to unfaze her, it was likely protecting her from the noise.

He tried to cover his ears, but his arm would not move. Viltarin lay there, paralyzed by the unearthly sound and his vision slowly faded to black.

Viltarin woke up to the earth quaking beneath his feet and a fire raging in his throat. His arms were bound in an outstretched position so that his shoulders pulled taught. Something rough scratched against his skin. He tilted his head to see a tree towering over him.

"Kallistê!" he shouted. Or at least he tried to–her name came out sounding like a garbled mess.

He gagged against the piece of cloth shoved in his mouth. Tension seized his head as he shifted—a tight band kept the material in place.

"What's that? Speak slowly and try to enunciate your words."

Kallistê's voice came from overhead. She peered down at him with her legs crossed and her hands folded in her lap as she floated in the sky.

A deep bellow reverberated through the air followed by another violent tremor beneath his feet. Falling leaves blanketed his vision and he sputtered as they landed in his mouth. Viltarin tugged against his binds to no avail. Where had she taken him?

Kallistê laughed as she watched him struggle, her voice soft and melodious like a flute.

The answer to Viltarin's question came in the form of a massive figure barreling toward him, as if it had been tossed through the air. A giant humanoid creature landed a few yards away from him. It clambered to its feet and cast the entire area under its shadow, shifting it from midday to the darkness of midnight in the blink of an eye.

Blood dripped from its wounds and splattered on the ground. Almost instantaneously, new plant life sprouted where it had landed. Viltarin gawked at the sight.

The giant had hundreds, if not thousands, of marks on its skin. They were raised ridges, like scars. It uprooted a tree nearby and went running off. A violent crack echoed in the distance shortly thereafter. It was fighting something, but at his current vantage point, Viltarin could not determine what.

"How familiar are you with the seven realms, Viltarin?"

In answer, Viltarin made a muffled protest of a sound. Kallistê smirked.

"There's our home, the Human Realm. The Beast Realm, which is where I found my beloved pets. The Demon Realm, where the goddess Aaryn lives. The Celestial Realm, home to the Angels. The Soul Realm, where we all go after we die. The Cosmic Realm, which birthed every realm and every life force in existence," Kallistê counted in her fingers as she spoke. She only held up six.

"Ah! I missed one. We currently stand in the Titan Realm. That giant you saw? It's in the middle of a death battle with one of its own kind. I don't quite understand it, and don't really care to, but they fight as often as they breathe. And as you can see with the newly sprouted flowers, the realm itself quite literally thrives on bloodshed. One of them will die, and their blood will bring forth new life. Poetic, if you ask me."

Both Titans came into view as they exchanged blows. The original Titan tackled the other to the ground. It straddled them and landed a barrage of blows before the second one managed to buck them off. They rolled on the ground wildly, leveling a row of trees in the process. A cloud of bark and dirt coated the air. Viltarin squinted as some of the debris sprayed onto him.

One of the Titans bellowed as the other tore its arm from its body. It held the severed appendage high up in the air and let the blood pour into its mouth. The wounds on its body dissipated immediately after.

"I forgot to mention they can use another's blood to heal themselves as well. This fight could last a few minutes, or a few days, or even a few weeks," Kallistê shrugged. "Whoever wins will mark their skin afterward. Things will calm for a bit. Then, sooner or later, the wind will blow the wrong direction and they'll start fighting again. My first time here, they leveled out an entire forest in ten minutes. But as you can see, it will grow back just as quickly."

Still smiling, Kallistê descended toward the ground.

"If you're lucky, one of those Titans will crush you where you stand in an hour or so. Or, you might just live through this battle. But the Titan Realm is no place for a human being. You've no way to return. You can't even speak, much less cry out for help."

She reached into her shirt and pulled out two blades.

"Oh, these are mere kitchen knives. But I've been thinking about my guests at the ball. The ones that you did everything in your power to tarnish my reputation with: the Bruvian warriors. I've always admired how they dual-wield their weapons. The more that I think about it, it makes perfect sense. The human body has two of almost everything. Two arms. Two legs. Two hands. Two feet," Kallistê pointed the knives at each body part as she spoke. "Two eyes. Two ears."

Viltarin blinked. Kallistê vanished. Sharp pain seared into either side of his chest and he breathed out a gurgling wheeze.

"Two lungs," she whispered.

"If you wanted me out of the picture, then you should have killed me. Your arrogance and closed-mindedness brought you here. Now, you'll die here, tied to this tree, because the only person who could possibly *begin* to help you is *me*, Viltarin. I have a dream for Kestramore and the rest of the realm that I fully intended to have realized. I'll be damned if you or anyone else stands in my way."

Kallistê floated backward, her eyes never leaving his.

"We'll meet again, someday. In the Soul Realm. I'll let you know how victory tastes. Until then, you can spend the rest of eternity wallowing in your own defeat."

Chapter 36

Human Realm, Mount Illiniza, Heavensbreath Village

A dark bruise bloomed on Sage's side. The fabric of her shirt pricked like pins and needles against her skin and one of her arms bent at an odd angle. Each step she took brought on a bout of dizziness and jostled her insides, but her desperation to get away from the construction site pushed her to continue onward.

She put one foot forward. Then another. And another.

Snap.

A snare closed around her leg. The world spun and flipped upside down as a rope yanked her toward the sky. She swung wildly from a tree limb.

Some part of Sage's mind was still functional—she reached forward and sent a wave of magic to free herself from the tree. She'd intended to cut the rope, but her vitality flared violently and the tree's massive trunk groaned as it bulged outward before bursting. Wood grated against wood and splinters rained down on her. Her reflexes weren't quick enough to blunt her fall. Pain exploded within as the impact knocked the wind out of her lungs.

Something broke inside of her. Her bones. Her spirit. She wasn't sure which.

A metallic taste coated her tongue. When she coughed to dispel it, blood splattered on the ground. She winced as pain stabbed at her side. Sage lifted her shirt to see the bruise on her side expanding across her abdomen.

Vision swirling, she curled into a ball. Shivers wracked through her body.

Felix. She needed to get back to him and check on his condition. He could barely sit up right when she left him. That's why she'd gone to the village to begin with. And then...and then...

Sage eyes fluttered closed, too tired to think. Too tired to worry. Darkness wrapped its arms around her, eclipsing the luminous gleam of the vitality and enveloping her in its shadows. She welcomed its stone-cold silence and sank into its embrace.

Perhaps it meant that this living nightmare would end.

Time ticked by—a second, a minute, an hour, a day—she didn't know how long. But despite her wishes, the Cosmos did not let her go so easily. It roared and dragged her back into the light.

The vitality fluxed around her. It swayed and parted ways as another force commanded it to kneel. A suffocating weight settled on Sage's chest. She jolted awake and gasped for air and the motion sent another wave of blistering pain through her abdomen.

She tried to sit upright, but her arms buckled and she fell face first into the dirt.

"Felix," she called out, but only managed a raspy whisper.

Thump *thump*.

Sage's breath hitched in her throat. A cold sweat broke out across her body.

"Felix," she breathed.

Thump *thump*.

Silence. Her brother was not here. He could not help her. Alone. Sage was all alone.

She and Felix had spent nearly two years on the run. They'd done all of this to avoid detection by the omens who had invaded Arcelia—and to exact vengeance on the one who killed their parents.

Sage never imagined that her moment would come this way. They were supposed to scale the rest of the mountain. Catch her by surprise. But things hadn't turned out like they'd planned. It seemed it never did.

The blood mage closed the distance between them, each step sending shockwaves of energy through the vitality. She lowered herself to Sage's level and sat down on the ground. Her vermillion eyes bored holes into her very Soul.

"You've grown since I last saw you. If I remember correctly, your birthday passed a little while ago. Hard to believe you're sixteen now."

Odd, how calmly she spoke—though the thundering in Sage's ears nearly muffled her words. The blood mage looked around and frowned.

"Where's your brother?" she asked.

Sage couldn't give him away. He still had a chance to survive this—to make it down the mountain and back to their home.

"He...he didn't make it."

The blood mage's eyes narrowed on her, cold and assessing. Something sharp clawed through Sage's mind and she shuddered. The blood mage hummed, low and soft, but otherwise did not press further. A silence settled between them.

That painful, raking sensation returned and with it came more memories: the tavern, Jorah, the collapsing pylon. The tiny cot she had in Miss Tamsyn's cabin. Bose materializing at the dinner table as they sat down for supper. Her brother's complaints about drinking water from a pig bladder...such a trivial matter to take issue with.

A tear slid down Sage's cheek.

"You're here to kill me, aren't you?" she whispered.

The blood mage shifted as she crossed her legs. A moment passed before she answered.

"Do you know why I killed your father?"

Sage's teeth clattered together as she nodded.

"Felix told me he used your grandfather as bait to reel you in."

"Is that all he told you?"

"He said that Father cut off his head and sent it to you and because it's the same thing you warriors do when you kill your enemies."

"King Rhys chained my grandfather down in a cage and proceeded to torture him for hours on end. He ripped out his tongue. Tore off his fingernails, and when my grandfather passed out from the pain, King Rhys waited until he was alert and awake to cut off his head. Did Felix tell you that?"

Despite her neutral visage, the vitality quaked with the blood mage's words. Sage swallowed thickly and shook her head.

"Your father was very intentional about his methods to antagonize me. He wanted a fight, and I responded accordingly. He gambled and lost."

"What about my mother? She didn't have to die."

The blood mage plucked a blade of grass and examined it. She released it with a sigh and a soft breeze carried it away.

"She didn't. I wanted to hurt King Rhys the same way he hurt me. I won't apologize for what I did. If I could do it all over, the only thing I'd change is to kill him much sooner, before he could hurt my grandfather," her glowing eyes flickered like a torch in the night. "But I am sorry for the position I put you in. King Rhys deserved to die, but you didn't deserve to lose your father."

Sage fiddled with her fingers. Something in her chest pulled taut.

"I don't forgive you," she whispered. "I hate you. I hate my parents for leaving me behind. I hate Felix because I don't know what he sees when he looks at me. I can't tell if he actually cares about me as his sister or if he just wants to protect me as a weapon. And I...I hate myself," she sniffed and wiped her cheeks. "For following him. For hurting so many people."

Sage rocked back and forth, her magic rising and crashing within like an ocean wave.

"I...I saw you down at the base. You came with your friend. I thought you might have recognized me. We should have turned back then."

The blood mage's brows rose.

"I remember a girl running away and dropping her bowl of soup. So that was you."

"Felix bought enchantments for us."

"That means you were in Eaglestone too."

Sage nodded. The blood paused, looking off into the distance.

"I met an older woman there. Her name was Miss Tamsyn. Is that how you learned transmutation?"

"She said I was too young. Felix convinced her to teach him instead. When we were alone, he passed everything he learned onto me."

Another itch ruffled underneath her skin as she spoke. Unable to resist, she began snapping, creating small sparks of flame as if her fingers were matchsticks.

"You haven't been in control for quite a while now, have you?"

She shook her head, dampness welling in her eyes.

"I'm scared," she whispered.

Something flickered in the blood mage's expression. Not warm, but not unkind either.

"She'll hesitate when she sees you. That will be your opening."

The blood mage had sat down and opened a dialogue, but Sage didn't know if that meant she had no desire to bring her harm, or if she simply hadn't made up her mind yet.

Felix would have long attacked by now. He would have unleashed the full might of his Cosmic power as soon as an opportunity presented itself.

Her stomach churned. She could do nothing and lose her chance, leaving herself open to the blood mage's whims yet again. Or she could attack and bring an end to this. She'd have to act while the blood mage's guard was still down. Each moment she waited gave the omen more time to think—more time to decide that Sage's life was not worth sparing a second time.

Sage reached for her magic but stopped short as she coughed up another globule of blood. She lifted her shirt and touched her side. Darkness skirted the edges of her visions, and she buckled over from the pain. Before, the bruise had been roughly the side of her fist. Now it spanned from her ribcage to her hips.

Her ears began to ring. Something was wrong. Very, very wrong. Time would heal her broken arm, but she was bleeding internally. Going by how quickly her bruise had spread, she must have lost a lot of blood already. With each passing second, she would lose that much more.

And the only person who could help her was the very person she'd come here to kill.

The blood mage's voice yanked Sage from her thoughts.

"Not only have you scaled a mountain, but of the five major peaks, you're on Illiniza. You're within striking distance of my home village. On top of that, you're an omen now. This was no coincidence—you came here for me."

Sage shrank away, but collapsed under her own weight, and her cheek hit the blood-tinged dirt. As much as she tried, she couldn't muster the strength to pick herself back up.

"Please don't hurt me," she rasped.

The blood mage stood, and the air around her rippled and distorted from the movement. Sage's breath caught in her throat as she made a desperate attempt to reach for her magic.

Heat singed her skin as fire birthed from the air and crackled against her ears. As the energy built within, her vision flickered, and Sage's command over the vitality slipped from her grasp.

An invisible force seized Sage from within, constricting her veins and paralyzing her. Her heart stuttered within her chest, leaving her breathless. Wetness trickled down her nose and splashed onto her hand. The blood mage's form blurred before her as Sage crumpled to the ground.

The last thing she saw was the blood mage's glowing crimson eyes before the darkness swept over her.

"Is this him?"

Haizea followed Shauni to a secluded clearing between villages. They stopped in front of a small camp, where a young man slept beside a tree. Blankets partially obscured his face, but Haizea could make out enough of his features to identify him.

She crouched down in front of Felix and pressed her palm against his skin. The vitality in his body was dim, particularly in his lungs and head—a telltale sign of altitude sickness. She turned to Shauni.

"Yes."

Shauni crossed her arms over her chest.

"And you're sure about this? I...despite my own feelings, I know what they meant to you."

Haizea nodded, ignoring the lump that had formed in her throat. Her friend glanced at Felix's sleeping form, her eyes darkening.

"Alright," Shauni sighed. "Let's get this over with then."

Haizea stood upright and nudged him with her boot. When he didn't stir, she kicked harder. Felix rolled over with a groan. It took several seconds for him to open his eyes. Several more for recognition to flicker in his expression. Then, it melted into a peculiar mixture of fear and rage.

Felix slipped as he tried to get to his feet, his movements lethargic and uncoordinated. He wheezed and slumped over from the exertion. Somehow, he still managed to glower at her from his spot on the ground.

"You," he snarled. The word came out slurred and barely comprehensible.

"Me," she answered. "You traveled this far. So I've decided to meet you halfway."

Felix's magic spiked. A blade appeared from underneath his blankets, and he hurled it toward her with telekinesis. It barely moved a few inches before it halted in midair. The metal crumpled into a ball and fell harmlessly to the ground.

Haizea studied him. Patches of stubble lined his jaw. He'd shorn his hair low, barely a quarter of an inch long. Dark circles colored the skin beneath his eyes.

"If there's anything you want to get off your chest, this is your opportunity," Haizea prompted.

"There's...," he pressed his palm to his head, and inhaled a labored breath. "There's nothing for us to talk about, witch," he hissed.

His vitality surged again, but it sputtered out almost immediately.

"I'm surprised. I gave your sister the chance to speak. She seemed to have plenty to say."

At this, he paused. His eyes darted across the campsite.

"Where's Sage?"

Silence.

"Where. Is. Sage?" he pressed.

"She's not here. I am. That's what you need to focus on right now."

"Fuck you."

Haizea leveled her gaze at him. His heartbeat accelerated in kind.

"You and your sister have left a trail of bodies in your wake, and you're a long way from home. If I were you, I'd tread carefully."

He spat at her. Even that small seemed to drain him—his heart pumped harder in his chest, and his shoulders sagged downward.

Shauni grunted beside her. The sound drew his attention to her companion.

"Two of you for one of me? You've always been weak," he taunted.

"And yet you're the one who's been hiding behind his teenage sister."

"You don't get to act high and mighty. We have nothing, *nothing* because of you. I did what I had to do. Pushed her when she needed pushing."

Felix climbed to his feet. Stumbled. Barely caught himself on a nearby tree trunk before he sank back to the ground.

"Sage and I spent two years working for this moment," his hands trembled as he spoke. "I never thought you'd actually lay a finger on her. Not in a million years."

"You gambled with your sister's life. King Rhys made a similar choice when he tried to hunt me down. Look what it cost him."

"My father only wanted what was best for the kingdom. His only error was refusing to match your wretched magic with his own. I would have done it myself, but I can't wield Cosmic power. If I could, I'd have turned you inside out before you could even blink. I had no choice but to use Sage."

Haizea hummed, mulling over his words.

"Do you know what she said about you?"

"Whatever it is, I have no reason to believe you."

"She said that she wasn't sure whether you cared about her as a person or if you were only invested in what she could do with her power. Even now, that's all you speak about. Did you ever once ask her what she wanted?"

For just a breath, Felix's stiffened and his eyes widened. Then he recovered, his teeth bared.

"Stop the act, witch. You don't get to talk like that–like you *cared* about her. You killed my little sister. My parents. You left our only home in shambles. *You're* the reason omens crossed the ocean and chased us out. And the mountains are no place for people of the kingdoms. We've no place left to go. I can't even...I can barely breathe," he gasped, his lips gaining a bluish tint.

"Sage was...she was good. And that made her too weak to do what was necessary. She didn't thirst for vengeance. But I'll do what she couldn't. I'll claw my kingdom back from the omens and cleanse the realm of filth like you."

Haizea let his words hang in the air before responding.

"Is that all you have to say?"

He returned her glare with one of his own. She shook her head.

At the very least, she could admit that Felix was right. The blood of everything and everyone they ever knew and loved stained her hands. She had earned every ounce of their anger and hatred.

It made what she had come to do hurt that much more.

"I let you live. And you spent it by directing all this time and energy toward killing me," she paused, scrutinizing him. "I can't afford a second time."

"Yo–"

Haizea cut him off with her magic before he could speak—before she could remember him as the boy she once knew. Before she could change her mind.

One moment, Felix sat there defiantly with his mouth open. The next, he was gone, rendered to mere dust particles that floated away in the wind.

She should not have been surprised that King Rhys's children had followed in his footsteps and spent their time plotting her demise. But she'd hoped for something different. Something more.

Something better.

Haizea closed her eyes. She squeezed her hands into fists and inhaled deeply in an effort to maintain her composure.

Tears would not resurrect Vendela or Jorah or give Jassia her arm back. It would not erase the errors she'd made—or the fact that people she loved had paid the price for them yet again.

Shauni put a hand on her shoulder and looked at her solemnly. They walked back to the construction site in silence, with only Haizea's regret filling the void.

Chapter 37

Human Realm, Island of Kestramore, Khisfire Province

Kallistê emerged from the Cosmos, robed in its iridescent light. Magical pressure pulsed against her temples and resonated through her Soul as her feet landed softly on the ground.

She found Eryx in the east wing of the mansion, opposite to where the chaos had unfolded. The Premier sat in a cushioned chair with her feet propped up on an ottoman. A sheen of sweat glistened on the older woman's forehead.

Kallistê frowned. Heat billowed up her chest and neck, and her own magic sparked with energy. She fanned herself and fluffed her hair to lift it away from her neck.

"Good, you're back," Eryx said. "I see you're experiencing its effects as well."

"Its effects?" Kallistê arched a delicate eyebrow.

Eryx's cane floated from beside her chair and landed in her palms.

"You won't believe it until you see it. Come," she beckoned.

The air warped around their moving forms. Kallistê's footsteps dragged with effort as she followed behind the Premier. She waded through the sea of vitality, the push and pull of its waves threatening to pull her under.

The sharp click of her heels bounced off the walls and echoed around them. The usual hustle and bustle of servants throughout the mansion was entirely absent. Aside from Eryx, not a single living Soul brushed against her magic.

They arrived at the ballroom where the party–and by extension the fight–had taken place.

The soft clicks of Kallistê's heels halted as she stared before her, lips parted and brows high.

A woman lay at her feet with her eyes open and unseeing and her body rigid. Just a few feet away was a man with his arm outstretched, as if he'd spent his final moments trying to run away from something. His expression contorted, and his mouth was open in a silent scream.

Countless more corpses painted the floor, all positioned in a similar fashion—amongst them were Quathir and Nehemias.

A faint smile rounded her cheeks. The level of power required to create such a grotesque scene…it was as disturbing as it was impressive.

Premier Eryx walked past her with her hands clasped behind her back.

"The blood mage did this," Eryx said lowly, her expression indecipherable.

Kallistê flared her nostrils. Something about it didn't sit right with her.

"No, I don't think so. They would look like…," she shook her head. "There wouldn't be a body to find if Haizea did this."

"Blood mages don't disintegrate bodies–they turn them into husks. Although I'll admit that these don't look like they've had their vitality depleted. But she's the only one who could have slaughtered this many people at once."

"Normally, you'd be correct, Premier, but you didn't see what I saw when Viltarin ordered his minions to attack her. Haizea rendered them into dust. Her magic didn't do this," Kallistê said.

The more she thought about it, the more that observation rubbed her the wrong way. Years ago, during the attack in Llyr, Haizea turned dozens of knights into mummies—not reduced them to ash. Clearly, her magic had strengthened. But what had changed since then to cause such an increase?

Growing up, Kallistê had learned of the wars between the mountaineers and the major kingdoms and the fact that the connection to the vitality was most robust in the mountains, which resulted in more powerful mages. Still, many peculiar happenings had transpired tonight. Not only this, but notably the non-mage who had negated Viltarin's curse.

Kallistê's instincts told her that there was a connection between that mystifying ability and the strength of the mountaineers' magic.

"This isn't all," the Premier said, pulling her attention back toward the present.

Kallistê opened her mouth to reply, but her voice caught in her throat as the vitality whirled in a vortex around her. She closed her eyes, dizzied by the sudden influx. It took her a moment to realize that an approaching Soul had caused the disturbance.

"Oh thank the realms, you're back!"

Lotus came running toward them, her magenta eyes wild and her cheeks pale. She pulled Kallistê into her arms and hugged her tightly.

"You look like you've seen a ghost," Kallistê said as she let her go.

"I...all I remember is one moment, pure pandemonium had erupted, and the next, that white-haired man summoned the Soul Reaper, and the vitality itself turned against us. He...it? Did this," Lotus waved her arm around the room. "Every person within his arm's reach perished in an instant. They dropped dead, like flies. Then mountaineers vanished along with him. It all happened within the span of a breath."

Kallistê's brows rose. *Alastair* had done this? She shook her head. It shouldn't have taken her by surprise—she'd witnessed firsthand his unusual connection to the god of the Soul Realm. But as she counted the dozens upon dozens of bodies strewn about, she stilled.

She had always known that Haizea's blood magic made her a formidable force. When she and Alastair felled an army, it came as no surprise. But non-omens made up Arcelia's forces, therefore, they had no hope in besting the duo's power. On the other hand, the islanders could tap into the Cosmos. That alone should have helped balance the scales in *some* sense, but the carnage before her proved otherwise.

Part of the imbalance could likely be attributed to the fact that Alastair had clearly mastered his magic in the time since their last meeting. She did not know of any mediums in Kestramore or in the kingdoms that could summon the Soul Reaper to do their bidding in such a manner. This felt like a mere glimpse of the scale of the mountaineer's power.

And that did not even begin to account for the non-mage in their ranks. Perhaps there was *no* scale.

Kallistê stared into blank space, brows drawn together. She now had twenty *doyamas* at her beck and call, with another two-dozen incubating. Three omens in training. If the election went in Lotus's favor, then she could more easily conscript part of Kestramore's forces to fortify her own.

But would it be enough?

"That's not even the worst of it. What's mind-boggling is this:" Lotus's voice broke her concentration. She led them to the center of the room.

With each step, the weight of the vitality multiplied tenfold. Kallistê's expression pinched and tension wrapped around her head. The faint distortions in the air from a few moments ago intensified into a breathtaking whirlwind.

Kallistê reached her hand forward. It disappeared into thin air. Rather than shock, her lips curved upward deviously, euphoria clouding her thoughts. The Cosmos wrapped grasped onto her hand

and its tendrils crawled up her arm, inviting her to sink deeper into its embrace. Premier Eryx pulled her back.

"Careful. We don't know what this is, Kallistê. We should wait and observe what comes of this before we do anything further."

"How did this happen?" she asked.

"This is pure speculation, but I think it's either a result of the fight that occurred here or a product of the Soul Reaper. Possibly both. Magical pressure increases when using our power—and it's even more intense with omens. We've had violence break out on our island before, but not like this—and certainly never in the presence of the Soul Reaper. That much corrupted vitality in tight quarters combined with the weight of the entity's power...something had to give. The vitality needed release, and with nowhere to go, the result was this. A tear in the very fabric of our realm.

"I'm not sure if this tear is permanent or if it will repair itself over time. More fighting could lead to it worsening, but I'm afraid that might be out of our control," Eryx sighed. "We won't be able to hide a slaughter of this magnitude from the populace. Not to mention, Quathir and Nehemias are among the dead. The people will want answers. Retribution."

As the gravity of the Premier's words settled in Kallistê, a slow grin crept across her face.

Perfect. This was absolutely *perfect*.

"The sooner we hold a referendum, the easier we can control the narrative. Let the people see what transpired here. Their anger will make them easier to manipulate."

Kallistê whistled and beckoned her *doyama* that she had previously lent to the Premier.

"Where are you going?" Lotus asked.

"The mountaineers were victims of Viltarin's scheming just as much as us. I'll placate them and buy us time," Kallistê answered as her body entered the astral plane.

Chapter 38

Human Realm, Mount Illiniza, Windhaven Village

Flame-shaped shadows danced on the white lilies that lined the perimeter of the funeral pyre. The warriors formed a circle and lifted wrapped remains into the pyre. The fire crackled and sizzled before it flared and swelled, swallowing the body whole.

Nearly every person in the village cluster came to pay their respects to Vendela and Jorah. Haizea stood beside Alastair, Shauni, Jassia, and her mother, Loreina. They all dressed in white—the color of mourning for the mountaineers.

Various attendees walked to the front of the crowd to offer their remarks and condolences. Vendela did not have any children, but she did have a cousin in a neighboring village who attended. Jassia buried her face into her mother's coat. They were Jorah's only family.

One by one, the warriors stepped forward and offered parting words. Haizea waited until the very end to go up to the podium. She sighed and peered out at the crowd.

"Vendela took my mother's place on the leader's mantle ten years ago. In the decade that followed, she's been the type of leader many can only hope to aspire to be. When my grandfather's life was in peril, she descended the mountain herself to come to his aid. When Jassia was poisoned by the earth's smoke, Vendela acted swiftly and removed her arm before it could spread. And when we realized that her blood loss was too great, Vendela made the ultimate sacrifice so that Jassia could live. Vendela always gave her all to help the people around her." Haizea paused and looked at Jassia and her mother.

"I did not know Jorah all that well, but I do know that he worked hard to provide for his family. And I believe that the way Jassia and Loreina so openly loved and cherished him is a testament to his character. Jorah departed from this realm far too soon. I hope that someday, we can find peace and understanding with what happened to him, but until then, we should all come together and ensure that his family never goes without."

A monk stepped forward, robed in white and gold. They took her place at the stand.

"Let us end this with a moment of silent prayer to the goddess Aaryn. We ask her to aid their Souls in the transition to the next realm."

As they bowed their heads, Haizea found herself wondering if the Demon could hear humanity's prayers. And if they could, she wondered if the goddess even cared.

Alastair wrapped his arm around her, and she suppressed a shiver at his touch, energy radiating up and down her arm. Loreina reached over and squeezed her hand. Her healing magic tugged as Loreina's lifeforce pulled on hers. The woman's heartbeat much too weakly for her liking. Haizea let her power flow freely, mending and weaving the warped particles within.

After a few moments, they lifted their heads. Despite the sea of red-rimmed eyes surrounding her, a newfound calmness permeated the crowd. Maybe it didn't matter if the Demon Queen paid them any mind. The act of paying obeisance to Aaryn brought comfort to her believers. That was more important.

A soft breeze blew against Haizea's skin. Her magic fluxed in response. Haizea lifted her head to see Alastair with his eyes open. He tilted his head toward the sky, long locks billowing behind him like a soft cloud. Alastair's lashes drooped, and he wore a distant gaze that told Haizea that a passing Soul had caught his attention—most likely the Souls of Vendela and Jorah as they departed their realm. She hoped that they would find peace in the next.

The crowd began to disperse shortly after, but Jassia and her mother lingered.

"I haven't had the chance to thank you properly for saving my daughter. I don't know what I would have done if I'd lost them both," Loreina said.

"I wouldn't be able to live with myself otherwise. It's my fault this happened to begin with. I'm very sorry. Whatever you two need, from here on out, our door is always open," Haizea said.

Something in Jassia's expression fractured. She pulled away from her mother and walked away, her eyes glassy. With a nod of approval from Loreina, Haizea followed after her.

They traveled in silence for a little while before Jassia paused on the walkway. She wrapped her arms around herself and curled her shoulders, making herself look smaller.

Haizea touched her arm. The gesture had two aims—both as a means of comfort and to monitor her vitality. It was still too soon to tell if replenishing Jassia's vitality would have genuine longevity—if any of her own corrupted vitality had slipped into the young warrior's body, it would take time for the effects of magical wasting to show. Perhaps Haizea's efforts had simply delayed the inevitable.

Then again, in a way, all healing was exactly that: a minute, a day, a month, a year, a decade. Every life would eventually come to an end—but each wound she mended rewound the hands of time for just a little longer, ensuring they departed this realm in peace and dignity.

"Vendela's dead because of me," Jassia whispered.

"That's not true, Vendela—"

"If I never went down the mountain, she'd still be here."

Haizea shook her head.

"If there's anyone to blame, it's me. What you're feeling right now, I felt the same way after my grandfather died. Then I went and killed everyone Sage and her brother ever knew and cared about. I put them through exactly what their father did to me. Vendela, your father, and all of those villagers who died—their deaths rest on my shoulders."

Jassia sniffed, her eyes glassy as they searched Haizea's.

"Why didn't you get rid of them before?"

Haizea hummed softly, searching for the right words.

"Back when I confronted King Rhys, Sage and Felix were just scared kids. No older than the age you are right now. If I could go back to that moment in the bunker...," Haizea trailed off, gazing into the distance. "Killing them then would have prevented what happened to your father and Vendela, but they were innocent and had no control over their parents' actions."

Jassia rubbed her arms.

"The way you talk about them...it almost makes me feel sorry for them, but I don't *want* to. I feel so angry. And sad. I just...I feel confused. Back when we did that cull, you said a person's intentions didn't matter—the effects of their actions did. Now I feel like that's wrong."

"It *does* matter. But every situation calls for discernment. There are times when we should not yield, and there are situations where flexibility is the best approach." A soft breeze lifted the hair from Haizea's shoulders, and Jassia's curls were tousled in kind.

"I'll put it this way: Every person is born into this realm for a reason. Vendela dedicated her life to leading our cohort and cultivating the next generation. My purpose is to protect the people I hold dear to me. And as warriors it's our duty to safeguard the mountains. It might be difficult to wrap your head around now, but one day you'll be a fully-fledged warrior, or even on the leader's mantle. By then, you'll have the experience that will help you understand."

"I only have one arm. I'll never be the leader," she whispered.

"That's not true. There will always be a place for you in the cohort. You aren't the first warrior who lost a limb, nor the last," Haizea said.

Jassia nodded and wiped dampness from her cheeks.

"Haizea?"

"Yes?"

"Thank you. For everything."

Haizea could not quite bring herself to meet Jassia's gaze but wrapped an arm over her shoulder and squeezed her lightly.

"Let me know right away if you start feeling unwell, alright?"

They made their way back to the others. Jassia's curls bounced as she sped ahead. She offered a small wave before leaving with her mother.

Alastair reached for her and planted a gentle kiss on her temple. The gesture elicited a spark of energy from her magic. She laced her fingers with his and the sensation spread to her hands before radiating up her arms.

Haizea welcomed it. She would always, always, welcome it.

Chapter 39

Human Realm, Kingdom of Olysseus, Unknown

Dense foliage surrounded the paved walkway. Haizea positioned herself within the branches so that the leaves and shadows cloaked her. She assessed the area without a sound—hunting for a suitable target amongst Olysseus's inhabitants.

A person meandered on the path several yards away, their unsuspecting form bathed in moonlight. Haizea closed her eyes and inhaled deeply as their life force called out to her. The vitality buckled and swayed as it responded to her power and her vermillion eyes flashed in the darkness.

Its rhythmic thrum sent desire ripping through her veins, unquenched and insatiable. The faint glow around the person's body sharpened into a glimmering light. They were mage, of that much she was certain.

Whether or not they were an omen, had yet to be seen. For this particular endeavor, Haizea preferred to fill her vessel with corrupted power, but she would make do regardless.

She did not don her mask or arm herself with her swords. Her pendant rested against her chest, neatly tucked away beneath her shirt. She wore plain clothes with her hair neatly braided under a hat. Haizea did not have the convenience of an official assignment to account for the blood she would spill.

Tonight, this kill was of her own volition. She carried the small vial that contained the realmdrifting blood that she'd bartered prior to her trip to Kestramore. With Alastair transporting them home, she had not used the remainder like they'd originally planned. It allowed her to travel to Olysseus in the middle of the night undetected.

She could not reconcile carrying out this type of hunt close to home—as a warrior, it was her sworn duty to protect her people. But Haizea had no such obligation toward the people of kingdoms.

The distance between herself and her target diminished and the glow in her eyes intensified. Pure energy rolled off of her in cascading waves as her magic reached outward. Her target's footsteps faltered. Their head turned from left to right, likely sensing the increase in magical pressure.

"Who's there?" they asked.

Haizea forced herself to focus solely on the essence of their life force. She did not allow herself to linger on the shape of the body or the timbre in their voice. She ignored the length of their hair and the fall of their footsteps.

The person before her was not a man or woman. Not a daughter or son. Not a friend or a foe. Their hopes and dreams, and aspirations did not exist.

They were simply a living being. And their life—their purpose—was to serve as fuel for her power.

A shuddering breath expelled from her lungs. Before the nagging inner voice could convince her otherwise, she opened the internal gate further. Her magic sprawled outward, gripping them from within so that they seized where they stood.

Haizea sank deeper and immersed herself in the world of the vitality. Sparks flickered in her vision as her target's heartbeat pulsed against her magic. The high seeped in, fogging her mind just enough to mute the sound of their strained gasps. She drained them in the span of a blink. A cloud of shimmering dust took their place.

The resulting euphoric rush sent tremors through her body. A grin crept across her face before she burst into a fit of giggles, her voice echoing into the night. Haizea clutched her head in an attempt to maintain her composure, but she slumped to the ground and laughed harder. Her reddened vision blurred with a tint of white.

Buried in the haze were her target's eyes, staring back at her. Pleading. Condemning.

Haizea leaned onto a nearby tree to regain her balance and small divots formed in the trunk where her fingers gripped onto the bark. Something shuddered deep within as her body absorbed their vitality and she gained access to additional power–telekinesis, based on how the winds picked up and the tree branches curled towards her.

Who's there? Who'sthere? Whostherewhosthere?

As their last words swirled in her mind, she pulled herself back up to her feet. Though a smirk still toyed at her lips, Haizea stared at where the person had been just a moment ago. Nothing remained of them. Not a speck of blood. Not even their bones.

The lack of physical evidence ought to have made it easier for her to turn away, but her legs wobbled beneath her.

Someone would realize this person had gone missing. They would search for them. Even if no one had borne witness to what had transpired here, *she* carried the weight of that knowledge.

In an effort to dispel that thought, Haizea tested the reach of her temporary abilities—telekinetic energy brimmed at her fingertips, but she could not wield the power of transmutation. Her target hadn't been an omen. It meant that they had been a native Olyssean and not one of the islanders who had infiltrated and forcibly taken over the kingdom. This person had likely spent the last few years running and fighting from omens, only to meet their end in this way.

She had stolen the life of an innocent. Erased them from existence so that she could draw a better future for someone she loved.

They were not the first. And if this worked—and she so desperately hoped that it did—they would not be the last.

Haizea opened her vial of blood and poured it into her palm to replenish the realmdrifting vitality in her veins. The infinite sea of the Cosmos invited her in, and she heeded its call.

The rising sun painted the horizon in an idyllic blend of orange and purple hues as Haizea emerged from the astral plane. She rematerialized just a few feet outside of her home. Her fingertips barely brushed the door handle before a disturbance thrummed at the cords of her magic. She halted and turned on her heels. The realmdrifter appeared before her.

Kallistê straightened the front of her dress and fluffed her hair. Haizea eyed her warily, irises shining like rubies. A little over a week had passed since their trip to Kestramore, where they'd turned the Premier's estate into an elegant graveyard. Although the islanders had attacked first and their trio had acted to defend themselves, Haizea did not know the realmdrifter's disposition on the matter.

She left Kallistê to break the silence.

"I owe you an explanation. When I invited you to the Premier's farewell gala, I was under the compulsion of a curse mage–Viltarin. He ordered the attack on you, Alastair, and Shauni. You previously said that not everyone in Kestramore agreed with my plans. You were correct. He was one of them."

The wind shifted and Kallistê's hair lifted from her shoulders. Particles of vitality floated toward Haizea. She inhaled, her fingers subconsciously curling into claws. Noting her reticence, the realmdrifter continued.

"I've since dealt with Viltarin accordingly and deployed a permanent solution. And, thanks to you all, the other dignitaries who stood in my way no longer pose a threat to my aims. I apologize for putting you all in peril, but my actions were not my own at the time. I hope you understand," she continued.

Haizea carefully maintained an impassive expression. Behind that visage, she listened to her power—an additional heartbeat thrummed their proximity. Although she could not make out a separate shape, Kallistê shined just a little more brightly than normal. Her eyes narrowed. A Beast?

Was its presence a precautionary measure? Or premeditation?

Perhaps...perhaps it did not matter.

This all began with the assassination attempt in Llyr, where Kallistê had brought her Beasts into the realm to wreak havoc. Haizea had slain King Rhys and eliminated his army, leaving Arcelia prime for the taking. And their trip to Kestramore had apparently worked out to Kallistê's benefit as well. Thanks to Haizea, the island and the entire continent rested in the palm of Kallistê's hands—everything, save for the mountains.

Would the realmdrifter truly stop there? Haizea didn't know. Could she in good conscience, leave it up to chance?

She had remained idle in the face of latent threats in the past and each time, her passivity inevitably came back to bite her. Worse yet, Haizea never bore the brunt of her errors—the people she loved paid the price instead.

She'd approached Kallistê and the islanders with diplomacy. Humored them. And by doing so, it put Alastair and Shauni's lives in danger. They'd taken efforts to mitigate the risk of being surrounded by omens in foreign lands, but they'd only returned home safely thanks to Alastair's intervention. Or, more specifically, the Soul Reaper.

They had not saved themselves. The God of Death had to rescue them—a fact that only a fool would ignore.

Haizea cleared her throat, finally breaking her silence.

"Alastair and I figured that something was not right and suspected as much. I understand what happened," she began.

"I—"

"I've also come to understand that, when a threat begins to bud, it's best to eliminate it before it can sprout. I made that mistake with King Rhys. And I recall you offering a similar warning about his children, long before our conversation with Premier Eryx. I should have listened, not only to you, but to my own instincts," Haizea straightened to her full height, forcing Kallistê to incline her head upward to maintain eye contact.

"Do you know what my instincts are telling me right now, Kallistê?" Haizea asked lowly.

Kallistê arched a delicate eyebrow. She shifted her weight and glanced downward, rubbing manicured fingers over her arms. Haizea could not detect any breaches in her skin.

A palpable energy coiled between them. A bated breath waiting to exhale. Embers ready to ignite.

"Please, enlighten me," Kallistê said, her tone sickly sweet.

"When I take a step back, ignore hatred and the guilt and all the other emotions clouding my judgment, and look objectively at everything that's happened, all I see is a bright, clear line that tells me that this all starts and ends with *you*."

Everything unraveled in the blink of an eye.

Haizea's power whipped outward, and Kallistê reached for her magic just as quickly, but as her Soul drifted into the astral plane, her body did not follow. She remained stationary, pinned in place by the vice tight grip of Haizea's magic. Blood trickled from the realmdrifter's nose, and blotches formed on her skin.

"It's not personal, Kallistê," Haizea said evenly. "It's a calculation."

The invisible Beast that accompanied Kallistê sprang to life. Its howl split Haizea's mind in two. Even the realmdrifter's expression crumpled. The two women sank to their knees, but Haizea kept just enough control to hold the creature at bay so that it could not sink its teeth into her.

Just as suddenly as it began, the Beast's screeching ceased and it skimpered back toward Kallistê. The two women's gazes met, vibrant rubies floating under white clouds.

The eyeless Beast held its nose pointed in Haizea's direction, nostrils flaring. She did not need to turn her head to see why—the magical pressure increased several fold. The commotion must have woken Alastair from his slumber.

She found herself suppressing her own as the high inched its way closer to fully eclipsing her mind. Before she could respond—or decide if she should give chase while she still held realmdrifting power—Alastair stepped between them.

For just a breath, Haizea thought she saw an apparition of the Soul Reaper.

Even Kallistê took a small, pensive step backward. She looked between the pair contemplatively.

"Next time," she murmured, her tone indicating both a promise and a threat. The realmdrifter bared her teeth in a vicious smile before vanishing from sight.

Alastair helped Haizea stand upright and they made their way back toward the cabin.

~*What the hell just happened? Did she hurt you?*~ he asked.

The vitality twisted and brightened as the motion of his arms created small ripples. Her own magic threatened to burst at the seams. She wiped the few droplets of blood from her arm–some of it Kallistê's, some of it not.

~Haizea?~ he urged.

~No, Kallistê didn't hurt me. That was my failed attempt at being proactive,~ she signed.

Tingles raced down her arms. She swallowed a giggle that rose in her throat but did not truly find humor in what had just transpired. She'd almost succeeded in her attack, but against a realmdrifter, *almost* wasn't good enough. It was a liability.

Alastair studied her carefully. His eyes lingered on her lips, which had curved into a faint smile.

~You aren't thinking clearly. It's too dangerous to do something like that by yourself. Not with a realmdrifter. She could have snatched you away. Taken you—~

~I know. I'm fine, Alastair. Look.~

Haizea held up her hand. It turned translucent as she allowed it to drift into the astral plane. His stern expression remained unchanged.

~Your power has a time limit. Hers does not.~

The air shimmered around them. Haizea swayed on her feet and took a deep breath to try to retain her focus.

~ I thought turning a blind eye to the kingdom's affairs would help me avoid unnecessary conflict, but in reality, I allowed chaos to take root, and the situation has festered unchecked. Kallistê is the common thread behind most of the turmoil that we've endured. I saw an opening and I went for it,~ she paused, noting his furrowed brows and the way his lips puckered downward. ~But I won't do something like that again without talking to you first.~

~I noticed the bed was empty a while before this happened. I thought you were off-duty last night,~ he signed.

~I went out. There's...something we need to talk about. Something I want to try.~

Haizea held his hand and led him inside. She situated him on the couch. He watched her expectantly—irises teetering toward a baby blue, hair flowing past his shoulders, and cheeks just a little too thin for her liking.

She retrieved a blade from her ankle sheath and cut her palm. Her blood bubbled forth, a beacon of light forming in her hand. Alastair's brows arched high, and he reached for her as if to stop her, but she shook her head.

~*Trust me,*~ she signed.

Haizea cupped his face in her hands and planted a gentle kiss on his nose. She did not possess the ability to protect his Soul from corruption, but perhaps she could save his body from magical wasting and carry this burden in his stead.

If it meant keeping Alastair safe, Haizea would pay the price a million times over.

Epilogue

Human Realm, Mount Illiniza, Eaglestone Village

A bird's soft, melodious song flowed in through the open window. Sage opened her eyes, and the bed creaked beneath her as she sat upright. She looked around. The room was startlingly familiar.

It was tiny, barely big enough for a cot and a small dresser. It didn't even have a proper closet. Sunlight beamed in from the small window to her left. A ball formed in Sage's throat. Miss Tamsyn sat just a few feet away with a blanket draped over her lap.

"Sage," she said.

Tears welled in Sage's eyes, and though she fought to keep them contained, they spilled down her cheeks. The cot groaned in protest as Miss Tamsyn came and sat beside her.

"I'm sorry," Sage cried. "I'm so sorry."

Miss Tamsyn wrapped her in her arms and gently swayed from side to side. Sage rested her head against her chest, Miss Tamsyn's soft murmurs helping her to find her calm. Miss Tamsyn dabbed her tears away with a small rag, the worn fabric rough on her skin.

"I was worried sick about you. I'm glad to see that you're okay."

Memories came rushing back. Sage caved under the weight of them.

"Bose," she whispered.

"I know what happened to him. I know Felix did it."

Sage kneaded her fingers along the edge of her blanket. Delayed, she realized that the pain inside was absent. Her once broken arm was whole—a band clung to her wrist.

A million questions formed, but she only managed to choke out one of them.

"How?"

Miss Tamsyn stroked her hair.

"I met Haizea when she came down to clear out the village. She contacted me after she found you and asked if I'd be willing to look after you."

Sage stared out of the window as she absorbed that. A rock settled in her stomach as she turned back to Miss Tamsyn.

"What about Felix?"

Miss Tamsyn pursed her lips and creased her brows. Warmth cocooned Sage as she placed a soft hand and hers. The silence stretched on for an eternity before she answered.

"From what I understand, he had altitude sickness," she said, squeezing her lightly. "By the time they found him, he was too far gone...he didn't make it. I'm so sorry, dear."

"He...?"

Felix couldn't be dead. She'd just seen him. He was asleep at their camp. He was...

She only left to get him a potion. If she'd made it back in time, she could have helped him.

Why did everything keep going so horribly wrong?

They were never supposed to part ways. As long as they stayed together, they would always be safe.

Yet Sage was down at the mountain's base. It didn't feel real.

"What did they do with him...his body?"

Miss Tamsyn stood up and went over to the dresser. She came back with an envelope and placed it in Sage's hands, but she didn't open it right away.

"They didn't say, but we burn our dead here in the mountains. Higher up, the soil's too hard to dig deep enough, and nobody in their right mind would bring one all the way down just for a burial," Miss Tamsyn paused, pointing with her chin. "You should read that letter."

Tears plopped onto the envelope and Sage's hands trembled as she opened it.

Sage,

If you're reading this, it means that Miss Tamsyn has agreed to watch over you. You'll live with her and work on her farm. You may have noticed that you're wearing a wristband. It will prevent you from accessing your magic and, by extension, will cut you off from the Cosmos. Miss Tamsyn will decide when it's ready to come off. Under no circumstances are you to remove it yourself.

If you do, I will know, and I will find you.

Once you're of age, Miss Tamsyn has agreed to continue your training. When the time comes, the choice is yours to make.

I know that you did not mean to hurt the people that you harmed. You have a second chance, Sage. A chance to do what you *choose.*

Don't waste it.

Haizea

Sage set the letter down.

In the end, as she'd feared, it boiled down to the blood mage's whims. Their lives had value because *she* had deemed it so.

Confliction cleaved through Sage's heart. Her brother—the only family she had left—was dead. But after everything he'd done, all the sins they'd committed, perhaps it was the ending he deserved. Sage choked on another sob.

"If Felix is a murderer, then so am I. I deserved to die with him."

Miss Tamsyn held up her hand.

"I won't stand for that kind of talk," she admonished. "You trusted and relied on Felix and he misled you. He went behind my back and taught you the Cosmic Arts, even though you're far too young. You made mistakes along the way, and you can't undo the damage that's taken place, but you can work toward making amends," she rubbed Sage's back. "Haizea told me that you're a princess. Is that right?"

Sage hesitated at first but nodded.

"Then the first step toward making things right is getting a handle on your magic so that you can return home where you belong."

"I'm an omen now. I don't know if I want to go back anymore." Sage rubbed her arms. "I don't even know if my people accept me."

"You embraced Cosmic magic despite your upbringing, didn't you?" Miss Tamsyn asked. Sage nodded.

"That in itself is proof that people are malleable. Minds can change. There's a saying here in the mountains: *'Cosmic magic is only as vile as the mage who wields it.'* Kingdom dwellers only know omens in the context of the islanders who've brought violence within their borders, but there's more use to Cosmic magic than fighting. Once they see that, they might view things differently," Miss Tamsyn sighed. "Still, there are consequences to learning the Cosmic Arts that you should know about. There's a reason I agreed to only teach your brother. The Cosmic high is like alcohol—an adult mind can more easily withstand the addictive effects. Your young age complicates things. But you should rest for today. I know this is a lot to take in. We'll worry about the rest tomorrow."

Sage ran her hands over her arms, and goosebumps prickled against her skin. Had Felix's Soul lingered in this realm or had he joined her parents? She could almost hear his voice now. He'd whisper in her ear that the mountaineers were fools for this. That she should weasel her way into gaining their trust and bide her time until an opening arose.

That was what *Felix* wanted, though.

Sage looked around the room, small but familiar. Quiet, and yet homely. She didn't know what the future held or what she wanted, but perhaps with time and with Miss Tamsyn's help, she could figure out the rest.

Afterword

I want to thank each and every one of you for sticking around for the continuation of Haizea's journey! If you enjoyed The Haunted Warrior, I kindly ask that you please leave a review about your reading experience on Amazon, Goodreads, or whichever platform you purchased from. This will help this book find a home with readers who will enjoy it, which in turn helps me as an author.

If you'd like to stay updated on future works, you can find me at: zetakpierce.carrd.co Here, you can sign up for my monthly newsletter, as well as connect with me on social media (@zetakpierce on all platforms).

Acknowledgements

There are many people that this book would not have existed without their help.

First, I would like to thank my beta readers: Xander, Britany, Dee, Gabriel and I.M. Abett.

I would also like to extend my deepest gratitude to my editor, Danyelle Briggs at In the Write Dyrection. You were one of my biggest cheerleaders and helped me make this story shine as best as it could.

Next is Ty. You have been rooting for me since the very beginning and it truly keeps me going.

Last, but certainly not the least, I want to thank my readers. I can't wait to share the conclusion of Haizea's story in book 3!

About the Author

Zeta K. Pierce is the pen name of the fantasy/science fiction writer behind The Haunted Warrior. In her spare time she enjoys gaming, anime, and spending time in nature. She is also an amateur self-taught artist. You can connect with her on zetakpierce.carrd.co

www.ingramcontent.com/pod-product-compliance
Lightning Source LLC
LaVergne TN
LVHW091701070526
838199LV00050B/2234